DAUGHTERS OF LIVERPOOL

ANNIE GROVES

Daughters of Liverpool

HarperCollins*Publishers*

HarperCollins*Publishers*
77–85 Fulham Palace Road,
Hammersmith, London W6 8JB

www.harpercollins.co.uk

Published by HarperCollins*Publishers* 2008

A catalogue record for this book is
available from the British Library

ISBN-13: 978 0 00 726589 3

Set in Sabon by Palimpsest Book Production Limited,
Grangemouth, Stirlingshire

Printed and bound in Great Britain by Clays Ltd, St Ives plc

Mixed Sources
Product group from well-managed
forests and other controlled sources
www.fsc.org Cert no. SW-COC-1806
© 1996 Forest Stewardship Council
FSC

FSC is a non-profit international organisation established
to promote the responsible management of the world's forests.
Products carrying the FSC label are independently certified
to assure consumers that they come from forests that are managed
to meet the social, economic and ecological needs
of present and future generations.

Find out more about HarperCollins and the environment at
www.harpercollins.co.uk/green

To Barbara and Tony
for their kindness and understanding

I would like to thank the following for their invaluable help:

Teresa Chris, my agent.

Susan Opie, my editor at HarperCollins.

Yvonne Holland, whose expertise enables me 'not to have nightmares' about getting things wrong.

Everyone at HarperCollins who contributed to the publication of this book.

My friends in the RNA, who as always have been so generous with their time and help on matters 'writerly'.

My grateful thanks go to fellow author Bryan Perrett for his generosity in sharing with me his knowledge of World War Two Liverpool in general and the Postal Censorship Service in particular.

ONE

December 1940

'I called in at the Salvage Depot to see Dad on my way over here, and he was telling me that you're going to have some girl billeted on you.'

Jean Campion looked up from her annual task of anxiously working out if the Christmas turkey she had ordered that morning from St John's Market was going to be too big for her gas oven, to look at her son, her hazel eyes warm with maternal love.

She loved all four of her children, but Luke was the eldest, tall and dark-haired, like his dad, Sam, and her only son – a man now, not a boy any longer, with the experience of Dunkirk behind him and a year in the army.

'Yes, that's right.' Jean pushed her still brown hair back off her face, her cheeks flushed a soft pink from her exertions.

The kitchen was the heart of the Campion family's home. Modestly sized but warmly furnished with all the love that Jean and Sam gave their family, it shone with the pride Jean took in her home.

Her kitchen was her pride and joy, newly refurbished the year before the war had started. A gas geyser on the wall next to the sink provided Jean with hot water for all her domestic tasks, and was 'extra' to the electric immersion heater upstairs in its own cupboard next to the bathroom. She and Sam had distempered the walls themselves, painting them a cheerful shade of yellow that made Jean feel as though the sun was shining even when it wasn't.

Sam had got the well-polished linoleum cheap from a salvage job he'd been on, and had fitted it himself, in the bathroom as well as the kitchen, and Jean kept it as shiny and as spotless as her pots and pans.

Jean was a careful housewife and she'd been thrilled when she'd spotted the remnant of yellow fabric with its red strawberry pattern on it, which she'd bought for the kitchen curtains.

The big family oak table had come from a second-hand shop, and Jean and Sam had reupholstered the chairs themselves.

'She's supposed to be arriving this evening, but you know what the trains are like. Your dad wasn't keen on us taking someone in but, like I said to him, it's our duty really. We've got two spare rooms now, after all, with you in the army and based at Seacombe, and Grace training to be a nurse and living in at the hospital, and only me and your dad and the twins here. Mind you, your dad said straight out that it would have to be a woman, on account of Lou and Sasha.'

The mention of his fifteen-year-old twin sisters made Luke smile.

'Well, I hope whoever she is that she likes jitterbug music,' he told his mother.

'I'm putting her in what was the twins' room now that they've moved up into Grace's old room in the attic,' said Jean, ignoring his teasing comment about the twins' devotion to their gramophone and the dance music they played on it. 'It will be more fitting. I could have done wi'out her arriving the week before Christmas, mind, but there you are.'

'In uniform, is she?' Luke asked.

Jean shook her head. 'No. She's going to be working at the old Littlewoods Pools place off Edge Lane, where they censor the post. You know where I mean.'

Luke nodded. 'They've got going on for two thousand working there now, so I've heard.'

'Well, never mind about her,' Jean said, 'let's have a proper look at you.'

They had the kitchen to themselves, otherwise Jean would not have risked embarrassing her tall handsome soldier son by subjecting him to the kind of maternal scrutiny that more properly belonged to his schooldays, minus a brisk demand as to whether or not he had washed behind his ears, but the truth was that she was concerned about him.

It might be over six months since Dunkirk but Jean knew that her son had still not got over the heartache he had suffered then.

It was thanks to Grace that she knew how he

had been led on and then let down by the very pretty, socially ambitious nurse he had been hoping to become engaged to. According to Grace, Lillian Green had never had any intention of getting seriously involved with Luke and had simply used him. She and Grace had done their nursing training together and she had boasted right from the start that she had decided to train as a nurse only because she wanted to marry a doctor. A decent ordinary young man ready to give up his life for his country wasn't good enough for her, and she had told Luke as much when he had gone to the hospital to see her on his return from Dunkirk.

How much the experience of the British Expeditionary Forces' retreat to Dunkirk, and its subsequent evacuation from its beaches, was responsible for the sometimes remote and grim-looking young man who had taken the place of the laughing boy Luke had been, and how much the heartbreak inflicted on him by Lillian was responsible, Jean didn't know. What she did know, was that it made her heart ache to see her once carefree son turned into a man who looked at the world through far more cynical eyes, and who sometimes betrayed a sharp edge of bitterness towards love and romance.

He was young yet though, Jean comforted herself. Plenty of time for him to meet someone else, a girl who would give him the real love he deserved. At least she hoped there would be plenty of time.

To distract herself from such worrying thoughts she asked, 'Will you be getting any leave over Christmas, do you think, now that Hitler has stopped dropping bombs on us every other night?'

4

It was over two weeks now since they'd last been woken from their sleep by the sound of the air-raid sirens, and everyone was hoping that situation would continue.

'We haven't been told yet, Mum – at least not officially – but the word is that we should get a couple of days off, so with a bit of luck I should be home on Christmas Day, at least.'

'Oh, I do hope so, love, especially with Grace and Seb going down to spend Christmas and Boxing Day with Seb's family. Oh, did I tell you that she's had ever such a nice letter from them, saying how pleased they are about her and Seb getting engaged and how much they're looking forward to meeting her? I must say I was pleased. I don't mind admitting that I was a bit worried when she first started talking about Seb, on account of him being related to Bella's late in-laws.'

Luke agreed. He was well aware, of course, of the full story, but he knew how fiercely protective his mother was of them all. And not just of her own children and husband. She was equally protective of her twin sister, even though, in Luke's opinion, neither his auntie Vi and her husband, Edwin, nor his cousins, Charlie and Bella, deserved his mother's staunch loyalty.

So far as Luke was concerned, his auntie Vi was a snob, his cousin Charlie a bragging fool, and his cousin Bella a spoiled and very selfish young woman. A young widow now, he reminded himself since her husband and his parents had been killed when a bomb had fallen on their house last month.

5

Luke was glad that his auntie Vi's social aspirations meant that they didn't have to see much of her and her family, who lived across the water from the city of Liverpool in posh Wallasey Village. Of course, Luke himself was also living across the water now, seeing as he was based at Seacombe barracks, close to Wallasey and New Brighton, and, like them, accessed by the ferry boat.

'I'd better get back to the barracks. It will take me half an hour or so to walk down to the ferry,' Luke told his mother, returning her hug and then shrugging on his army greatcoat, with its recent addition of his corporal's stripes. 'Our sergeant gave me a few hours off on account of all the extra time we've had to put in clearing up after the bombs, seeing as it doesn't take me long to nip home, but I don't like taking time off and leaving the other lads to it. It's all right for me being stationed at Seacombe barracks and so close to home, but some of them haven't seen their families in weeks.'

Luke had changed so much since the outbreak of war, Jean acknowledged as she waved him off. Sam was tall and broad-shouldered, but Luke was now both taller and broader than his dad, his boyishness stripped from him by the experience of war.

More than anything else she wanted this war to be over and her children kept safe, but Churchill had warned them that they were in it for the long haul. Jean shivered at the thought. She should be counting her blessings, she scolded herself. Her children were all safe and well, and here in Liverpool where she could see them, and put her arms round them to reassure herself that they were safe. Unlike some. She didn't need to look at the damage the Luftwaffe's bombs had caused in the city to remind herself of the cost in human suffering of this war.

Her ten-year-old nephew Jack, legally the son of her twin, Vi, but in reality the illegitimate child of their younger sister, Francine, had been killed outright when a bomb had been dropped on the Welsh farmhouse to which he had been evacuated.

Sadness clouded Jean's eyes as she set about wiping the already immaculately clean oven, before refilling the kettle ready to put it on the boil when her family started to arrive home.

Unlike some housewives, at Sam's insistence Jean did not wear a scarf over her shiny brown curls when she was doing her housework.

'You've got a lovely head of curls,' Sam had told her gruffly the one and only time she had attempted to cover them inside the house. 'One of the first things I noticed about you, them curls and that smile of yours.'

Jean paused in her cleaning, a tender smile curling her mouth. She'd been so lucky in her husband and her marriage. She started to hum softly under her breath, and then stopped, her smile fading, remembering how Francine had always sung around the house as a young girl.

Poor Francine. Vi hadn't been pleased at all when their younger sister had returned to Liverpool from Hollywood, where she had been living and working as a singer, since she had left England in disgrace after giving birth to her child.

Vi had been even less pleased when Fran had started to question the way in which Vi and Edwin had been treating the little boy they had vowed to bring up as though he were their own. Jean suspected that Fran had been within a heartbeat of really throwing the fat into the fire and insisting that she wanted to take Jack back and bring him up with a proper mother's love, when the poor little lad had been killed.

Jean's heart ached for her younger sister. Poor Fran had been more misled and deceived than bad, and only sixteen when she had given birth to Jack. In many ways Jean blamed herself for the unhappiness both Fran and her son had endured. If she herself hadn't been so poorly at that time she would have been able to do more and would have taken Fran's baby on herself.

Fran was in London now, having volunteered for ENSA, the group of performers who entertained the troops. She had written to Jean to tell her that she would be working over Christmas but that she wasn't allowed to say where.

That must mean she's overseas, Jean guessed.

Much as she loved her younger sister and felt sorry for her, in some ways Jean was relieved that Fran wouldn't be able to spend Christmas with them.

Her own twin daughters were going through a phase when all they wanted was to go on the stage themselves, and having their glamorous Auntie Fran around, talking about the shows she was going to be in, wasn't really what Jean wanted them to hear at the moment, especially not when

Fran herself had already said that she thought their dancing was good enough to get them on stage.

Sam, who could be protectively strict with his children if he thought it necessary, would never entertain the idea of them going on stage, especially not with there being a war on, and all sorts of men likely to be ogling every girl they saw dancing around in a skimpy costume.

Thinking of the twins made Jean hope that their billetee wouldn't be too put out by the noise the pair of them made with their gramophone records and their dancing. The nice young woman who had come to see her about her spare room had told her that her boss – 'Mac,' she had called him, explaining that his real title was 'Officer Commanding Beds' – would be thrilled to have such a clean bedroom in what was obviously a very well-run home, to add to his list of billets.

'Flannelling you, she was,' Sam had laughed when Jean had reported this comment to him later.

'No such thing,' Jean had insisted firmly. 'She was telling me that some of the rooms she'd been to see weren't fit to house an animal, never mind a decent young woman.'

Vi had, of course, sniffed disparagingly on being told that Jean was to have someone billeted on her, announcing that she would never be able to let some stranger sleep in one of her own beds. By rights Vi, with her three empty bedrooms now that her son and daughter had left home, should have put her name down for billetees but with Edwin on the local council she had boasted to Jean that she had managed to avoid doing so.

'Just look at the situation at Bella's,' Vi had told Jean crossly, at the service for those who had lost their lives in the same bomb that had killed Bella's husband and his parents. 'Newly widowed and still having to have living with her those Polish refugees she was forced to take in. Not just one of them either, Jean,' Vi had complained bitterly. 'There's the mother and the daughter, both of them adults and eating their heads off, and the mother's got that son of hers expecting to stay at Bella's whenever he comes to visit.'

Privately Jean's sympathies lay with her niece's billetees, who, from what she had learned of them on the single occasion she had met them, had seemed very pleasant, especially the son, Jan, who was in the air force and had taken part in the Battle of Britain.

There was no denying that her sister was a snob and a social climber, Jean admitted now, as she went back to her cleaning, rubbing fiercely at the kitchen sink taps. The war meant it was getting harder now to buy proper cleaning things. Not that Jean would ever waste her money on fancy cleaning stuff when a bit of a wipe with vinegar could do the job just as well.

Vi's snobbery didn't seem to have brought her any happiness so far as Jean could see. Even as a child Vi had been one of those people who was never satisfied or happy, unless she was sure that she had the best of things, and could look down on others, and she was just the same now.

*　　*　　*

10

'Have we got time to walk home past the Royal Court Theatre, do you think?' Lou asked her twin sister, Sasha.

Sasha shook her head. 'Better not. Mum will only start asking us why we're late and where we've bin, you know what she's like. It's a pity that Auntie Fran has gone to London. If she was still here she'd have bin able to work on Mum for us and help us to get some stage work, p'haps in one of the Christmas pantos. After all, she said we were good enough.'

The twins exchanged disappointed looks. They were, as Jean herself often said, as alike as two peas in a pod with no one really able to tell the difference between them unless they themselves allowed that to be seen.

At fifteen they were in many ways young for their age, still very much 'schoolgirls', with their plaits and freckles and their giggles. But that outward youthfulness hid a shared fierce determination to follow their auntie Fran onto the stage, along with an awareness of how strongly their parents would oppose that ambition.

The jobs they would be going into in Lewis's department store after Christmas – proper jobs with proper wages, not just the bits of work they had been doing running errands for Mrs Lucas, the elderly owner of the old-fashioned dress shop in the city centre, which was closing down after Christmas – showed what their parents wanted for them: safe steady jobs that would keep them at home until the time came for them to marry. But the twins had other ideas and dreams, which had become all the more compelling with the onset of war and their auntie Fran's recent visit.

On the top floor of their parents' three-storey house in their shared attic bedroom, the twins regularly practised all the new dance steps they had seen in films, or begged their school friend, whose sister was a dance teacher, to show them, adapting them to a private shared routine they could dance in time to the new songs coming out of America, ready for the breaks they just knew they were going to get. Somehow or other . . .

Walking home past one of the most famous of Liverpool's theatres, the Royal Court was part of their secret plan. A plan that involved them being seen and offered the opportunity to audition for a show, in which they would so impress the right people that they would be whisked off to Broadway to become overnight stars.

The train had slowed down preparatory to pulling into Liverpool's Lime Street Station. Katie Needham wriggled a little apprehensively to the end of her seat. It had been a long stop-and-start journey from London to Liverpool, and the train was full with a mix of young men in uniform and other non-services travellers like herself. Naturally, the precautions necessitated by being at war meant that there were no lights on inside the train to illuminate the December late afternoon gloom, but Katie was too nervous to want to read, even if there had been enough light to enable her to do so.

She smoothed the fabric of her navy-blue skirt, glad of the warmth of the cherry-red jumper she was wearing. She had taken off her navy-blue woollen coat along with her matching wool beret, and her cherry-red hand-knitted scarf and gloves, a present from an elderly neighbour, when she had got onto the train, folding up her coat and her scarf and rolling her beret and her gloves to stow them carefully in the pocket of her coat before putting them on the luggage rack above her head along with her small case.

'Soon be there.' The pleasant woman in her thirties, who had chatted to her during the journey, informing her that she was travelling to Liverpool to see her husband, who was on leave from the navy, gave her a brief smile but Katie guessed that her travelling companion's thoughts would be on her husband and the happy reunion that lay head. No one asked too many questions or gave away much information in these security-conscious times, and Katie had been relieved when the navy wife had accepted her own vague but proud statement that she was going to Liverpool to do 'war work'.

Now, though, Katie's thoughts were more apprehensive than happy. Had she done the right thing? As the train rattled over the points and into the station, Katie admitted that she didn't know whether to feel pleased with herself or downright scared. She knew what her parents would want her to feel, she acknowledged, as, along with the other occupants of the compartment, she stood up and started to put on her outdoor clothes. The looseness of the wedding ring on the finger of the woman seated next to her reaffirmed the effects of the anxiety and hardship the whole country was experiencing, with 1941 only just around the corner and no end to the war yet in sight.

The train jolted to a halt with a hiss of steam and a squeal of brakes, causing everyone to reach for something to hold to steady themselves. Katie and the navy wife exchanged final smiles and then went about the business of straightening hats and wrapping on scarves.

Katie's parents had made it plain enough to her that they were far from pleased about her decision to leave home to go to do war work in Liverpool when, according to them, they needed her at home to help them.

To keep the peace between them more like, Katie thought ruefully.

It wasn't that Katie didn't love her parents – she did – but she didn't have any illusions about them. When her best friend at school had said enviously that she wished that her mother had been an actress and her father a famous band leader, Katie had had a hard time not telling her how much she wished that her parents were more like her friend's: that her mother wore a pinafore and worried about mealtimes and muddy kitchen floors, and that her father went off to work in the morning and then came home at five o'clock.

Where other parents seemed to manage to have calm ordered lives, her parents seemed to prefer chaos and quarrels.

Her father was fiercely jealous and had insisted on her mother giving up the stage when they had married, whilst she in turn vented her frustration on him with outbursts of temper during which crockery was thrown and threats to leave were made. As a young child Katie had been dreadfully afraid that during one of their quarrels both her parents would leave and that she would be forgotten and left behind.

As she followed the other passengers out onto the platform Katie wrinkled her nose against the smell of smoke and cold air.

The station was very busy. Every platform seemed either to have a crowd of people standing on it waiting for a train to pull into it, or passengers crowding onto it from a train that had just pulled in.

As Katie joined the queue for the ticket barrier, she was glad of the warmth of her winter coat. All around her she could hear people speaking with an unfamiliar accent, so very different from the cockney she was more used to. She had been told that Liverpudlians were friendly and welcoming. She hoped that that was true.

She was so afraid of having made the wrong decision and having to admit that to her parents. She loved them dearly but their quarrels had coloured Katie's childhood and as she grew older they had obliged her to take on the role of peacemaker, both parents appealing to her to support their points of view. Katie felt as sorry for her glamorous excitable mother, denied a proper outlet for her theatrical talents, as she did for her poor father, who was so afraid of losing her. If the relationship between her parents was what happened when a person fell in love, then Katie had decided falling in love was definitely not for her. She wanted no truck with it and even less with passionately jealous men.

They had been shocked when she had told them what she had done.

'You're going to Liverpool to read letters?' had been her father's disbelieving comment, followed by his signature crashing of his hands down onto the keys of the ancient upright piano that took up far too much room in their small rented London house. Her father always used the piano to express his feelings. 'But I need you here.'

He had been dressed to go out to 'work' when she had told them, wearing his immaculate band leader's white tie and tails, his hair slicked back with brilliantine.

Now Katie smiled as she handed over her ticket, and was relieved to receive a warm smile back from the burly uniformed ticket collector.

In looks Katie took more after her mother than her father, having her mother's dainty build and expressive heart-shaped face with high cheekbones and a softly shaped mouth. Her colouring, though, was her father's. She had his hazel eyes and the same dark gold hair that turned lighter in the summer sun.

She had been working as her father's unpaid 'assistant' ever since she had left school, organising his diary, attending rehearsals with him, making notes for him from the comments he made about various members of the two different bands he worked with, some of whom were foreign and inclined to break out into their own language in moments of stress, so that as well

16

as her knowledge of modern music Katie also had a smattering of Italian, Polish and French.

There was nothing about the history of modern dance and song music that Katie didn't know, from every word of every popular song for the last decade or so, to the name of every composer of those songs, and the names of every member of the country's most popular dance bands.

Sadly, though, whilst her father and her mother could both sing with perfect pitch, Katie, whilst loving music every bit as passionately as they, had a voice that was completely musically flat, a voice incapable of being raised in song; a voice that had caused both her parents, but especially her father, to demand that it was never ever heard attempting to sing a single note because of the pain it would cause him.

Katie might not have a 'voice' but she did have a good 'ear' – and, so she was pleased to think, a good awareness of how wearying artistic temperament could be, especially to those on the receiving end of it.

Katie treated her inability to sing as philosophically as she treated the quarrels between her parents – what else after all could she do?

'Yes, Katie, your father is right,' her mother had told her. 'You can't possibly go to Liverpool.'

'I have to,' Katie had told them both, patiently explaining that it was her duty, but diplomatically not explaining how she had slipped the all-important consent form under her father's nose when he had been signing some business letters she had typed for him.

She had seen the job advertisement in one of the London papers, asking for young women with 'some specialist knowledge' on a list of subjects that had included music, and had written off before she could change her mind.

She had been so excited when she had received a reply requiring her to present herself at the address given in the letter for a formal interview.

It had seemed such a grown-up and important thing to do when she had had it explained to her that because of her knowledge of popular music the Government wanted her to work in Liverpool for MC5, the 'secret' organisation where letters to and from certain countries were censored and checked for hidden messages. The fact that she could speak and write a small amount of French and Italian was apparently an added bonus. The stern-looking official who had interviewed her had told her that spies were very clever in the ways in which they made contact with one another, often using devices such as mentioning in their letters something as seemingly innocent as popular music, their references a code containing secret information. Her task would be to read such letters and look for anything within them that seemed suspicious.

She would be working alongside other girls, she had been told, and under a supervisor, to whom she would be able to refer any letter that might arouse her suspicions.

She had felt so proud and pleased with herself when she had been offered the job but now, after nearly eight hours on a train that had seemed to crawl from London to Liverpool, she was beginning to wonder if her parents had been right and she had done something very silly indeed.

Now that she was in Liverpool, instead of feeling relieved Katie was actually beginning to feel slightly shaky and uncertain. If she had stayed at home she would have been accompanying her father tonight to the well-known London hotel where one of the bands he conducted would be playing. Instead of having merely a semi-stale cheese sandwich to eat, she would have been able to look forward to a delicious supper from the hotel restaurant.

Now that she was through the ticket barrier Katie put down her case in order to get her bearings, and then almost lost it in the surge of people milling around her.

As she reached to retrieve it, a young man in RAF uniform beat her to it, handing it to her, giving her a wink and a smug grin as he did so.

'That will cost you a kiss,' he told her cheekily.

'Then you'd better put it back,' Katie replied sharply, 'because you won't be getting one.'

He looked as shocked as though a kitten had suddenly shown the teeth of a tiger, but Katie was unrepentant. Give his type an inch and they'd try to take a mile. Well, not with her, they wouldn't. People – men – thought that just because she was small and dainty-looking that she was a pushover. Well, she wasn't, and she wasn't going to be either.

Picking up the case the airman had put down, Katie turned her back on him and made her way towards the exit.

'Will 'Itler be bombing Liverpool again before

Christmas? Read all about it,' the newspaper vendor outside the station bawled.

Katie stared at the headlines. She didn't really know very much at all about Liverpool or about it being bombed. She'd been too busy soothing her parents' fears about their ability to manage without her to worry about any bombs.

'What's up, love?' the news vendor asked her.

'Oh, nothing . . .'

'If it's directions you're wanting then you'd better go and ask at the WVS post back there in the station,' he told her. 'They'll probably give you a cup of tea an' all . . .'

It was good advice. She knew that she had been billeted with a Mrs Jean Campion in somewhere called Wavertree, but she had no idea just where that was, other than that it was close to the place where she would be working, which was apparently off a road named Edge Lane.

The women in charge of the WVS post were every bit as helpful as the news vendor had promised, although there was no tea.

'We've run out,' the plump grey-haired woman standing beside the tea urn apologised to Katie. 'I dare say your landlady at your billet will have something nice and hot waiting for you, though. It's the bottom end of Wavertree you're wanting, just over the border with Edge Hill. You can take the bus or even walk it, although walking will take you a good half an hour or so, and uphill as well,' she told Katie informatively.

Katie thanked her.

*   *   *

20

It was dark and cold, and the Liverpool night air smelled alien. Katie had walked past the Royal Court Theatre just as the stage door was opening to admit a group of chorus girls smelling faintly of greasepaint, sweat and that once known never forgotten smell of dusty dressing rooms, excitement and nerves that she always associated with her mother, even though the only visits her parent now made to theatre dressing rooms were to see old friends from her own stage days.

That wasn't homesickness she was feeling, was it, because if it was then it had better be on its way, Katie told herself stoutly as she wrapped her long scarf more tightly around her neck and marched determinedly past the theatre.

The WVS had given her the number of the bus she would need and the name of the stop to ask for to get off. There was quite a queue already waiting at the stop, young women mostly chattering away in an accent that Katie's acute ear quickly had her mimicking inside her head.

She gathered from their conversation that they were shop girls on their way home from work. They sounded jolly, their conversation mixed with lots of laughter. Katie hoped that the people she would be working with were as pleasant.

She had been told that the exact nature of her work would be explained to her once she had presented herself at her place of work. She had been given the name of the person she was to report to tomorrow morning and had been warned that she was not to discuss the nature of her work with anyone.

The bus arrived, disgorging some passengers before taking others on. By the time Katie got on there was only one seat left, but when she saw the heavily pregnant and not very young woman getting on behind her Katie offered it to her and was rewarded with a tired smile, and a grateful, 'Ta, love. Gawd, but me legs are aching. Never thought I'd see meself in this condition again at my time of life, but there you go. Got me like this before he went off to war, my Bert did, and now he's living the life of Riley in some army camp and I'm here like this.'

Katie listened politely. The people of Liverpool weren't so very different from their neighbours in London, by the sound of it, for all that they spoke with a very different accent.

'Here's your stop, love,' the conductor eventually warned her as the bus started to slow down.

Picking up her case, Katie thanked her and stepped down onto the platform.

The blackout made it impossible for her to see anything of her surroundings as she followed the WVS lady's instructions and crossed the road, shining her torch to find the opening to the street she wanted, before heading down it.

The house where she was billeted was down at the bottom of the road. Now she *was* feeling a bit nervous, Katie admitted as she knocked on the door. After all, she had never lived anywhere other than at home. What if the people she was billeted on didn't like her, or if she didn't like them? What if . . . ?

Her increasingly apprehensive thoughts were put

to flight as the door was opened by a slender, attractive-looking woman of her mother's age, wearing a clean pinny over a brown skirt and a camel-coloured twinset, who greeted her with a warm smile, her hazel eyes twinkling.

'You'll be Miss Katherine Needham, who's billeted with us,' she said. 'Come on in, you look fair frozen. I've kept back a bit of tea for you and if you don't mind the kitchen it's the warmest place in the house. Yes, just put your case down there for the minute. I'll get my Sam to take it up for you later. Oh, if you were wanting to freshen up perhaps . . .'

'No. That is . . .' It was so unlike her to feel shy and tongue-tied that Katie barely recognised herself. 'I mean . . . please call me Katie,' she managed to get out as her hostess led her down an immaculately clean and shiny hallway smelling of lavender polish, and into a wonder-fully warm kitchen that smelled deliciously of soup, making Katie's stomach rumble, much to her embarrassment.

The kitchen was empty, although it was plain that Mrs Campion had a family, from the number of chairs around the big table, and the size of the soup pan on the stove.

As though she had guessed what she was thinking Mrs Campion informed her, 'Sam, my husband's, gone off to an ARP meeting, so that will give us time to get to know one another a bit before he gets back. The girls, my twin daughters, are upstairs in their room. I'll call them down to meet you once you've had a chance to have a cup

23

of tea and a bowl of soup. Take you long to get here, did it?'

'About eight hours.'

'Well, you get your coat off, love, and make yourself comfortable.'

Jean didn't know quite what she had expected, but it certainly hadn't been someone as young as this, a girl no more than eighteen, and so small and dainty she looked as though a puff of wind would blow her over. Nice manners, though, Jean thought approvingly, and lovely and clean, with that shiny hair and those well-scrubbed nails. Her shoes were well polished too, and her coat a good sensible cloth, obviously bought to last, instead of being some skimpy fashionable thing like the twins always wanted to have.

Jean had taken trouble with her own appearance. She was wearing her second-best Gor-Ray skirt and the smart twinset that Grace had persuaded her to buy three years ago in Lewis's winter sale, having had it put to one side for her mother as 'staff' were allowed to do.

Jean had always stressed to her own children the importance of being neatly turned out and taking a pride in themselves. Her young billetee looked just as she ought, Jean decided approvingly.

'It really is kind of you to go to so much trouble, Mrs Campion. If you can just show me where I'm to put my outdoor things . . . ?'

'I'll take them for you for now, love. Time enough to get used to our ways once you've got something warm inside you.'

Katie's grateful smile illuminated her whole face.

It was such a relief to discover that she was billeted with someone so obviously kind and decent. Up until now she hadn't realised how much she had been worrying about where she might end up. There would be no dusty corners or damp beds in this house, Katie knew, and hopefully no raised voices and fierce quarrels either.

Trouble? Keeping her a bowl of soup? As she hung Katie's coat up on the hall coat stand, all Jean's maternal instincts were aroused. Something told her that this wisp of a girl needed a bit of good northern mothering.

'You're to call me Jean and my husband Sam,' she informed Katie after she had returned to the kitchen, ladled a good helping of soup into a bowl and brought it over to the table for her. 'I'll let you have your soup and then I'll tell you a bit about us, although I don't expect you to remember all our names right from the start. Got brothers and sisters yourself, have you?'

'No, I'm an only one.'

'Well, your parents are going to miss you then. Me and Sam have four. Our Luke's a corporal in the army and based here at Seacombe barracks on home duty at the minute. Although he was at Dunkirk.'

Katie looked at Jean. 'You must be very proud of him,' she said quietly and simply.

'That we are,' Jean agreed. 'Me and his dad both, although my Sam didn't take too well to it when Luke told us that he'd joined up. Sam had got a job lined up for Luke in the Salvage Corps, you see, working alongside him.'

Katie nodded understandingly.

It wasn't like her to talk so intimately about her family to a stranger, Jean acknowledged, but there was something about her young billetee that made it easy to do so. She had a quiet but dependable air about her that said that she knew how to respect a person's confidences. And, of course, Jean was hugely proud of her son.

'Of course, there's no one prouder of our Luke now than his dad,' Jean continued. 'And as luck would have it the two of them often get to work together, what with Sam and the Salvage Corps doing their bit to help clear up the mess after the bombings, and the soldiers stationed at Seacombe doing the same.

'Then there's our Grace,' Jean continued. 'That's our eldest daughter, who's training to be a nurse and lives in the nurses' home. She's just recently got engaged, and her fiancé, Seb, is a wireless operator with the RAF. Then there's our two youngest, Lou and Sasha – twins, they are – they left school a while back but they've been waiting for jobs to come up at Lewis's department store, where our Grace used to work. They're starting there after Christmas. You'll get to meet them all soon enough, of course, especially the twins.' Jean gave a small sigh.

Jean loved her family, Katie could see that, but she had also heard in her voice her special love for her son, and her concern for her younger daughters.

'Now, you're to treat this house like your own home whilst you're here with us, Katie, and seeing as I've got a daughter of my own not much older

26

than you, I want you to know now that if you should get any problems you need to talk over with someone, I'm always here to listen. It isn't easy for you young ones having to move away from your families to do war work, we all know that.'

To Katie's embarrassment something had happened to her that she hadn't suffered in years. There was a lump in her throat and tears were threatening her vision. Quickly she blinked them away.

'You're very kind,' she told Jean huskily, and meant it.

TWO

It was now almost half-past nine in the morning and an hour since Katie had arrived – early – at the large Littlewoods Pools building, off Edge Lane, which had been taken over by the Government to house its wartime postal census operation. She'd presented herself to the clerk on duty and given the name of the person she had been instructed to ask for. From the corridor where she had been told to wait, Katie had watched a stream of people – women, in the main, and not wearing any sort of uniform but instead dressed in their ordinary daytime clothes – entering the building and going about their business. She had been able to see into the large room on the other side of the corridor, where women had been settling down at long tables to work. The large windows allowed in plenty of daylight and Katie had also seen that there was plenty of overhead lighting, essential, she had guessed, when handwriting had to be read very carefully.

After a wait of ten minutes or so she had been escorted down a corridor to the office of the manageress. By this time Katie had been feeling horribly nervous, and she hadn't felt any better when the manageress had summoned a stern-looking older woman, Miss Edwards, to show Katie where she would be working and explain the nature of her work.

Miss Edwards had a rather schoolmarmish manner and a clipped way of speaking that had alarmed Katie at first, but Katie was a sensible girl and not given to being 'nervy', and after listening quietly to Miss Edwards for several minutes Katie had deduced that the older woman wasn't anything like as frightening as she had first appeared, but was instead merely determined to make sure that Katie understood the serious nature of the work she was going to be doing.

'The mail is opened and sorted according to content, and then passed on to those readers who specialise in specific contents. If necessary – that is to say, should a piece of mail contain something that arouses a reader's suspicions – then she refers that piece of mail to her supervisor.

'Everyone has her own identification labels, which carry her own personal number, and a label must be attached to every piece of mail a person checks, identifying her as its checker. At this point I must remind you that it is a strict rule that nothing that happens within these walls is discussed with anyone else.'

Katie nodded in acknowledgement of the severity of the embargo.

'Since your field of expertise is, I believe, contemporary music, it is letters containing any references to such music that you will be required to read and either pass as unremarkable or hand on to your supervisor should you come across anything suspicious. You will, of course, be reading only those letters written in English. We have separate sections dealing with letters written in other languages.'

Katie got the impression that being an expert in a foreign language ranked much higher in the department's pecking order than merely having knowledge of contemporary dance music.

'Right now, follow me and I'll take you to the table where you will be working,' said Miss Edwards briskly, turning on her heel to march down through the rows of tables without waiting to see whether or not Katie was following her.

The Littlewoods building was large and the room in which she was going to be working very long, and Katie was slightly out of breath by the time she had caught up with Miss Edwards, who had come to a halt beside one of the tables.

Eighteen or so girls were already seated around it, their heads bent diligently over their work. Each operative had a basket full of letters and another one into which they obviously put the letters once they had read them, plus a smaller tray with a red warning sign on it. Miss Edwards explained that it was into this smaller tray that Katie should put any letters that struck her as suspicious.

Katie was introduced to Miss Lowndes, a pretty, placid-looking, fair-haired young woman wearing an engagement ring, who Katie guessed was in her early twenties, and who was in charge of the table.

'Come and sit down here next to me so that you can watch how we work,' she told Katie, pulling a small face and adding, once Miss Edwards had left, 'We all call one another by our first names on this table. I'm Anne.'

'I'm Katie,' Katie told her, obediently pulling out the chair next to her and settling herself on it.

There were too many girls seated round the table for her to be able to memorise all their names in one go, but she could remember that the tall thin girl with mousy brown hair who was sitting on the other side of her was Flo, and that the girl next to her with red curls and a snub nose was Nancy, and the girl on the other side of Anne – a stunning brunette with creamy skin and corn-flower-blue eyes was Allie – short for Alison, whilst the girl opposite her with her serious expression and fair hair was Mabel.

They seemed a friendly bunch, most of whom had originally worked for the pools company, and who Katie learned had been selected to do this special war work because of their ability to spot very quickly when 'something wasn't right'.

'It's a trick you learn fast when you're checking the pools,' Anne explained to her. 'Folk think that it's easy, but you need to be pretty sharp and to have a good head for figures.'

Figures and logic, Katie suspected.

'To start with, you'll be working with Carole here. She'll show you the ropes,' Anne told her, indicating a giggly, curvy girl with red-gold curls, who quickly informed Katie that Liverpool was just about the best place to have been posted

31

because of the excellence of its famous dance hall, the Grafton.

'I can see that you're not hitched up regular, like, with someone 'cos you're not wearing any rings,' Carole informed Katie, 'but how about a steady? Have you got one?'

'No,' Katie told her firmly and truthfully.

'Well, that's good then, 'cos that means that the two of us can go out dancing together.' Carole winked and added mock virtuously, 'I reckon it's our duty seein' as there's a war on and all them poor lads in uniform need a bit of female company to cheer them up. The Grafton's the best dance hall there is. You're certainly never short of a partner. Loads of lads, there are, round here,' Carole continued enthusiastically. 'All sorts – locals, uniforms, even some of them Canadians wot's come over to help with the fighting. You can go out with a different one every night if you want. The soldiers are my favourites.'

'I'm not interested in dating soldiers,' Katie began firmly.

'Oh, hoity-toity! After an officer then, are you? Well, you've certainly got the looks and the style.'

Katie opened her mouth to tell her that she wasn't interested in getting involved with any man full stop, but before she could do so Carole had changed the subject.

'What kind of digs have they put you in? Some of the girls are staying at the Young Women's Christian Association.' Carole pulled a face and giggled. 'That's not my cup of tea at all, but luckily I've got an auntie who lives local and I'm staying with her.'

32

Katie thought ruefully that the Christian Association would probably be as horrified at the thought of hosting Carole as she was at the idea of having to stay there, given the other girl's out-spokenness on the subject of young men. But although Carole's outlook on men was very different from her own, there was something about the other girl's bubbly friendly personality that Katie couldn't help liking.

'I've been billeted with a family. I haven't met them all yet but the mother is very nice, and I've got a lovely room.'

Her bedroom *was* lovely, and she had been thrilled last night when Jean Campion had shown her up to it, explaining that it had originally been the twins' bedroom but they had moved up to the attic floor into their elder sister's room and so Jean had taken the opportunity to refurbish the room a bit.

'You've got Grace's bed, and dressing table and wardrobe,' she had explained to Katie, 'but my Sam's given the walls a fresh lick of distemper. I wasn't sure about duck-egg blue at first. I thought it might be a bit cold-looking.'

'It's very pretty,' Katie had told her truthfully, earning herself another warm smile, before Jean had continued, 'And then I made up the rag rugs from a couple of bags of offcuts of fabric I got from a mill sale. Go a treat with the paint, they do, with them being blues and yellows. The blue silk eiderdown and the curtains came from my sister Vi. She lives across the water in Wallasey.'

Katie had been thrilled to have such a pleasant

room. There was also a pretty bedroom chair, and a view of the garden and the allotments beyond it from the window.

'We can have a proper chat when we knock off to go to the canteen for our dinner,' Carole told Katie now. 'I'd better show you how we work otherwise we'll have one of the supervisors down here. They sit over there at those desks you can see on that bit of a dais,' she added, jerking her head in the direction of a railed-off raised-up section of the room where people sat at single desks instead of around a table.

'Going home for Christmas, are you?' Carole asked as she passed a small pile of opened letters to Katie. 'Only I was thinking that I could get us both tickets for the Grafton's big Christmas Dance. I've seen them advertised, and I reckon if we don't jump in now it could be too late.'

Again, without waiting for Katie to reply, she rattled on, 'Now what you do with these 'ere letters is you read them and if there should be anything in them that doesn't quite gell, like, then you tell me for now.'

Dutifully Katie started to read the first letter, in which its writer referred to having been in London and having danced at the Savoy Hotel to the sound of Carroll Gibbons and the Savoy Orpheans.

Katie had often heard the Orpheans play and an unexpected wave of homesickness hit her. At home right now her father would just be getting up, grumbling about the noise from the street, which would have woken him up, complaining that no one seemed to realise that those who worked into the early hours of the morning needed to sleep in.

Her mother would be sitting at the kitchen table wearing one of her theatrical, and totally unsuitable for a shabby London terrace, 'robes' and before too long the pair of them would be bickering.

'Summat up? Only you've been staring at that letter for nearly five minutes.'

Shaking her head in answer to Carole's query, Katie put the letter to one side.

She was just over halfway down the pile when she found it: a letter written in bold spiky handwriting, in which, out of the blue, the writer referred to Gracie Fields singing 'The White Cliffs of Dover', when surely everyone knew that it was Vera Lynn who sang that particular song. It could simply have been a mistake, of course, but it made sense to check.

'I've just noticed this,' she informed Carole, pointing out the error.

Carole grinned at her. 'Good for you. The top brass always check out newcomers by giving them a little test to see if they are as on the ball as they've made out.'

Leaning across Katie, she waved the letter in front of Anne and told her triumphantly, 'She spotted it straight off.'

'Well, thank goodness for that,' Anne smiled. 'We've been desperate for someone to fill in for Janet since she decided to join the ATS.'

A bell suddenly rang, making Katie jump.

'Don't worry, it isn't one of Hitler's bombs. It's only the bell for the first sitting for lunch,' Anne reassured her. 'Carole, you and Katie can go first sitting today, but make sure you're back on time,' she warned them.

THREE

Emily could still feel her face burning hot with angry humiliation, despite the cold air that hit her when she stepped out of the stage door of the Royal Court Theatre, where her husband, Con, was a producer, and into the narrow street that ran behind the building. It was her own fault, of course. She should have known better than to be taken in by Con's lies and come down here with the sandwiches she'd made up for him, thinking that it would save him having to go out and buy himself something since he had said he was so busy with pantomime rehearsals that he wouldn't be able to get home for his tea. Too busy to get home for his tea, but not too busy to take the afternoon off, apparently, and not, from the look she had seen on his assistant's face, on his own.

Where was he now? Shacked up in some cheap hotel room with an even cheaper little slut, if she knew her husband.

She wasn't going to cry. Big plain women like her didn't cry; it made them look even uglier than they already were. Besides, she was all cried out over her husband and her marriage. How could she not be when she knew what Con was and what a fool she had been to marry him?

Properly taken in by him at first, she'd been, and no mistake, a big gawky plain motherless girl, whose father had made himself a nice bit of money as a theatrical agent and who had died unexpectedly of a heart attack, leaving it all to her, his only child.

Con had come round to offer his condolences. She could remember now how her heart had thrilled when she had opened the door of the tall double-fronted Victorian terraced house at the top end of Wavertree Village where she had lived all her life, and seen him standing on the step.

She had never seen such a good-looking man and she had certainly never had one calling on her.

Six months later they were married. Con had insisted that it wasn't disrespectful and that it was what her father would have wanted.

She had been so besotted with him by then that she would have agreed to anything, given him anything, she acknowledged. And of course she had already done both. Better for them to marry quickly just in case anything should happen, he had told her after the night he had got her so inebriated on sherry that she hadn't even realised they were upstairs and in her bedroom with him undressing her until it was too late.

She had been grateful to him then, too stupid to realise what it was he was really after and why he was doing what he was doing to her.

Of course, that had all stopped once they were

married and he had what he wanted, which had been access to her father's money. Her father had more sense than her, though, and he had put most of it safely away in investments, bonds and things, and a bit of a trust fund that couldn't be touched. And that brought her in a good income even now. Good enough to keep Con still married to her, that was for sure. Married to her but bedding other women – younger, prettier women. And they, for all their pretty faces and slender bodies, were no better at seeing through him than she had been herself. Actresses, chorus girls, singers, those were the kind that appealed to Con. Just as she had done, they took one look at that handsome face of his, those laughing eyes, that slow curling smile, that thick dark hair and those broad shoulders, and they were smitten.

Con knew all the ways there were to make a woman fall in love with him and then break her heart. He had certainly broken hers more than once in the early days, with his protestations that it was her he loved, and his pleas for forgiveness.

But not even Con's unfaithfulness had broken her heart quite as painfully and irreparably as the discovery that she could not have children.

Emily loved children. She had ached for babies of her own, dreamed of them, longed for them and cried the most bitter of tears for her inability to conceive.

Now, a sound in the alleyway caught her attention. It often seemed to Emily that the stage door to the theatre was symbolic of theatrical life itself. The face it showed to the world on the main street was the face it wanted to be known by. Out in the front of house, where people queued to pay and watch the show, everything was shiny and smart, but go backstage, use the entrance those who worked within the theatre used, and it was a different story: peeling paint, a narrow alleyway blocked by bins, guarded by marauding cats and sometimes, poor buggers, the odd tramp poking around hoping to find something to eat. Something like Con's unwanted sandwiches, for instance.

Emily could see a small shadow lurking by the bins. A *small* shadow? She frowned. Ah, yes, she could see him now, a dirty, poor-looking boy, his bare legs blue with cold, and his face pinched. He had seen her too. He looked terrified, so he wasn't some young thief, then, hoping to grab her handbag. He was turning away from her. He looked hunted, desperate, and as thin as a stick. Emily's heart melted.

'Here, boy, you look hungry. You can have these,' she told him, holding out Con's greaseproof-paper-wrapped sandwiches to him.

He licked his lips, darting nervous looks towards her, and then down the alleyway, stretching out his hand and then withdrawing it, the look in his eyes one of mingled hunger and fear. Emily sensed that if she moved any closer to him he would turn and run.

'Look, I'm going to put the sandwiches down here. Tinned salmon, they are, and best quality too,' she told him inconsequently. 'Brought them for my husband, I did, but he's gone out. I'm going to put them down here and then I'm going to walk away. If you've any sense, you won't look a gift horse in the mouth.'

She put the sandwiches down and started to move away but then something stopped her and she turned back to him.

'There'll be some more this time tomorrow and some hot soup, if you want it, but don't you go telling anyone else because I'm not feeding every young beggar in Liverpool, that I'm not.'

As she walked away from him Emily was dying to turn round but she made herself wait until she had reached the end of the alleyway. When she did turn, she wasn't surprised to see that both the boy and the sandwiches had gone.

Poor little kid. More than half starved, he'd looked. Probably lost his home and p'haps his family as well – there'd been plenty of folk who had, thanks to Hitler's bombs, according to the papers.

She made her way home – no point in bothering looking round the shops, seeing as they had nothing much to sell, thanks to the war. Not that she'd got anyone to go buying Christmas presents for, except her ungrateful and unfaithful husband. Spoiled him rotten, she had in those early years, and nothing but the best either – hand-made suits, a lovely camel coat with a smart fur collar, just like the big theatre owners on Broadway wore. She'd seen photographs. All Con had ever given her had been boxes of chocolates, and not fancy ones either. That poor little kid hadn't even had a decent jacket to keep himself warm, never mind a coat with a real fur collar. She could easily buy him a pair of gloves and a scarf from that Iris Napier, her neighbour who was always going on at her to join her knitting circle. She might as well go home via St John's Market, which was behind the theatre and off Charlotte Street, and order a turkey after all. She hadn't been going to bother, seeing as Con would be down here at the theatre, Christmas Day or no Christmas Day, but she could invite Iris Napier in and if there was any turkey left, well, then she could make up some nice thick sandwiches for the boy, that was, of course, if he should come back, which he probably wouldn't. But if he did, well, then she'd have a bit of something for him.

'It was bad enough trying to shop for Christmas last year, but goodness knows how the Government expects us to manage this year, what with rationing coming in. Your father's had something to say about the cost of a bottle of gin, I can tell you,' Vi told Bella as they walked down Bold Street, Liverpool's most exclusive shopping street.

Bella was barely listening to her mother's monologue; instead she was watching the young woman – the young mother – on the other side of the road. Her coat was shabby, like the pram she was pushing. She looked tired and poor, no engagement ring shining about her thin gold wedding band. Bella looked down at her own hand; her wedding ring still shone richly, the diamonds in her engagement ring sparkling in the sudden ray of sunlight that broke through the greyness of the December afternoon.

42

She was a widow now, of course, and not a wife. She had lost her husband to one of Hitler's bombs. Not that she missed or mourned him. Not one little bit. Why should she after the way he'd treated her, taking up with that stupid ugly Trixie Mayhew and telling people that he wanted a divorce from her so that he could marry.

Bella could just see the baby inside the shabby pram, a little girl obviously, seeing as she was dressed in a well-washed faded pink knitted jacket and bonnet. Bella could see the darkness of the baby's hair showing through the pink bonnet. She would have had a baby if it hadn't been for Alan trying to push her down the stairs. The too-familiar pain that she wished would go away, but which refused to do so, had started up again. Her mother didn't like her talking about the baby. She said that it was best forgotten and that it had probably been for the best. Her mother was probably right. Just imagine if she'd ended up having a plain nasty-tempered baby like its father?

Her mother had interrupted her monologue to complain sharply, 'Bella, you aren't listening to me. I was just saying that I wish that Charlie would let me know what he's planning to do for Christmas. I've written to him twice now.'

Bella couldn't stop looking at the baby. She had huge brown eyes and a wide smile. If she'd been her baby she'd have had her dressed in something much better than washed-out and faded hand-me-downs. Was the mother too poor to buy her child decent clothes or did she just not care?

'I want to go into Lewis's, Bella.'

43

The road outside the main entrance to the store was busy with Christmas shoppers. There were no Christmas lights, of course, on account of the blackout, but the people of Liverpool were still trying to put a brave face on things and make the best of the festive season. The young woman with the pram stopped beside a man selling roasted chestnuts from a brazier. She looked cold and hungry. Bella huddled deeper into her good thick coat with its fur collar, and a label inside it that said that it had come from a famous store in New York. The coat had been a present from her parents and had come into the country as a 'special order' put in by her father to one of his many contacts in the Merchant Navy. Bella's father had a business that fitted the pipe work into naval and merchant vessels and their household seldom went short of anything, rationing or no rationing.

'I still don't know why you've gone and ordered a turkey, Bella. After all, you'll be coming to us for your Christmas dinner.'

'I told you, Mummy, the turkey's for the billetees.'

Vi's mouth thinned with disapproval. 'If I'd been you I wouldn't have gone to the trouble of buying a turkey for them.'

'I was just trying to do the right thing, Mummy. You're always saying how important it is, with Daddy being on the council and everything.'

Vi, who had picked up a carrot from the vegetable barrow in front of them, put it back without examining it to tell Bella sharply, 'There's doing the right thing by people, and there's being overgenerous. If you ask me there's no reason why that Jan shouldn't

44

have got a turkey for his mother and sister himself. After all, he's in the RAF, as he's so fond of telling us all, so it's not as though they're destitute.'

'Mummy, I'm getting cold standing here,' Bella protested, stamping her feet in her boots and hugging her arms around herself as she changed the subject. She didn't want to talk about her billetees. She wasn't quite sure herself why she had gone to the trouble of ordering a Christmas turkey for them, as well as letting them practically have the run of the house, as she had done these last weeks. At least she would be at her mother's for Christmas, and sleeping in her own childhood bedroom, so she wouldn't have to listen to the mother and daughter going on and on like they did about Jan and how wonderful he was.

'Come along then.' Vi started to cross the road, having spied another vegetable barrow. Bella made to follow her and then stopped, opening her handbag to remove a ten-shilling note and then hurrying over to the girl with the pram.

'Here, this is for the baby. Buy her something pretty,' Bella told her.

The young mother's face betrayed her shock, followed by anger.

'I'm not a beggar, you know,' she began.

'Bella, what are you doing?'

The sound of her mother's voice had Bella turning away from the pram.

'Very well then, I'll take it, but only because me husband's been laid off from his ship on account of him not being well.' She took the note, pushing it quickly into her pocket.

'Bella . . .'

'Coming, Mummy.'

'What on earth were you doing?' Vi demanded crossly when Bella caught up with her.

'I was going to buy some chestnuts but then I decided not to bother,' Bella fibbed. She had no idea why she had given in to that impulse to give the other woman something. She could still see the baby's big brown eyes and sweet smile. The pain was back again. It was silly of her to feel like this. She hadn't even wanted a baby really, had she? But she had been having one and now she wasn't, and somehow that had left her feeling different and sad, even though she didn't want to feel like that; as though there was an emptiness in her life and as though she really wished that she was still going to have a baby after all.

'I just don't know what I'm going to buy your father for Christmas, Bella. He's not easily pleased at the best of times, and with this war on . . .'

'You could always buy him something to water down his gin.'

Vi's face took on a high colour and she gave her daughter the kind of displeased look she normally reserved for others. Vi had spoiled her daughter and boasted about her to everyone who would listen, but having a daughter who was widowed, and, even worse, whose husband had been carrying on before his death and threatening to leave her, was not easy to boast about.

'I'm surprised at you, Bella,' Vi told her daughter, 'making a comment like that about your father. It's only thanks to him that you're living in that house;

those refugees seem to have taken over without you putting your foot down and stopping them.'

'I can hardly go against the Government and turn them out,' Bella pointed out. 'Everyone with a spare room empty is expected to go on the register with the billeting officer, you know that, Mummy. The only reason you haven't had to is because Daddy's on the council, and he's claimed that he needs the bedrooms in case he has to put up some of the men from the Ministry of Defence who come to see him because of the work he does for the navy. Not that I've heard of any of them staying with you, Mummy.'

'Now that's enough of that,' Vi reproved her daughter crossly. 'Your father is only doing his duty. You know that. Your auntie Jean has had to take someone in, but she's only got the one, not two like you – some young girl, it seems, who's working sorting letters or some such thing . . . What do you think about this cravat for your father, Bella? We've been invited round to the Hartwells' for drinks on Boxing Day, you know. Mr Hartwell is on the council with your father. He took Alan's father's place.'

'Yes, I know, Mummy. I can't see Daddy wanting a cravat, though.' Bella picked up a pair of leather driving gloves, wondering if they would do for her brother, Charlie, and then suddenly remembered something she had intended to mention to her mother. Putting the gloves back, she told Vi, 'I almost forgot. Mrs Lyons from three doors down from me called round again the other day to ask if I'd thought any more about joining the WVS.'

'Well, I suppose you should really, especially with your father being on the council. You'd be better joining my group, though.' Still frowning over the cravat, Vi complained, 'I do wish Charlie would let me know what he is doing for Christmas. Of course, it's only natural that his friends want his company, what with him being a hero and everything.'

Bella's mouth compressed. She was so used to her brother being the 'naughty' one, whilst she herself had always been her mother's favourite, that it had come as an unwelcome surprise to discover that since Dunkirk her parents had taken to singing Charlie's praises and boasting about him instead of her. And all because Charlie had rescued a fellow soldier from drowning when they had had to evacuate the beaches. Privately Bella thought that the parents were making too much of a fuss over Charlie and his 'bravery' but she knew she would earn herself a black mark with her mother if she said so.

'Did I tell you that Charlie's kept in touch with the family of the boy he saved – such a pity that he went and drowned anyway. Daddy had a lovely letter from the father – Mr Wrighton-Bude – saying how grateful he was to Charlie.'

'Yes, Mummy, you did tell me.' And more than once, Bella thought crossly. She'd never be able to stop her mother now that she was in full flood about Charlie's bravery, and the last thing she wanted was her mother concentrating on Charlie just when she, Bella, wanted to gain her sympathy and persuade her to ask Bella's father if he would increase the allowance he made her.

The discovery after Alan's death that his father's business had been on the point of bankruptcy, and that both Alan and his father owed money to their business associates, had come as a very unpleasant shock to Bella. She had thought that Alan's family were very comfortably off. They had certainly behaved as though they were, especially Alan's mother, acting like she was something special, and Bella nothing at all. Bella had thought the fact that the mother-in-law never spent any money was down to meanness, not to the fact that there wasn't any money to spend.

Heaven knows what would have happened if Bella and Alan's house hadn't been bought for them by Bella's father, who had kept the deeds in his own name.

Now Bella was dependent on her father and she really could do with a larger allowance.

Her mother, having finally exhausted the subject of Charlie's bravery, much to Bella's relief, changed the subject.

'I want you to come back with me and help me decorate the Christmas tree, Bella. I'm so glad your father managed to get that new set of lights last year. You just can't buy them now.'

'I've got the tickets for us for the big Christmas Dance at the Grafton. I decided I might as well get them sooner rather than later, seeing as you'd given me your money,' Carole told Katie.

They were in the cloakroom at Littlewoods, getting ready to go home, having finished work for the day. Katie pulled on her beret but didn't

49

speak. She might have been working with her new friend for only a few days but it had been long enough for her to learn that Carole was a chatterbox who steamrollered over anyone's attempt to get a word in edgeways once she was in full flood.

'You'll need to get a bit dressed up. Proper smart, the Grafton is. And everyone will be wanting to look their best, seeing as it's Christmas. I'm going to wear me pink. Had it for me cousin's wedding the summer before last. It's got a net petticoat and there's little silver stars embroidered on the skirt when I was her bridesmaid. It's my favourite colour, is pink. What will you be wearing?'

'I don't know,' Katie told her truthfully.

'Well, you must have summat a bit fancy, seeing as you was always going out to them posh places with your dad.'

Katie had been obliged by Carole's persistent questions to tell the other girl at least something about her family, but now, just like the Campion twins, Carole seemed to think that Katie had lived a far more glamorous life than she had, despite all Katie's attempts to explain to her that her life had not been glamorous at all.

Mentally Katie reviewed the contents of her wardrobe. When accompanying her father she had worn either a plain black dress or a black skirt with a white blouse – very dull indeed. Her mother had kept all the stage costumes she had ever worn, and had a wardrobe full of the kind of clothes that Katie suspected Carole would expect her to wear, but Katie wasn't the sort who had

50

ever wanted to wear sparkly sequined things, or in fact any kind of clothes that made her stand out in a crowd. She had grown up dreading standing out because it normally was as a result of some kind of embarrassing behaviour on the part of her parents. Being a little stoic with two artistic parents hadn't always been easy. Katie could laugh at herself, of course. She had grown up to feel fiercely protective of her parents and yet at the same time she was rather relieved finally to be able to 'be herself' and be judged accordingly. She couldn't, for instance, imagine anyone as down-to-earth as Jean Campion having a cosy chat with her dramatic mother.

Katie liked Jean. There was a warmth about her that made Katie feel happy to be going 'home' to the Campions after work.

She missed her parents, though, and she was looking forward to returning home for Christmas, even if she would have only a couple of days with them. Not that she wasn't enjoying her work or happy in Liverpool. The girls were a good crowd who had made her welcome, and Anne's calm manner brought a steadying presence to their 'table'. So far there had been nothing remotely suspicious in any of the letters Katie had read, and Anne had informed her that this was the case with most of the letters.

'But we still have to be vigilant,' she had warned Katie, 'because you never know, and we don't want any spies sending letters that might get our lads killed or help Hitler to drop bombs on us, do we?'

*   *   *

'There you are, Katie; I was just beginning to worry about you,' Jean greeted Katie when she knocked briefly on the back door and then stepped into the kitchen. Jean had told Katie that she must treat the house as her home and that there was no need for her to knock, but Katie still felt that she should.

'I'm sorry I'm late, only I saw people queuing, and someone said it was oranges so I joined the queue thinking that you might like them for the twins for Christmas. They'd almost gone by the time I was served, but the grocer let me have four.'

'Oh, Katie, bless you. You are thoughtful. Did you hear that, Sam?' Jean called out. 'Katie's gone and managed to get some oranges for the twins.'

Sam was more reserved than his wife, but he was a kind man and he gave Katie a warm smile.

'There's a letter arrived for you, Katie. Looks like your dad's handwriting.'

Thanking Jean, Katie took the letter from her. It was indeed from her father. A familiar mix of happiness and apprehension tightened her stomach as Katie opened it. So far her father's letters had contained nothing but complaints about how hard his life was without her, and how surprised he was that she had not thought of this before taking on her war work.

This time, though, her father's mood was more positive. He had, he wrote, bumped into an old friend – a musician who had done well for himself, who lived in Hampstead and who had invited Katie's parents to spend Christmas with him and his wife.

So there's no need for you to bother coming home, Katie – the Durrants haven't got any children and since your mother and Mae Durrant were on stage together as girls, we're both looking forward to having a splendid Christmas reminiscing about old times.

'Katie, are you all right? It's not bad news, is it?' Jean's concerned voice made Katie look up from her letter.

'No. Not at all. My parents have been invited to spend Christmas with some old friends and so my father has written to tell me not to bother travelling all the way back to London to see them.'

Jean's maternal heart filled with indignation. That poor girl. Fancy her parents doing that to her. It was obvious to Jean how upset she was. She was only a girl still, for all that she behaved in such a sensible grown-up way.

'Well, never mind, love,' Jean told her sympathetically. 'You're welcome to spend your Christmas here with us. In fact I don't mind admitting that I'll be glad of an extra pair of hands, especially with our Grace going down to spend Christmas with her in-laws-to-be, and me having invited a couple of elderly neighbours who'll be on their own to have their dinner with us. Mind you, I dare say the twins will plague you to death, especially when they find out that their brother has gone and bought them both some new records. I'm hoping that he'll be home for his Christmas dinner as well – our Luke.'

As yet Katie hadn't met the Campions' son, or

their eldest daughter, Grace, and her fiancé, Seb, but she was looking forward to doing so, given how kind Jean herself was.

'Now come and sit down and have your tea, Katie love, before it gets cold.'

As Jean said to Sam later in the evening when Katie had gone upstairs at the twins' request to tell them more about the famous dance bands her father had conducted, 'I felt that sorry for her, Sam. Her face was a picture although she didn't so much as say a word against her parents. If you ask me that girl hasn't had an easy time of it at all, for all that the twins keep on about how lucky she is.'

'Well, she's lucky enough now, having you to take her under your wing, Jean,' Sam told his wife lovingly.

'Oh, go on with you, Sam. She's no trouble to have around at all, kind and thoughtful as she is. I admit I was a bit worried at first when she started saying how her mother had been on the stage and her father conducted dance bands, knowing what the twins are like, but I reckon it's doing them good having her here to tell them what it's really like, and not all glamour and excitement, like they seemed to think.'

'Well, you've got your Fran to thank for them thinking that,' Sam reminded her.

Jean sighed. 'All this business of them wanting to sing and dance is just a bit of a phase, I reckon. Once we're into the new year and they're both working at Lewis's they'll forget all about wanting to be on the stage.'

'Well, whether they forget it or not they are not going on it. I'll not have it. I've nothing against your Fran, Jean, you know that, but her kind of life isn't what I want for our girls.'

'No,' Jean agreed.

'Tell us again about the Orpheans, Katie,' Lou begged.

The three of them were in the twins' top-floor bedroom, the music from the gramophone for once turned down so that the girls could question Katie about the exciting life she had lived with her parents.

'There isn't anything to tell that I haven't already told you,' Katie answered her prosaically.

'Imagine going out every night and dancing. What did you wear, Katie? If it had been us then we would have had the same frocks made, but mine would have been in black and Sasha's would have been in white – like mirror images, you know, and then when we do our dance we do it like there is a mirror and it's just one of us. Shall we show you?'

They were on their feet, finding their current favourite dance tune, and buzzing with excitement before Katie could say a word.

They were talented, no one could deny them that, but Katie knew what the reality of making a living was for girls like them, and she had seen the anxiety in Jean's eyes when she had watched her daughters.

'You are very good,' Katie told them when they had finished their routine and had turned, slightly breathless, to face her, 'but being on the stage isn't what you think it is. All that glitter is just a few sequins stuck onto cheap cloth that's darned all over the place, cheap lodgings where you don't get enough to eat, damp bedding and bedbugs, and cheap . . .'

'Values', Katie had been about to say but they were too young for her to talk to them about that kind of thing, she decided, watching them grimace over the bedbugs and giggle that she was teasing them.

'We can't understand how you can leave something so glamorous to come here and sit all day reading letters,' Lou told her.

'No, if it was us you'd never get us doing what you're doing,' Sasha agreed.

'That's because you don't know what it's really like, and that means that you are very lucky,' Katie told them firmly.

'Well, we still want to be on the stage, don't we, Sasha?' Lou asked her twin.

'Yes, we do,' Sasha confirmed, 'and we're going to be, as well.'

Not if their parents had anything to do with it they weren't, Katie thought. She didn't blame Jean and Sam either, but the twins were stubborn and Katie suspected that the more they were told they couldn't do something, the more they would want to do it.

FOUR

Saturday 21 December

'Well, I must say, Mum, she does seem a decent sort,' Grace Campion told her mother generously.

Grace had initially felt rather jealous when her mother had spoken so enthusiastically to her about this girl who was billeted with Grace's parents, but now having met Katie Grace had to admit that she had liked her.

The three of them had gone for a cup of tea at Lyons Corner House, Jean having decided that it was best that Grace met Katie on neutral ground.

Tactfully Katie had now gone off to do some shopping, leaving mother and daughter to talk on their own.

'She won't be going home for Christmas so she'll be having her Christmas dinner with us. I'm hoping that our Luke will get leave to be home. I'll miss you, Grace love, but it's only natural that Seb's family want to meet you.'

'We'll be back to see in the New Year with you, Mum. Then I'm on nights again.'

'You'll have been busy today, love, with Hitler bombing us again last night. Your dad was out all night helping to put out the fires started down on the docks by the incendiaries. The Dock Board offices and Cunard's were both hit, and then there was that awful thing down by the railway arches in Bentinck Street. Your dad says they still don't know how many people who were sheltering under those arches got killed when they collapsed.'

'Just when we were thinking that Hitler had finished with us,' Grace agreed.

Jean patted her daughter's hand. Grace had only just escaped being a casualty of one of Hitler's bombs herself late in November when she and Seb had been caught in the Durning Technical School bomb blast.

'I'd better get back, Mum,' Grace told her mother, 'otherwise I'll be late going on duty, and you can imagine how busy we are.'

'Well, you take care of yourself, remember?' Jean gave her a fierce hug.

'And you, Mum. Are you going home now?'

'Not yet. Whilst I've got Katie with me we're going to nip over to St John's Market so that I can get me turkey and a few other things.'

Grace laughed. It was a standing joke in the family that Jean complained every year that the poulterer from whom she ordered her turkey always got the size wrong, resulting in Jean worrying about being able to get the bird into her oven.

To get to the market Jean and Katie had to cross Ranelagh Street, where Lewis's was, and go down the upper part of Charlotte Street, before crossing Elliot Street. St John's Market ran back from Elliot Street, the whole length of the lower section of Charlotte Street, which divided it into two: the fish market to one side, and the meat, fruit and veg market on the other.

Although it was nothing like the size of Covent Garden, St John's Meat Market did remind Katie a little of the famous London market, as much, she suspected, for the cheery confidence of those working there as anything else.

With Christmas so close the market was especially busy, with the bustle of porters; horse-drawn deliveries arriving; errand boys ringing their bicycle bells and then pedalling furiously as they raced about, shoppers protesting when they had to dodge them. Stall holders were shouting their wares, whilst small children, bored with the quays, were trying to escape their mothers' surveillance.

With so many people pressed into the market it was no wonder police officers were patrolling between the stalls, Katie acknowledged. Somewhere like this would be a paradise for thieves and pickpockets.

Jean, raising her voice so that Katie could hear her above the noise as she hurried her through the maze of stalls, pointed out that at the other end of the market were the Royal Court Theatre, then Roe Street and Queen Square.

'The station hotels and Lime Street itself are only the other side of the fish market,' Jean added. 'But you'll soon find your bearings. Just remember, if you're walking uphill along Edge Road then you're heading away from the city centre and the docks; if you're walking downhill you're heading for them.'

St John's Market was especially thronged with people collecting their Christmas orders. Every other stall, or so it seemed to Katie, was filled with poultry. Those that weren't selling 'fattened geese and turkeys' were selling all those things that went with them: strings of sausages, hams and tongues to cook for Boxing Day, special Christmas pâtés and stuffing, whilst in the fruit and vegetable section of the market, which they had come through earlier, Katie had seen stalls selling boxes of dates, even if there were signs up stating, 'No oranges/lemons/bananas/tangerines or nuts – don't blame me, there's a war on.'

'Sam's got all the veg sorted out. He's grown most of it on his allotment and bartered for what he hasn't grown with some of the other allotment holders.

'I've made a bit of a pudding but it won't be up to my normal standard . . . There's the stall over there,' Jean told Katie, 'that one with the poultry painted on the sign board. I don't know why I come back to him every year because I'm sure he's a bit of a rogue, even though he says his prices are the best in the market.'

There was a queue at the stall, and whilst they waited for their turn, Jean said to Katie, 'You'll be looking forward to going to the Grafton tonight with your friend.'

'I'm not sure that I am really,' Katie admitted. 'It's kind of her to ask me, but I'm not much of a dancer.'

'You'll enjoy it once you're there,' Jean assured her firmly, stepping up to the counter for her turn to be served.

'I appreciate what you've bin telling the twins about it not being all that glamorous going on the stage, Katie,' said Jean, once they had finished their shopping and they were on the way home, carrying the turkey between them.

'Well, it's the truth otherwise I wouldn't say it, but I can understand that they can't see that. It's like I said to them, all the audience sees is the sparkle from the sequins, they don't see all the darning and patching in the cheap fabric that's underneath.'

They exchanged understanding looks.

Emily hadn't seen the boy for the last two days. The last time he had had a nasty bruise on his face and he had looked thinner and dirtier than ever. She'd got more than enough to do as it was, without coming down here and hanging around a back alley with a packet of sandwiches and a flask of hot soup.

Hot water was what that boy wanted, and plenty of it, along with a generous lathering of soap. Not that it was up to her to fuss over him. The boy meant nothing to her. He wasn't her responsibility, after all. But somehow she couldn't stop worrying about him.

She wasn't going to admit to herself that she was disappointed because he wasn't there, and the sandwiches that she put out earlier were, or that she'd woken up in the night thinking about him, wondering where he slept and if he had a proper bed, or even a proper home. That was daft doing that, and no mistake. Why should she care about some dirty boy? She didn't.

She was only coming down here because it gave her an excuse to keep an eye on Con, and that new piece he'd taken up with.

The boy wasn't going to come now. The late December afternoon had turned into winter darkness and it was cold, with a thin mean wind whining up the alleyway and making her shiver, despite her padding of fat and her warm coat.

She bent down to pick up the sandwiches. She couldn't leave them here. They'd have rats coming after them. A thin whisper of sound from the bins against the wall caught her attention. Emily frowned and listened, but she couldn't hear anything. It must have been the wind. She picked up the sandwiches and turned away. There, she'd heard it again. She turned back, and reached into her bag for the torch she carried for the blackout, switching it on and pointing its beam towards the bins.

It was his legs she saw first, bare to the knee and mottled red and purple with cold, and so thin she could see his bones. She hurried towards the bins, her heart pounding so heavily she felt breathless.

He was curled up between the bins, looking more dead than alive, his face all bruised and his lip cut, with dried blood on it. What had happened to him? Had he been set on by some bigger, heavier boys? He looked as though he was too weak to move. Emily wanted to pick him up, take him home with her and look after him properly, but instead she sat down beside him in the alleyway and unscrewed the Thermos, pouring out some soup.

It was her own home-made nourishing broth, made from a chicken carcass and vegetables. He was so weak that she had to hold the Thermos cup to his mouth so that he could drink, and take it away from him as well when he tried to drink too much too quickly.

'You'll be sick if you take it too fast,' she warned him. 'And I'd like to know who's been knocking you around as well, because I'd have a few words to say to them. Now you can have a bit more. Gently, there's no need to drink it so fast, like you've got no manners. No one's going to take it from you, not whilst I'm here, so you take your time and then you can start on these sandwiches, and this time you and me are going to have a bit of a talk, because you can't go on like this. It will be the death of you, and me too with all the worrying about you I've been doing. I've got a good mind to take you home with me, where I can keep an eye on you, and see that you get looked after properly.'

The boy hadn't said a word, but he was listening to her and taking in everything she was saying, Emily knew that.

'Of course, if you've got folk of your own and a home of your own then it's them that you should be with.'

Silence.

'And if you're one of those boys that's got himself into trouble . . .'

Now there was a reaction. Not just his hands but his whole body was trembling, and Emily suspected that he would have got up and run from her if he'd been strong enough.

It was well after half-past five, the matinée was long over, and the queues would already be forming at the front of the theatre for the evening's first house. It wasn't unknown for the actors and members of the chorus to slip out through the stage door for a bit of fresh air between shows – and sometimes something rather less innocent than a breath of air, as she had good cause to know, since Con wasn't above slipping out for a bit of a kiss and a cuddle with his latest girl if he thought he could get away with it. The last thing Emily wanted was to get caught sitting here on the ground with the boy. Con would laugh his head off at her and then no doubt tell her that she wasn't to have anything more to do with the boy, citing as his reason for this veto a concern for her safety she knew perfectly well he did not feel. It would suit Con very well indeed, she suspected, if she were to suffer the kind of accident that would lead to him becoming a widower. Not that he would actively do anything to achieve that status for himself. Con was too lazy for that, and besides, Emily thought, sometimes he wasn't above using her existence to get rid of a girl once he had grown bored with her. Wives had their uses in some ways.

At best, though, he'd probably chase the boy off and then she'd never see him again, and Emily

64

knew that, daft though it was, she would miss him. Was that really what she was reduced to? Being afraid of missing a boy who hadn't so much as said a word to her and only wanted her because of the food she gave him?

So what was new? After all, she already had a husband who only stayed married to her because of her money.

She ought to leave.

'I'll come in the morning tomorrow,' she told the boy, 'about ten o'clock – oh, and take this and go and buy yourself some warm socks and gloves and a scarf.'

The two half-crowns she pushed towards him gleamed briefly before he reached for them.

Emily never knew what it was that made her turn round once she had got to the end of the alleyway. It wasn't any kind of sound – there hadn't been one. Perhaps it had been some need within her to take a last look at the boy; whatever it was she was glad she had obeyed it when she saw the two heavily built youths who had crept out of the shadows behind her back.

One of them was pinning the boy against the wall whilst the other went through his pockets.

'Come on, where are they? We saw the money she give you,' she heard the heavier of the boys demanding.

When the boy made no response the youth holding him shook him roughly. 'Need yer memory giving a bit of a shake, do yer? Well, Artie here don't mind doing that, do yer, Artie?'

There was the soft but sickening sound of a

bunched fist meeting vulnerable flesh and then a burst of cruel laughter.

'Aaw, look at that, he's crying. Hurt, did it? Well, that'll learn you then, won't it, 'cos there's plenty more where that come from. Now give us them half-a-crowns.'

Emily had heard enough. She advanced on the bullies with a ferocity she'd never have used for her own protection, demanding, 'Let go of him otherwise it will be the worse for the pair of you.'

They turned round to stare at her, one of them bunching his fists until Emily swiped him hard with the heavy weight of her old black shopping bag with the Thermos in it.

The bully yelped in pain, releasing the boy to lift his hands to protect himself as he dodged Emily's second swing with her bag.

'Here, Artie, let's get out of here,' he yelled to his friend. 'She's a ruddy madwoman. I ain't having me head bashed in for no five bloody bob, that I ain't.'

'The next time it will be the police that will be waiting for you,' Emily warned them, as they fled down the alleyway towards Roe Street.

She was out of breath and her heart was racing in a way she knew her doctor would have warned her was dangerous but she actually felt more elated than afraid.

She looked down at the boy. He was looking back at her.

'You can't stay here,' she told him emphatically. 'Not now. I'm taking you home with me.'

Where had those words come from? Wherever it was they had made Emily feel positively giddy with power and excitement.

'Be much safer for you there. And warmer too. Lost your family in one of the bombings, I expect, haven't you?'

At least she was giving him a chance to tell her if there was someone he should be with, Emily reassured herself. And it wasn't as though, if there was someone, they were much good to him, was it? After all, it had been over a week now that she'd been feeding him.

Emily reached down and took hold of his hand. It was icy cold and the bones plain to feel through his skin. She was trembling a bit, half shocked by what she was doing and half thrilled, as she tugged him to his feet.

Once he was on them he looked even thinner and weaker than she had thought. It was a fair walk up to the top end of Wavertree Park but she didn't want to risk taking him on a bus in case she saw someone she knew. She wanted to get him cleaned up and a bit more respectable-looking before that happened. But then there was no hurry. They could take their time. Con wouldn't be in until gone midnight. They could stop off at one of the chippies on the way. Emily's stomach growled eagerly at the thought.

The neighbours would want to know where he'd come from; she'd have to think of something. Perhaps she could tell them that he was related to her in some roundabout way; after all, any number of folk were having to take in the homeless so there was no reason why she shouldn't have him to live with her, was there?

No reason except that Con would play holy hell about it.

Well, let him, she didn't care. And it was her house, when all was said and done.

Katie knew the minute she saw the twins' faces that her black dress was every bit as dull and unsuitable for Liverpool's best ballroom's big Christmas Dance as she had thought.

Even Jean was looking at her sympathetically. Katie's heart sank even lower. She really wished that she had not agreed to go to this dance. As her father's assistant it had been necessary for her to wear businesslike clothes that helped her to fade into the background, not pretty dance dresses.

'Are you really going to the Grafton in that?' Lou, always more forthright than her twin, asked.

'Lou . . .' Jean objected, shaking her head at her daughter.

'It's all right,' Katie assured her. 'I know that my dress is very dull, but I didn't think to bring a dance frock with me.' Her words were both the truth and a small face-saving exercise, since in reality she did not possess a 'dance frock', but no one need know that.

'Nobody will ask you to dance if you wear that. It's too dull, more like what me and Sasha will have to wear when we go to work in Lewis's,' Lou told her.

'Lou, that's enough.' Jean sounded stern now and Katie felt obliged to defend the child.

'Lou's right, my frock isn't suitable for a Christmas Dance, but unfortunately I'm going to have to wear it because it's all I've got.'

'You could have borrowed something from Grace if she'd been here,' said Sasha, 'couldn't she, Mum?'

'Yes, I'm sure she could. Wait a minute!' Jean exclaimed. 'I've just had a thought. There's that trunk full of clothes our Fran left behind. I'm sure she wouldn't mind you borrowing something from her if we can find something suitable, Katie. That is, if you don't mind borrowing?'

'Of course she doesn't, do you, Katie?' Lou answered for her.

Without appearing rude Katie had no choice but to agree.

Ten minutes later the four of them were upstairs in Katie's neat, tidy bedroom, but which now reminded her of an expensive dress salon. Clothes were lying on the bed – expensive, beautifully made, elegant clothes that Katie's mother would have loved.

'What about this, Katie?' Lou demanded, pirouetting round the room on her toes, holding a pale grey silk taffeta evening dress in front of her. It had a white sash waist and a matching short-sleeved bolero jacket decorated with one white and one grey silk flower that nestled stylishly together.

It was, Katie knew without even inspecting it properly, a very expensive outfit. It was also perfect for her colouring, and some female instinct she hadn't known she possessed until now yearned for her to wear it. Even so, she felt obliged to demur.

'It is beautiful, but it looks very expensive.'

'Oh, Fran won't mind, will she, Mum?'

'I'm sure that she won't, Katie,' Jean agreed. 'Why don't you try it on?'

By the time Katie had got the dress on and discovered that it fitted her as though it had been made for her, Jean had found a pair of grey satin shoes to match it, along with a small evening bag, and once the twins had seen her in her borrowed finery, Katie recognised that there was no way she was going to be allowed out of the Campion house wearing her own dull black frock.

'If you're sure that your sister won't mind . . . ?' Katie asked Jean yet again.

'She won't mind at all,' Jean assured her. 'But you'll need a coat. It's a cold night and if I know anything about the Grafton at this time of the year you'll be queuing outside for a while before you can get in.'

'That's all right; I'll wear my own coat,' Katie told her.

Her change of clothes made her later meeting Carole than they had planned, which meant that there was indeed rather a long queue for them to join, even though it was only just gone six o'clock.

'That's because it's the big Saturday night Christmas Dance,' Carole told her. 'Everyone wants to get a good table. I'm glad we've got tickets. They're making those in the queue who haven't got them wait.' She gave Katie a warning dig in the ribs and giggled. 'Just look over there at those army lads eyeing us up.'

The young men in question had just climbed out of an army truck. One of them, with more cheek than was good for him, Katie thought, winked at them and called out, 'Waiting for us, girls?'

'Ooohh, cheek,' Carole breathed, but it was plain to Katie that she was not at all averse to the attention.

The young men looked decent enough, although the tall one with thick dark hair and the kind of stern, almost brooding, expression that made him look a bit like a film star, didn't seem too pleased about his friend's flirting.

'We could be all right tonight with that lot in,' Carole told Katie, giggling again as she added, 'Mine's the one with the fair hair and the nice teeth.'

The dark-haired one had turned his head to look right at them, and Katie suspected that he didn't approve of what he saw. He was wearing a corporal's stripes on his jacket so perhaps he thought himself a cut above the other men and above the kind of girls who flirted with them. The dismissive look he was giving them irked Katie. He might look like a film star but looks weren't everything.

'You can have them all. I'm not interested,' she told Carole in a cool voice, adding a smart toss of her head for good measure. She wasn't having any chap thinking that she was the sort that would go chasing after him.

'Just like I said before,' Carole laughed, good-naturedly, 'you're after someone rich who isn't in uniform.'

Katie didn't say anything. She liked Carole but she suspected that the other girl wanted to egg her on so that she would join her in flirting with the army boys, and Katie didn't want to do that. It wasn't that flirting was beneath her, exactly – Katie hoped she wasn't the sort that thought herself 'above' other girls in any kind of way – but at the same time she didn't feel comfortable with the kind of giggly eyelash-fluttering behaviour to attract male interest that Carole plainly enjoyed.

The queue was moving forward and the army boys were slotting into it almost directly behind the girls. Katie could see that the tall good-looking corporal was giving her a contemptuous look. Well, let him. She didn't care.

Luke's mouth compressed as Katie turned away from him. So she was after a rich man, was she? Well, he might have guessed that just from the way she looked. She was outstandingly pretty, and she had that air about her when she stuck her nose up that somehow said she thought she was a cut above chaps like him. Not that Luke cared for one minute. Certainly not. If he was interested in getting himself a girl, which he wasn't, it would be one who was more like her friend, with her ready smile and her bubbly personality.

Luke hadn't wanted to come to the Grafton tonight; he'd much rather have gone down to Hatton Gardens and had a chat with his father, to find out just how much damage had been done last night by the Luftwaffe's bombs. However, his men had begged him to come with them and seeing as some of them were still pretty wet behind the

72

ears, in a strange city, and desperate for a bit of female company, Luke had decided that it was his duty to keep an eye on them. The Grafton was a respectable dance hall, Liverpool's best – his own sister came here – but still he didn't want to see his men getting themselves into any kind of trouble by drinking too much and flirting with the wrong girls. There had already been reports of fights breaking out between local men and lads in uniform when there'd been a bit of a misunderstanding over a girl.

Girls! Luke was glad that he'd decided not to get involved with one. Falling in love with Lillian and then discovering that she'd just been making a fool of him had done him a favour. He wasn't the green fool now that he'd been when he had first met her. Take now, for instance; he'd seen straight off what that uppity-looking girl was like, and he wasn't wrong either. She was another Lillian; the sort for whom a decent ordinary chap wasn't good enough. The sort that wanted a chap with money and prospects, not one who was proud to put on a uniform and fight for his country.

'The quiet one's a smart piece,' Andy Lawrence, the fair-haired private who had so cheekily called out to the girls, told Luke admiringly in a low voice, as they stood in the queue behind Katie and Carole.

'Stuck-up piece, more like,' Luke answered him. 'You heard what she said: she's after a chap with money.'

Unlike Andy, Luke had not made any attempt

73

to keep his voice down, and Katie, overhearing Luke's comment, could feel her ears burning.

Well, let him think what he liked, she decided defensively. She didn't care, and she didn't have to explain herself to him either.

It was a cold night, and those girls lucky enough to be queuing with a partner were snuggling up close, whilst several groups of girls were shivering and complaining that their feet would be so numb they wouldn't be able to dance. Sensibly Katie was wearing her stout work shoes and carrying her borrowed dance shoes in a drawstring canvas bag. She was still conscious of feeling cold, though, and hoped that her nose had not gone too obviously pink.

'I'm freezing,' Carole complained.

'You can have a borrow of my coat, love,' the cheeky soldier behind them announced, over-hearing Carole's complaint, 'but you'll have to share it with me.'

'Ooohhh.' Carole pretended to complain, but Katie could see that her eyes were shining and she was smiling.

The army boys were, of course, trying to look as though the cold wasn't affecting them and that they were far too tough and manly to be affected by a bit of winter weather. Actually, their corporal looked as though he *wasn't* affected by it, Katie admitted, watching him hunch one shoulder and turn out of the wind as he lit himself a cigarette.

It had just gone twenty past six when Katie and Carole finally got inside, and handed over their coats to the cloakroom attendant.

'Here, can you keep my ticket with yours?' Carole asked her. 'Only your bag is bigger than mine.' Her eyes widened as she gazed at Katie's frock. 'Oh, you look ever so nice, Katie. Proper smart and stylish.'

'It isn't mine,' Katie felt obliged to admit, sensing that Carole was just a little bit put out by the elegance of Katie's outfit. 'All I had was the black frock I wear when I go out with my dad, so my landlady very kindly let me borrow this. It belongs to her sister, but she's with ENSA – you know, the Entertainments National Service Association, whereby entertainers join up and go out to entertain the troops – and she's touring somewhere at the moment.'

To Katie's relief her explanation had obviously mollified Carole because she told her generously, 'Well, it looks ever so glamorous, it really does. It makes you look proper posh and no mistake.'

People were just starting to make their way into the ballroom, and out of habit Katie looked towards the band in their alcove next to the dance floor. She had already seen from the programme pinned up in the foyer that the band leader was a Mrs Wilf Hamer. Katie didn't think she'd met her; for one thing she suspected that her father, who was inclined to be old-fashioned about such matters, would not have approved of a female band leader. She had forgotten all about the army boys in the queue now and the hostility of the tall dark handsome one, as she focused on the band, or so she told herself.

*   *   *

It was a pity the boy was so weak. Emily would have liked him to walk a bit faster so that they could get away from the theatre, just in case they were seen.

They'd almost reached the end of the alley when the boy stopped walking and went rigid.

Now what was wrong with him? Emily wondered what on earth she could do to get him to move and then looked back over her shoulder, keen to get away before anyone came out of the theatre and saw them.

Had those bullies hurt him worse than she had thought? Was he in some kind of pain?

'What is it, what's wrong?' she began, only to stop when he suddenly looked up at the sky in terror.

Then Emily heard it: the low droning sound of approaching bombers, quickly followed by the shrill anxious scream of the air-raid warning.

A thrill of fear went through her, rooting her to the spot, followed by a sense of urgency as she cast a frantic look around herself for an air-raid shelter. The only one she could remember was two streets away on the far side of Roe Street.

'Come on, we need to get ourselves into a shelter,' she told the boy, her head down as she broke into a lumbering run towards Roe Street, dragging the boy with her.

Already the night sky was alight with the first crop of incendiary bombs, exploding into the darkness and, as they did so, illuminating the destruction they were causing. Emily froze in horror as one landed on the roof of a building in the next street, and then exploded, sending up a shower of bricks. Woven into the hellish noise of the devastation were the sounds of running feet, cries of warning, and screams of fear and pain as people fled the building and tried to escape the bombs.

Breaking free of the horror transfixing her, Emily started to run for the safety of the air-raid shelter, somehow managing to dodge the shards of flying glass from blown-out windows.

Overhead she could still hear the drone of engines, the bombs falling in a seemingly neverending hell of explosions, followed by the collapsing of buildings. It looked as though the whole of the city and the sky above it were on fire.

As she looked up, desperately trying to track the downward fall of a cluster of incendiaries, one she hadn't seen fell into a neighbouring street, blowing out the windows of the buildings ahead of them. Instinctively Emily grabbed the boy, swinging him round in front of her and protecting him with her own body as she turned her back to the blast.

When she turned back again she was shaking so much she could hardly move. But they had to move. She *had* to, for the boy's sake. She had to think about him and not give way to her own fear.

Picking her way through the broken glass and ignoring the cacophony of fearful sounds all around her, Emily hurried on.

They had almost reached Roe Street when suddenly the boy tried to pull out of her hold, digging in his heels.

'What is it?' Emily asked him, desperate to get them both to the safety of the air-raid shelter. The street they were in now was virtually empty, and Emily's instincts were urging her to run for safety, but she couldn't leave the boy. An air-raid warden standing at the crossroads ahead of them yelled out, warning her to get off the street, but his words were lost behind the noise from the exploding incendiaries raining down from the sky, as a fresh wave of bombers roared in overhead and attacked the docks and the waterfront. The clamour of bells from the fire engines racing to put out the fires made Emily's heart pound dizzily.

'Come on,' Emily begged the boy, tugging him forward, only to stop and gasp in fear at the sound of a plane so low overhead, it hurt her ears. Instinctively Emily pushed the boy to the ground and then flung herself down on top of him. As she lay there, hardly daring to breathe, an enormous explosion shook the ground, followed by a flash of searing heat. Emily could hear buildings collapsing all around her. Dust and smoke were stinging her eyes, and clogging her throat and nose. Something, Emily didn't know what, a brick perhaps, thumped down on top of her, followed by another. The sky was raining debris and death.

Katie and Carole were just sitting down at the table they had secured right on the edge of the dance floor when the air-raid siren went off. The two girls looked at one another in mutual consternation, whilst Luke, who had been watching his lads head for the bar, martialled them all together, ready for whatever action might need to be taken.

All in all Luke reckoned there were about two hundred people in the ballroom.

The shrill scream of falling bombs had everyone who could including Katie and Carole diving under the tables for cover.

Katie, who was hoping that her borrowed dress would survive such rough treatment, managed to resist the childish urge to clap her hands over her ears when the ballroom reverberated to the sound of a bomb exploding above their heads, followed by the terrifying sight of a hail of shrapnel coming through the plaster ceiling. The lights flickered and dipped but mercifully managed to stay on.

Katie could see the band leader, Mrs Hamer, diving for cover under the piano, as the shrapnel seemed to chase her, scoring deep marks in the dance floor and marking it right the way across, almost up to the bandstand itself. It all happened so quickly, the shrapnel travelling at such speed, that Katie could only shudder and marvel at the band leader's lucky escape, whilst saying an automatic prayer for her own father and his safety far away in London, where he too would be working tonight.

'It's the theatre next door that's been hit,' a fire watcher, who had come running into the building from outside, yelled out. 'But the explosion's taken off half the Grafton's roof.'

Some band members, emerging from cowering under their seats, briefly struck up a rousing tune, quickly applauded by the dancers huddled under the tables.

'I'm scared,' Carole wailed to Katie. 'I want to go.'

'It's too late for us to go anywhere now, with bombs still dropping. We'll all have to stay here until they sound the all clear,' Katie told her.

They could hear bombs exploding close at hand, and then abruptly the lights went off. Katie held her breath but they didn't come back on again.

'We'll be killed if we stay here.'

Katie could feel Carole trembling, and she could hear in her voice that she was close to tears.

'No we won't,' Katie told her stoutly. 'They'll leave us alone now, just you wait and see.' Behind her own back Katie had her fingers crossed. She was every bit as scared as Carole but there was no point in saying so. She was practised at re-assuring her mother in air raids and slipped easily into the role of being the strong sensible comforter.

'Listen, the band's started playing,' she encouraged Carole. 'You stay here. I'm going to see if there's any candles.' Katie took from her handbag the torch such as they had all learned to carry since the blackout laws had come into force, and crawled out from beneath the table, trying not to damage her borrowed dress.

Luke, having used his own torch to ensure that his men were all unharmed, and knowing that they couldn't leave the dance hall until the all clear had gone unless they wanted to risk being caught in the open whilst bombs were being dropped, caught sight of a very harassed-looking Mr Malcolm Munro, the Grafton's manager. He went up and introduced himself, offering the services of himself and his men.

'I'd be grateful to you for whatever you can do, Corporal,' Mr Munro told him gratefully. 'We've lost nearly half the roof, by the looks of it. Not that you can see much with the power gone.'

'We've all got torches so we can go and take a look at the ceiling to make sure it's safe. If you happen to have any tarpaulins around we could try and secure the roof for you until you can get summat proper sorted out.' Luke had to raise his voice to make himself heard above a group of screaming girls who were having hysterics.

He looked round the ballroom. Already someone was moving about quietly, lighting candles and placing them on the tables. Luke frowned when he realised that it was the snooty girl from the queue. Somehow she hadn't struck him as the sort who would get stuck in in such a quiet and efficient way.

It didn't take long for Luke and his men to confirm that the ceiling wasn't in any immediate danger of collapsing onto the dance floor, despite the shrapnel damage, but Mr Munro had been right about the roof. And they didn't need their torches to show them how much damage had been done. The arc lights from the anti-aircraft batteries, combined with the light from the fires burning in bombed buildings, provided more than enough for them to see where a whole mess of timbers and slates had fallen inwards into the roof space, leaving a gaping hole where the roof itself had been blown right off.

Luckily the ballroom manager had taken the precaution of providing himself with a good set of extending ladders and some tarpaulins, 'just in case, like the ARP lot told us we should do,' as he explained to Luke.

'Two of you hold on to them and the rest of you stay here,' Luke told his men as he prepared to climb the ladders once they had been extended into the roof space as close to the damage as Luke deemed it safe to place them.

'Why don't you let one of us go up, Corp?' one of the men suggested, but Luke shook his head.

If there were any risks then as their corporal it was only right that he should be the one to take them. Besides, when your dad was a member of the Salvage Corps you grew up knowing a thing or two about climbing ladders in unsafe buildings.

He went up slowly and carefully, testing his weight against the wall until he was level with what had been the roof and was now a gaping hole. He was just about to poke his head through the hole when suddenly the ladder started to slide sideways on the wall.

Down below him Luke could hear a warning shout as his men fought to steady the ladder. Remembering his father's tales of his own work, Luke spread his arms wide onto the wall, his stomach lurching when, instead of wall, his right hand met cold night air.

'You're going to have to move the ladder over to the left, lads,' he called down as calmly as he could. 'The wall's gone on the right-hand side up here. You're going to have to lift the ladder, two of you to each leg – just ease it up off the ground.'

He had to swallow down the sick sour taste in his mouth as he felt the ladder jerk and sway.

'That's it.' It was up to him to stay calm and keep the men steady. If he panicked then they would panic. 'Now just ease it over – nice and gently.'

He was having to lean all his weight to the left of the ladder to keep it flat against the wall. His right hand caught the rough edges of a broken brick, dislodging it in a shower of brick dust. His heart was pounding, and so was his head. If he fell now or, even worse, if the ruddy wall gave way . . . The ladder jerked and swayed, and he heard a muttered curse from below. His right hand was on solid brick now, but he couldn't risk putting any pressure on the wall yet. He counted four more bricks and then pressed his hand flat to the fifth, his breath easing from him as it held solidly.

'That's it, lads,' he called down, adding laconically, 'Thanks for the lift.'

It wouldn't be good for their morale to let them think he'd been scared that they couldn't do it.

Checking that the ladder was steady, he climbed the last few rungs and looked out into the cold night air. In the light of the fires and the searchlights from the batteries, Luke could see the damage that had been inflicted on the West Derby Road area of the city. Instinctively he looked towards Hatton Gardens, where the Salvage Corps, for which his father worked, was based, his heart thudding into his chest wall when he saw that the area had been hit and was on fire.

'Here, can you smell that?' Andy Lawrence called out from down below him. 'Smells like me mum's kitchen on Christmas morning.'

There was indeed a rich mouth-watering smell of roasting poultry.

'They've got St John's Market,' Luke told his men after he had gone back down the ladder to rejoin them. Andy, typically, given his enjoyment of a bit of fun and a joke, groaned and announced, 'Well, I reckon that'll be our Christmas dinners gone.'

Luke smiled but his thoughts were with his father, anxiety creasing his forehead as he saw the fire engulfing the Hatton Gardens area. The salvage teams weren't normally called out until the fires had been put out, which meant that with any luck his dad would be safe at home, in the air-raid shelter at the end of the road.

'Ruddy hell, there ain't going to be much of the city left if the Luftwaffe carries on like this,' Graham Moores, one of the older men, announced bleakly whilst Jim Taylor, the newest recruit who was only just eighteen, had gone very quiet and looked a sickly green colour in the light of the other men's torches.

'Well,' Luke told his men briskly, 'the theatre next door's taken a hit, but there's a bit of a parapet running round the roof of this building and I reckon it should be safe enough for us to stand on whilst we fix things.'

As he finished speaking, Mr Munro and some

of his staff came puffing up the stairs, carrying between them some heavy tarpaulins.

'When I got these in,' the Grafton's manager told Luke ruefully, 'I didn't think I'd be needing them on the night of my Christmas Dance. The trams have stopped running, and the whole of the West Derby Road is a sea of broken glass, so I've just heard from one of the fire watchers who was on the building across from the theatre.' The manager shook his head, obviously struggling to come to terms with what had happened, and what was still happening closer to the dock area of the city if the spasmodic bursts of explosives from the German bombs, interrupted by the fierce retaliatory booming of the anti-aircraft guns, was anything to go by.

'We've got some more ladders down in the basement, if you think you can put these tarpaulins up,' the Grafton's manager told Luke hopefully, adding, 'I'll see that your lads are well rewarded for their trouble, by the way – free drinks tonight, and free entrance over Christmas and the New Year.'

Luke grinned as the men gave a loud cheer.

'Now that you've said that I reckon they'd have those tarpaulins up, ladders or no ladders,' he told Mr Munro.

As the men under Luke's able direction set to clearing what they could of the mess by torchlight, preparatory to putting up the tarpaulins, Luke could hear the music from the dance band down below them. He had a mental image of the snooty girl with her shiny dark curls and her plain silver-grey dress, which had somehow looked so much more eye-catching than the fancier dresses of any of the other girls, going quietly from table to table lighting candles. It was an image at odds with his initial impression of her. She hadn't struck him as the sort that would do anything as homely as light candles, never mind be quick-thinking enough to find some and put them to good use in the circumstances. She was probably only doing it because she wanted to see if there were any rich blokes about, Luke told himself cynically, unwilling to give her any real credit for thinking of others.

'Are you all right, love? Can you stand up?'

Emily wasn't sure. She ached all over, but at least her rescuer had removed the debris that had fallen on her. As she turned her head to look at him, Emily could see that he was extending his hand to help her. Emily blinked and focused on the ARP band on his arm. There was glass and debris everywhere, and the air smelled of smoke and fear and roasting poultry.

Watching her sniff the air, the warden told her, 'They got St John's Market, so that's half the city's Christmas dinner gone up in smoke, along with the rest.'

The warden was still waiting for her to make an effort to stand up. Reluctantly Emily did so, exhaling shakily in relief when the boy moved with her.

To her astonishment she actually seemed to be in one piece and unharmed, and the boy too, unlike some of the buildings nearby.

Taking the ARP warden's outstretched hand, Emily struggled to her feet, dragging the boy with her. All around her Emily could see blown-out windows, the road a mass of broken glass and roof slates, a front door sticking up at an odd angle from amongst the rubble of what had been a wall. The whole northwest side of the city seemed to be on fire. The street was empty apart from themselves.

Apprehensively Emily turned round to look towards the theatre, her breath easing from her lungs in a creaking gust of relief when she saw that the building was still standing. She was just about to ask the ARP warden if he knew if anyone had been hurt, when there was a sudden whoosh of sound, followed by the loudest bang Emily had ever heard, which would have had her diving for the ground again if the warden hadn't kept hold of her.

Another warden came racing up the street. 'That was the chemical factory in Hanover Street,' he told them breathlessly. 'The Corporation's had to send to Lancashire for reinforcements, we've got that many fires burning.'

Emily was properly on her feet now, and the boy with her, miraculously also unharmed.

'You two are a lucky pair,' the warden told her. 'There's a bomb dropped on Roe Street that's left a crater the size of a house, and if you'd been a dozen or more yards down the road, you'd have had it and no mistake—' He broke off and cursed under his breath as a fire engine came racing down Roe Street towards them, and the bomb crater.

'No, stop!' The warden ran towards it, waving his hands and yelling in warning, but it was too late. Right in front of her eyes Emily saw the fire engine, with its crew on board, plunge right into the crater, with a sickening sound of breaking glass and tearing metal.

'Jeff! Pete!' the warden was calling out, Emily and the boy forgotten as two other ARP men raced with him towards the crater, from which flames were already emerging.

Emily took the boy's hand and turned away. There was nothing they could do, after all.

To the north, the whole of the city along the shoreline seemed to be on fire and the planes were still coming, attacking the dock area now, the night sky illuminated by the growing number of fires and the coloured arcs of the tracer bullets from the anti-aircraft batteries.

The ARP men by the crater were saying something about it looking like everyone in the fire engine had 'bought it'.

Emily shivered and held the boy's hand more tightly.

Later she found it hard to recall how long it had taken them to walk up Wavertree Road, scrunching over pavements strewn with broken glass, and past bombed-out burning buildings. There was no comforting stop at the chippie. Its windows were blown out and its owners in an air-raid shelter. Where they should be, Emily knew, but if she was going to die she'd prefer to die in her own bed in clean sheets, thank you very much, not some council shelter where you'd be mixing with all sorts. The people of Wavertree Village had certain standards, make no mistake about it.

Every time she heard a plane overhead Emily clung more tightly to the boy's hand. He had saved her life once tonight, after all.

'Katie, is it really you?'

Katie had just reached the table closest to the band, with her candles, as they were about to take a break, and a wide smile curved her mouth as she returned the warmly enthusiastic hug of the sax player, Eric, whose family had originally come from Hungary, and who had played for a while in one of the bands conducted by her father.

'How is your father?' Eric asked her eagerly. 'He is well? Safe? There have been so many bombs in London.'

'He is very well, thank you, Eric,' Katie answered. 'And you?'

'I am well too, but I hadn't expected this. We came away from London to escape from the bombings.'

Luke's men had done all that they could do, and now that the tarpaulins were safely in place, Luke had agreed that they could accept Mr Munro's offer of a free drink.

'Not too much, mind,' he warned the men as they re-entered the candlelit ballroom. 'It isn't Christmas yet, lads.'

The girl, the stuck-up one, was standing over

by the alcove talking to a member of the band. They were laughing together and the man had his hand on her arm. Pretty nifty work on his part, Luke reckoned, and the girl didn't look as if she objected to his familiarity. So, a bit free with her favours then, as well as wanting a rich husband. Not that he cared. She didn't appeal to him one little bit.

Seeing Hatton Gardens in flames had left Luke feeling on edge and wishing that he could go across and find out what was going on. It irked him to be stuck here in a ballroom when he could be doing something far more useful, but rules were rules, and if he went off and left his men to their own devices anything could happen. Half of them would have too much to drink and the other half would be taking Dutch leave, and then there'd be hell to pay in the morning when they weren't fit to report for duty.

No, he had to stay with them and keep an eye on them. The barman was offering him a beer, but Luke shook his head, and asked for lemonade instead.

'Lemonade, Corp? That's a girl's drink,' Andy grinned.

'Well, one of us has got to keep a sober head on his shoulders and since I *am* your corporal it had better be me,' he told them.

'You know what,' one of the other men announced, eyeing the dance floor, 'I reckon this dancing by candlelight could be a pretty good thing. You can get a girl close and do a bit of smooching.'

'That's enough of that,' Luke warned him, but

he could see that the men were looking hopefully towards those tables occupied solely by girls.

The band was ready to start playing again. Katie had been introduced to Mrs Hamer and the other members of the band now, all of whom had heard of her father.

'What was all that about?' Carole hissed when Katie returned to their table.

'Eric knows my father and he was asking after him.'

'Them army lads have come back from fixing the roof,' Carole told her, 'and that fair-haired one's been looking over here ever such a lot. I reckon he'll be asking me to dance before the night's out.'

'He certainly will if you keep on making sheep's eyes at him,' Katie agreed.

Carole pulled a face and protested mock innocently, 'What a thing to say. I can't think what you mean,' and then started to giggle, nudging Katie as she said, 'He's got ever such a nice smile, though, hasn't he?'

Katie's expression softened. She could never behave like Carole, but she still couldn't help feeling her own mood lightened by the other girl's bubbly manner. Perhaps her mother had been right to tell her that she was too serious, but if that was how she was, she couldn't change her nature, could she?

Mr Munro had gone over to Mrs Hamer and was saying something to her, and then he turned round and announced, 'Let's hear a cheer for our army lads, and if any single young lady here has anything about her I reckon she'll be the first on her feet to ask one of them to dance when the band starts playing, because the next dance will be a ladies' excuse me in their honour.'

There was a cheer from the occupants of the tables, and then a lot of laughter, as the men were herded onto the floor, looking bashful, and three or four daring girls got to their feet and went over to them to claim their partners.

Carole needed no further encouragement or excuse. She was on her feet, dragging Katie up with her.

'Come on,' she demanded, ignoring Katie's objections. 'I'm not letting some other girl walk off with that lad I've got me own eye on.'

It was only innocent fun, and sanctioned by the Grafton's manager – a nice way for them all to show their appreciation for what the men had done, Katie knew – but still she felt very self-conscious about it all, even though they were far from the first or the fastest of the girls to approach the soldiers.

In fact, since Katie had hung back, by the time she actually reached the dance floor and the soldiers, to her relief all the men seemed to be partnered.

She was just about to turn round and go and sit down again when Mr Munro himself appeared at her side, announcing, 'Here you are, Corporal. Here's a partner for you. Now don't say "no". I'm well aware that you're the one who ensured that your men did such a good job, and I'm sure this charming young lady here is as keen to show her appreciation as I am to show mine.'

It was *her*, the stuck-up one. Luke's heart sank. He didn't want to dance with anyone but least of all with her. The last time he had danced here it had been with Lillian, just before he had left with the BEF for France. Last Christmas, in fact.

He didn't want to dance with her, Katie could tell. Well, she didn't want to dance with him either, and she held herself stiffly away from him to let him know it.

She was dancing with him as though he was a bad smell under her nose, Luke thought angrily.

The band swung into a pacey swing number, designed to get things moving, and allow those who had the skills to show off their best steps.

Katie might not be able to sing but she was a very good dancer, something that had been an additional source of discord between her parents when she had been growing up, as her mother claimed that Katie's ability to dance had been passed on to her daughter by her, whilst her father had retaliated by saying that he did not want a daughter who thought that prancing around on a stage meant that she had 'talent'.

Whilst the other couples, taking advantage of Mr Munro's invitation to the girls to choose their own partners, were eager to take advantage of the mood of the moment – a potent mix of male bravery and heroism, and female bravado, spiced with the kind of music that allowed the more adventurous men to take a firm hold of their partners and draw them closer – Luke and Katie were determinedly keeping one another at a rigid arm's length, both making it plain that they were more than delighted when the music finally stopped.

Ten minutes later, having politely refused an invitation to dance from a smartly uniformed RAF officer, who in Katie's opinion had thought rather too much of himself, Katie had the galling experience of sitting at their table and watching as the angry, good-looking corporal danced expertly past with another girl. Katie rarely got the chance to dance and when she did it was even rarer for her to have the kind of partner who danced well. Musicians did not in general have much spare time to learn to dance. And now here was this soldier who had danced with her as woodenly as though he were a puppet on strings, dancing with another girl so well that it was no wonder she looked as though she was in seventh heaven.

'Phew,' Carole announced breathlessly, sinking down into her chair as her partner returned her to their table, 'that was fun. You'll never guess what,' she added after she had finished fanning herself energetically with her hand, 'Andy's only asked me if I'll go to the pictures with him the next time he gets a pass out. The boys are based only down the road at Seacombe.' She gave Katie an arch look. 'I saw you dancing with that corporal; he's ever so good-looking, isn't he?'

'Is he? I hadn't noticed,' Katie lied.

Carole laughed and shook her head in a way that implied that she didn't believe Katie for one minute.

Whilst the band was playing it was relatively easy to forget what was happening outside, but

94

whenever the music stopped the sound of German planes dropping bombs was a stark reminder of the reality of the situation.

Whilst Katie and Carole were in the ladies, two other girls were discussing the bombing, one of them complaining to the other, 'I told you we shouldn't have come out tonight after the bombing last night. If we'd done as I said then we'd be safe in a proper air-raid shelter now.'

Her friend tossed her brown curls and argued firmly, 'Well, I'd rather be bombed here, whilst I'm enjoying meself, than stuck in some air-raid shelter, and besides, they aren't always safe. There was that one at the Durning Road Technical School where all those poor folk were killed in November, and I've heard of others as well. If a bomb drops on a shelter, then you could end up being buried alive. At least if we bought it here, I'd have had some fun.'

'Fun. That's all you think about, Marianne Dunkin. I'm more interested in staying alive,' her friend retorted tearfully, 'and if you think I'm letting you persuade me to come dancing again whilst this war's on then you've got another think coming.'

They were still arguing as they left the cloakroom, the door swinging closed after them.

Carole, who had gone unusually quiet and rather pale, shivered and asked Katie anxiously, 'You don't think we'll get bombed again, do you?'

'Of course not. No one ever gets bombed twice in the same night,' Katie reassured her with a conviction she was far from feeling.

*　　*　　*

95

The toffee-nosed girl seemed to be enjoying herself dancing with the young Canadian airman who was partnering her now, Luke recognised as he watched Katie dance past. The Canadian looked pretty smitten with her. Well, more fool him, since he was only a lowly private.

Luke was itching to leave the Grafton and set to with the work he knew would be going on, to do what could be done to counter the effects of the bombing, but his first duty was to his men. He had sneaked outside a couple of times to look with despair at the destruction that the bombs had caused. The electric tram wires were down along the West Derby Road, outside the Grafton, and broken glass from blown-out windows covered the road. Instead of the Christmas skies being filled with Santa's sledge piled high with the presents of children's fairy tales, the skies over Liverpool were filled with the Luftwaffe, bringing death and destruction as Christmas 'gifts' to the people of the city.

They had made it. Emily leaned gratefully on the inside of the front door as she stood in the dark hallway of her home, the boy at her side.

There had been plenty of moments when she had feared that they wouldn't make it, but they had.

Wave after wave of planes had come in over their heads, heading for the docks, where they dropped their deadly cargo. The north side of the city seemed to be ringed with fires lighting up the night sky.

The worst moment was when they had walked past a newly bombed house and Emily had seen the tears sliding down the faces of the children standing outside it, making oily tracks through the soot from what had once been their chimney. They had been inside when the bomb had hit, Emily had heard one of the children telling their rescuers, taking refuge under the table they had put under the stairs, just like the local ARP man had told them, and now their granddad was dead and their mam taken off to hospital.

As she and the boy had turned into Emily's own road, she had heard a thin reedy elderly female voice calling out, 'Tiddles, where are you?'

Emily's father had had electricity installed in the house at the earliest opportunity, and its welcoming light banished the shadows from the hallway.

Gently pushing the boy in front of her, Emily headed for the kitchen where mercifully the Aga was still on and the kitchen warm.

She had expected the boy to be overawed by the house, but instead he seemed to take its comforts for granted.

'You can sit on here whilst I stoke up the Aga and put the kettle on,' Emily told him, pulling a chair out from the table but removing the cushion from it before letting him sit on it. 'But no moving off it, mind,' she warned him. 'I'm not having you messing up my house, filthy like you are.'

He was trying to stifle a yawn, his face white with fatigue, and Emily had to harden her heart against the pathetic sight he made.

'I know you're tired,' she told him, 'but I'm not

having you sleeping between my nice clean sheets until you've had a bath.'

He still hadn't spoken, but he was listening to her and watching her.

Quickly Emily banked up the Aga. She was tired and hungry, but she couldn't eat without feeding the boy as well and he certainly couldn't eat using her clean china in the filthy state he was in, so she would have to wait until she had made sure he was bathed and clean.

'Come on,' she told him. 'Come with me.'

In the airing cupboard she found some old towels that she kept for the theatre because of all the greasepaint that Con managed to get on them. It never washed out properly, no matter what instructions she gave them at the laundry.

'Here's the bathroom,' she told the boy, opening the door to show him. 'I'll run you a bath and then you'll take off your clothes and get in it and give yourself a good scrub.'

Normally Emily stuck rigidly to the letter of the law, but the boy was so dirty he was going to need two baths, not just one, and she certainly wasn't going to let him put those filthy clothes back on. He'd have to sleep in one of Con's old shirts tonight.

It was gone midnight before Emily finally climbed into her own bed. The boy, bathed, fed and wearing an old flannel shirt that trailed on the floor behind him, was tucked up in bed in the spare room with a hot-water bottle to keep him warm. There'd been a black rim round the bath like she'd kept coal in it, and when she'd washed his clothes, his vest had fallen apart in her hands, it was that full of holes. Poor little mite. She'd been surprised to see what a nice-looking lad he was once he was clean, but it was beginning to worry her that he wouldn't speak. Could it be that he was deaf and dumb? There'd been a girl when she'd been at school whose sister had been like that, and her family had made signs to her when they wanted to tell her something, Emily remembered.

She yawned tiredly and reached out to switch off the bedside light, only realising as she did so that Con hadn't come in. Well, his absence was no loss to her.

FIVE

It was half-past five in the morning and the all clear had finally sounded. Wearily, Jean woke the twins whilst Sam gathered up their things. Around them in the air-raid shelter their neighbours were also stirring and throwing off the dark fear and dread of the night. They had survived, although just how much of their city had also managed to survive after the pasting it had had from the Luftwaffe remained to be seen, Sam told Jean as they walked tiredly home.

The kitchen felt warm and comforting after the chill of the shelter. Jean had just finished washing up from their tea when the air-raid siren had gone off, and the dishes were still on the draining board.

'I'll put the kettle on,' she told Sam as she stifled a weary yawn.

'You look done in, love. Why don't you go up and have an hour in bed?' Sam suggested.

'I can never sleep in the shelter. It doesn't seem proper somehow, sleeping when you're with all them other people, even if there is a war on and they are our neighbours.'

'I know what you mean,' Sam agreed. 'It will be all hands to the pumps for us today, clearing up the mess Hitler's left us with. I'll go up and have a bit of a wash and then I'd better get down to the yard. We won't be able to see how much damage has been done until it's properly light, of course.'

'I just hope that Katie's all right.'

'She'll be safe in one of the shelters, love.'

The kettle had boiled. Jean reached for it, warming the pot and then sparingly spooning some fresh tea leaves into it before adding some of the tea leaves she had kept from the previous day, to give it a bit more strength.

The resultant brew wasn't the cup of tea she longed for but it was better than nothing and, more important, it was all that they could have. Not that Jean intended to complain. What did she have to complain about, after all, when both her son and her daughter were alive and well and living close enough to home for her to be able to see them regularly? Others were not so fortunate. There was more than one family in their road now that had lost someone. One of the other women in Jean's WVS group had arrived at their weekly meeting earlier in the week with red-rimmed eyes, explaining that her son, who was fighting in the desert, had been reported as missing in action. It made Jean's heart contract just to think of what she was going through.

The all clear had sounded. The two hundred or so dancers who had braved the Luftwaffe to dance the night away together, and in doing so had formed a bond in the way that young people do, began to shake hands if they were male, and exchange hugs if they were female, relieved that they were now free to leave and yet at the same time unwilling to part from one another.

A standing ovation had been given to the band for keeping them dancing, and Mr Munro had stood up and thanked both the band and the dancers.

'He's got another saxophone player coming to audition tomorrow,' Eric told Katie as he packed away his instrument. She'd gone over to say goodbye to him and she didn't want to seem rude by rushing off when he plainly wanted to chat.

Katie smiled and nodded.

Luke scowled as he watched her smiling at the musician. She was pretty pally with him on the strength of one night's acquaintanceship, but then her sort were like that, as he well knew from Lillian. They excelled at making a chap believe they thought he was the best thing out and then making him look a fool. Well, that was never going to happen to him again.

As they left the Grafton in the chilly darkness of the December morning, coats over their dance dresses, groups of girls huddled together shivering and looking down at the glass-strewn pavement and road in distress.

'There's no way any buses are going to be coming down here,' Carole told Katie unnecessarily. 'We'll have to walk.' She looked dismayed. 'And me wearing me only pair of dancing shoes. They'll be cut to ribbons.'

'We'll just have to be very careful,' Katie tried to comfort her.

The fair-haired private who had been dancing with Carole called out to his friends, 'Come on, lads. Let's see these girls safely on their way. They'll never be able to walk over this lot. Allow me to offer you some transport, modom,' he joked, putting on a fake 'posh' accent as he and another private made a seat with their crossed and joined hands, indicating that they would carry Carole over the worst of the broken glass.

She was giggling now, her dismay giving way to a dimpled smile as she settled herself into her 'transport'.

Luke came out of the Grafton just in time to see what was going on and hear Carole's giggles as his men carried her down the street.

Impatiently he strode after them, watched by Katie, who had held back from accepting an offer of her own transport, being naturally more self-conscious than her more exuberant and boisterous friend.

'You're in the British Army, you two, not the Christmas panto,' Luke barked at the two young men, causing them to put Carole down and hang their heads.

'We was only helping the girls across the worst of the broken glass, Corp,' Andy defended his actions. 'With them thin shoes they're wearing their feet would be cut to ribbons.'

It was cold and Katie was tired and unwilling to hang around outside the Grafton any longer under the disapproving gaze of the corporal, whom she was quite sure now had taken a dislike to her.

With so many torches switched on it was easy enough for her to see the ground and pick her way carefully through the glass, or at least it would have been, if she hadn't suddenly put her foot on such a smooth piece of glass that she was slipping on it.

Luke swung round as he heard Katie cry out, sprinting the few yards that separated them and reaching her just in time to catch her as she fell. Katie gasped as she was swung off her feet with so much force and speed that she fell against her rescuer's chest and was obliged to lie there, winded, with her feet dangling above the ground.

He smelled of khaki and soap and clean male sweat. A funny unfamiliar sensation seemed to pierce her body, leaving her even more breathless than his forceful rescue.

Her 'thank you' was muffled and made uncomfortable by both her awareness of how much she wished it had been any soldier but this one who had saved her, and how much he himself must dislike having had to do so.

'You can put me down now,' she told him. She dare not move. He was of necessity holding her very tightly. He had no option, having rushed to save her, of course, but it was still a very intimate hold, given that they were strangers, and she was now clasped so tightly to his body that she could actually feel the hard muscles in his thighs against her own legs. Katie was glad that it was dark, because she knew that she was blushing. Which was so silly, given the situation. He already despised her enough without her making things even worse by behaving like a silly overly dramatic type of girl who had to make a fuss about something that wasn't really anything at all. Even so, she would be very glad to be standing on her own feet and not held so close to him. He must have very strong arms to hold her like that. She was panting and had to struggle slightly for breath, but he was not breathing fast at all. Well, not very much. She could feel his heart thudding quite heavily, though. And he still hadn't put her down. In fact . . .

Katie gasped as she felt him starting to walk, still carrying her.

'Put me down,' she repeated.

'Keep still,' he warned her, ignoring her demand and carrying her across the worst of the broken glass to where Carole was standing watching.

How embarrassing. Katie felt so flushed and self-conscious. She had to thank him again, of course, after he had placed her on her feet, and she certainly didn't welcome Carole's giggled, 'It looked ever so romantic, him carrying you like that. Just like something from *Gone With the Wind*,' once they had left the men behind and were picking their way carefully through the mess.

It was nearly seven o'clock before Katie finally made it back to the Campions'. Jean welcomed her with open relief, clucking over her like a mother hen, as Katie explained what had happened.

'We were safe enough but there's been some dreadful damage, according to what I heard from the bus driver on my way back. There's been fires at Hatton Gardens and St John's Market, and there's been a church really badly burned.'

'Did you hear that, Sam?' Jean called out to her husband as he came into the kitchen to catch the tail end of Katie's comment. 'Katie says there's been a fire in Hatton Gardens.'

Hatton Gardens being the headquarters of the Salvage Corps, Sam was naturally concerned to learn more.

'I don't have any details,' Katie apologised. 'It's just what I heard. The law courts caught it as well.'

She had also heard that both Mill Road Hospital and the Royal had been hit, but she didn't want to say so, knowing how anxious it would make Jean on her daughter Grace's behalf, since Grace had probably been on duty.

'If they were going for the docks, let's hope that Derby House wasn't hit. That's where Grace's Seb works,' Jean told Katie. 'You look fit to drop, love,' she added. 'I'm going to have an hour in bed myself before church so why don't you go up and get some sleep too?'

'I think I will,' Katie agreed.

'Liverpool was bombed so badly last night I feel we ought to offer our services to those WVS groups in the city who might need some extra pairs of hands.'

Bella yawned, and then shivered. It was cold standing here outside the church, even though she was wearing her new winter coat, with its fur collar, and a matching fur hat. The coat was honey-coloured, with a nipped-in waist and a flared panelled skirt, and Bella knew that it suited her. The congregation at St Mark's always dressed smartly, with the ladies discreetly vying with one another when it came to elegance and new hats. But then, as Bella's mother was fond of saying, the congregation of St Mark's did come from the best addresses in the area, and St Mark's itself was very definitely High Church, with a locally renowned choir and a long waiting list of ladies willing to 'do the church flowers'.

Bella would have avoided being collared by the leader of her mother's WVS group, and slipped inside the church with her father before the woman had spotted them, but her mother had had other ideas.

Bella watched as members of the congregation continued to arrive: families with children dressed in Harris tweed coats and highly polished shoes, the girls' hair in plaits and the boys' slicked back, the mothers in good but sensible rather than stylish coats, and the fathers hurrying to catch up, having had to park their cars.

Bored and irritated, Bella yawned again. For one thing she had hardly had any sleep at all last night because of having to go into her dreary neighbour's air-raid shelter, and for another, her mother had told her that her father had refused to increase her allowance.

How on earth was she supposed to manage? Her clothes were virtually in rags – not that there was much to buy anyway, but she couldn't appear at any of the Tennis Club's dances in last year's frock. She had a certain position to maintain, after all.

She had told her mother this, of course, but instead of being sympathetic, her mother had actually asked her if she thought it was a good idea to go dancing when she was so very newly widowed.

'A young woman in your position has to be very careful of her reputation, Bella,' was what she had said, pursing her lips as she did so. 'No one expects you to go into full traditional mourning, of course.'

'Well, I should hope they don't,' Bella had agreed. 'Not after the way Alan and those parents of his treated me. Shameful, it was. Anyway, people should be appreciative of me trying to make a bit of an effort and do my bit in wartime instead of crying all over the place.'

'Well, yes, darling, of course,' her mother had agreed. 'No one's saying you should do that, but to go dancing . . . Daddy feels that with his position on the council and everything that it would be much better if you didn't go to the Tennis Club for a while. People talk, you know, Bella, and there was all that unpleasantness about Alan and that young woman.'

'That wasn't my fault,' Bella had reminded her mother angrily.

If she didn't watch it she was going to end up spending the rest of her life doing good works and attending boring WVS meetings, and that would not suit her at all.

To her relief her mother finally ended her conversation. Tucking her arm through Vi's, Bella headed for the warmth of the church. They were almost the last of the congregation to go in, and they had to squeeze past other worshippers to reach Bella's father.

Everything about St Mark's was rich, from the High Church smell of incense to the organ and the scarlet and white of the choristers. Even the kneeling pads were deep soft velvet – a bequest from a member of the congregation, like the prayer and hymn books.

When you said you worshipped at St Mark's, everyone knew you were 'someone'.

Jean might have told herself that she would go and have an hour in bed to make up for the sleep she had lost, but of course she didn't. For one thing she was worried about Sam, knowing the danger he would be in helping with the clearing-up operations; for another she was equally anxious about Luke and Grace, wondering how they had gone on.

When Katie arrived downstairs ahead of the twins, dressed to go to church, in her dark blue coat and her matching beret, Jean found herself warming even more to her billetee.

She couldn't take Grace's place, of course – Grace was her daughter – but Jean acknowledged that she was growing very fond of Katie.

The twins, as usual, had to be reminded several times that they were going to be late for the service before they finally came rushing down the stairs, their coats still not on.

'Why can't you two get ready on time?' Jean scolded them, hurrying them into their bright red hooded jackets, and then putting her own on – brown to go with her best skirt and twinset, and with a really smart beaver lamb collar and a matching hat – another sale bargain from Lewis's. Jean felt a bit guilty sometimes being able to have things that were so smart, thanks to Grace, when her neighbours had to make do with plainer things. But then Sam always liked to see her looking nice, and it was lovely to have a good coat.

'We had to make sure that our hair was right,' Lou told her importantly. 'Didn't we, Sash?'

Sasha nodded, her newly cut hair bouncing in soft curls round her face.

They had disappeared the previous Saturday, refusing to say where they were going, reappearing later in the afternoon with their plaits cut off.

They had saved the money from their shared paper round and their work for Mrs Lucas, they had told Jean, and she had to admit that the short style suited them. Sam predictably had been a bit put out to see his little girls suddenly transformed into stylish young women. The twins, though, had their own way of dealing with their dad, and of course having had two older siblings they had a much easier time of it, getting away with things that Sam would never have allowed in either Luke or Grace.

'We won't wait for your dad,' Jean told the twins. 'He's gone down to the depot and chances are that he'll be helping out somewhere with all the mess that will have to be cleaned up.'

'Tell us all about the Grafton, Katie,' Lou demanded, tucking her arm through Katie's whilst

Sasha did the same at the other side. Somehow between them they managed to ensure that the three of them fell back slightly from Jean, who had now been joined by their next-door-but-one neighbours for the walk to church.

'Who did you dance with? Was he handsome? Has he asked you out?' The twins' questions came thick and fast.

'There was an air raid going on,' Katie reminded them. 'We spent more time crouching under the tables for protection than we did dancing.' It wasn't entirely true, of course, but the twins already had vivid enough imaginations without her encouraging them in their romantic flights of fancy.

'But that's when the best stuff happens,' Sasha informed her, confirming Katie's own private thoughts. 'We've read about it in *Picture Post*, haven't we, Lou? It's in times of danger when a girl and a man are thrown together that "it" happens, and they fall in love.'

Sasha looked so solemn that Katie had trouble not laughing. Instead she said firmly, 'You shouldn't believe everything you read in the papers, you know. We were far too busy keeping safe last night to think about doing anything else.'

'You can say that but I bet you had more fun than we did down our air-raid shelter.' Lou's voice was gloomy. 'It was boring, wasn't it, Sash?'

'Yes, except when little Davie Simmonds from number twelve said that his nan had come out without her knickers on.'

Laughter shook the twins. For all their new haircuts and the fact that officially their schooldays were over, they were still very much 'young girls', Katie thought affectionately whilst trying to look severe.

'Terrible night, wasn't it, Jean?' Anne Briars, a fellow member of Jean's WVS group, said tiredly as they exchanged hellos outside the church.

St Thomas's was a small, slightly shabby church, on the border between Edge Hill and the bottom end of Wavertree, but Jean reckoned you could feel its warmth and kindness the moment you saw it. There was something about St Thomas's that made you think about all those who had worshipped there over the years so that you felt like you were part of one big family. The congregation wasn't poor like some folk who lived in Liverpool were, but they weren't well off either.

They did believe in helping one another, though.

'My Jeff's an ARP warden, as you know, and he was saying this morning that both Mill Road and the Royal Hospitals got hit.' She broke off when she saw Jean's face to apologise. 'Oh, I'm sorry, I forgot that your girl is working there. It didn't sound too bad from what my Jeff was saying – no one hurt or anything. The West Derby Road got it bad, though. There's no trams running, and down by the docks it's even worse. Oh, there's my sister, I'd better go over and join her.'

As Anne hurried off to join her sister, Jean's heart was thudding with anxiety for Grace.

As people arrived for the morning service, dressed in their best clothes, carefully looked after to make them last as long as possible, everyone was talking about the night's bombing raid and the damage it had done. A dull pall of smoke hung over the centre of the city and the docks, and it was still possible to see the darker plumes of smoke rising from fires that must still be burning.

People were moving into the church. Jean looked round for the twins, and was relieved to see Sam hurrying towards her. He had obviously been home first because his hair was newly slicked down.

Jean caught hold of his arm, drawing him to one side.

'Sam, Anne Briars has just told me that both the Royal and Mill Road Hospitals were bombed last night.'

'Yes, I know, but it's all right, our Grace is fine, and she said to tell you not to worry. The nurses' home wasn't touched, nor Grace's ward, although Grace had to spend the night in the air-raid shelter and ended up helping out with the patients and then having to go on duty again this morning. Not that she minds. She said she wouldn't feel comfortable not doing her bit when they've had so many casualties brought in.

'It was a shock seeing how much damage there's bin, I can tell you, especially round Hatton Gardens. The Law Library got a hit, and there was a fire engine went down into a crater in Roe Street, killing all seven of its crew.' Sam shook his head. 'They've had to bring in reinforcements from Lancashire, extra police and all sorts. I've got to get back to work meself. I've only come back to tell you that our Grace is all right, 'cos I knew what you'd be thinking the minute you heard about the hospitals being bombed.'

'What about Luke? Is there any news of the barracks?'

'No news except that the barracks are OK and Luke should be fine. The army have been called in to help with the clearing-up operation, of course. Oh, and I nearly forgot, there's a strange tale going round about the church of Our Lady and St Nicholas.'

'The Catholic church?'

'Yes, that's the one. It got bombed last night really bad, being close to the docks, and it was pretty well completely gutted, only the walls and the tower left standing. I was speaking to Joe Fields, who's with the fire service, and he reckons it was only the stout door to the tower that kept that from going up as well. Anyway, when the men went in as soon as it was cool enough this morning, they found two charred beams lying in the shape of a cross right where the altar had been. There's folk saying that it didn't happen by chance and that it's a sign from you know who.' Sam looked upwards as he spoke, his voice as solemn as his expression, and the fact that her normally practical and somewhat cynical husband could be so obviously moved by such an occurrence brought a lump to Jean's throat.

As she followed Jean and Sam and the twins into the church, Katie saw how full it was and how warmly people smiled at one another.

The church was plain inside, its pews well worn and its kneeling cushions threadbare, but this morning it was filled with an overwhelming sense of quiet purposefulness and determined reverence.

As she kneeled to pray Jean gave heartfelt thanks for the safety of her own family and said a special inward prayer for all those who this morning were mourning loved ones lost.

Luke straightened up from helping with the back-breaking work of trying to clear the streets of their covering of broken glass and other debris. It had to be all the broken glass that was causing him to think about the stuck-up girl. He had showered and changed once he had got back to the barracks after leaving the Grafton, and yet he could have sworn that he could smell that light fresh scent he had been so aware of when he had carried her over the broken glass. That, of course, was just plain daft; the whole city stank of smoke and dust from the bombing.

Luke and his men had been sent down to the docks. Gladstone, Canada, Brocklebank, Prince's and King's Docks, together with the adjacent ware-houses, had all suffered serious fires and damage. The Pier Head church of Our Lady and St Nicholas had been burned out, and some of the law courts within St George's Hall had been destroyed.

Whilst they worked Luke kept a weather eye out for his father, knowing that the Salvage Corps would be deployed to work on the worst of the damaged and collapsing buildings because of their great experience in this field.

A pigeon that had been watching from the top of the high wall on the opposite side of the road from where they were working – the wall all that remained of what had been a large warehouse – suddenly flew off at speed, its departure followed by a brick falling from the top of the wall.

Immediately Luke warned his men, 'Get back, the wall's going to go.'

The men looked unconvinced but Luke hadn't listened to his dad's tales of his work in the Salvage Corps all his growing years without learning a thing or two, and he knew very well what the single falling brick might mean, even if the others didn't.

'Get back,' he repeated.

'Give over, Corp,' Andy grinned. 'If the Luftwaffe can't knock it down then a ruddy pigeon . . .'

His words were lost in the dull rumbling sound that filled the air along with the choking mist of brick and cement dust as the wall collapsed down on top of itself.

The men were moving now, but Andy was closer to the wall than the others, and one of the falling bricks caught him squarely between the shoulder blades, sending him sprawling.

Luke could feel the bricks hitting his own body as he turned back to grab hold of Andy, and drag him clear of the collapsing wall.

Another group of men who had been working close by, and who had heard the wall collapse, came hurrying to their assistance, the sergeant with them, taking charge and doing an immediate roll call.

'You're a ruddy hero, that's what you are, mate,' Andy told Luke emotionally. 'I'd have bin a gonner then if you hadn't turned back to help me.'

Luke brushed his gratitude aside, but much to his embarrassment the sergeant insisted on being told exactly what had happened.

'I owe you one, mate,' Andy thanked him gratefully.

'Then another time when I say jump, make sure you jump,' Luke told him grimly, 'because next time you might not get so lucky.'

'What do you mean, he's your second cousin from off the West Derby Road's boy? I've never heard you mention any second cousin from off the West Derby Road.'

Very little natural daylight managed to work its way into any of the rooms of number eleven Walsingham Close, but especially the downstairs best parlour, with its carefully polished aspidistra, its sombre dark brown furniture and its heavy dull red velvet curtains, all of which belonged to the late Victorian age and had been passed down from Emily's father's parents to Emily's father, and from him to Emily herself. In fact, nothing inside the house had been altered or moved in any way since Emily's own childhood.

The Turkey carpets bought by her grandparents still covered the floors in the best and second-best parlours, a matching stair runner still covered the flight of stairs leading from the hall to the first floor, turned regularly by Emily and the cleaner to make sure that no one part of it wore more than any other, whilst a plainer more serviceable runner covered the landing and the stairs up to the second floor.

In the best parlour, silver-framed photographs of Emily's parents and their parents still took pride of place on the carefully polished mahogany sideboard, whilst the dull green wallpaper had been put up when her proud grandparents had moved into their new smart villa in the exclusive enclave of Wavertree Village.

Wavertree Village was still considered exclusive – or at least the part of it where Emily lived – and the people who lived there did not mingle with those who lived in less favoured streets – or even with their own neighbours. Mingling was simply something that was not 'done' in Walsingham Close.

However, Emily could still see Con's expression despite the dull thin December light. It was a mixture of truculence, anger and disbelief, but Emily ignored it. Rather surprisingly, she was, she discovered, actually enjoying lying to him and then acting as though he was the one who was in the wrong. Of course, it helped that he hadn't returned home until almost lunchtime and still smelling of drink and cheap perfume. That had definitely given her the upper hand when it had come to informing him that from now on the boy would be living with them.

The boy himself was upstairs in his bedroom where Emily had told him to stay, until she came up for him. She had made the room as comfortable as possible for him, lighting a fire in the grate and leaving him a bacon sandwich. She had used the bacon she had bought on the black market, and which she had been saving for Con's Sunday morning breakfast treat. A husband who stayed out all night even if he 'explained' that he had had no choice because of the air raid, did not deserve what amounted to a family of four's whole ration of rashers for a week, along with a nice bit of sausage and a couple of eggs, all supplied via the friend of a friend of the man who delivered their coal, and at an extortionate cost.

The kitchen was really Emily's favourite room in the house. She had happy memories of the hours she had spent there watching Mrs Evans, who had come in daily as a housekeeper to her father, cooking and baking, and then when she was older learning from her and being allowed to 'help'.

Mrs Evans had died four years ago, but right up until her death Emily had visited her twice a week in her little house close to the Edge Hill railway goods yard, taking her little treats and making sure that she was all right, even though Con had complained about her spending money on a 'servant'. Mrs Evans had been more to her than that. And besides, Emily's father had been very stern about their duty to treat those they employed 'well'.

One of the aspidistra's leaves wasn't quite straight. Automatically Emily removed a clean duster from the pocket of her apron and went to straighten and wipe it, ignoring Con's irritation.

Whilst she wiped the leaf, Emily rather marvelled at her own inventive ability and the way she had conjured up out of nowhere her younger, much younger, cousin twice removed, who had disgraced herself by marrying a merchant seaman against her family's wishes. At a single stroke and without a twinge of guilt, Emily had between one breath and the next removed from the world of the living both of 'cousin Jenny's parents', her father via an accident involving the blackout and a tram, shortly after Jenny's undesirable marriage, and her mother from the shock of losing her husband.

Exhilarated by this success, Emily had gone on to inform Con that after her parents' deaths Jenny had written to her begging her for help.

'The poor girl had not only lost her parents, she had also been informed that her husband had been listed as missing at sea, presumed drowned,' Emily informed Con, adding that she had often visited Jenny in the shabby boarding house close to the docks where she had been living, and that was how she had got to know Jenny's little boy.

'Jenny made me promise that if anything should happen to her I would take Tommy in. She'd even told Tommy that herself, but you still could have knocked me down with a feather when this police constable turned up last night to say that the house had been bombed and that Jenny's last words had been that Tommy was to come to me.' She embroidered her story now, returning her duster to her pocket and then removing it again when she spotted a few specks of dust on the mahogany-framed mirror that hung over the marble fireplace.

'Well, if you ask me she'd got no right foisting her kid off on us. Kids are expensive, and we aren't made of money.'

'It's my duty, Con, and I'd never be able to live

with myself if I turned the boy away. Mind you, I know what you mean about the expense.'

Con's face brightened and Emily almost found it in her heart to feel slightly sorry for him. Almost.

'We could easily cancel them two new suits you've got on order, and there's no need for you to go on running a car. You could walk to the theatre from here, or catch a bus.'

'Now hold on a minute, Emily. I need that car, you know that. We both agreed that it wouldn't look good for the theatre if I was to be seen dropping me standards.'

'No, Con, we did not both agree. You told me, just as I am now telling you that the boy stays.'

Con looked at her, and then gave her his most charming and coaxing smile, coming towards her and reaching for her hand. Emily let him take it, even though the sensation of him holding it between her own in a gesture of mock tenderness, reminded her of all those other times when he had used his charm and her vulnerability to it, his lack of feeling for her and her excess of it for him, to blandish and bully her into giving way to him. But not this time. This time she had something far more worthwhile to fight for than Con's non-existent love. This time she wasn't fighting for herself, she was fighting for the boy.

Baffled as well as irritated by the fact that within such a short space of time his normally easy-to-manipulate wife had somehow conducted a campaign in which he had been well and truly routed, Con retreated behind a wall of sulky silence, which he had to break himself after ten

121

minutes of being totally ignored by Emily to tell her in an aggrieved voice, 'If you're not going to listen to reason then I might as well go back to the theatre.'

'Yes, you might,' Emily agreed unperturbed, mentally planning to take the boy straight down to one of the WVS rest centres as soon as Con had gone so that she could buy him enough second-hand clothes to tide him over until she could get him something decent. She could do with seeing that coal man as well. She was going to need some decent food to fatten the boy up a bit, rationing or no rationing, and if Con made a fuss about it, well, then she'd make a fuss about that car of his, and they'd see which one of them won!

SIX

'Well, Katie, how are you settling in?'

Katie smiled politely at the supervisor, who had called her over to the raised table overlooking the rows of desks where the girls worked.

It was still early – not yet nine o'clock – and Miss Foster had the supervisors' desk to herself.

'I'm really enjoying the work, Miss Foster,' Katie answered truthfully.

Miss Foster – Frosty Foster, as the others had nicknamed her – inclined her head.

She was taller than Katie, and very slim, thin almost, with sharp narrow shoulders and long hands that were unexpectedly large. Her hair was mousy brown and cut in a neat bob, her eyes a pale icy blue.

Typically, Carole said that it was no wonder she had never married. 'She'd freeze a chap with one look,' she had giggled.

No one was quite sure how old Miss Foster was, although Carole had said that she must be in her thirties. Like Katie, Miss Foster had been recruited into her censorship post, and had not come to it, as so many of the girls had, from the original staff employed by Littlewoods.

Carole claimed that because of this the supervisor looked down on them, and there had been several small clashes between them, with Miss Foster trying to impose her authority on Carole, and Carole deliberately flouting it by pretending she hadn't heard Miss Foster's instructions. Carole defended her rebelliousness by saying that she wasn't having Miss Foster bossing her about, but Anne had warned Carole to be careful, pointing out that whilst she was currently getting away with her behaviour it would not have gone unnoticed, and could rebound on her.

'It's obvious that Frosty Foster thinks she's better than us, and I'm not putting up with that,' Carole had told Katie.

'Well, I suppose in one way she is, since she's our supervisor,' Katie had felt bound to point out.

'No, I don't mean that kind of better,' Carole had told her. 'I mean, you know, she thinks she's "better" than us. Just look at the way she walks around like she's got a bad smell under her nose.'

Katie knew what Carole meant and now she felt a small burn of anxiety as the supervisor looked at her for a minute before saying pointedly, 'I would caution you, Katie, in your own interests, to be on your guard against certain of your fellow workers, some of whom do not take their responsibilities as seriously as I can see that you do. I shall not mention any names, but I think you can guess to whom I refer.'

Katie knew that Miss Foster must be referring to Carole but of course she didn't say so.

'A certain person could well find herself looking for work more suited to her nature before too long, unless she mends her ways,' Miss Foster continued.

Katie wanted to defend her friend and tell the supervisor that, despite her outwardly careless manner, there was another side to Carole. She had shown Katie nothing but kindness, and was always ready to explain something that Katie didn't understand and to answer her questions, but Katie knew as well that Carole had deliberately gone out of her way to bait and provoke the supervisor.

'Don't be led into trouble yourself out of loyalty to a friend,' Miss Foster warned Katie, dismissing her with a brisk nod.

'What was old Frosty Face saying to you then?' Carole, who had arrived at work whilst the supervisor was still talking to Katie, asked once she had returned to their desk.

Katie hated having to be deceitful, but she could hardly tell Carole the truth and say that Miss Foster had been warning her against becoming too friendly with Carole herself.

'Nothing much,' she answered, but she knew that she was blushing guiltily as she did so.

'Do you reckon the Luftwaffe will be over again tonight?' someone further down the table asked worriedly, changing the conversation, much to Katie's relief.

'I hope not,' Anne answered.

'Me too.' Carole smothered a yawn. 'I need me

kip in a proper bed. I haven't got over Saturday night at the Grafton yet, and tomorrow's Christmas Eve.

'Do you fancy coming down the Grafton with me again tomorrow night, Katie?' she asked.

'I can't,' Katie told her. 'I've already said that I'll go to midnight mass with the Campions.'

Carole pulled a face. 'I suppose I'll have to try and get me cousin to go with me then, only she's courting now and doesn't want to go anywhere without her chap. I was hoping that them army lads might be there again, especially that Andy, the handsome fair-haired one,' she added wistfully.

'I thought this time last year that it would all be over quickly, but look at us now: we've been at war over a year and no end anywhere near in sight,' Jean sighed.

She and Katie were hanging up the paper chains that Katie had patiently spent the afternoon repairing.

'Mind you,' Jean shook her head and laughed, 'I was just remembering how our Luke had got leave from France without us knowing and arrived home whilst we were all at church. You should have seen the twins' faces when they saw that the mince pies we'd left for Father Christmas had gone. Of course, it was Luke who had eaten them.'

'It must have been a wonderful surprise to have him home,' Katie smiled, deftly dabbing glue onto another of the torn paper links.

It was next to impossible now to buy new decorations, or even to buy brightly coloured paper in order to make them, because of the war. Paper of any kind was precious and not to be wasted.

'Oh, yes, it was,' Jean agreed. 'I'm hoping that Luke will get leave this Christmas as well, even if it's only for Christmas Day.' Jean gave her young billetee a sympathetic look. 'It will be hard for you, Katie, this being your first Christmas away from your parents.'

Katie didn't say anything. Christmas had always been one of her father's busiest times and Christmas Day had had to be planned around his work, so that Katie had never really known the kind of traditional Christmas Day that Jean's children had obviously enjoyed, and whilst of course she knew she would miss her parents, a part of her was looking forward to experiencing Christmas Day at the Campions' with almost childlike excitement and anticipation, although she felt too self-conscious to say as much.

'There, I think this one will be long enough now,' she told Jean, eyeing her handiwork.

The flames from the fire were sending out warm tongues of light that danced with the shadows, the occasional hiss of a damp coal a familiar and homely sound.

The Government had increased everyone's food ration for Christmas, and Katie had insisted on passing on her rations to Jean to go into the 'family' pot.

'It's the least I can do,' she had insisted when Jean had protested.

Katie wasn't a spendthrift, and the wages she earned for her work seemed like riches compared

127

with the 'pocket money' her father had given her, and so she had been able to buy gifts for the Campions in return for their hospitality.

'You've done a really good job on that, Katie,' Jean approved, looking up from her own task of tying labels to the brightly wrapped Christmas presents spread out on the floor all around her, much of the paper carefully kept from the previous Christmas, as the war meant that paper was in short supply and could only be used sparingly. 'And ever so quickly and neatly,' she added with a warm smile. 'If I'd have asked the twins we'd have ended up with glue everywhere and the paper chain in more of a state than it was before they started.'

'I enjoyed doing it,' Katie told her truthfully.

It was lovely and cosy with the fire lit, the paper streamers spread out on the floor adding an air of Christmas magic and excitement.

'I'll get the step ladders from under the stairs and we'll make a start on getting them up. Oh, just listen to that.' Jean looked up at the ceiling as they both heard the sound of the twins' newest gramophone dance record coming down from their attic bedroom. 'It's just as well their dad isn't here, otherwise he'd be going up there to tell them to turn it down.'

The music was one of the pacey new American dance tunes that were becoming so popular and Katie acknowledged that its rhythm was making her own feet itch to dance just a little, as she helped Jean with the step ladders, insisting that she should be the one to stand on them whilst Jean held the ladders.

Katie had secured one end of the first streamer to the room's neat plain coving with two drawing pins, and they had moved the ladders over to the opposite corner of the room, only to discover that the garland might not quite reach it, when they both heard Grace's voice calling out from the kitchen.

'Hello, Mum, it's only us.'

A delighted smile lit up Jean's face. 'In here, love,' she called back, 'putting up the decorations.'

Grace and her fiancé, Seb, appeared in the doorway, Seb's arm around Grace, who was wearing a lovely coat in a soft mid-blue, with a darling little matching hat trimmed with petersham ribbon, which emphasised her lovely skin and strawberry-blonde hair.

'You look very smart,' Jean told her daughter, as she went to hug first Grace and then Seb.

'It's Seb's Christmas present to me,' Grace told her mother, giving her fiancé a glowing smile.

It was plain to see how much in love they were, and Katie could easily understand why Jean liked Seb so much. Tall and good-looking, he had a steadfastness about his smile and the way he looked at a person that made you feel immediately comfortable and aware that he was someone you could trust, Katie decided.

'Katie, come down off the ladder and be properly introduced to Seb,' Grace instructed her warmly.

'I hear from Grace that you and I are in the same line of business,' Seb told Katie as he shook her hand, adding in a very reassuring way, as Grace went to take off her coat and Jean went with her, as though he had realised she was feeling a bit uncertain, 'It's all right, I know you aren't allowed to talk about your work in any detail. It's the same for me. I'm in the "Y" Section. We do what could be considered to be the equivalent of your work but in an airwaves form.'

Katie smiled in relief, admitting, 'It's difficult when people ask me what I do. I know we can say that we work at the Censorship Office . . .'

'But you worry that you might accidentally say more than you should?' Seb supplied.

'Yes, that's it exactly.' Katie was relieved that he understood.

'I felt pretty much the same myself when I first started, but after a while one develops an instinct that becomes second nature. If it's any help to you I find that most decent sorts understand and accept that it's your duty not to talk about your work. I tend to use that as rule of thumb, if ever I'm in any doubt. Anyone who tries to bully you into going against your own instincts is someone to treat rather warily, in my experience.'

What a kind man he was, Katie thought, to have understood her dilemma and found such a tactful way of offering her the benefit of his advice.

Jean and Grace had come back into the room, the fitted blue dress Grace was wearing showing off her neat waist so well that Katie was not surprised to see Seb's glance resting lovingly on his fiancée, before he gallantly offered to take Katie's place on the ladder.

Soon he was deftly pinning up the recalcitrant

end of a paper streamer, and somehow managing to make it stretch to the corner of the room, before moving the ladders to pin up the second garland.

'Well, that looks lovely now,' said Jean happily, five minutes later, standing back to admire the effect of the two red and green streamers going corner to corner across the room, crossing over in the centre above the light fitting.

'I thought we were going to have a problem with the new tree lights that your dad got after the warehouse they were in was bombed, but, bless him, he managed to sort them out. Just as well, really, because the candle holders were on their last legs, and I always worried about them setting the tree on fire. We certainly had our money's worth out of them, mind you. Your dad bought them the year the twins were born. That was the year you had that lovely smocked party dress, Grace. Ever so pretty you looked in it.'

Katie felt a small pang of envy as she listened to these reminiscences. Her own sharpest Christmas memory was of the terrible row between her parents the Christmas Eve they had promised to take her to Harrods to see the lights. Katie couldn't remember now what the row had been about but she did remember that there had not been the trip to Harrods.

'We can't stay long, Mum,' Grace warned her mother, 'but like I said to Seb, it wouldn't seem properly Christmas somehow if I hadn't seen you.'

'Go on with you, you softie,' Jean admonished her daughter, but Katie could see that she was pleased. 'Your dad should be back any minute if you can hang on, and the twins are upstairs.'

'I'll go and tell them, shall I?' Katie volunteered, thinking that it would also give her a chance to disappear tactfully and leave the family alone together, but once she had told the twins that their sister had arrived, they were insistent that she must go back downstairs with them.

By the time the three of them were down to the front room, Grace and Jean were busily exchanging brightly wrapped Christmas presents, and when Grace turned to Katie with a warm smile and handed her a small parcel, Katie was relieved that she had followed her own instincts and was able to say truthfully, 'I won't be a minute; I'll just nip upstairs and get yours.'

Since she didn't know Grace well, Katie had taken a guess that as a newly engaged girl she would be keen to start collecting for her bottom drawer, and when Katie had seen a pair of pretty pillowcases being sold off in a small shop that was closing down, she had taken the opportunity to buy them, and wrap them up just in case Grace included her in her own Christmas shopping.

'No opening anything until Christmas Day,' Jean warned everyone, firmly taking possession of the presents Grace was handing out, much to the twins' disappointment. 'And that goes for you too, Grace.'

'Have you heard if Luke's going to get leave over Christmas yet?' Grace asked her mother.

'No. He did say, though, that even if he hasn't got proper leave he'd try to bob round just to say Happy Christmas.'

'We'd better go, Mum. Everyone's saying that the trains are running any old how on account of all the bombing, and Seb thinks that we should get to the station before it gets dark.'

'Seb's right, love,' Jean agreed. 'I just hope we don't have another air raid tonight although, according to your dad, it was Manchester that got it worst last night. We're safe enough up here away from the docks, of course, although you never can tell. Wallasey was bombed last night. Your dad reckons it was a mistake, and I dare say that your auntie Vi won't be too pleased, seeing as she seems to think that Wallasey is a cut above the rest of us.'

Providentially Sam arrived just as the visitors were about to leave, and of course fresh hugs and Christmas wishes had to be exchanged.

Whilst Seb was assuring his father-in-law-to-be that he would take good care of her, Grace drew Katie towards the back door and said conspiratorially, 'I need a word.'

Mystified, Katie followed her outside. There, standing to one side of the back door were two shabby cardboard boxes with newspaper sprouting from the top.

'This is a special present for Mum from me,' Grace explained. 'Mum's always wanted a proper china tea set. I got this one from Miss Higgins down the road. I used to run errands for her before I started nursing and I always pop in to see her when I'm home. The last time I called round she told me that she was closing up the house and

133

moving to her cousin's down in Shropshire to get away from the bombing. She asked me to give her a hand sorting out everything. She was wanting to sell what she could, which was lucky because me and Seb have been able to buy a fair few bits to put by for when we get married. I've told Mum about them but I didn't tell her about the tea set. Miss Higgins wanted to give me it on account of me running her errands for her, but it didn't seem right so I made sure I paid her properly for it, you can tell Mum when she asks. Anyway, what I wanted to ask was if you could hide it in your room and give it to Mum on Christmas morning for me?'

'Of course, but surely you want to give it to her yourself?' Katie protested. She could tell from the excitement in Grace's voice how much giving her mother the tea set meant to her, and it seemed wrong that she wouldn't be the one to do so.

'Well, it's true that I would, and that I've had a bit of a tussle with myself over asking you to do it for me,' Grace admitted. 'I'll admit that I felt a bit put out when Mum first kept going on about you and how she'd taken to you straight off, but then when I'd met you I could see what she meant.

'It's only right that Mum should have her present on Christmas morning, and besides, I'll be able to imagine how she'll look and everything,' Grace laughed. 'She'll be that made up, I bet the first thing she does is put the kettle on and then she'll wash every piece and put it away in the corner cupboard our dad got for her from a salvage sale, and she'll only use it for best. It's ever such a good one, so Miss Higgins said,' Grace added proudly. 'Minton or something, and she had it from her mum, who had it as a wedding present. But then I owe Mum such a lot.

'When you give it to her, Katie, I'd like it if you were to tell her that it's on account of the dress – she'll know what you mean. Quick – let's get them upstairs whilst everyone else is still in the front room. I've warned Seb that he's got to keep them there until we've done.'

As she helped Grace with the boxes, Katie's eyes stung with tears when she thought how she was part of such a special Christmas surprise.

Her triumph over Con had given Emily a taste of what she could achieve with a little ingenuity. Now all those hours spent in meetings, dutifully listening whilst others took the floor and said what was what, were a treasure-trove of useful information, and it turned out to be surprisingly easy to enlist the aid of a minor council official she knew through her late father. Bert Hopwood was on one of the committees that dealt with rehoming the homeless, and through him Emily was able to obtain proper papers for the boy, now officially given the identity of Thomas Binns, grandson of the late Esme Archer Binns, a blameless second cousin of Emily's own mother, who had lived in a remote Cheshire village the name of which Emily conveniently could not remember. However, as she explained to Bert Hopwood, there was no doubt that the boy was the son of poor Esme's disgraced daughter.

A few subtle comments about how she knew the council were struggling to rehouse all those made homeless by the bombs, and how difficult it must be to find suitable homes for those children who had been orphaned, had been enough to ensure that Bert was only too eager to turn a blind eye to the small matter of the lack of any papers or records for 'Esme's grandson'.

Now, in the eyes of the council if not the Law, and until someone with good reason to do so claimed otherwise, the boy was hers.

The pair of them, Tommy dressed in his shabby second-hand clothes, and Emily in her stout shoes and dull brown coat, might not have looked a particularly appealing pair as they walked into Lewis's on Christmas Eve, Emily clutching Tommy's hand tightly, but so far as Emily was concerned, there was no happier woman in the whole country.

'What we're going to do first is go and have a look at the toys, so that you can tell Father Christmas what you'd like him to bring you, but mind, he won't have much time on account of us leaving it so late,' Emily informed Tommy as they waited for the lift.

She had grown used to his silence and rather liked the freedom it gave her to talk unchecked, something she had not enjoyed with Con, or indeed with her father.

As they stepped out of the lift Emily saw an acquaintance coming towards her. Boldly she stepped up to the other woman with a smile, saying, 'I thought it was you, Mrs Fisher. I'm just doing a bit of last-minute Christmas shopping with my cousin's son here. He's bin orphaned and come to live with us.'

'Well, there's a lot of that happening,' the other woman agreed. 'My sister's had to take in one of her in-laws' kiddies and there's worse to come, I dare say. He looks a quiet enough lad, anyway.'

'Oh, yes. He's ever so good. I'll be keeping him at home with me for a while, though, and not sending him straight to school. He was in the house, see, when it was bombed, and it's affected his hearing.'

Really she had never imagined she could be so inventive or that it could be such an exhilarating experience.

Emily liked the way the boy pressed closer to her when they reached the crowded toy department. She put her arm round him to hold him even closer, filled with pride and delight. Although he wasn't saying anything she could see him eyeing the Hornby train that was on display.

They were sold out, the salesman told her, and no more to be had with the war on, but Emily wasn't put off. The train was something else that would go on her list for the coal man, who, by that mysterious manner in which the black market worked, had sent her a message to say he would be round later.

The boy had stopped moving and was standing staring at a display of books. Emily had been a keen reader herself as a girl, and all her old annuals were up in the attic. She could get them down for him, but in the meantime, a *Beano Annual* was something she could buy, along with a tin whistle for his stocking and some 'magic' playing cards. A set of paints and a puzzle book, some Meccano and a game of snakes and ladders were also all discreetly purchased, with instructions as to where they were to be delivered.

Emily did have a bit of a moment when Tommy went in to see Father Christmas. What if he didn't come back to her? A small boy could easily disappear in such a throng of people and if she lost him now she just didn't know what she would do. He had changed her life so much already.

On Sunday, going to church, for the first time since she had realised what her husband was, she had felt that she was on a par with the other women. What did an unfaithful husband matter when she had a child?

She had felt so proud taking her place in her normal pew, the boy crushed in beside her and then afterwards, outside the sturdy parish church, with its square Norman tower and its worn tombstones bearing the names of families who had called Wavertree home for many generations, before the builders had arrived and erected the handsome villas like number eleven, for the Victorian middle classes.

Emily's own parents were buried in what had always been referred to as the 'new' graveyard, to one side of the church, and which was now having to be extended – thanks to the war.

Not a single Sunday seemed to go past without at least one ashen-faced grieving family filing into the church to hear the name of one of its members added to the list for prayers for the deceased, and already there was talk of the parishioners getting together to provide funds for a memorial of some sort for the congregation's war dead when the war finally ended.

Now all Emily had to do was make sure that coal man understood how heavily the full weight of her displeasure would fall on their financial relationship if he was not able to supply the items she was swiftly adding to her growing list.

It was wrong, of course, to encourage black marketeers by buying from them, but what choice did she have, Emily reasoned. It seemed that no sooner did something go on a government list of being in short supply than it disappeared from shop shelves immediately, having been diverted to the black market. Why should the boy go without when she had the money to make sure that he didn't? She'd far rather spend it on him than Con and his fancy suits and unnecessary car.

Wallasey had been bombed, and this time by accident from all accounts, when the Luftwaffe had missed their intended target of the docks. Vi bristled with indignation at the thought of the Luftwaffe mistaking Liverpool's docks for somewhere as obviously smart as Wallasey, as she picked up her telephone receiver and asked to be put through to Bella's number. Edwin had been complaining that their daughter having a telephone for which he had to pay, was an unnecessary expense now that Bella was widowed, but Vi had to admit that at times like this it was extremely convenient. There was no way she wanted to put her hat and coat on and walk round to her daughter's at this hour on a Christmas Eve, and yet the news she wanted to convey to her was very important.

'I've put you through, Mrs Firth,' the telephonist told Vi chirpily, 'but don't be surprised if your Bella doesn't answer. I tried her number a while back and she wasn't there. It was that young Pole whose mother and sister are billeted with her. I dare say he wanted to wish them a Happy Christmas. He's with 302 Squadron, isn't he? I dare say he'll be down at Coolham now, that being where so many of them Polish pilots are based.'

'Thank you, Doreen.' Vi's just south of arctic tone cut into the telephonist's chattiness.

'There, I told you,' Doreen began, patently oblivious to Vi's irritation, only to break off as Bella picked up the receiver. 'Oh, aren't you the lucky one? She must be back, Mrs Firth. Happy Christmas to you both.'

'Bella, at last. What on earth took you so long?' Vi demanded, taking her irritation out on her daughter.

'I was doing my nails,' Bella told her, equally crossly, 'and now you've made me go and smudge one of them. What is it you want, Mummy?'

'Please listen because this is very important. I've got some good news. Your brother's coming home for Christmas and he's bringing someone with him.'

On the other end of the line Bella's spirits lifted slightly at the thought of the dullness of Christmas with her parents being enlivened by the addition of an unknown young man. Mind you, if he was anything like Charlie . . .

'You'll never guess who it is?' Vi continued, her voice becoming slightly arch.

'Who?' Bella demanded.

'Daphne Wrighton-Bude. You know, Bella, the sister of that young man whose life Charlie tried to save. I told you about his parents writing to Charlie to thank him and inviting him to their house. It seems that Charlie has become a regular visitor there, not that he said a word to me or Daddy about it, the naughty boy,' Vi told Bella archly, adding, 'Not that I can be too cross with him really. I suppose it's natural for a sensitive young man not to want to speak out too soon about his feelings. Not, of course, that there's anything official yet. Charlie was very clear about that. However, we all know what's about to happen when a young man brings a young lady home to meet his family, don't we?'

Hearing her mother speak about Charlie with so much new-found maternal enthusiasm was enough to silence Bella even before she'd taken on board the sudden transformation of her selfish brothers, with the hide of a tank, into a sensitive young man.

'I've managed to get Mrs Wilson round to turn out the boxroom for you, but you'll have to bring your own hot-water bottle.'

'The boxroom? What do you mean?' Bella demanded. 'I'll be sleeping in my old bedroom.'

'Oh, no, dear, I'm putting Daphne in there. After all, we can't expect her to sleep in the boxroom, can we? Not with her being a double-barrel. It just wouldn't be fitting. She's bound to be used to the very best. Pure linen sheets, I shouldn't wonder.

'They'll be driving up today, Charlie said in his letter, although he didn't say what time they'll arrive. We'd better go to midnight mass tonight, I think, rather than church in the morning, with poor Charlie having driven all that way. What time were you thinking of coming over, because I could do with a hand getting the vegetables ready?'

Vegetables? Bella was outraged. She looked down at her nails and only just resisted the temptation to slam down the receiver.

'I'd really like to meet Charlie's young lady, Mummy, but to be honest I just don't know if I'm up to it.' She sighed theatrically. 'Not with all that I've been through. And I don't think that that bed in the boxroom would be a good thing for me, you know with me losing my baby like I did.'

'Now, Bella . . .' Vi began.

But Bella sighed again and said tiredly, 'Truly, Mummy, I think I'd really rather stay here at home and just come over to meet Doreen at lunchtime. I don't want to spoil everyone's fun with my own glumps.'

'Her name is not Doreen, Bella, it's Daphne, and I really think you should be here. Charlie will expect it.'

'I'll have to see if I feel up to it, Mummy. I didn't want to say anything but I've been very low today. In fact, I really think I need to go and lie down for a while.'

'Bella, my vegetables . . .'

'I'm sorry, Mummy . . .'

Two spots of angry colour were burning on Bella's face as she let the Bakelite receiver drop back into the cradle. No way was she going to take second place to Charlie's double-barrelled girlfriend, and nor was she going to peel vegetables for her. So there!

SEVEN

Christmas morning, and it wasn't properly light yet but Katie could hear stifled giggles as her bedroom door was opened to admit Lou and Sasha, clutching their Christmas stockings.

'Here's yours,' they told her, climbing onto her bed and settling down either side of her, silent for once as they focused their energy on the agreeable task of investigating their stockings.

This was the kind of Christmas fun that had previously passed Katie by and she soon found that she too was giggling every bit as excitedly and child-ishly as the twins as she delved into her own stocking to find a single peppermint cream wrapped in rustly paper, along with an apple and then another peppermint cream.

In their own bed, listening to the giggles, Jean told Sam quietly, 'I'm ever so glad we didn't get any bombs last night.'

'You're telling me,' Sam agreed. 'There's nothing like sleeping in your own bed, and them rolls of bedding in the air-raid shelter are nothing like our own bed.'

'I wasn't just meaning that, Sam. I was meaning with it being Christmas and everything. I know we're still at war, and there's plenty that will be having a bad time on account of losing their loved ones and their homes, but it meant a lot to be standing in church last night singing carols, instead of being in a shelter.'

'Aye, I know, love.' Sam lifted his arm, pulling her close to him.

'Sam, the girls might come in,' Jean protested, but she still rested her head on his shoulder, enjoying the comforting warmth of his big strong body next to her own. Theirs wasn't the kind of marriage in which either of them made a fuss or said very much, but it was a good marriage; a strong marriage, and a marriage rich in love.

'When will this war be over, do you think, Sam?' Jean asked.

She could feel his chest lift and then fall as he breathed in and then exhaled.

'I don't know, love. Churchill says we're in it for the long haul, and I reckon he knows what he's talking about.'

It was a cold morning, to judge from the thin film of ice on the inside of the bedroom window, but it was the puff of white caused by her own breathing that made Jean feel reluctant to leave the warmth of Sam's arm and their bed, and rub her feet against his instead. She hated it when Sam had to work nights in the winter. Apart from the danger, she missed his warmth in bed. No hot-water bottle could take the place of a nice big cosy husband.

'But we got our lads back from Dunkirk, and beat the Germans in the Battle of Britain,' Jean reminded him.

At least the kitchen would be warm, and Sam had banked up the fire in the front room last night as well. There was something so special about Christmas morning.

'Aye, we did that.' Sam's voice was fervent with emotion, but then their own son, along with his cousin Charlie, had been one of those soldiers who had been brought home safely from the beaches of Dunkirk.

'But that doesn't mean that Hitler's anywhere near beaten yet,' Sam warned her.

'I just want it to be over and for everyone to be safe,' Jean told him.

'I know that, love.'

'Luke may be on home duties now but that isn't to say he won't be sent abroad to fight later on,' Jean told him worriedly.

'If he is then we must just be strong for him, Jean, and for one another.'

'We've been so lucky so far: Luke coming home safe from Dunkirk, Grace not being hurt when she and Seb were caught in the Technical School bombing, this house not being damaged; but I do worry, Sam.'

'But not today, because today it's Christmas,' he told her with a smile.

Jean smiled back, and agreed softly, 'No, not today.'

They lay in shared silence for a few minutes, and then Jean told Sam, 'I'd better get up otherwise, if

I know the twins, they'll be downstairs eating the mince pies I made yesterday and then there won't be a thing left if we get neighbours calling round.'

The rag rug at the side of the bed felt cold, and so did her slippers, Jean acknowledged, as she slid her feet into them and pulled on her dressing gown, before heading for the bathroom.

Eight o'clock, that meant that he'd probably missed breakfast, Luke thought hungrily as he increased his walking pace, his face glowing from the sharpness of the cold December air. There hadn't been time to let his mother know that he was going to be home for Christmas Day after all because the sergeant had only given Luke the news just over an hour ago.

'Word is that all them who can make it home and back to the barracks again before tomorrow morning can have unofficial leave.'

Luke hadn't waited to hear any more, grabbing the presents he had bought for his family and stuffing them into his kitbag.

He could smell soot and the aftermath of burning wood; a dull pall of smoke and still air hung over the areas that had suffered the worst of the bombings. It didn't do to dwell on the tragedies of the last few days, but no one who had witnessed them was going to forget them.

Luke wasn't looking forward to having to share this Christmas with someone outside the family. It was bad enough that Grace wouldn't be there, without having to make polite conversation with a stranger when all he really wanted to do was be

147

with those he loved, even though – having been good-heartedly warned by Grace, in the brief conversation they had shared when Luke had managed to go up to the hospital to check that his sister was unharmed after the bombing, that their mother had invited the billetee to stay over Christmas – he had included a small gift of some handkerchiefs, nicely boxed, for the billetee amongst his presents for his family.

The city devastated by the bombs, so many of its buildings destroyed and damaged, stood proud in all its grey shabbiness in defiance of the enemy. Striding through the empty streets, Luke felt a lump come into his throat, along with a surge of love and pride for the place of his birth.

It had been a long year. The things he had seen and learned during the retreat to Dunkirk were scorched on his heart and his soul for ever. Some of them were things that could only be shared with those who had been there, things that had turned him from a boy to a man and put him on a par with his father, man to man; things there was no going back from. War did that to a person. It changed them for ever, sometimes for the good, and sometimes not. He had seen comrades, friends, screaming in agony from the wounds they had suffered, and begging to be put out of their pain; he had seen friends as close as brothers fighting to the death with one another over a place in one of the queues for the boats; he had seen sickening, horrific things that the boy he had been would never have imagined possible, but which the man he had become knew were.

He seen acts of incredible heroism and self-sacrifice, and acts of terrible self-interest and cruelty, and Luke knew that before this war was over he'd see more of the same.

He'd turned into their own street now, his spirits rising with every step he took. His mother would be properly made up to see him home for Christmas Day and no mistake. He'd go round the back, he decided, and surprise her rather than going to the front door.

He started to whistle cheerfully to himself.

They'd had breakfast in the kitchen, all of them cosy and warm in their dressing gowns and slippers as they'd eaten their porridge and drunk their tea, Sam manfully lifting the heavy roasting tin containing the turkey out of the oven so that Jean could baste it and check anxiously that it was cooking properly, before returning to their bedrooms to get dressed and come back down, all of them dressed in their 'nice' clothes, ready to gather in the front room where presents were piled under the tree, waiting to be handed out by Jean, according to Campion family tradition.

Katie, like the twins, was wearing red, but whereas they were in tartan skirts and bright hand-knitted jumpers, Katie was wearing a plain grey wool skirt and a white blouse and a soft red cardigan that fastened with pretty red and cream buttons.

Jean had put on her second-best outfit, the brown skirt and camel-coloured twinset from Lewis's, although she had covered them protectively with a clean white pinny embroidered with holly leaves and red berries, which Miss Higgins had given her the previous Christmas. Sam was wearing a knitted patterned pullover over a checked shirt with the cavalry-twill trousers Jean had bought him in Blackler's the year before the war had broken out.

A fire was burning warmly in the grate, and every time the front-room door was opened, the smell of roasting turkey wafted enticingly in from the kitchen.

The sound of Christmas carols being played over the wireless mingled with the twins' chatter, and the ringing of church bells. Although from the start of the war the ringing of church bells had been forbidden unless as a warning of invasion, this year the Government had given special permission for church bells to be rung on Christmas Day and they were now pealing loud and clearly the country's message of defiance to its enemies.

'You'll be missing your parents,' Jean told Katie gently, once they were all assembled in the front room.

'Yes I am,' Katie agreed truthfully. But she was still glad to be here.

'Come on, Mum,' Lou urged. 'I'm dying to know now what Grace has bought us. Do you remember last year, Sasha, when we thought she had given us slippers and instead it was a record each that she'd put in those boxes to make them look like slippers?'

'*I* certainly do,' Sam told them both mock grimly. 'How could I forget when the pair of you made that much racket playing them?'

'Oh – I've just got to get something, if you'll excuse me for a minute.' Katie stood up, well aware that the twins were impatient to begin unwrapping their presents, but unable to explain that even though she'd managed to get enough wrapping paper to cover the dilapidated cardboard boxes containing the china tea set, she'd been reluctant to bring them downstairs earlier, knowing that their size was bound to arouse everyone's curiosity.

Katie, having carried one of the boxes downstairs and placed it carefully on the kitchen table ready to take into the front room, had just reached the kitchen with the second box when the back door to the house suddenly opened and a man in army uniform came striding into the kitchen, only to come to an abrupt halt, the smile dying from his eyes as he saw her.

Katie and Luke stared at one another in mutual shock and recognition. There was no need for any words: they both knew what the other was thinking and why. The silence between them, hostile on Luke's part and heart-sinking on Katie's, was only broken when Katie felt the box beginning to slip from her grasp and struggled valiantly to hold on to it.

Luke might be bitterly shocked and resentful that the young woman his mother had apparently taken to her heart should be none other than the stuck-up little madam from the Grafton, but he was still enough of Jean and Sam's son to leap forward automatically to help her with the battle she was obviously losing with the cardboard box.

151

Katie, equally very much the daughter of two parents who by their own selfish self-absorption had taught her to value the help of others, reacted just as automatically, thanking Luke and explaining, 'It's for your mother, a tea set that Grace wants her to have as a special surprise. I was keeping it upstairs as I knew she'd wonder what it was if I put the boxes under the tree.' Did she sound as breathless as she felt, Katie wondered, as she continued truthfully, 'I'd never have forgiven myself if anything had happened to it.'

'Katie, are you all right . . . ? Oh.'

Jean's face, as she told Sam later, must have been a picture when she walked into the kitchen to find her son and Katie in what looked like an embrace, until she realised that what they were actually holding so tightly was not one another but a large Christmas present.

'I was just . . .' That was Katie.

'I was just . . .' And that was Luke, both of them speaking at the same time in exactly the same tone and using exactly the same words. Katie's face went bright red, Jean noticed, and Luke's wasn't much different, for all that he was hiding his self-consciousness that little bit better.

'This is for you from Grace,' Katie explained, starting again. 'I got such a shock when the back door opened that I nearly dropped it. Luckily your son grabbed hold of it.'

'And you with it, by the looks of the pair of you,' Jean laughed. 'You'd better take it into the front room before something does happen to it, whilst I put the kettle on,' she told Luke.

'There's another one on the table,' Katie indicated. Grace had been wrong about the kettle going on: Jean hadn't even waited until she'd unwrapped her present. But then Grace hadn't known that Luke would be coming home.

Katie had heard a great deal about Jean and Sam's only son and she knew how proud of him his parents were. It had never occurred to her that the angry young man from the dance hall would be the much-loved son of her landlady, but then why should it have?

'It's just as well I got that bigger turkey, after all, Katie,' Jean said happily. 'Of course, Luke did say that he'd try to be here, but I didn't want to get my hopes up too much. His dad will be that pleased. Poor Sam, it's hard for him sometimes, Luke not being here and he having to live with four females.'

Katie felt the draught from the door into the hall opening and somehow she knew without turning round that it was Luke who had returned to the kitchen.

'I'll get my kitbag and get me coat off and then I'll carry the other box through for you, Mum.'

'Did you have anything to eat before you left the barracks? You're looking a bit thinner.'

Katie turned round, expecting to see the same angry rejection in the blue eyes she had seen at the Grafton, but instead they were gleaming with good humour, and Luke was shaking his head and laughing as he hung his coat on one of the pegs behind the back door. Beneath the khaki shirt Katie could see the stretch of his muscles and the breadth

153

of his shoulders, and a funny and disconcerting feeling squirmed through her stomach.

The tea had been made and drunk, and everyone apart from Jean had opened all their presents, Katie's face glowing with pleasure when she had opened her present from Jean and Sam to find a pretty little powder compact with the initial K picked out on it in sparkling crystals.

'I got it second-hand,' Jean told her, 'but me and Grace both said that it was perfect for you the minute we saw it.'

'It's lovely,' Katie replied, and meant it. Now she understood why Grace's gift had been a Max Factor powder refill. It would fit perfectly into her new compact.

'Come on, Mum,' Lou urged Jean, her eagerness to see what was in the cardboard boxes overcoming her impatience to try out the new dance record Katie had bought for them.

Whilst Jean hesitated and looked uncertainly at the boxes, Katie discreetly started to gather up the discarded wrapping paper, knowing it would possibly have to be used again next year. The firelight burnished the bright reds and golds, adding to the festive warmth of the homely parlour, whilst the lights on the tree illuminated the dark green branches and the carefully tied-on decorations. The smell of pine needles and mince pies filled the room; you could hardly see the top of the sideboard for all the cards, and happily the garlands had stayed up – thanks more to Seb than to her, Katie thought ruefully, as she, like everyone else, waited for Jean to open her present.

Katie found that she was holding her breath as she watched Jean untying the red ribbon that Katie had seen on a market stall and immediately snapped up. It was as though somehow she had taken on an honorary role as Grace's representative, she admitted. She was certainly mentally recording everything so that she could give Grace a detailed report on it later.

Even that heart-stopping feeling she had had when Luke had grabbed the box she was holding and had inadvertently held her as well?

That had been only because she was still angry about the way he had carried her over that glass against her wishes, and besides, it was private and had nothing at all to do with Grace's gift to her mother.

'Well, I don't know, all this newspaper . . .' Jean was looking puzzled and uncertain. 'Are you sure that Grace said this was for me, Katie?'

'Yes,' Katie confirmed. She'd tucked the letter Grace had also given her to give to her mother inside the flap of the second box.

'Do you want us to help you, Mum?' Lou offered, but Jean wasn't listening. She had removed the layers of newspaper to reveal what was inside it and the look on her face brought a huge lump to Katie's throat.

'Grace said to tell you that she bought it from Miss Higgins,' Katie told Jean quietly. 'She's giving up her house to go and live with her cousin.'

'Yes. Yes, I know,' Jean agreed.

Her voice shook slightly and Katie could see the tears sheening her eyes.

'I've always wanted a proper tea set, ever since me and our Vi used to play with one when we were girls.'

'Grace said that Miss Higgins said that this one was Minton and that it had been a wedding present to her parents. There's a letter for you from Grace in the other box with the teapot and the rest,' Katie told her gently.

Luke frowned as he watched the two women, aware that somehow a bond was being formed between them that excluded everyone else, and he was both confused by it and resentful of it because of his dislike of Katie.

And yet, watching her now, there was none of that snooty, stuck-up, nose-in-the-air manner he'd been so sharply aware of at the Grafton. She wasn't acting any different than if she had been his sister Grace, except that she didn't look like Grace. Grace was a very pretty girl, but she was his sister; Katie wasn't his sister and she was very, very pretty. Too pretty in fact, Luke decided angrily.

This was just about the best Christmas she could remember, Emily decided happily. She and Tommy were kneeling on the carpet in the spare room next to Tommy's bedroom, home now to the Hornby train set, delivered at eight o'clock in the morning by a very unlikely Father Christmas in the form of the coal man, who had been bribed beforehand to dismember the large iron bedstead that had supported the room's 'spare bed' to provide adequate accommodation for the new arrival.

Emily and Tommy had gone to church, where Emily had proudly showed off her second cousin's boy and now, to all intents and purposes, her adoptive son. Neighbours who had scarcely bothered to exchange the time of day with her before had come over to wish her a 'Merry Christmas' above the sound of the church bells ringing out so strongly across the smitten city, causing all those who heard them, including Emily, to add a special plea that the prayers they had just said in church might be granted. Before too long Emily had found herself included in a group of mothers and grandmothers, and treated very much as an equal as they all bemoaned the effects of rationing and war on their lives and those of their children.

Now Emily watched as the train chugged round the tracks. Together, she and Tommy had connected railway lines and sidings, with proper points and signals, and the most up-to-date of all the Hornby engines was now running happily along its tracks, pulling its smart LMS-liveried coaches behind it.

Con, who hadn't arrived home until the very early hours of Christmas Day morning, had slept through Christmas morning and Christmas dinner before going back to the theatre. Not that Emily cared one jot. She and Tommy had had the jolliest of times, pulling crackers, wearing silly hats and then reading out the jokes, or at least she had read out the jokes and Tommy had listened, and now they were having the best of fun together with the Hornby train set.

A nice warm fire burned in the grate, hot milk, with a touch of brandy in it for her, had been drunk, and mince pies consumed, and very soon Emily suspected both of them would be ready for their beds. And still to be enjoyed in the days to come were the brightly coloured annuals, and the Meccano set. Emily heaved a happy sigh of contentment.

All the presents had been unwrapped, they had eaten their dinner, listened to the King's speech, all to one degree or another fighting back tears, the washing-up had been done, and although he had been watching her, waiting for her to show her true colours the whole way through, Luke had to admit that Katie hadn't put a foot wrong. She had helped his mother discreetly without in any way claiming for herself a role in the household she did not have, she had kept the twins entertained and amused when they had started to get bored, she had even listened to their elderly neighbours' rambling tales of their own youth with every evidence of genuine enjoyment, whilst somehow still managing to keep herself in the background. But despite all of that, far from being pleased that he had been unable to find fault with her, Luke was growing more antagonistic towards her by the minute.

Not just his mother but both his parents had sung her praises to him, the twins were hanging on her every word, yet none of that could shift the lump of angry dislike Luke could feel burning inside him.

She was a fraudster who was deceiving his whole family, and he was sorely tempted to drop into the conversation, sort of accidentally, the kind of comment that would alert them to her real nature and expose her for what she was.

Small wonder that she had kept her distance from him all day, even preferring to pull crackers with old Mr Gilchrist from five doors down, rather than with him, and leaving him to pull his with his mother.

Oh, yes, she had been as tireless about keeping away from him as she had been in helping his mother. Not that he could blame his family for being taken in by her. Luke had to admit that, having watched the tactful way she went about ensuring that his mother was given the chance to enjoy Christmas Day herself by taking over many of the dull chores of the day. She was certainly very good at portraying herself as a 'good sort'.

Luke looked moodily down at his beer. A knocking at the front door signalled the arrival of the neighbours his mother had invited round for a Christmas drink and a bit of a singsong. Like her sister Francine, his mother had a good singing voice and musical ear, which all her children had inherited, and it was a bit of a family tradition that on Christmas Night everyone got up and did a bit of something, either a song or, in the twins' case, both a song and a dance. Everyone that was except for their dad, Luke acknowledged, since Sam claimed that he couldn't sing a note.

*   *   *

159

Luke was just pouring a beer for one of their neighbours when Lou came up to him and announced importantly, 'Me and Sasha have learned a new routine specially for tonight.'

Luke grunted. He was used to his younger sisters' dedication to their dancing and singing, and shared his parents' feelings about the girls' desire to make a career for themselves on stage.

'Just wait until you see it. Katie says it's the best, and she should know, what with her dad being a band leader and her mother having been on the stage. Imagine having parents like that!' Lou exclaimed enviously.

'No, thank you. I'm perfectly happy with the parents we've got, and so you should be and all,' Luke rebuked her sharply.

'I didn't mean it like that,' Lou defended herself, 'did I, Sasha?'

'No,' Sasha immediately supported her twin.

'I'll bet, though, that if Katie had wanted to go on the stage her parents wouldn't have said she'd be better off working in Lewis's.'

Luke wasn't really listening to the twins' grievances. He was looking at Katie, who was listening to something his mother was saying. Of course it would be easy for her to pretend to be something she wasn't, with her background. No wonder she was after a well-to-do chap; that sort – her sort – always were.

'Well, you don't have to do a turn if you don't want to, Katie, love,' Jean assured Katie as the two of them organised the chairs the neighbours had brought with them, all the way round the outside of the carpet to leave plenty of space free in the middle for the 'turns'. 'The twins will be disappointed, though. I think they were hoping you'd sing with them.'

'I'd love to,' Katie told her, 'but the truth is that I can't sing a note.'

Jean looked unconvinced.

'It's true,' Katie assured her. 'My father banned me from even trying, I'm so bad.'

'You've got ever such a good sense of rhythm, though; I've watched you dancing with the twins.'

'Oh, that. Well, yes, I can dance,' Katie agreed, 'but that's not a real talent like singing or playing an instrument.'

'Well, never mind, although I must admit I like a bit of a singsong meself. Goes back to when me and our Vi were young. Our mother had a good voice – that's where Fran gets it from, of course, and my lot too. The kids have always enjoyed putting on a bit of a show for the neighbours over Christmas. I remember one year Luke and Grace did a bit of a mime and a dance. The older ones like to get up and do a bit as well. There's a couple of the men got good strong voices and can hold a note well, and Dan Simmonds from number twelve plays the accordion.'

It was going on for midnight, and everyone who wanted to had done a bit of a turn, with the twins receiving the most applause for their song-and-dance routine, and now, to Katie's dismay, the twins, having had an illicit glass of sherry apiece, were insisting that Katie got up and sang with them.

'No, honestly, I can't,' Katie protested, but they weren't in any mood to listen, taking hold of her hand and trying to drag her up out of her seat. Everyone was laughing and joining the fun, egging them on, and she looked despairingly round the room for help, but Jean, who could have saved her, was out of the room, having taken an elderly neighbour who couldn't walk very well to the bathroom.

Someone had seen her discomfort, though, and was coming to her rescue – and a very unlikely someone indeed, Katie acknowledged, as Luke, who had been sitting talking quietly with his father, got up and came over, telling his sisters firmly, 'Leave her be, you two.' Katie was just about to thank him when he continued coldly, 'If she wants to be stuck up and too posh to join in then that's up to her. Tell you what,' he added, turning his back on Katie, 'how about I sing with you?'

There was no one to see the hot tears burning Katie's eyes as painfully as the embarrassed colour burned her face as she slipped out of the room and went into the kitchen, where she busied herself with some washing-up.

Or at least Katie had thought there was no one to see, until she felt a hand on her arm and heard Sam Campion saying quietly, 'I'm sorry about that, lass. I'll have a word with our Luke. His mum told me earlier that you can't sing.'

To Katie's embarrassment fresh tears welled in her eyes. She wanted to rub them away but her hands were wet and soapy from the washing-up water.

'Don't think too badly of the lad. The thing is that he was made a bit of a fool of a while back by a girl he was keen on, when she told him that he wasn't good enough for her.'

Katie had to fight against an urge to point out that since she wasn't that girl it was hardly fair of Luke to tar her with the same brush.

'There's no need to say anything, Mr Campion,' she said. 'I feel daft enough as it is, not being able to sing, without having to tell everyone about it.'

'Aye, well, there's more important things in life than singing, and if you ask me sometimes it can cause more trouble than it's worth when folk go putting the wrong ideas in other folks' heads.'

Katie knew that he was referring to the twins and their belief that they were destined to follow in their aunt's footsteps.

'We all have our dreams,' she told him, 'especially when we're young, but as I've told the twins, working in entertainment is nowhere near as glamorous or exciting as it looks. Even my father says that if he had a son he would prefer him to have a trade rather than be a conductor. It can be such an unkind life, even for those who are very talented.'

She could hear Luke's good baritone enriching the sweetness of the twins' voices as they sang together, and she felt a small pang of envy, knowing how her father would have loved and praised her had she had one half of the talent of the Campion offspring.

'Jean's right, you're a good lass. I admit that I wasn't keen when she said that we'd have to take someone in, but I reckon we've dropped lucky in getting you.'

Praise indeed from the normally reticent head of the Campion household. But not even knowing that Sam had come to her rescue and liked her could take away the hurt Luke's words had caused.

It was all very well for his father to explain that he was suffering from a broken heart on account of some girl who had made a fool of him, but that was no reason for him to be so antagonistic and unkind to her, was it?

The twins, accompanied by Katie, had gone up to bed, and if he hadn't known better Luke admitted that it would have been easy for anyone to think that the gentle but determined way in which Katie had insisted that she was tired and ready for her bed but that she'd love to hear the twins' new gramophone records first, was a kind and thoughtful way of giving him some time alone with his parents, but of course that was impossible, given what he knew about her.

Still, no matter what the reasoning behind her disappearance upstairs with the twins in tow, virtually the minute the last of the washing-up and the last of the guests had been dealt with, it was well timed from his point of view.

He couldn't remember the last time he had had both his parents to himself.

'You'll have to be getting back to the barracks,' Sam warned him. 'You don't want to be late and get put on a charge.'

'I won't be, Dad,' Luke assured him, nodding

his head in acceptance of his mother's offer of a cup of cocoa before he left.

'I just hope the Luftwaffe doesn't decide to attack us again tonight,' said Jean worriedly. 'They've held off so far over Christmas.'

'I don't reckon we'll be seeing them tonight,' Sam reassured her, exchanging a rueful look with Luke behind Jean's back as she headed for the kitchen.

'The city can't take much more,' Sam told Luke in a low voice once Jean had disappeared. 'We've had to call in reinforcements to deal with what we've already been dealt, and we're a long way from getting everything back to normal. Half the services are running on a make-do-and-mend shoe-string, and it wouldn't take much to knock them out. The City Council's done its best, but you can't clean up after the kind of bombing raids we've suffered, on thin air. We've lost equipment we can't replace, and the lads reckon that a lot of it can't be repaired easily either.'

'The Germans are bound to go for us, Dad, on account of the docks,' Luke warned his father. 'They know the country needs to keep the west coast ports open for the convoys.'

'Aye, it really gets my goat to think of them brave lads risking their lives on them ships, and paid nothing for the days they aren't at sea, just to have their cargo slipped sideways to some ruddy black marketeer who's getting rich off their backs.'

'There's bin a lot of unofficial talk down at the barracks about putting the army in to sort out the docks to stop the black market,' Luke told him, 'but at the end of the day we're soldiers, not dockers, and then there's the unions.'

They broke off their conversation when Jean returned with three steaming hot cups of cocoa.

'Katie, bless her, made some for herself and the girls and took it up with them.'

'I'm surprised they're daft enough to want to bother with her after the way she made out she was too good for them when she refused to sing with them,' Luke announced curtly. He didn't want to tell tales – that would be beneath him – but he certainly didn't want to see his family taken in either.

'Luke,' Jean protested. 'Whatever gave you that idea? Katie's not a bit like that.'

Luke could see that his mother was upset, and that made him dislike Katie even more.

'Aye, I meant to have a word with you about what you said to her, Luke,' Sam pitched in. 'Proper upset, she was.'

Now his father was sticking up for her as well.

Luke stiffened.

'Thing is,' Sam continued as though he hadn't noticed Luke's angry withdrawal, 'the lass can't so much as sing a note. Proper self-conscious she is about it as well, what with her father being a professional musician, at least that's what your mother says.'

'Yes, that's right, Luke,' Jean agreed. 'Katie came to me and told me earlier when I told her about our singsong. She's not the sort to say too much, but I could tell that she'd been upset by what her dad had said to her when he'd banned her from trying to sing, though she made a bit of a joke about it, in that gentle way she has. Mind you, I reckon those parents of hers don't deserve a good daughter like her, telling her not to come home for Christmas because they're going to some friends. She's been ever so good with the twins, telling them that going on the stage isn't a bit like they think it is, and she's a real homebody as well. She's even asked me about joining the WVS so that she help out a bit. It's hard for a young girl like her to come to live amongst strangers.'

'Well, it was her choice and she isn't the only one,' Luke pointed out, unwilling to relinquish his animosity but at the same time suffering that defensiveness that always accompanies the discovery that one might be guilty of misjudging someone. He wasn't going to vindicate himself, though, by telling his parents what he had overheard Katie saying at the Grafton. He wasn't like that.

He'd finished his cocoa and it was time for him to leave.

'Grace said to tell you that she and Seb are going to the Grafton's New Year's Eve dance, if you can get leave and fancy going,' Jean told him as she and Sam accompanied him to the back door.

Pulling on his army greatcoat, Luke laughed. 'What, me go out with that pair of lovebirds?'

'They're an engaged couple now,' Jean reprimanded him firmly.

But Luke grinned at her and said teasingly, 'That's what I mean. Besides I won't be getting any leave over the New Year, seeing as I've got some now.'

Relieved to see Luke restored to good spirits,

Jean hugged him, trying not to let him see how much she worried that every time she saw him it could be the last, given the fact that he was in the army and they were a country at war. There were those who said that the men posted to home duties had an easy time of it compared with those posted overseas, but living in Liverpool was no picnic, with Hitler's bombs raining down on them night after night, and soldiers like her Luke having to go out and risk their lives sorting out the mess those bombs had left behind.

'It's a shame that Luke seems to have taken against Katie,' said Jean to Sam as she picked up their cocoa cups to take through to the kitchen to wash them whilst Sam stoked up the fire.

'The lad took a hard knock over that good-for-nothing piece that dropped him to take up with someone else, and besides, wartime is no time for a soldier to think of starting courting,' Sam warned her, 'or for his mother to get ideas about match-making.'

'Sam Campion, what a thing to suggest,' Jean protested. 'I hope I'm not the kind of mother who goes about trying to choose her own daughter-in-law.'

Sam said nothing.

The horrid narrow single bed in the small boxroom that had originally been her youngest brother, Jack's, was every bit as uncomfortable as Bella had known it would be. Of course Jack's things had all been packed away after the tragedy of his death. Naturally her mother had not been able to bear to have them there to remind her of what had happened. Bella admitted that she sometimes forgot that Jack had even existed. There had been a big age gap between her and Charlie and Jack, and Jack had been one of those difficult children who always seemed to be doing the wrong thing and causing a lot of trouble.

Thinking of people who caused a lot of trouble made Bella feel even more hard done by. It had come as an unpleasant shock to have her mother virtually ignoring her to fuss all over Charlie's new girlfriend, who wasn't even particularly pretty, never mind as pretty as Bella herself.

Vi had been openly impressed when Charlie had told them all about Daphne's parents' detached house, immediately quizzing Daphne about her mother and how many committees she sat on, and other stupid things like that, and then practically fawning on the wretched girl as though she were Princess Elizabeth or something.

Their father had been impressed as well. He must have been to have given Charlie the one hundred pounds Charlie has boasted to her he had been given. Now Daphne was no doubt sleeping comfortably in Bella's old room and in her bed, whilst she was relegated to the boxroom as though she was of no account at all, her, a widow whose husband had been killed. All Daphne had lost was a brother.

Bella turned over, hunching her shoulder petulantly. It seemed pointless to her, everyone calling Charlie a hero, when in the end Daphne's brother had gone and drowned anyway. There had been tears in Daphne's eyes when she had told them all how grateful her parents were to Charlie for what he had done.

'My parents look upon Charles almost as an adopted son,' Daphne had told Vi emotionally. 'My father especially has become tremendously attached to him. Charles has been so very kind to Daddy, coming to see him when he can, and talking to him about Eustace. People don't, you see. They think it's better not to.'

Now, of course, her mother was dying to show off Daphne at the Hartwells' Boxing Day party, Bella acknowledged bitterly, whilst she no doubt would be pushed into the background. Daphne was so dull and boring, and her clothes, stuffy and not the kind of thing at all that Bella would ever wear. A horrid tartan skirt with a dreadful mustard-coloured jumper, just because they had Scottish connections, whatever that was supposed to mean.

'We think it must have been because of his dreadful injuries that Eustace did what he did and—' Daphne had said when she'd been going on about her wretched brother.

'I just wish that I'd seen what he was doing and been able to stop him,' Charlie had interrupted her, 'but I was helping to get one of the other lads onto the boat. They'd pushed him off the one he was on, said it was overloaded.'

'Oh, no, it wasn't your fault. You must never think that, and at least you saved him from that dreadful beach and being taken by the Germans. Daddy couldn't have borne that.' Daphne had reached for Charlie's hand as she spoke, adding

170

emotionally, 'You are such a hero, Charles, and so very brave.'

And Bella had known immediately what her mother was thinking and planning.

And then her father had joined in, saying, 'Well, you can tell your dad that Charlie, er, I mean Charles here has got a good job waiting for him in a good business when he comes out of the army. I shouldn't wonder that I'll be making him up to a full partner by the time he's thirty. What line of business is your father in, if I may ask, Daphne?'

'Oh Daddy's a member of Lloyd's,' had been Daphne's answer, which had plainly left her mother as confused as it had done Bella herself, although her father had looked both impressed and delighted. So whatever Lloyd's was, it obviously meant that Daphne's father had plenty of money.

It was plain that Daphne was sweet on Charlie.

Bella thumped her pillow again. It wasn't possible, of course, that she could ever be supplanted in her mother's affections, and especially not by someone like Daphne, with her big wide eyes and silly way of looking so adoringly at Charlie. Charlie, of all people. And now she had to put up with Charlie preening himself and boasting that their father was going to be like putty in his hands.

'He still hasn't forgiven you for joining up,' Bella had reminded her brother.

'Huh, that's all you know, Miss Clever,' Charlie had retorted. 'Dad took me to one side after dinner and told me that he thought it could be the best thing I've ever done.'

'That's just because of Daphne,' Bella had told him. 'And once she's not around—'

'And who says she isn't going to be around? Dad reckons that Daphne would be the right girl for me to marry, and I reckon he's right,' Charlie had announced, adding, 'Of course I told Dad that I'll have to give her a decent engagement ring, her family being what they are, and Dad agrees.'

Bella's chest heaved with indignation and outrage as she thought of the machinations she had had to go through to get her ring off Alan.

Still, at least she hadn't had to marry down, she thought cattily, which if Daphne's parents were as posh as her parents seemed to think, was what Daphne would be doing if she married Charlie.

Her mother certainly seemed to think she would. When she had forced Bella into the kitchen to help her with the supper 'so that Charles and Daphne can have a bit of time together on their own', all she had been able to talk about was weddings.

Bella thumped her pillow again glowering into the darkness.

EIGHT

March 1941

It was hard to believe she had been in Liverpool for nearly three months now, Katie acknowledged. Time had passed so quickly. Not that her new life wasn't without its complications at times, Katie admitted as she left the Littlewoods building, her work finished for the day. Now that she knew who the Campions' son was, Katie made sure that she was away from the house whenever Jean mentioned that it was likely that Luke would get leave, and so far, fortunately, she'd been able to avoid seeing him again. It was silly that she should feel so angry and yet so hurt as well, because a man she didn't really know had misjudged her so unkindly, but she did.

Katie had decided that it was because she liked the rest of the Campion family so much that she was disappointed that one member of it should let the family down so badly with his unkindness, nothing more than that. Luke Campion might be good-looking but that didn't mean anything to her.

She wasn't about to get her heart broken by any chap, but most especially one who scowled and glared at her in the way that Luke Campion did.

The cloudy winter skies had meant that Hitler's bombers had kept away from Liverpool through all of January and February, and now they were into March. Thankfully her parents had been lucky so far in escaping the worst of the London bombing.

Katie had been dreadfully worried about them when she had first seen the news in the paper that during the same night that Buckingham Palace had been struck by a stick of incendiaries, the Café de Paris, a famous night spot, had sustained a major hit from two bombs, one of them killing the whole band outright, including its leader, 'Snakehips' Johnston, who had been a friend of her father's, and the second hitting the dance floor and causing dreadful casualties even though it did not explode. However, much to Katie's relief, her father, obviously shocked by the tragedy, had written to her to tell her that they were now considering taking up their friends' offer and moving in with them, since they lived outside the city itself.

She had almost reached Ash Grove. She would soon be home. A pink tinge of colour flushed Katie's face as she realised how easy it was for her to think of the Campions' house as 'home'.

'You don't think that someone we know will see us, do you?' Sasha asked Lou uneasily, as they turned into the alleyway that led to the Royal Court Theatre's stage door.

'Well, they might if you don't get a move on,' Lou warned her twin unkindly, relenting when she saw how apprehensive Sasha was. 'Of course they won't, silly, and anyway even if they do, what does it matter?'

'They might tell Mum.'

'Then we'll just say that we were going to see Eileen Jarvis's sister, and that she's working here, her being a dancing teacher. Look, Sash, do you want to do this or not? After all, it wasn't my idea that we go in for a dancing competition, was it? It was yours.'

'Yes, I know that, but that was only because Evie Rigby in Haberdashery said that her cousin who lives in Blackpool had done one. I never said anything about us coming here to ask if they did any dancing competitions at the Royal Court. That was your idea.'

'Well, we can't just up and off to Blackpool looking for one, can we? Not without saying anything at home, and you know how Dad would be if we did ask. I reckon that if we can get into a competition here, and win it, then Dad won't be able to say "no" when we say we want to enter a really big one in Blackpool,' Lou, ever the optimist, told her twin confidently.

'But wouldn't it be better if we went to one of the dance halls like the Grafton and asked if they do dancing competitions? After all, it was at the Tower Ballroom that Evie Rigby's cousin went in for hers.'

'Dare say it would,' Lou agreed scornfully, 'excepting that our Grace and Luke go dancing

175

there, and you know that Mum has said we can't until we're sixteen.'

'Well, we don't know that they do any here yet, do we?' Sasha pointed out equally as scornfully.

This was their second visit to the Royal Court Theatre in their quest for a dancing competition they could enter. They'd chosen the Royal Court because it was close to Lewis's where they now worked, and because they knew that their auntie Fran, who was a singer and their mother's sister, had worked there for a while when she had been in Liverpool.

'That Kieran we saw the last time we were here said that he'd find out for us and that we were to come back and ask for him,' Lou reminded her twin.

Sasha brightened noticeably at the mention of the good-looking young man they had seen coming out through the stage door to the Royal Court on their first visit, and who they had approached to ask if he knew if the Royal Court ever held dance competitions.

'Yes, he did say that, didn't he?' Sasha agreed. 'And he said that his uncle was in charge of the shows, and that he'd have a word with him about having a dancing competition.'

'Come on,' Lou instructed her, lifting her hand to bang on the stage door.

Con wasn't in a good mood. And it was all because of that ruddy kid that Emily had gone against him and taken in. If Con had his way the kid would have been out on his ear long before now. Con had had enough of Emily fussing round him and making out like he was God's gift. Like he'd told her this morning, the ruddy kid couldn't even talk.

'He's not right in the head,' had been his exact words, 'just like you, so it's no wonder the pair of you get on so well.'

He'd wanted to tap Emily up for some money, and he'd gone home last night ready to fuss round her a bit to soften her up for that purpose. He'd gone straight into the kitchen and put his arm round her waist – or at least as far round it as it could reach – but instead of going like putty in his hands, like she normally did, Emily had actually had the gall to push him off.

He'd told her meaningfully that he fancied an early night, whilst eyeballing the kid, who had been sitting at the table eating his tea, but instead of welcoming this husbandly message of intent, Emily had looked at him like he was a bit of muck under her shoe and told him that he could have as many early nights as he liked, but they'd be in his own room and his own bed. Then she'd turned her back on him and asked the kid if he'd like a bit of rice pudding.

Con hadn't given up, though. He'd needed the money too badly for that. He'd forced himself to smile, cracking a few jokes for the kid, who looked at him without a flicker of interest, and then telling Emily that it was the marital bed he wanted to sleep in – with her, his wife.

Time had been when him saying something like that would have been enough to have her going bright red and rushing upstairs as quick as you like on the promise of a bit of how's-your-father.

Con knew his own worth. Why shouldn't he? He'd had the prettiest girls in Liverpool queuing up for his attentions since he'd turned fifteen. So now to have his overweight pudding of a wife turning him down felt a bit like being slapped in the face with a wet kipper, as the saying went. Con had spent his whole life in 'the business' and so tended to think in the phrases that were common currency in music hall and variety. It was a world in which sex was a commodity to be traded for profit, and whether that meant selling the punter a quick flash of a chorus girl's legs, or coaxing his wife to hand over fifty quid didn't matter to Con. Not so long as he reaped the reward and the bonuses in the shape of his pick of the bunch.

He'd already had his bank manager on the telephone, going on about 'the small matter of your overdraft' and something had told Con that this time sending round the prettiest of the chorus girls with some free tickets for one of the best boxes in the house wasn't going to work.

''Ere, Con, there's a couple of kids just come in asking for your Kieran,' Harriet Smith, his secretary told him.

Harriet was fifty if she was a day, and in reality she was the one who ran things. She'd been with the Royal for years, and Con had heard from one of his uncles that the reason she was so devoted to him was because she'd had a bit of a thing for Con's late father.

'What do you mean a couple of kids?' he asked uneasily.

'Well, they ain't calling you their dad, if that's what's worrying you,' Harriet told him frankly. 'Said something about wanting to enter some dancing competition your Kieran told them about.'

Con's expression hardened. His nephew had caused him nothing but trouble since his sister had foisted Kieran off on him with some daft claim that he had flat feet and couldn't join up. If he wasn't chasing after a bit of skirt he was doing some deal to fill his pockets, Con thought bitterly, conveniently ignoring the fact that Kieran was following in his own footsteps.

'Tell them to hoof it,' he told Harriet.

'I already did, but they won't. Not until they've seen Kieran.'

Con filled his chest and bellowed, 'Kieran, get your arse into my office double quick.'

Kieran Mallory had inherited his uncle's good looks along with his nature, and he knew better than to let Con get the upper hand, so instead of appearing 'at the double', he sauntered into the dark cubbyhole, tucked into a corner up a short flight of stairs in the warren of passages, dressing rooms and costume cupboards that existed behind the stage of the theatre, which Con referred to as his office.

There was barely enough space in the small room for the large mahogany partners' desk, which had originally belonged to Emily's father, and which Con had decided would suit his office very nicely indeed, specifically because of its two concealed 'secret' drawers in which he could safely tuck away the 'girlie' magazines a friend of a friend who knew a sailor brought back from America. Con read these from inside what looked like a leather-bound play script, ogling the impossibly long legs of the 'models'.

On the wall opposite the door and behind the desk stood a set of rackety bookshelves, which ran the entire length of the wall. On here play scripts, copies of the *Stage*, playbills, the detritus not just of his own years as producer, but also those of the men who had gone before him, filled half a dozen or so battered cardboard boxes, sitting haphazardly on the shelves alongside account books and bills. Spilling from the top of one of them was an unsavoury collection of pieces of false hair, false noses and the like, found abandoned, brought to the producer's office to be rehomed, and left to grow dusty with age.

The room itself smelled strongly of Con's cigars and the hair pomade he used, their smell not quite masking the odour of old paper, old building and a lack of fresh air.

In the far corner stood a coat stand on which Con hung his hat and his camel-coloured cashmere coat – a necessity for anyone in production in the theatre.

It was Con's habit to tilt back his chair, his long legs stretched out in front of him and his feet on his desk. The tilting chair had other benefits as well, as he was fond of proving to his 'girls'.

The only changes Con had made to the room were to have the clear glass in the upper half of the door replaced with frosted glass and to have a bolt fitted on the inside.

'What the hell do you mean, telling some daft girls to come here for some dancing competition?' Con demanded irritably of his nephew.

'Only practising what you preach, Uncle Con,' Kieran replied insouciantly. 'You was the one wot told me never to turn down an opportunity.'

'Aye, and I told you to mek sure you keep it off your own doorstep,' Con reminded him angrily.

Kieran laughed, showing strong white teeth. 'Nah, that isn't what I was meaning. I was thinking of you, see, not meself. This young pair – twins they are – were after knowing if you ran any dancing competitions like they do at the Tower Ballroom in Blackpool.'

'Well I don't,' Con snapped. 'I've got enough problems with proper dancers without getting myself involved with ruddy amateurs.'

Young though, and twins. He'd always fancied having a matching pair, so to speak, not that he'd ever want to get himself involved with girls too green to know what was what – too much trouble by far, that was. No, he liked them knowing and game, though age, or the lack of it, was no bar to that. He could string 'em along a bit, tell them that he'd do something for them. Con grinned to himself. Well, of course he would be doing, but it wouldn't exactly be the something they had in mind.

'Yeah, but the difference is that with professionals you have to pay them, but with amateurs they're the ones paying you. See what happens is that these girls that are mad for dancing pay to go into these competitions. Of course, you have to give the winners a prize, but I reckon that letting them go on and do a bit of a routine in a matinée show that no one goes to see will do the trick with that. Of course, to make it worthwhile you'd have to advertise the competition – but I reckon that putting a few leaflets up in all the dance halls will do that. I thought if we told this pair that you'll be doing a competition here, they'll spread the word for us, as well.'

Con looked at his nephew with grudging admiration. Of course he wouldn't have looked at doing a ruddy dance competition if Emily had come up with some money, but since it didn't look like she was going to, there was no harm in him taking a look at these girls. No harm at all. And no need either to say anything to Kieran about his private thoughts.

'We can't lose,' Kieran was telling him. 'We can charge the dancers to enter and we can charge them that comes and watches them competing as well.'

Without taking his eyes off his nephew Con yelled out, 'Harriet, if those girls are still here, bring them in.'

'But, Mummy, Daddy will have to give me a job, otherwise I'll have to go and work in some dreadful munitions factory,' Bella protested angrily.

Her mother had arrived at Bella's house ten minutes earlier, and now they were sitting in Bella's kitchen, drinking the tea that Bella had grudgingly made.

'Bella, your father isn't in a very good mood at the moment, not with the Ministry of Labour being given these new powers over businesses that are engaged in essential war work.'

'But only last week he was going on about how it would be a good thing because the men wouldn't be able to go on strike and things.'

'Well, yes, but that was before he'd realised how much he was going to have to pay them, now that the Government's going to set a minimum wage for men working in these essential jobs.'

Vi returned her cup to its saucer. The tea set had been one of Bella's wedding presents, and the delicate flowers on the white china perfectly matched her kitchen décor. Not that Bella was currently in any mood to appreciate that fact.

'But you've got to do something, Mummy.'

'Well, I don't know what, Bella. I must say that it's very difficult, what with so many of the other mothers in my WVS group having daughters who are doing their bit.'

'I am doing my bit, aren't I? I've got those refugees.'

Crossly Bella got up and made a big play of carrying their empty tea cups over to the sink, and then returning to remove the embroidered cloth from the tea tray, and start to fold it. Normally she left such tasks in the hope that one of her billetees would do it for her.

'Well, yes, darling, but Mrs Jeffries' daughter has joined the Wrens, and Mrs Blackston's the ATS.'

'You said after Christmas that Daddy had said

that people were calling girls who joined the ATS "officers' groundsheets", and worse, and that he was relieved that his daughter wasn't showing him up by joining,' Bella pointed out crossly, abandoning the tray cloth.

'Well, yes, but that was before the Government brought out these new laws about young women of your age having to sign up for war work, Bella. You'll have to find something, you know; otherwise it will look very odd. Daphne's thinking about becoming a Red Cross trainee, and—'

'Oh, bully for Daphne.'

'Really, Bella, I'm ashamed of you for speaking like that. You know we really do have to make sure that we're a credit to Charles now, with him being on the brink of proposing to Daphne. I don't like saying this to you, but Daddy does feel that you've let him down a bit with your marriage and I have to say that I agree with him.'

'You wanted me to marry Alan,' Bella reminded her mother furiously.

Ignoring Bella's outburst, Vi continued firmly, 'I'm so thrilled that Charles's got leave over Easter and that he and Daphne will be coming here. Of course, by then Charles will have some very special news for us. He and Daphne are spending this weekend with her parents and Charles has as good as said that he intends to ask Daphne's father for his permission for them to be engaged. And that's another reason why Daddy won't be very pleased if you start pestering him for a job. Not when he's already going to have to give Charles the kind of private income that Daphne's father will expect him to have.'

Bella wanted to scream and stamp her feet, and point out to her mother that no one was taken in by her sudden adoption of such phrases such as 'private income', or by referring to Charlie as 'Charles'.

'Look, I must run, Bella,' Vi announced, getting up from the kitchen table, putting on her coat and her gloves, then collecting her handbag. 'I want to write to Daphne. She's sent me the sweetest letter. Anyway, haven't you got a WVS meeting this evening?'

Bella waited until her mother had gone to vent her fury, by kicking one of the chairs across the kitchen and then bursting into angry tears.

It just wasn't fair. Why did things always seem to go wrong for her? She was the prettiest girl for miles around and yet she had ended up married to a man like Alan, who had been so horrid to her and whose parents had pretended to be so well-to-do when all the time all they had really possessed had been debts. And now, just when she needed her mother to make a fuss of her, Mummy was fussing round Daphne.

How could it be possible for lazy crafty Charlie to end up making such a good marriage whilst she had ended up with someone like Alan? She had been relieved at first when she had been widowed, but that had been before she had realised that people expected her to go into some sort of mourning for her husband and behave more as though she was her mother's age than not even twenty-one yet. And now the Minister of Labour, Ernest Bevin, was saying that he wanted women

185

like her to do factory work; jobs that men had left behind when they had joined up. Factory work! The very idea! For all that her mother had been unsympathetic, Vi certainly wouldn't want to tell Daphne's posh mother that she, Bella, 'Charles's' sister was working in a factory, Bella acknowledged, calming down slightly. She must point that out to her mother. Then there would be no more talk about her father not being able to give her a job, Bella decided triumphantly.

Jean was worried about the twins. They were up to something, she was sure of it. She had said as much to Grace when she had come home on Sunday with Seb, whilst Seb and Sam, and Luke, who had managed to get a bit of leave, had been busy talking together about the fact that the headquarters for the Western Approaches Command, along with the headquarters of the RAF's Group 15 Coastal Command had been relocated to a complex of reinforced buildings beneath Derby House. Seb was now a member of one of the teams working within the Western Approaches Command, that work being very confidential and hush-hush, Grace had told her mother conspiratorially.

There was nothing that Jean could quite put her finger on to explain her anxiety; it was more of a mother's intuition. The twins came home every day full of their work at Lewis's, where they seemed to be thoroughly enjoying themselves in their normal way, playing tricks on people by changing places, to such good effect that, as they admitted to Jean, they had been threatened with being moved to separate departments.

'You should be ashamed of yourselves,' Jean had scolded them. 'Grace was so well thought of at Lewis's and didn't have a blemish on her record, and look at you two, in trouble before you've been there a few weeks.'

'It was just a bit of fun, Mum, honest,' Lou had assured her. 'And even Mrs Cooke, the manageress of our department, said that it was good to see customers smiling when they come in and see two of us and that anything that lifted people's spirits in wartime was a good thing.'

'Mm, well, I just hope she doesn't start thinking that her department is getting too much of a good thing,' Jean had told them.

She had hoped that going out to work full time would keep them so busy that they'd grow out of wanting to go on the stage, but if anything, they seemed to be spending even more time practising their dancing, racing upstairs the minute they'd had their tea just like they had done tonight, and then not coming down again until suppertime, all evening that gramophone of theirs playing dance music.

Con knew when he was on to a good thing. He hadn't reckoned much to the twins when he had first seen them – in fact he'd been downright dis- appointed. There was no way they measured up to his fantasy. They looked so young for their age that they could have passed for fourteen really, with their curls and their freckles, girls really rather than young women, and without any kind of sexual appeal for him. Granted, they were identical, and that could be enough to get a sentimental audience going.

But then they had started to dance and Con had seen their value immediately. The pair of them were naturals, and bright as well. That mirror imagine routine they'd done had been pretty smart. Not that Con had said that to them. Instead he'd frowned and shaken his head and told them to come back in a couple of weeks when he'd had a word in a few ears and seen if anyone was interested in having a dancing competition. In the meantime he'd told them they were to keep quiet. And he reckoned they would. He'd asked them their names before they'd left and Con, an expert on such matters after all, had known from the look they exchanged and the way they had hesitated that they'd been lying when they'd given him the names of Kitty and Lucy Carlton.

But he'd slapped Kieran on the back as they stood together at the bar of the shabby pub not far from the theatre that Con favoured, and ordered him a second drink.

The last thing she had felt like doing tonight was going to a boring WVS meeting in the church hall, Bella thought crossly, but at least it was better than staying at home having to listen to the Poles going on and on about their recent visit to see Jan, who was based with a squadron of Polish fighter pilots.

All she'd heard from the moment they'd come

back had been how heroic Jan was, and how happy they were to have been reunited with some friends from Poland, who had moved down to the base to be near their own son.

In Bella's opinion it was a pity that Bettina and her mother didn't take themselves off and move in with their friends, or at least it would have been if that didn't mean that Bella would be obliged to take in other billetees to occupy her spare bedrooms.

'Hello, you don't mind if I join you and introduce myself, do you? Only our chairwoman mentioned at the last meeting that she thought that we'd get on well together.'

The latecomer's whisper had Bella looking up at her in astonishment as she sat down on the chair next to Bella's own.

The church hall was an imposing rectangular building halfway between the church and the church school, which had gone from rarely being used to almost full-time occupation with the war and the need for so many different organisations needing somewhere to meet to discuss their war work and responsibilities.

Since the vicar's wife was on the WVS committee she had first call on the church hall, access to the chairs, which were kept locked in a separate storeroom to prevent pilfering and, even more importantly, a key to the kitchen.

The WVS meeting had only just started, the room in semidarkness thanks to the blackout curtains and the low-wattage light bulbs dangling on flexes from the ceiling. The committee, which included Vi, were seated on chairs in front of a long trestle table at the far end of the room – close to the stove, which was supposed to heat the whole room but in fact heated only a few feet.

The chairwoman was reading out something dull and boring about the previous meeting, and the importance of knitting more squares for blankets, leaving Bella free to study the newcomer, who in return gave Bella a confident smile.

'I'd have introduced myself at the last meeting,' she whispered, 'but you'd left before I could. I'm Laura Wright. I'm a teacher.'

A teacher. Well, that probably explained her confident manner, Bella decided, but Laura Wright was much younger and much prettier than any teacher Bella could remember from her own school-days – but, happily, not as pretty as Bella herself.

'I'm hoping that I can interest you in a project I'm involved with.'

Bella waited warily.

'I've been asked to organise an emergency crèche service for the area, to take in any little ones whose homes have been bombed, or whose mothers can't look after them all day for any reason – you know, if they have to go out to work. Mind you, from what I've heard a lot of the manufacturing compa-nies will be setting up their own nurseries now that Mr Bevin has said that he intends to make it obligatory for young women of twenty and twenty-one to register for war work. And the thing is that I'm going to need some help. I've mentioned this to our chairwoman and she suggested that I should approach you. Would you be interested, do you think? It would be full-time work with pay. Of course, I'd have to get official approval but our chairwoman didn't seem to think that would be much of a problem. She mentioned that your father is on the local council.'

'I've never looked after small children,' Bella protested, somewhat taken aback by Laura Wright's confident open manner. Bella didn't have any close girl friends and she didn't really know how to go on with members of her own sex who were her own age, especially not in this kind of situation. And then there was that sharp pang of unwanted emotion she had just felt at the mention of young children, and the angry fear that went with it. Bella didn't like it when something made her feel vulnerable or made her think about things she didn't want to think about. Why should the thought of young children and babies upset her? It didn't, and she wasn't going to let it, either.

'I should have thought you'd need trained nursery nurses,' she told Laura Wright dismissively, eyeing the woman seated on the other side of her, with her neatly stacked squares of knitting on her knee waiting to be handed in. How utterly boring to spend one's spare time knitting blanket squares. The very thought made Bella shudder. She was beginning to wish now that she had thought of some kind of more exciting war work to get involved with, although quite what she didn't know.

'Oh, yes, we will,' Laura Wright agreed, 'but I will also need someone to work as my assistant, help with all the paperwork, admitting the babies, keeping a register, all those practical things, as well as dealing with council officials and the like. Our chairwoman said that she thought you would be the ideal person. I must say that you do look the kind to me who knows how to get what she wants.'

Perhaps because of Laura Wright's compliment, or maybe because of the thought of having to knit blanket squares, Bella didn't know, but for some reason, instead of bristling or dismissing Laura's words outright, Bella discovered that she actually felt intrigued and even a little bit excited by the other girl's suggestion.

'Look, you don't have to make up your mind right now,' Laura told her. 'We'll be having the crèche in a spare classroom at the junior school. That way it will be easy for the mothers to leave both their little ones and their older children, if they have any, so you can always come and see me there and let me know if you want the job, although I need to know by the end of the week. Luckily they've got a kitchen at the school, and the council will provide us with all the things we need – you know, cots and bedding and the like. It would be something very worthwhile.'

Had Laura Wright offered her a job, especially one described as 'very worthwhile' at any other time, Bella knew she would probably have turned it down flat, but Mr Bevin's plans to oblige women to do war work, combined with her mother's warning that Bella's own father was not likely to be willing to offer her a job, combined to make Laura Wright's suggestion seem both appealing and providential.

Bella decided that she would enjoy telling her mother not to bother coaxing her father on her behalf, because she had found a job for herself. The Assistant to the Manageress in charge of a crèche. Assistant Crèche Manageress – let Daphne try to better that!

The chairwoman had finished speaking, but the committee members, including Bella's own mother, were still in their seats.

Those Poles wouldn't be able to look down their noses at her once they knew she was doing proper war work. Assistant Crèche Manageress. Yes, it had a very good sound to it. It would put her cousin Grace in her place as well, seeing as Grace was only in her second year of training to be a nurse.

Bella's own mother was getting up to speak now. Bella exhaled a bored sigh of resignation. No doubt her mother was going to go on for ever about the number of blanket squares that still needed to be knitted. She'd even tried to coerce Bella to knit some, using dirty old wool that had been unwound from someone's old clothes.

Bella turned to Laura Wright and hissed, 'I'll do it.'

NINE

Katie had never felt so self-conscious and awkward in the whole of her life. She was stuck here in the Campions' kitchen, having to make small talk with the one person above all others she most certainly did not want to make any kind of talk with. Luke Campion himself.

He had arrived unexpectedly a few minutes before Jean Campion had had to go out to a WVS meeting, explaining that he had hoped to see his father.

Jean had told him that Sam had volunteered to do some extra work but that he would be in soon, and had begged him to wait, saying that Katie would make him a cup of tea and a sandwich.

That, of course, had put a stop to Katie's own plan to escape upstairs to her own room, and now they were alone in the house, since the twins had gone to the cinema with Eileen Jarvis, whose sister taught dancing.

Katie longed for Sam Campion to return. She felt as though her tongue was stuck to the roof of her mouth, and that she had become a total butterfingers when she had tried to make Luke a sandwich without feeling self-conscious.

Luke Campion had made it worse by getting up and 'helping' her, instead of sitting down at the kitchen table and letting her wait on him. Now he had drunk his tea and eaten his sandwiches, and his father had still not come in. She'd been glad of the excuse that washing up his tea things had given her to keep her back to him whilst she busied herself at the sink.

'So you work at the censorship place, then?'

The sound of his voice breaking the silence almost made Katie drop the cup she was washing, but what was even worse was that he was now standing beside her, a tea towel in his hand as he set about doing the drying.

'Yes, that's right,' she confirmed in a strained voice. Since he was attempting to make conversation and be polite, Katie's own good manners insisted that she should do the same. Frantically she hunted around for something to say but could only come up with a forced, 'It's really interesting.' That made her flush as soon as she had spoken and she added uncomfortably, 'Not reading other people's letters. That's the worst part to the job, knowing that we're reading something that's meant to be private.'

'A person would have to be a fool to put anything in a letter that was properly private, seeing as everyone knows the post is being censored,' was Luke's prompt response. 'And anyway,' he added, 'it's for the good of the country. And that's what we're in this war for, after all.

Sometimes we have to put our duty before what we've been brought up to think is wrong, like reading other folks' letters.'

His supportive comment caught Katie by surprise, relaxing her into turning to him to say, 'That's exactly what I try to tell myself, but it isn't always easy.'

'War never is.'

This was a man who had been through Dunkirk, Katie reminded herself, so it was no wonder that both his voice and his expression should be shadowed and bleak.

'It must be very hard to . . . to . . .' Katie stumbled to a halt. 'I think our men in uniform are the best in the world and so very brave,' she said simply and with such real feeling that even Luke, prejudiced against her as he was, knew she was speaking honestly.

Luke frowned and turned away from her. He didn't want to have to acknowledge that his mother's billetee, whom he had resolved thoroughly to dislike, had somehow touched his emotions.

'I dare say you'd rather be with your fancy theatrical friends than stuck here. I'm surprised you didn't get yourself a job with ENSA, seeing as your dad's in that line of business.'

Joining the Entertainments National Service Association hadn't had any appeal for Katie, but the hostility was back in Luke Campion's voice and so she didn't feel that she wanted to prolong their conversation. She told herself that she was glad of his hostility. She didn't want to warm to Luke Campion, and she did not want to find herself thinking that he was brave and handsome, and a loving son and brother. And she certainly did not want to find herself regretting that some other selfish young woman had treated him so badly that it had turned him against those girls whom he thought might be like that, including Katie herself.

And yet despite being sure that she didn't want any of those things, Katie still found herself saying quietly, 'I'm very happy to be here and proud to be doing what I am doing.'

Luke had to turn away from Katie as he heard the mixture of anger and sincerity in her voice. Could it be that he *had* been wrong about her? He acknowledged that it got his back up a bit the way his mother in particular was always praising her billetee and going on about how kind she was, and how pretty, in a sort of meaningful way. It hadn't escaped Luke's notice that Katie was indeed very pretty. How could it when a girl was such a good-looker? Luke admitted that he was struck afresh by just how pretty Katie was every time he saw her. Far too pretty to want to have anything to do with an ordinary bloke like him.

Now what was he thinking? Luke wasn't at all happy about the direction his own thoughts had somehow taken without him having authorised them to do any such thing. Hadn't he learned his lesson the hard way from Lillian? The trouble was that he hadn't ever envisaged finding himself in a position in which he'd have to talk to Katie on a one-to-one basis. He'd have preferred to keep his distance from her. He wished his dad would come in.

Katie wished desperately that Sam Campion would arrive home and put an end to the unwanted and uncomfortable intimacy she was having to share with Luke.

The Campion kitchen, normally such a warm and comforting, homely room, now seemed to be filled with all sorts of unspoken tensions. Perhaps she should just excuse herself and go up to her room? Katie turned to Luke at the same moment as he turned to her, both of them beginning to speak at the same time and then both falling silent as they heard the now familiar piercing warning of the air-raid siren, rising in pitch and volume.

'Air raid,' Luke warned Katie unnecessarily, his voice clipped and his manner suddenly very soldierly in a way that Katie found unexpectedly reassuring. 'Come on, get your coat.'

The shelter was down at the bottom of the road, and thanks to the Luftwaffe's frequent bombing raids towards the end of last year, Katie was already familiar with both its position and its other occupants.

She was three or four houses down the street, which was now filling with people from the other houses, all of them heading for the shelter, when suddenly she stopped and turned round, running back to the house without a word of explanation to Luke.

He caught up with her in less than half a dozen yards, grabbing hold of her arm and demanding sharply, 'What are you doing? The shelter's the other way.'

Pulling herself free of his grip, Katie yelled

back above the noise of the siren, 'I've got to go back for your mum's china. She keeps it ready packed for an air raid and always takes it with her. I'd never forgive myself if anything happened to it.'

She was gone before Luke could stop her, weaving her way through the people going the other way, her slight body making that process far easier for her than it was for him, but it never occurred to Luke not to go after her.

He finally caught up with her just as she reached the house.

'Are you mad?' he demanded. 'Mum doesn't think more of a few tea cups than she does of your life.'

Katie ignored him, rushing into the house and through the kitchen to the hallway, and of course Luke followed her. How could he not do? He was the eldest boy in a family of sisters, and as such he had always taken his responsibilities to the female sex very seriously.

Oblivious to Luke's presence, Katie pulled open the door that led to 'under the stairs', and then she got down on her knees to pull out what looked to Luke like an old basket stuffed with newspaper and rags.

'Careful with it,' she warned him as he took the basket from her, and then reached down to help her to her feet.

They hadn't got much time. Whilst she'd been in the cupboard Luke had already heard the menacing drone of the incoming bombers, heavy with their bombs, the threatening, hostile sound growing steadily louder. They'd be heading for the docks, of course, he reassured himself and, as his father always said, up here in Wavertree they were safely distant from the docks. He urged Katie towards the back door, having estimated that it would take them less time to make it to the safety of the air-raid shelter if they ran down the narrow lane at the back of the houses rather than using the street itself.

As soon as they were outside, the noise of the bombers, engines desynchronised to prevent them being tracked by the British defence systems, as Luke knew, was becoming louder by the heart-beat. Down towards the docks, the night sky was filled with the beams of searchlights trying to pick out the bombers for the anti-aircraft guns.

The planes were Dorniers, from the sound of their engines, Luke reckoned. The guns from the batteries were now thumping out anti-aircraft fire whilst the Dorniers' bombs howled earthwards and explosions lit the darkness.

'Run!' Luke urged Katie, as he put down the basket to pull the back door closed behind them, but when he turned round again she was standing next to the basket, not having moved at all.

As he bent down to lift the basket she reached down too, telling him, 'We can take a handle each and then we can both run.'

It was the kind of thing that Grace would have said to him, and for no reason he could think of Luke felt a sudden prick of unmanly tears. Blinking them away, he grabbed the basket handle nearest to him and, just as though she was as well trained as one of his men, Katie took her handle and then broke into a run.

Added to the other sounds now were the ringing of fire engine and ambulance bells, flames shooting up from newly bombed buildings. The flat whistle of distant sticks of bombs falling on the docks was reassuring in the sense that the characteristic sound of the falling bombs meant that they were at a safe distance.

They had to pause at the bottom of the garden whilst Luke opened the gate, and then they were out onto the muddy track that ran between the gardens and the allotments, and came out on the main road itself just a little bit down from Ash Grove, where Luke could see a couple of corporation buses obviously caught out in the open, their windows blacked out, a line of thin blue light emerging from them where the passengers were disembarking, no doubt making for the same air-raid shelter as they were themselves.

They were over halfway down the path, when Luke heard the Dornier, the hairs lifting in his nape as he did so. He knew instinctively somehow, even before he heard the scream of the bomb, just how close it was going to be. He reacted automatically, dropping his end of the basket and then pushing Katie down beside it before throwing himself on top of her.

Luke lifted his head as he saw the bomb hit one of the huts on the allotment, only a few yards away from the stationary buses, causing it to explode with a dull crump, and then ducked again, knowing that the explosion would send wood and glass flying through the air.

He could feel Katie squirming beneath him as though she wanted to get up.

'Keep still,' he warned her. 'They're still overhead.' He stopped speaking as a burst of machine-gun fire drowned out his voice, making speech impossible as the Dornier turned and strafed the trapped buses.

The cries and screams from the injured and dying mingled with the general nightmare sounds of the night, as the Dornier, its work done, banked and turned, dropping a final stick of bombs as it went.

Luke had gone so still that if it hadn't been for the firm steadiness of his heartbeat and the warmth of his body protecting her own, Katie could almost have thought herself alone. She could smell mud and rain and grass, the scents of life and the living, but they were mingling with the smells of smoke and explosives and burning – the scents of potential death.

The bombers weren't overhead any more, although she could still hear them and their bombs, just as she could still hear the sound of fire engine and ambulance bells, and the determined thudding of the heavy anti-aircraft guns.

She wriggled under Luke's muscular weight; he had somehow braced himself on his forearms in such a way that whilst he was protecting her he wasn't squashing her. No doubt it was some technique they must teach them in the army, she decided, suddenly growing conscious of the fact that she felt slightly dizzy and shaky, and very much aware now of the unfamiliar man scent of Luke, which at the same time was disconcertingly also very familiar, as though she had been aware of his scent all the time without even knowing that she was, and could have recognised it, picked it and him out from a hundred other men without a second's hesitation.

She shouldn't be thinking about things like that, Katie chided herself. She should be thinking about more important things, like Jean's tea cups.

The china!

Luke could have broken it, the way he had almost thrown it down like that. She struggled more anxiously, telling him, 'Let me up, you shouldn't have dropped the basket like that. Your mother's tea cups are probably broken now.'

'Keep down,' Luke told her.

His voice sounded thick and choked, alerting Katie at once.

'What is it? What's happened?' she demanded to know, pushing even harder to be free.

'The so-and-so's strafed a couple of buses that had stopped to let people off to get into the shelter,' he told her. 'Come on. I'll see you safely into the shelter, then I'll go and see if there's anything I can do to help.'

Katie's heart lurched into her chest wall. Those poor people on the bus. It didn't take much imagination to work out how defenceless they would have been.

'I'm coming with you,' she told Luke stoutly. 'I go to first-aid classes.'

However, when they got closer to the scene it was obvious to both of them that there was nothing that anyone could do.

The buses were burning wrecks it was impossible for anyone to get near. Fire crews were working busily to put out the flames whilst the ambulance crews were kneeling on the ground beside charred still-smouldering bundles of what looked like rags, but which Katie recognised with a heave of her stomach were the remains of human beings, who must have been flung from the burning buses by the force of the explosion.

Katie almost dropped her handle of the basket. She looked at Luke, and he looked back at her.

'Come on,' he told her gruffly. 'Let's get you and Ma's tea cups into the shelter.'

'I don't think I can,' Katie told him. Her legs were shaking so much that she didn't think they could support her. Luke took one look at her and then gently told her to put down the basket.

Poor kid, this was probably the first time she had seen something like this, and he hadn't forgotten how he had felt his first time. He had thrown up his dinner and cried like a baby. After, he had felt properly ashamed of himself, but an older, much more experienced soldier than he was himself had comforted him and had told him that it affected everyone like that at first.

There was nothing he could say; no words of comfort he could offer. He knew after all that, just like him, Katie had seen the two small charred bundles laid out next to the bigger one and guessed like him that they were a mother and her two children. There were no words for things like that, but what you felt about them was there inside you, engraved on your heart for ever. Luke pulled Katie towards him and then wrapped her tightly in his arms.

Katie wanted to close her eyes and blot out what she had seen but it seemed wrong somehow, an insult to those poor people who had been killed. She wanted to cry but she couldn't. She wanted to say something but she couldn't. She was, she realised distantly, shaking from head to foot, her teeth chattering together despite the warmth of Luke's arms holding her tightly and Luke's body against her own.

TEN

'Well, I really don't know why you felt it necessary to come rushing over here to Wallasey, Jean,'
Vi told her twin sister, 'just because you'd heard
that a few bombs had been dropped on us when
clearly they were intended for the docks.'

They were in Vi's immaculate but somehow
cold-looking kitchen, with its cream and blue
colour scheme.

Jean exchanged rueful looks with Grace, wishing
now that she hadn't wasted her daughter's precious
few hours off from the hospital by taking the ferry
and then the bus to Kingsway, Wallasey Village to
make sure that her sister hadn't suffered in the
severe bombing Wallasey had endured.

Jean was so very proud of her eldest daughter
and the way in which she had matured since she
had started her nurse's training. Grace was so very
much a young woman now, and able to hold her
own as such, rather than the sometimes impulsive
and slightly scatterbrained girl she had been. Of
course, the fact that she was training to be a nurse
had done a lot to give her a calm air of capability,

206

and Jean had noticed how proudly and confidently Grace held herself these days. Some of that must be due to her happiness with Seb, who always treated Grace just as he ought. It was plain to Jean just how much Seb thought of Grace and that they were very much in love. Grace felt very strongly, Jean knew, that she had a duty to finish her training and that, of course, meant that they could not get married until she had done so.

'And Bella's safe then, Auntie Vi, and her house as well?' Grace pressed her aunt, taking pity on her mother, and showing that maturity Jean had seen in her.

Despite the fact that everything in her aunt's kitchen was new and modern, including the Rayburn oven Vi and Edwin had had fitted after they had moved in, Grace acknowledged to herself how much she preferred her mother's kitchen – equally as spick and span as Auntie Vi's but much more homely. Even the chairs in her aunt's kitchen felt uncomfortable to sit on and unwelcoming, Grace thought ruefully. She was glad though that she'd worn the new blue coat and hat Seb had bought her for Christmas. She'd seen the sharp way her aunt had inspected them – pursing her lips slightly as she did so.

'Yes, Bella and her house are both safe, thank you, Grace,' Vi answered. 'She and I were both at our WVS meeting when the air-raid siren went off. One has one's duty to do, after all.

'Now that you are here, Jean, I may as well tell you that Charles is on the point of becoming engaged to be married,' Vi continued, changing the subject.

Now it was Grace's turn to catch her mother's eye and to mouth behind her auntie Vi's back, 'Charles!' and pull a small face.

'It isn't official as yet, but there will be a notice going in the papers over Easter. Edwin and I are both delighted. It won't be a long engagement. I always think that June is the perfect month in which to have a wedding. Charles is being so brave, but as our doctor has said, with his back he shouldn't really be in uniform. Charles doesn't like to make anything of it, of course, but naturally him trying to drag poor Eustace onto the boat the way he did was bound to damage his back. Edwin says that the army are bound to give him an honourable discharge, when he goes before his Medical Board. Of course, Charles will be disappointed. He's been keen to do his bit right from the start, but as Edwin says, there's more than one way for him to serve his country and now that Edwin's business has been scheduled by Mr Bevin as being engaged on essential work of national importance, he's going to need Charles working in the business with him. Of course, as a soon-to-be-married man Charles needs to be able to support his wife. Daphne is such a delightful girl. That's Daphne Wrighton-Bude, of course,' Vi elaborated, for all the world as though they had never heard her name before, as Grace said wrathfully to her mother later when they were on their way home.

'Charles saved her brother's Eustace's life at Dunkirk as you know,' Vi continued complacently. 'Mr Wrighton-Bude, that's Daphne's father, is a member of Lloyd's. Oh, I'm sorry, Jean, you won't know what that is, of course.'

'Of course we do,' Grace piped up quickly. 'We were talking about it only the other week, weren't we, Mum, when Seb was telling us about that relation of his.'

Jean nodded. It always gave her a bit of a kick in the stomach when Vi was like this with her, even though she knew she should be used to it by now. After all, her twin had spent all of her married life looking down on Jean and her family, and making it clear that she thought she and Edwin and their children were above Jean and Sam and theirs. It wouldn't suit Vi at all if she knew that, far from feeling envious of her, she wouldn't have swapped places with her for double rations for the rest of the war, Jean knew, but it was the truth.

Sam had warned her that Vi wouldn't thank her for her concern, or for taking the trouble to travel all the way out to Wallasey to check up on her, and as usual he had been right. However, Jean knew that she would never have been able to forgive herself if she had not done so. She was, after all, the elder of the two of them, and as the elder she had always had it impressed on her by their mother that it was her responsibility to take care of her younger sister.

'You're lucky to have caught me in,' Vi added. 'I've only just popped back from the church hall. Naturally in my role as second in command on our WVS committee I'm heavily involved, dealing with those poor unfortunates who were made homeless by the bombs. I shouldn't say so, of course, but our chairwoman simply couldn't manage without me. Some of the women who join the WVS simply aren't up to the work and need constant organising. One practically has to stand over them.'

Vi looked pointedly at her kitchen clock as she told them firmly, 'You'll want to leave yourselves plenty of time to get back, I know. You should be able to get a cup of tea at the ferry terminal. I've made it a rule not to offer visitors any kind of refreshments whilst the war is on. It seems so unfair to our sailors.'

'Cooeee, Mrs Firth, are you there?' a new voice called out from the other side of the half-open back door. 'Only I've brought you some of those biscuits you said you and the other ladies from the WVS liked so much, you know, the ones that my special contact brings for me.'

Black market was what Vi's neighbour meant, Jean knew, as Grace only just managed to subdue a splutter of laughter. Vi had heard her, though, Jean could tell that from the angry colour burning her twin's cheeks.

Ten minutes later, as they walked to the bus stop together, Grace's arm tucked through Jean's, Grace squeezed her mother's arm and told her lovingly, 'I'm ever so glad that you are my mum, Mum, and not Auntie Vi.'

'And I'm glad that you're my daughter, Grace,' Jean returned, blinking away a tear.

'Lancaster Avenue took a direct hit and they're saying that over eighty have been killed.'

Bella nodded as she listened to her mother. She was doing her personal ironing, and had just finished ironing a delicate silk blouse, which she hung on a padded silk coat hanger before hanging it on her ironing maiden, whilst the household laundry, which had been delivered that morning, was stacked on the kitchen table.

Vi had arrived ten minutes earlier, announcing that she wasn't staying long because she was on her way to the local reception hall to oversee the restoration of order after the previous night's influx of people rendered homeless by the bombing.

'Just look at the creases in this sheet,' she complained crossly to Vi, half unfolding the offending item to display the creases ironed into it. 'I've a good mind to send it back.'

'You've got your iron on – you may as well run it over the sheet. That will get rid of it,' Vi advised her.

'I've got enough to do ironing my blouses without having to start ironing sheets as well,' Bella told her.

Bella wasn't domestically inclined although she did rather like ironing her own pretty things, and besides, ironing them herself meant that they were done properly.

Refolding the sheet, she placed it back on top of the others, and reached for another blouse from her ironing basket, carefully dampening it and then rolling it up to spread the damp, before unrolling and starting to iron the collar.

'I've had a word with your father about you going to work for him, Bella, and I'm afraid that he says that it just won't do, not with him being a councillor. He says that other people will think that he's made up a job for you so that you don't have to register for proper work, and a man in his position just can't do that, especially not with your brother on the point of getting engaged.'

Bella looked up angrily from her ironing. 'So Daddy can't find a job for me, but he can find one for Charlie, is that what you're saying, Mummy?'

Vi looked pained. 'Really, Bella, this isn't like you. You've always been such a sweet-natured girl. I don't think that your father would be very pleased if he knew what you were saying. It's always been understood that Charles would join him in the business; Charles was working for him before—'

'Before he joined up?' Bella stopped her mother furiously, realising just in time that she was in danger of singeing her blouse, and removing the iron. 'But he did join up, didn't he, and now he's trying to wriggle his way out of the army by claiming that he's got a bad back just so that he can marry Daphne and come home and have a cushy number working for Daddy.'

'Bella, that's a dreadful thing to say. Your brother is a hero. Everyone knows that. I don't know what's happened to the sweet-natured daughter you were, I really don't.'

Bella could have pointed out that what had happened to her was that she'd married a man who had knocked her senseless and been unfaithful to her, a man who tried to kill her and had succeeded in killing their unborn child. She could, of course, equally truthfully have pointed out that she had never actually been 'sweet-natured' in the first place, but of course she did not.

Instead she tossed her head and said triumphantly, 'Actually, Mummy, I've already got a job, so I don't need one from Daddy.'

'What kind of job? I do hope it isn't something dreadful like factory work, Bella, not with Charles about to propose to Daphne.'

'I'm going to be the Assistant Manageress at the new crèche. Laura Wright, who's the Manager, asked me last night.'

Bella pressed the iron down very hard on the hem of her blouse as she spoke. She was sick of having to listen to her mother going on about Daphne.

As soon as she had finished ironing her blouse she put it on a hanger, unplugged her iron, and told her mother firmly, 'Actually, Mummy, I must dash. I've arranged to meet up with Laura and if I don't go and get ready I'm going to be late. We're going to be frightfully busy with all this bombing. You will excuse me, won't you?'

Bella was still seething with fury over her parents' sudden preference for her brother when she reached the small church school where the crèche was to be established.

She found Laura in the school room that was to be the new crèche, surrounded by recently delivered second-hand cots and small beds.

'I do hope you haven't come to tell me that you've changed your mind and you don't want the job after all,' she told Bella anxiously from the middle of the jumble of furniture. 'Only I've already spoken to the powers that be and they've given the go-ahead to you becoming my assistant.'

'No, I haven't changed my mind,' Bella reassured her, eyeing Laura's smart black and white tweed skirt and grey jumper, and feeling glad that she had taken the trouble to change into a smart outfit herself.

'Thank goodness for that.' Laura scrambled out of the confusion to stand next to Bella. 'We'll celebrate with a cup of tea and a biscuit in a minute. The biscuits are Garibaldis. Apparently someone knows someone who can get them. Oh, and I've got some forms for you to fill in. You'll be paid two pounds ten shillings a week, which isn't a huge amount, I know, not as much as they earn working in munitions.'

Bella didn't need to fake the shudder she gave at the thought of working in a munitions factory.

'Isn't it dreadful about the bombing last night?' said Laura. 'The siren went off the minute I got in from the WVS meeting. One of the bombs went off in the next road to where I'm billeted, although Lancaster Road seems to have had the worst of it. I'd been told that it was unlikely that the Germans would want to bomb Wallasey. Can you take this list and check off the bedding on it for me?'

More bedding? Bella hesitated and then, remembering the conversation she'd had with her mother earlier, she told Laura, 'I suppose they were aiming for the docks at Birkenhead,' taking the list that

Laura was holding out to her, and then removing the dark sage-green swagger coat she was wearing over a matching skirt and a lighter sage-green jumper with pretty pearl buttons on the shoulder and the cuffs of the sleeves.

She had bought the outfit, along with several others, when Lewis's had had its last order in from Paris. Alan had been furious at the time, she remembered, complaining when he received the bill, which she had had sent to him, but Bella hadn't cared about his anger at the time and she cared even less now. She loved nice clothes and couldn't bear the thought of not having any.

Just over two hours later, Bella took the cup of tea Laura handed to her and sat down on a chair. Out of the chaos that had greeted her arrival she and Laura between them had achieved a very creditable scene of order and neatness.

A feeling Bella couldn't put a name to, other than to recognise that it was both unfamiliar and rather pleasant, had completely banished the angry resentment she'd felt earlier.

'Well, last night's bombing really did hit you for six, didn't it?' Carole said to Katie. 'That's the third time I've asked you if you fancy coming to the matinée at the pictures with me on Saturday.'

Katie gave her friend an apologetic but slightly wan smile, as they sat together in the staff canteen, having their morning tea break. It wasn't just the horror of what she had witnessed last night that was making it so difficult for her to think about more mundane everyday things, she admitted, it

215

was also Luke Campion. There – it had happened again: that disconcerting way her heart had suddenly started bumping into her ribs every time Luke's name popped into her head.

It must be something to do with the shock of being caught out in the open with bombs falling all around them, Katie told herself.

'Well?' Carole demanded impatiently. 'Do you want to?'

Did she want to what? Oh, of course, the cinema.

'Yes I'd love to,' she told Carole.

It had been ever such a shock when Luke had put his arms round her like that and had held her so comfortingly. She would never, ever forget how kind he had been. And she would never forget either the awful reality of those poor people and the way they had died.

'And guess what?' Carole continued giggling. 'Old Frosty's going to get ever such a shock 'cos I've made up this letter making out that it's from a spy, like, and I'm going to give it to her. She'll think she's the bee's knees until she finds out it's just a joke.'

Carole's words brought Katie out of her sad reverie. She looked at her friend in considerable alarm.

'Carole, you mustn't do that,' she protested.

'Why not? It's just a bit of fun.'

'A bit of fun that could lose you your job and get you into a lot of trouble,' Kate prophesied. 'You can't make jokes about spying. Someone might think that you really are.'

'I just thought it would be a bit of fun, that's

all. After all we're always being told to look out for oddities, but none of us ever finds anything, and I reckon it would liven things up a bit if I pretended that I had.'

'Well it will certainly liven things up if you were to get shot as a spy,' Katie agreed bluntly.

She could see from Carole's expression how much she had shocked the other girl and she was pleased. She knew that Carole didn't mean any harm. She was just high-spirited and a bit bored, because their work wasn't as exciting as she had thought it was going to be. But Katie knew that Carole would be in terrible trouble if she didn't frighten her off her 'joke'.

'Very well then, I won't do it,' Carole agreed.

'And you should have seen our Vi's face when this neighbour of hers arrived and handed over the Garibaldis after Vi had just been sticking her nose up in the air and telling me and Grace how she felt it was her duty not to offer visitors anything,' Jean laughed later that evening, as she related to Sam the events of her visit. They were in the back room, sharing a pot of tea whilst Jean told Sam about her day, and darned Sam's spare pair of heavy-duty socks. 'Our Grace could hardly keep her face straight, and no wonder when Vi had already had us trying not to laugh when she kept on calling their Charlie "Charles". Of course, she had to make the point that Charles and Daphne wouldn't have to wait to get married, like our Grace and her Seb . . . What's wrong?' Jean asked when she saw that Sam was frowning.

'I was just thinking about them biscuits,' he said grimly. 'Black market, like as not, and you know how I feel about that, Jean.'

Jean did, of course, and she shared his feelings. Black market goods meant that racketeers were making money from other people's misfortune.

'One of the lads was saying whilst his mother was in the air-raid shelter just before Christmas a couple of so-and-sos went into the house and took everything they could get their hands on – all the food and the kids' presents,' Sam continued. 'And she wasn't the only one they'd done it to. It's common knowledge that the sound of an air-raid siren going off brings out every thief in Liverpool.'

Jean sighed. 'That's such a nasty thing to do, Sam, especially when there's a war on.'

'Aye, well, there being a war on doesn't stop some folk being rotten. In fact, it gives some of them a chance to be even more rotten than they already were, if you ask me.'

'There's some, though, that are worth their weight in gold,' Jean told him softly. 'Like Katie, for instance. I couldn't believe it when Luke told us how she'd run back to get the tea cups.'

'Aye. She's a good lass,' Sam agreed. Luke had taken Sam to one side after the all clear had gone and he'd delivered Katie safely back to Ash Grove, to tell his father about the machine-gunning of the buses and their passengers.

'She didn't say much but it wasn't the kind of thing you'd want anyone to see, if you know what I mean, Dad. You might want to keep a bit of an eye on her for a couple of days, to make sure she's all right,' Luke had told him gruffly.

The siren went off just as Katie had managed to close her eyes, jerking her right back into immediate wakefulness, her heart pounding and her stomach tensing.

Up above her in their own room she could hear the twins, and then Jean's voice calling out urgently, 'Come on, girls!'

There wouldn't be any Luke tonight to tell her off for going back for his mother's tea cups and then holding her so protectively, shielding her from that ghastly sight of those poor people.

Quickly Katie pushed him out of her thoughts, and pulled on her 'siren suit', as the warm all-in-one dungaree suits were called. For those fortunate enough to have them they were ideal for keeping you warm when you had to spend the night in a chilly and often damp air-raid shelter. It was said that Winston Churchill himself wore one given to him by his wife.

Katie could hear the twins coming down the stairs, banging on her door, and urging her to hurry, as they went past.

Jean and Sam were waiting for them in the kitchen, Jean telling Katie firmly but affectionately, raising her voice to make herself heard above the noise of the siren, 'And there'll be no coming back for any tea cups tonight, I'll have you know.'

'Come on.' Sam was shepherding them all towards the door.

Once outside Katie could see everyone else from

219

the street hurrying out of their front doors to make their way down to the shelter.

Lou pulled a face and complained, 'Oh, no, look. Mr Simmonds's got his accordion. That means that we're going to have to listen to him playing all night.'

'That's enough, you two,' Jean checked them. 'He keeps all the older ones' spirits up, even if you don't appreciate his playing.'

Tonight they were safely inside the shelter well before Katie heard the first drone of the bombers' engines.

'They're heading for the docks and Birkenhead again,' Sam announced, shaking his head as one of the men asked him if he wanted to join the card game being set up in one corner of the shelter.

Jean got her knitting out, and, as Lou had predicted, Dan Simmonds was playing his accordion, whilst the mothers with young children were tucking them into the bunks and telling them to go to sleep, before sitting down themselves on the lower bunks to exchange news.

It was an almost homely atmosphere, Katie recognised, especially when flasks and sandwiches started coming out of baskets.

Whilst Jean was discussing the problems of knitting with wool unwound from old clothes with a neighbour, Sasha edged along the bunk they were sitting on to get closer to Katie, leaning towards her to whisper, 'Katie, when you went out with your dad did you ever go to any dance competitions?'

'Dance competitions?' Katie queried. 'What do you mean?'

'You know, the kind you can put your name down for and enter, and if you win you get a prize,' Lou explained.

'No. Never,' Katie told them. 'Why do you ask?'

'Oh, no reason,' Lou answered airily. 'We just wondered, that was all.'

Whilst Katie was engaged in conversation with their mother, Lou dug Sasha in the ribs and reminded her, 'We said that we wouldn't talk about the competition to anyone.'

'Well, I wasn't talking about it, I was just asking,' Sasha hissed back indignantly, before adding, 'Oh, I do hope that we'll win. Kieran says that he reckons we will.'

Kieran and his opinions had become a frequent topic for discussion between them, even more frequent, in fact, than their illicit visits to the theatre to practise their special dance routine in front of Con's sternly critical eye. It wasn't that they wanted to deceive their parents, and especially their mother, Lou had told Sasha earnestly, it was just that for the moment it was better not to worry her.

'Once we've been in the competition it will be different,' she had assured Sasha optimistically, 'especially if we win.'

'I don't think Dad will let us go on the stage, even if we do,' Sasha had predicted.

'It's a pity that Auntie Fran isn't here. She'd be on our side,' Lou told her twin now.

They'd chosen the Royal Court Theatre as a starting point for asking about dance competitions because it was where their aunt had sung when she had first started out, which reminded Lou of something.

She gave Sasha another dig in the ribs and hissed, 'You nearly let the cat out of the bag when we were at the Royal Court, didn't you, when you started to tell Kieran that we had an aunt who'd sung there, after we'd given him made-up names so that no one would know who we are. Just as well I managed to pretend to have that coughing fit.'

'You know when we do that bit when you dance and then I copy you?' Sasha began, changing the subject.

Lou nodded and soon the girls were deep in conversation about their dancing, and oblivious to the noise outside the air-raid shelter.

'Things have changed a bit whilst you've been away.'

Bella and her billetees were in the kitchen when she made her announcement, Maria and Bettina Polanski having just returned from a visit to see some other Polish refugees with whom they were friends.

Mother and daughter both had the same high cheekbones and dark hair, but while Bettina's hair curled thickly round her face, her mother's was drawn back into a neat chignon, and marked by silvery streaks.

All three of the Polanskis were tall and lean, with olive skin and dark eyes, but brother and sister were far more outspoken than their gentle mother.

Bella had been so proud of her kitchen when she had first moved into the house as a bride. She'd plagued her father for her Cannon gas cooker, with its cream enamel and its matching set of pans and oven dishes, insisting that she had to have it although it was Maria who used it more than Bella. The yellow distemper on the kitchen walls gave the room a sunny air to it, although, of course, like most kitchens, it faced north to keep the food in it as cool and fresh as possible.

The red cherry design on her white curtains, and the gathered skirt covering the space under her draining board and sink still looked as stylish as it had done when she had first chosen the fabric in Lewis's.

The kitchen was large enough for a table and chairs, and for the cream dresser Bella had insisted on having, with its shelves at the top and cupboards beneath it, whilst the linoleum on the floor shone, thanks to Maria, who kept the whole house spot-less.

Bella didn't even try to keep the smug note from her voice as she continued, 'You'll have to fend for yourselves a lot more from now on because I'm going to be working,' she told them, not in the least bit self-conscious about the fact that thus far during the Polanskis' stay, fending for them-selves had been the order of the day rather than an exception, and that in fact, after her miscarriage, it had been Maria Polanski who had cooked for Bella, caring for her as tenderly as though she had been her own daughter. However, now in the excite-ment of her new official position, and the authority

223

she felt it gave her, Bella was conveniently 'forgetting' all those things that might not reflect well on her in her role as Assistant Crèche Supervisor.

Bettina, though, looked meaningfully at her mother before asking Bella with some disbelief, 'You're going to be working?'

'Every young woman of twenty and twenty-one will soon have to register for work,' Bella pointed out, adding loftily, 'I'm surprised that you aren't aware of that yourself, Bettina, although of course with you being older and a refugee . . .'

Bettina's finely arched dark eyebrows snapped together, her brown eyes registering her anger. 'I already work,' she reminded Bella coolly.

'Well, I suppose you could call helping out with other refugees every now and again a sort of work, but I'm talking about a proper job,' Bella informed her. 'There's a crèche going to be opened in the church school for people who have been bombed and for mothers who are doing their bit by going out to work, and I've been appointed the Assistant Manager.'

'You mean that you are going to be working with babies and small children?'

Someone thinner-skinned and with less self-confidence than Bella might have been daunted by the incredulity in Bettina's voice, but Bella merely nodded her head, before adding sharply, 'So you see, you'll have to fend for yourselves from now on, as I shall be far too busy for any domestic work, especially with all the bombing we've had here in Wallasey. In fact, that's why I'm going out now to the crèche, although officially we won't be

224

opening until the beginning of April. As I said to Laura, who works with me, when I rang her this morning, heaven knows how many children we may have to deal with with all this bombing that's going on.'

It had in fact been Laura who had rung Bella to warn her of this concern, but of course there was no need for the Polanskis to know that, Bella decided as she put on her coat and gloves and picked up her handbag.

The house that had belonged to her in-laws and in which they and their son, Bella's husband, had died the night in November when it had been hit by a bomb, had been demolished now, leaving a raw gap in the avenue of immaculate red-roofed detached houses, with their garages and neat front gardens, but Bella barely gave the house or those who had died in it a second thought as she walked past it on her way to the school.

Whilst her own avenue remained unscathed, beyond it the devastation was obvious, with Lancaster Avenue reduced to untidy heaps of rubble amongst which men were working tirelessly to make things as safe as they could, whilst here and there families were poking disconsolately around in the remains of what had been their homes, looking for anything they could salvage.

The sight of one man leaning on his shovel to wipe the sweat from his eyes made Bella pause in recognition. Sam, her auntie Jean's husband. She wasn't going to acknowledge him, of course. Someone might see her. She had her position to maintain now and it wouldn't be the thing at all for her to be seen talking to a common workman.

Sam watched Bella walk past him with her nose in the air, and grimaced. He had no time at all for Jean's sister Vi, or her family, but he'd got more important things to do than think about them.

No one had expected Wallasey to be so badly hit, and some reckoned that the Luftwaffe had missed their real target and then dropped their bombs on defenceless Wallasey out of spite or desperation or maybe both. One of the bombs had hit and broken the trunk main supplying water for fire-fighting purposes, which had meant that such water had failed completely, leaving people having to stand and watch their property burn. This was why Sam and his team had been called out to help out with the clearing-up operation, and were likely to be working on it for several more days yet.

ELEVEN

Katie stared at the letter. She'd read it three times already, and now her heart was thumping unsteadily and she was going hot and then cold. They all knew why the mail had to be scrutinised but somehow or other the thought that they might actually come across a letter that was potentially 'suspect' became lost beneath the mundane normality of virtually everything they read.

The only other things she'd had to deal with had been the same commonplace things as the other girls – such as a man in uniform writing home, 'I can't tell you where I am, of course, but it's really hot here and there's a lot of sand – and camels,' which had to be crossed through.

But this was different. She could be wrong – so very easily – and then she would look a fool, and worse, an ignorant fool if she said anything, but then if she didn't and she was right . . .

'What's up with you?' Carole demanded.

'It's this letter,' Katie told her quietly. 'I think there's something in it that isn't quite right. It isn't one of your jokes, is it?'

'Don't be daft. I'd never do that to you,' Carole assured her, before sitting bolt upright and exclaiming in a voice loud enough for the whole table to hear, 'Guess what! Katie's caught a spy.'

Katie couldn't have felt more mortified. 'No, I haven't. I mean, I could be wrong. I only thought . . .'

To Katie's relief Anne came to her rescue, getting up from her own chair and coming over to her to ask calmly, 'What exactly is it that caught your attention, Katie?'

Anne's calm manner soothed Katie's nerves.

'It's this bit here,' she told the head of their table, 'where the writer talks about dancing at the Ritz to the Orpheans, and then goes on to mention two of their favourite dance numbers, and asking for them by special request.'

'Yes?' said Anne.

'Well, the Orpheans play at the Savoy, not the Ritz; the music he refers to just isn't the kind of thing the Orpheans normally play and the night he says they asked them to play their request, the Orpheans' normal band leader wasn't leading them, so they couldn't have asked him for a request. I know that because my father was standing in for him and I was with him. I remember it particularly because of the date: the first of May, my mother's birthday.'

'So what you're saying is that the writer of this letter and its recipient couldn't have danced to a request as he claims they did?'

'I don't think so.' Katie looked directly at Anne, admitting worriedly, 'But maybe the writer has just made a mistake. People do sometimes.'

228

'Yes, they do,' Anne agreed with another calm smile, 'but I think under the circumstances it's better to be safe than sorry so I'm going to take this letter over to the supervisors' desk. They'll want to talk to you about it, of course, but don't worry, I'll be with you. We are all on the same side here, remember, Katie. If the questions you'll be asked seem a little harsh it's only because the supervisor will want to be sure of the facts before anyone makes any kind of decision.'

Katie gulped and nodded.

'Fancy you uncovering a spy,' said Carole excitedly.

'I haven't uncovered anyone,' Katie reminded her friend.

They were in the cloakroom where Carole was checking her makeup. She had a date for the evening with Andy, the soldier she had met the night of the Grafton's Christmas Dance and who she'd been seeing regularly since she'd bumped into him again several weeks earlier.

'As good as,' she insisted, pulling a face at herself in the mirror, then complaining, 'Just look at my eyebrows. I'd love to have eyebrows like that Vivien Leigh.' She opened her purse and very carefully removed a spent matchstick, which she then applied to her eyebrows, rubbing in the resultant dark stain with the tip of her finger before carefully replacing the matchstick in her purse.

'Of course it could just be an ordinary couple and you've gone and got it wrong,' Carole acknowledged, returning to their original subject,

229

and causing Katie's heart to lurch uncomfortably into her ribs.

'Don't,' Katie begged her. 'I'm sure I have got it wrong and I wish that I hadn't said anything now.'

'Well, it's like Anne said, it's better safe than sorry, and I shouldn't lose any sleep over it, if I were you. You won't hear anything more about it now until Monday, anyway, seeing as it's Friday now.'

Katie nodded. She wasn't sure how she was going to survive a whole weekend of anxiety about whether or not she had done the right thing, but she knew that somehow she would have to do so.

'I feel ever so sorry for Katie. She's been here over three months now and she doesn't go out much at all, at least not like a girl her age should. She's got a friend that she works with, but by the sounds of it she's found herself a young man now.'

Jean paused to spoon the last of the fairy cake mixture into the bun tins lined up on her table. All the women in the street had got together as they had found that if they pooled their rations and each one of them cooked something in bulk and then shared it around, somehow the rations seemed to go further. This week it was Jean's turn to make the fairy cakes for a children's birthday party on Saturday afternoon.

'No, you don't,' she reprimanded Luke as he looked longingly at the virtually scraped clean bowl. 'There's enough in there yet to make a couple more.'

It had been a wonderful surprise to have both Grace and Luke practically arriving on the doorstep at the same time and unexpectedly too, Grace looking as pretty as a picture in her lightweight cream jacket she had bought the spring before the war, and a cream blouse embroidered with bright blue flowers to match the blue of her skirt. Jean was never happier than when she had her family round her.

'I've just been thinking,' she told them both, deftly putting the first of the trays of fairy cakes into the oven, 'seeing as you and Seb are going to the Grafton tomorrow night, and our Luke's on leave, you could go as well, Luke, and take Katie with you. It's such a shame that she doesn't get out a bit more.'

Behind their mother's back Luke and Grace exchanged mutually understanding looks.

And as though she had seen them Jean added immediately, 'Not that I'm trying to matchmake or anything, before either of you start, but I do feel that I owe her a bit of something, seeing as how she risked her life to save me tea cups.'

Once again the siblings exchanged looks but this time they were looks that said they knew when they'd been outmanoeuvred.

'Well, I don't mind asking her if she wants to come along with us – that is, if Luke doesn't mind – but she may not want to,' Grace warned her mother.

'Of course she will,' Jean insisted briskly.

'According to the twins she's ever such a good dancer as well, so you'll be put on your mettle, our Luke.'

Luke didn't attempt to hide his surprise. 'I thought she wasn't supposed to be musical,' he reminded his mother.

'That's singing and playing something,' Jean corrected him patiently. 'She *can* dance.'

A little to his own surprise Luke discovered that he wasn't as anti the thought of making up a foursome for the Grafton with Katie as he'd expected. But then, of course, it was something he was doing to please his mother and not himself, he reasoned firmly.

'Your dad's working out at Wallasey, helping to clear up after the bombs, so I don't know what time he'll be in.'

'Well, I don't expect he'll go and call round on Auntie Vi whilst he's there. Did you warn him not to expect to be offered one of her Garibaldis, Mum?'

'Huh, your dad would have something to say if he was,' Jean retorted. 'You know how he feels about black market stuff.'

Grace asked Luke with a grin, 'Has Mum told you about Charlie – oh, sorry, I mean *Charles* – yet?'

Luke shook his head.

'Vi reckons that Charlie is about to get engaged to the sister of that lad whose life he saved,' Jean told her son.

'It will be an Easter engagement. Auntie Vi thinks that Easter is the perfect time to get engaged and June the perfect time to get married,' Grace informed her brother.

Turning to her mother, Grace said, straight-faced,

'I reckon it's going to be difficult for Auntie Vi, Mum, having a daughter-in-law who's had to give up a double-barrelled surname to become a plain ordinary single.'

'Maybe she'll just add Charlie's name onto the others, to make hers triple-barrelled?' Luke suggested, laughing.

'Now that's enough of that, you two,' Jean scolded them. 'I know your auntie Vi can be a bit of a snob, but she can't help it. She's always been like that. Here's Katie, coming up to the back door. Why don't you ask her now about the Grafton?'

Katie had been worrying about the letter all the way back to Ash Grove, and wondering if she had done the right thing, so much so that she was inside the kitchen before she even realised that Luke and Grace were there.

'Sit down, Katie love,' Jean instructed her. 'I'm just putting the kettle on.'

'I hope we don't have any more bombers coming over tonight,' Grace sighed. 'We've got so many new patients in that we've got beds set up in the corridors as it is. They've had to bring in some of the injured from Wallasey, there's been so many injured. Mum's been telling me about you saving her tea cups, Katie.' Grace smiled at Katie, who had reluctantly seated herself on the chair Luke had pulled out from the table for her.

'I still can't believe that anyone would be daft enough to risk their lives for some tea cups,' Luke mock growled, shaking his head, but in such a way that Katie knew that he was not really criticising her.

'You're a man, Luke, you wouldn't understand, would he, Katie?' Grace teased her brother.

That warm feeling Katie had felt before was back, but this time it was a bit different, softer and gentler, springing from being here in this kitchen and with this family, Katie recognised, rather than just from being with Luke. It enabled her to relax a little and say truthfully, 'Luke's right. I shouldn't have gone back, but I'm glad I did, and I'm even more glad that he came back with me because he saved the china and he saved me as well.'

'Did he? Then you owe him a favour,' Grace said immediately. 'The three of us are going to the Grafton tomorrow night, and it would be much more fun if you'd make up a foursome with us, Katie. That way Seb and I won't feel guilty about leaving Luke alone at the table whilst we're dancing. Oh, and don't worry, he can dance; me and the twins have made sure of that. You will come, won't you?'

What was it about women that enabled them to perform that special female sleight of hand that somehow made it impossible for a person to refuse an invitation, Luke wondered wryly. Whatever it was, his mother had obviously passed it on to his sister, and in spades.

Katie was caught totally off guard by Grace's suggestion. It was, of course, impossible for her to refuse without being rude, and so she had no alternative but to nod her head and say self-consciously, 'Yes, yes, of course.'

'Good, that's decided then. We can all meet up outside the Graffie.'

Luke shook his head. 'I'll come up here and collect you, Katie,' he said firmly, causing Katie to struggle to control the self-conscious colour she could feel warming her face.

'I don't know why you want to keep that ruddy kid. He can't do anything. Like I've said before, he can't even speak.'

'You leave him alone, and don't go raising your voice to him either; you're frightening the life out of him,' Emily told Con sharply.

Con scowled. The recent bombing had meant a drop in people coming to the theatre and only this morning he'd had the lead female singer's understudy flounce off in a huff after having exchanged words with the lead singer.

'You promised me that I'd be on stage,' she had screamed at Con when she had accosted him in his office. 'You know you did, you rotten liar, so don't you go saying that you didn't.'

The lead singer, who had been walking past at the time, had put her head round the door to say tauntingly, 'He tells them all that, love, when he wants to get into their drawers, don't you, Con? More fool you if you were daft enough to believe it.'

Con had only just managed to dodge the heavy ashtray the understudy, a blonde with a redhead's temper, had hurled at him.

With box office receipts down, and Emily still refusing to open her purse strings, Con was beginning to get desperate. He'd convinced himself that she'd grow tired of having that idiot boy around long before now, but if anything Emily seemed to have grown even more fiercely protective of the child she still insisted on claiming was related to her through some dead cousin or other.

In desperation Con had sent Kieran off to Blackpool to scout around and see, first, what the deal was with these dance contests, and secondly, if he could set up some kind of joint deal with one of the Blackpool theatres that would benefit them both, whilst of course benefiting Con himself more.

Emily wasn't going to have Con, or anyone else for that matter, calling little Tommy an idiot because he wasn't. He understood everything that was said to him perfectly. Emily *was* worried about him, though.

Lewis's was just about to close for the day and the twins were tidying up the shelves of the haberdashery department, carefully refolding bolts of cloth, and then covering them before wiping down the tidied shelves.

'But how are we going to get Mum to agree to us going in for a dance competition?' Sasha asked Lou. 'And don't say that we won't tell her because we'll have to.'

'I know that, silly. Of course we'll have to tell her.' Lou straightened up from dusting her shelf and looked across at her twin. 'If we could perhaps persuade Grace to mention it to Mum, you know, saying that she'd heard there was a dance competition on and wouldn't it be a good idea if we were to enter it?'

Sasha looked doubtful. 'Do you think Grace would do that? She's gone really stuffy since she started training as a nurse and got engaged to Seb.'

'Mm . . . I know. Why don't we get Katie to do it instead of Grace?'

'Do you think she would?'

'Well, we could sort of mention it to her in a roundabout sort of way and then mention it to Mum; you know, sort of saying that Katie had told us about it and suggested that we should enter.'

'But what if Mum asks Katie and Katie says that we were the ones who told her about it?'

Lou dropped her duster onto the shelf and stood up on her ladders, her hands on her hips, demanding, 'Look, do you want us to go in for this competition or don't you?'

'Of course I do.'

'Well then, we'll just have to find a way to make sure that we can enter it, won't we? Look out, Mrs Gregg is coming over.'

Mrs Gregg was the senior assistant in the department and she had a keen eye for specks of dust and time wasting.

'Come along, you two,' she called out. 'No dawdling. I want those shelves spick and span before you leave, and remember, it's Saturday tomorrow so I want you in bright and early.'

'Yes, Mrs Gregg,' the twins chorused dutifully.

TWELVE

'Two minutes, everyone, oh and, Fran, swap your last number for "Dover", will you? We've been swamped for requests for it.'

'I'm not Vera Lynn,' Francine wryly reminded the stage manager, as she powdered her nose in the makeshift 'dressing room' that had been set up for the visiting ENSA entertainers. They were here to entertain the troops at the desert camp 'somewhere close to Cairo in Egypt', as the taciturn major, who was their military liaison officer, had answered Francine's question as to their destination when they had left Cairo at daybreak in their military transport.

It had taken them four months to sail from England to Alexandria, with a stopoff in South Africa on the way, travelling the whole time as part of a convoy, for protection against the German Navy's submarines.

When they had left Southampton Francine hadn't really cared if she lived or died in her grief for the loss of her son, her despair in sharp contrast to the excitement of other members of the troupe, most of whom had never travelled abroad before.

However, as she tried to remind herself she had a duty to the serving men that ENSA was sent abroad to entertain, and listening to the grim stories of some of the sailors and the serving men themselves – some of which had been so heartbreaking that initially she had been unable to understand how those telling them were able to go on – had made Francine feel that she had at least to try to match their bravery.

In South Africa they had put on a couple of shows for some injured men travelling home in a hospital ship that had put into port whilst they were there.

After their first show some of the artists, including Francine, had volunteered to tour the ship's makeshift wards at the request of the doctors in charge.

Francine had stopped by the bed of one young man, who had called out eagerly to her when he had heard her talking to someone else. Blinded in both eyes by shrapnel, and horribly wounded, he had told Francine how much hearing her singing had meant to him.

'Took me right back to when our mam used to sing to us when we was kiddies, you did, and no mistake,' he told her in a soft Northeast accent. 'Bin feeling that I wasn't going to make it home, I was, but then I heard you and it was like I was home already. By, but it means a lot to a lad, that, something from home close by him when he needs it. Fettled me up good and proper, it has.'

Francine had reached automatically for his hand as he spoke to her, and that night when she had been told that the young soldier was dying and had been put in a side ward, she asked if she could go and sit with him.

The major had demurred at first, but Francine had been resolute, and in the end permission had been given.

She had sat with the young soldier, holding his hand, as she sang the only Northeast song she knew, and whilst she was singing it the young lad's 'boat came in', as the words of the song said, and bore him away with it on its tide from life to death.

After that Francine had tried to put her own grief to one side and focus on her determination to give every bit of support she could to those they were travelling to entertain.

Ordinarily Fran would have been the second singer in the troupe, but Lily, the lead, had gone down with a huge sulk and a 'gippy tummy', leaving Fran as the sole singer, and two shows a night to get through for the next week.

The huge sulk was the result of the failure of Lily's four-month-long campaign to tease the major into a flirtation with her, whilst the gippy tummy was the result of the full bottle of gin the singer had drunk as a result of that failure. Lily wasn't used to men turning her down, but then neither was Lily used to war-hardened, taciturn soldiers. None of them was, including herself, Fran admitted. She'd watched Lily's overtures initially with resignation and some disdain, and had felt slightly sorry for the major, assuming that, given the relentless nature of Lily's campaign, allied to her determination, the major would ultimately have to give in. After all, Lily was a woman – attractive, available and extremely willing. The major was a man – heterosexual, alone and being tempted. But to her astonishment and Lily's obvious disbelief, the major had not given in. So now Lily had changed tactics and was loudly proclaiming that he was 'an odd sort' and a 'kill joy', and that if she had her way they'd have had a very different kind of officer escorting them.

Francine wasn't totally convinced that Lily had given up, though; it wasn't in her nature. Not that she cared one way or the other.

When she'd signed up for ENSA she hadn't really cared about anything; when she was feeling particularly 'low', as she was now, she still didn't. She knew she would never stop grieving for Jack. How could she? She still went to bed at night thinking of him, unfolding from her memory those precious days she had spent with him.

Not that there hadn't been some compensations for the long weeks of travel.

The sight of Cape Town, with Table Mountain in the background, was a memory that would stay with her for ever. And now, as for Cairo, Fran felt almost as though the richness of its sights and smells, combined with its history and the intensity with which those men posted to the area threw themselves into enjoying their leave, had overloaded her own senses.

Cairo was a hot, exotic, erotic, fiercely intense

mix of colour and excitement. Louche news reporters and photographers lined the bars of the city's most famous hotels – and so did some of the most beautiful women Fran had ever seen – some of whom, she had discreetly been informed by one of the comedians travelling with them, were not women at all, but rather young men who, having been castrated, had opted to 'become women'.

Fran was no stranger to 'different' forms of sexuality – she had lived in Hollywood, after all – but she admitted that she had been perhaps naïvely shocked at the way in which so many of the men on leave in the city seemed able to forget that they had wives and girlfriends at home.

It was as though in some way Cairo itself seemed to act as a hothouse for all those things that were such a visible part of its exotic nightlife. Life there seemed luxurious indeed compared with at home in England, and predictably Lily had thrown herself into that luxury with a vengeance.

Lily had made her hostility towards Fran clear the minute they were introduced on board the troop ship at Southampton, along with her determination to make sure that Fran knew that she, Lily, was the star of the show.

Fran had taken it all in her stride. She had been in the business long enough to know what its insecurities could do to people, and Lily was typical of many other lead singers Fran had met over the years, in her jealous determination to guard her own position.

So far as Lily was concerned, being the lead

singer meant getting the best of everything that was going, whether that was a hotel room, a stage outfit, or a man, and she was an expert at manipulating the situation to make sure she got what she thought of as her due.

Sometimes Francine thought that, ridiculously, her own lack of any desire to compete with Lily seemed to exacerbate Lily's antagonism towards her rather than pacify her.

Lily had made it plain that she wasn't happy about the fact that she and Francine were billeted in the same hotel, and had equally luxurious rooms, both with en-suite bathrooms – true luxury indeed, and a very welcome one. Francine, knowing how cramped the rooms of some of the chorus girls were, had made a point of letting them know that she was more than happy to 'lend out her bathroom' when the occasion arose.

They'd been made very welcome in Cairo. Lily and Fran had arrived to rooms filled with flowers and invitations.

So far they had been taken to the famous Shepheard's Hotel, photographed for the English papers at home, and entertained at the British Embassy. The dancers had soon been complaining that they were too tired to dance in the show because of all the partying and dancing they did 'off duty'. Cairo, as Fran had been told by one of the newspaper reporters who propped up the bar in Shepheard's Hotel, was a hotbed of political and sexual intrigue and scandal, where gossip was fanned by the heat of the desert wind.

Not that Cairo and its environs didn't have other

attractions. On their rest days between the shows, Fran and some of the ENSA members had been driven out to see the pyramids in transport organised for them by the major: tough desert-ready Jeeps driven by equally tough and desert-hardened men. She had also explored the bazaars, accompanied by a small barefoot dark-haired and dark-eyed 'guide' – one of several boys who had attached themselves to the group. Fran didn't think she would ever get used to the sight of so many children begging, although the major had told her that for them it was a way of life and that many of them would have caused Dickens' Fagin to marvel at their pocket-picking skills.

She had ridden a camel and managed to quell the nausea she had felt at its rolling gait – but then they had travelled halfway around the world on a troop transport ship – but now that they had actually been transported out into the western desert to entertain the men in their camps Fran felt that she was finally doing what she had joined ENSA to do: her bit for the war effort by helping to raise the spirits of the country's fighting men.

They were performing several shows at the desert camp, with men coming in from more outflung, smaller camps to see it. Lily had complained nonstop about the sand, which got into everything, blown in on a hot wind that at night became a very cold wind.

The sand lay against the skin like a layer of sandpaper, coating both food and tongue when one ate, so that within a few hours of their arriving at the camp, it had become an intimate and unwanted part of their lives. But where Lily complained, Fran tried not to, reminding herself instead that the men they had come out here to entertain had to endure these desert conditions month in and month out, and fight as well.

In contrast to the army, they were being treated like royalty. Fran and Lily had their own private showers in a specially erected tent. They had a full military escort to drive them and protect them. Every single aspect of their tour – the accommodation; the stage when they performed; the way they travelled – was under the expert control of their liaison officer, and whilst he might be taciturn and withdrawn, there was no denying the expertise and skill with which the major did his job.

They had all been told when they signed on for ENSA in London that they could be appearing anywhere, from a tent in the desert to a palace in Cairo, and to be prepared to go on in the clothes they'd travelled in, if necessary, but to take some stage outfits in case they got the chance to change into them.

'It's good for the men's morale when they see a pretty girl all dressed up for them,' was a now familiar comment from commanding officers, and one that Fran had taken to heart.

Tonight, for instance, Fran was wearing a full-length emerald satin gown that was in reality more style than substance, but which, like her paste jewellery, looked good on stage.

The cool of the evening was a relief after the enervating heat of the day, and she had only had to endure it for a few hours and in relatively relaxed comfort, not the searing exposure the men had to endure out in the desert in combat conditions, Fran reminded herself. Initially she had felt drained and exhausted, but now with the first half of the show behind her Fran was buoyed up by that fierce surge of adrenalin that hit the veins like a drug the minute she felt a stage floor beneath her feet and saw an audience in front of her.

She'd already sung 'A Nightingale Sang in Berkeley Square', and had been called back for encore after encore, and in all honesty she was not really surprised that the men had requested that she sing 'The White Cliffs of Dover'.

There would be tears in more than a few pairs of male eyes by the time she had reached the end of the song, Fran knew, and who could blame the men for longing to see the white cliffs of home and to exchange the desert for England's green and pleasant land? They were here, after all, to fight to protect that land, and she was here to remind them what they were fighting for.

From somewhere behind her she could hear the major's familiar voice, and a prickle of awareness sensitised her skin in much the same way as the sand. Fran didn't like admitting it but it wasn't hard to understand why Lily had made such a play for him. Major Marcus Linton was a very good-looking man, a very male man. Tall, broad-shouldered, grey-eyed, dark-haired and in his late thirties, he had an air of self-control and command about him that most women would find attractive.

Including her? Hardly. Even if Lily hadn't openly warned her off within minutes of him being introduced to them, Fran would not have been tempted to attract his attention. Marcus Linton might be a very different sort of man from Con, the theatre producer she had fallen for as a girl, and who had fathered her illegitimate child, but her experience with Con had made her very wary of the male sex.

Fran was an extremely beautiful woman with a lushly curvy body and the kind of features that men found sexually attractive. She couldn't change the way she looked but she could and did make sure that men understood that the sexuality of her face and body did not mean that she had the kind of nature that meant she was sexually available to them.

Fran knew that she could have had a very big career as a movie star if she had been willing to trade on the image created by her looks and if she had chosen to take the casting couch route to success and fame.

Singing was as much a part of her as breathing, and she would hate not to be able to use her voice in the way that nature had designed it to be used, but she was certainly not going to use her body or allow others to use it so that she could claim the false coin of 'stardom'.

The comedians were on now; then it would be the turn of the ventriloquist, then the chorus girls. The sound of male laughter rolled in a wave from the audience to reach backstage, where Fran was struggling to change and redo her makeup for the second half.

Fran and Lily were supposed to share a dresser, but typically Lily had appropriated Martha's services, claiming that her 'poorly stomach' meant that she needed someone on hand to minister to her. Since Lily had stayed behind in Cairo comfortably ensconced in the excellent Metropolitan Hotel, which they had been booked into, Fran failed to see exactly why she should need Martha, but Lily's temper tantrums were so well known and feared that John Woods, the ENSA officer travelling with them, had simply given in to her, begging Fran to manage without Martha.

Fran knew perfectly well that Lily wasn't above manipulating things to ensure that she not only remained the lead singer, but also to undermine anyone else's act if she thought they might be in competition with her. Fran wasn't going to put herself through all the emotional drama that went with that kind of situation just for the sake of being without a dresser for a couple of shows. In fact, Fran rather thought that Lily was hoping that Fran would challenge her and provoke an outright showdown between them.

Fran had far more important things on her mind, though. Today was the anniversary of the day she had met Connor Bryant – Jack's father – and remembering that brought the loss of Jack unbearably sharply into her thoughts.

She had been thinking about him all day: the hard labour of his birth, with its pain and her own fear, and then the tremendous sense of exhausted pride she had felt when she had given birth to him, followed by such a surge of maternal joy and love that she could feel its echo within her now.

She had been so young – too young – and nothing had prepared her for the intensity of that love: to give birth to a child, to hold it in your arms, a new life, so filled with trust and so dependent on you that the stab of fierce protective love was forever balanced with an edge of fear.

She had sworn that she would do the best she could for him. She had made that promise – that vow – to him, but she had broken it. If only she could go back and right what she had done wrong.

If only . . . Fran tried to shake away her painful thoughts. She could feel the satin fabric of her frock clinging tackily to her skin. She had lost weight since she had begun this tour and the reflection she could see in the mirror was not one that pleased her. She looked thin and tired, her face slightly gaunt. She opened the flap of the tent that served as her dressing room and stepped out into the familiarity of the backstage bustle, and the velvet darkness of the desert night.

'Ten, Fran,' the floor manager called out, holding up ten fingers.

Nodding, Fran headed for the stage, where their compère was already announcing her.

Fran was dripping with sweat as she came offstage, her heart racing and skipping, gripped by the familiar high of knowing that she had reached out to her audience and touched their emotions.

No matter how cynical she might feel when she was not on stage, once she was, her desire to sing

249

to her audience, and their desire to hear her sing, worked like a special magical spell that never failed to reach deep within Fran, to release a poignancy to her singing that drew those listening to her and to call her back for encore after encore. When she was singing Fran became the song, the instrument via which its words and music flowed into the hearts of others. That was her special gift.

Now, as the night air hit her, the familiar process of her euphoria giving way to exhaustion and emptiness was already taking place.

In her 'dressing room' Fran started to remove her stage makeup, though her work for the evening wasn't over yet. There was still the after-show 'party' to attend – a duty more than a pleasure but an important one for the morale of the serving men.

Fran had just removed the last of her makeup, but was still wearing the robe she had pulled on when she had taken off her stage dress, when she heard the major calling her name outside.

'Yes, I'm here, Major,' she called back.

The dressing room wasn't very big, Fran's precious jar of cold cream was still out on top of the makeshift 'dressing table' – an upturned barrel with a pillowcase over it, on which Fran had placed the photograph of Jack that travelled everywhere with her.

'I've just been speaking to the camp's commanding officer and he's asked if you will have time to go round the san tent and have a word with the men there who weren't well enough to see the show?'

It wasn't an unfamiliar request and Fran responded automatically, 'Of course.'

The major nodded and turned towards the exit to the tent, but as he did so, somehow or other he caught the edge of the photograph frame, sending it falling to the floor.

They both dived for it together, but the major got there first, apologising as he did so.

'I'm sorry, clumsy of me.'

Fran's heart was thudding heavily with a mixture of emotions she didn't want to analyse, but which were dominated by her fierce need to reach out and hold Jack's photograph protectively to her body. As she hadn't done Jack himself. She couldn't trust herself to speak, not even to make a polite response to the major's comment, so instead she simply held out her hand for Jack's photograph, gripping her bottom lip between her teeth when she saw how badly her hand was trembling.

'Nice-looking boy – a relative?' the major asked casually as he handed the photograph back to her.

All she wanted was for him to go, so that she could smooth her fingers over the frame in reassurance, the only reassurance she could give Jack – and herself – now. And yet she also felt a very different and even more desperate need, which she had to struggle to suppress.

'Yes, he's my . . .' You'd have thought after all the years – ten of them – of saying 'my nephew' that the lie would slip easily off her tongue but it never did and tonight, whether through tiredness or the pain of constantly having to deny him, and her own guilt and need, Fran heard herself saying proudly, 'He's my son. Or at least he was. He's dead now. A bomb hit the farmhouse where he'd been evacuated. He was ten.'

The words, hard with pain, cut into her heart like shards of glass, the mere speaking of them emotionally lacerating her throat. It was just as well she couldn't speak because she didn't trust herself to say anything else, Francine admitted.

The photograph lay held between them. Tears blurred Fran's vision.

'It hurts like hell, doesn't it?' The major's voice was unexpectedly kind and understanding.

Fran looked up at him.

'I lost my wife and the child we were expecting in the first wave of bombs that dropped on London,' he told her simply.

They looked at one another, and somehow Francine couldn't – didn't want to – look away. Like an invisible bridge stretching across a dangerous chasm the major's gaze held her own.

A need to talk about her past, about Jack and herself and what had happened, overwhelmed her, coming out of nowhere like a fierce desert storm, unstoppable and overpowering.

Still looking at him, Francine began slowly, 'Jack was born when I was sixteen.'

His steady regard was still fixed on her.

'His father was a married man.' Not a flicker of rejection or disgust. 'Not that I knew that when I fell for him; plain daft, I was, fancying that we were meant for one another and that he loved me when all he wanted was a bit of fun.'

The bridge was holding steady and she was clinging to that calm uncritical gaze.

'Of course, the truth came out when his wife got to know and came storming down to the theatre to warn me off. I hadn't been the first and I won't have been the last. Poor woman, I pity her being married to him.

'I didn't know then that there was to be a child, and when I realised I was that scared. My mother wasn't well as it was, and my father was already dead. One of my sisters always reckoned that the shame and disgrace of what I'd done killed Mum.'

She was trembling inside with all the emotion, all the things she had never said and had kept inside herself for so long. It was as though once she'd started unburdening herself to him she couldn't stop, like poison bursting from a painful wound.

She made an effort to check herself, pulling a face and saying in a shaky voice, 'It isn't a pretty story, is it?'

'Life seldom is a pretty story. You paid a heavy price for being young, trusting and naïve.'

'I dare say if Con hadn't been married pressure would have been put on him to do the decent thing, but he was married, and when my sister Vi offered to have the baby, and bring him up as her own, it seemed the best thing to do, especially for Jack. Vi and her husband already had two children and Edwin, Vi's husband, was doing well for himself. Vi said that she and Edwin could give Jack so much more than I could, and that if I kept him everyone would know that I wasn't married and that he'd suffer because of that. I hated the thought of giving Jack up but I thought I was doing the right thing – the best thing for him. I loved him so much, you see, and I wanted to make it up to him, do something right for him after all that I'd done wrong, so I agreed that Vi should have him, and then I went to America to work, to have a fresh start. But of course you can't walk away from something like that. I'd left a part of myself behind in Liverpool, literally as well as figuratively. You don't realise until you have a child just what it means.'

For the first time the steady gaze flickered. Remorse filled her, but she sensed that he didn't want her to say anything, so instead of apologising to him she continued unsteadily, 'I never stopped missing Jack or loving him, and in the end it got too much for me. I'd been working in America but when I got the chance to go home to Liverpool I did. When I found out how unhappy Jack was, and how badly he was being treated by my sister and her husband, it broke my heart. I felt so guilty. I thought I'd given Jack the best chance of a future I could give him but instead . . . I'll never forgive myself for what happened to him.'

The major took the photograph from her and stood it gently on her 'dressing table', before placing his free hand comfortingly on her shoulder.

'I feel the much the same about my wife.'

It was her turn to hold the bridge for him now, her gaze every bit as steady for him as his had been for her.

'She'd wanted to leave London, but she was so

close to her time I was worried about her travelling. I begged her to wait until after the baby. They were both killed three days later when a bomb made a direct hit on the friend's house where she was staying.'

Francine could hear the rawness in his voice and her heart ached for him.

'Do you think it ever ends – the pain and the guilt, I mean?' she asked him.

The major shook his head. 'Perhaps if you want it to, but something tells me that you don't.'

'Do you?' Fran challenged him.

This time he didn't answer her.

THIRTEEN

Katie had been so worried about going dancing with Luke that it had pushed all her earlier concern about the letter right out of her thoughts.

For a start there was the problem of what she was going to wear, but Jean had obviously remembered what had happened before Christmas because she had announced at Saturday dinnertime, before Katie had had time to say anything, that she had been through her sister's things and had put a dress on Katie's bed that she had thought she might want to borrow for the dance.

The minute Katie had seen it she had fallen in love with it. Yellow silk and full-skirted, with a neat waist, the dress also had a matching shawl to cover the shoulders.

However, as soon as Katie had seen that the label inside the frock said Molyneux, she had guessed that the dress had come from the famous London designer of the same name and she had known that she could not possibly wear it.

'Why on earth not?' Jean had demanded. 'That yellow will suit you perfectly.'

'Your sister has some lovely clothes, but they are far too expensive for me,' Katie had said honestly but Jean would have none of it.

'Well, Fran left them here and said that we were to use them, and I reckon it would be a sin not to do so,' she said firmly.

Of course, in the end Katie had given in, which was how she came to be standing beside Luke, who looked so smart and handsome in his uniform, feeling very self-conscious indeed now that she had handed her coat over to the cloakroom assistant.

'Katie looks ever so nice, doesn't she, Luke?' Grace demanded.

'Very,' Luke agreed warmly.

'Well, the dress really belongs to your aunt, the one that left her clothes behind when she joined ENSA. Your mother said it would be all right for me to borrow it since I haven't got any dance frocks of my own.'

They were walking towards one of the tables now, and Luke and Katie had fallen behind Grace and Seb in the crush of people, so only Katie saw the surprised look Luke gave her in response to her comment.

'I should have thought you would have a wardrobe full of dance dresses, with your dad being a band leader, and you working with him, as the twins told me that you did,' Luke explained.

'Well, yes, I did, but not front of house, as they say. Goodness, the Grafton is busy tonight, isn't it?'

'A bit different from the last time we were here,' Luke agreed. 'The Grafton holds close on a thousand couples,' he told her, 'and Saturday night is always popular, especially when they've got a good band on, like tonight. You'll know of them, I expect.'

One of the country's most popular bands, the Joe Dempsey Swing Band, was playing.

'Yes,' Katie agreed, 'and they are very good. They've played at the Savoy and the Ritz.'

There was no sign now of the damage that had been caused in the bomb blast. The roof had naturally been repaired to protect the building, but the ceiling and the floor had both also been restored to their original state, and with the lights on and the ballroom filling up it was hard to equate it with the candlelit, bomb-damaged, almost empty room in which they had all danced so determinedly at Christmas, refusing to let Hitler's bombers destroy their evening.

'Come on, you two.' Grace turned round to beckon them over to the table she and Seb had secured.

'That colour really does suit you,' Grace complimented Katie a few minutes later when the two men had gone to the bar.

'Your dress is lovely,' Katie returned the compliment generously.

Grace was wearing a beautifully elegant gown in green silk.

'There's a real story attached to this dress,' Grace told her. 'One day I'll tell you all about it.'

'Oh, please, tell me now,' Katie begged her.

Grace looked self-conscious and shook her head, and then said, 'Oh, go on then. Mum will have told you that I used to work at Lewis's, in the Gown Salon, I expect.'

'Yes,' Katie confirmed.

'Well I'd been invited to a Tennis Club dance, by my cousin Bella, who's a bit of a snob.' Grace gave a sigh. 'Anyway, this girl who I worked with sneaked this frock out of the salon, and persuaded me to borrow it for the dance. I knew it was wrong, but I did.

'Seb was to be my escort for the evening. We hadn't met until then. He was sort of related to Bella's late husband.

'There was a bit of an accident when Bella stood on my dress, and it got badly torn. I was so upset that I let on to Seb what had happened and how the dress wasn't really mine. Then, of course, when I got home I had to own up to Mum as well. That was the worst bit. I'd just been offered the chance to train as a nurse, you see, and she'd been so proud of me, and now here I was as good as admitting to have pinched a frock from work. I thought I'd have to stay on at Lewis's to pay for it, and it would have served me right if I had, but Seb only went and bought the dress to save me.' Grace's whole face lit up with love and pride. 'Wasn't that a wonderful thing to do?'

'Yes, it was,' Katie agreed fervently.

'Anyway, that's enough about me,' Grace told her with a smile. 'How are you enjoying working at the censorship place?'

'I like working with the other girls, and the work is important, of course, but sometimes it makes you feel uncomfortable reading other people's private letters, you know. Some of them have such sad things in them, like when a girl's

259

writing to say that she's found someone else. When I'm reading that kind I always wish that I didn't have to send them on.'

'What are you two looking so glum about?' Seb asked as the men came back with the drinks – beer for themselves and shandy for the girls – and sat down.

'Katie was just saying that it upsets her when she reads Dear John letters,' Grace explained to her fiancé.

'The worst are when it's a letter telling someone that there's been a death at home – you know, from the bombs.'

'You haven't found any in secret spy code then yet?' Luke teased Katie.

She had hesitated just that bit too long, Katie recognised, as she saw the way that they were all looking at her.

'No,' she answered. 'Nothing like that.'

She was feeling a bit uncomfortable when Seb gave a brisk approving nod of his head as though in response to her lack of response, followed by a small smile.

Had he guessed from the way she'd hesitated what had happened? Katie worried guiltily.

'It's much the same for us in the "Y" Section,' Seb was saying, as though he wanted to reassure her. 'We have to listen in to things we'd rather not, at times, but it is for the good of the country, and ultimately it can save lives.'

Grace was smiling at her and so too was Luke, Katie realised, suddenly feeling her heart lift and a rush of happiness spread through her. It felt as though she had suddenly been accepted into some special and very private club.

After that the evening went from good to even better, and just when Katie thought that it could not possibly be improved on, at the end of a particularly energetic swing dance number – during which she and Luke had ended up with the floor to themselves and being applauded by the other dancers – as Luke guided her back to their table, his hand still holding hers, he told her with a grin, 'Mum was right: you are a terrific dancer.'

'You're good too,' Katie returned the compliment.

'The twins taught me and Grace.'

'My mother taught me.'

'I dare say you must find my parents a bit dull after your own.'

They had almost reached the table. Katie stopped and turned to him, saying quietly and truthfully, 'I love living with your parents and the twins. It's what I've always longed for, to be part of a proper family. My parents' lives may seem glamorous but they aren't. My father works most evenings and practises during the day. My mother is proud of his success, of course, but at the same time she misses the stage herself and wishes she was still there. I love my parents very much, but so often when I was growing up I longed for them to be like other people's mothers and fathers. I know that must sound awful. It doesn't mean that I don't love them, because I do, but I still can't help envying people like you and Grace.'

'It doesn't sound awful at all. It sounds honest.'

Katie discovered that she was looking at the

neat fastening of Luke's tie against the khaki of his shirt, unable to lift her gaze to his face because she knew his compliment had made her blush.

'Friends?' Luke asked her softly.

Now Katie did look at him and what she saw in his eyes made her own sting slightly with tears. Unable to speak, she merely nodded.

Luke squeezed her hand gently.

'Come on, you two.' Grace's demand broke into the silence between them, causing them to hurry back to the table.

Nothing particular had been said but things had definitely changed between her and Luke, Katie knew. Now when he looked at her, he smiled, and his smile was slow and warm and very special, as though it was for her alone and as though they shared a secret that belonged to them alone.

They danced some numbers that were so fast that they were left breathless and laughing, but the slow numbers they sat out, leaving them to couples like Grace and Seb, who took advantage of the dimmed lights and slow beat to snuggle up close to one another.

That was, until the last dance of the evening. Then, as the lights dimmed and couples took to the floor, Luke stood up and held his hand out to her, and somehow Katie discovered that she was on her feet, and then they were on the dance floor and Luke was holding her close. So close that it seemed the most natural thing in the world for her head to rest on his shoulder when the music slowed even more, and his arms closed round her. The dance floor was packed with only enough room for couples to sway together, but no one was complaining; certainly not Katie.

'I just hope there isn't an air raid tonight,' Katie murmured, thinking of the number of people packed into the ballroom.

'Me too,' Luke agreed. 'At least not before I get to do this,' he added huskily, and then before Katie could say or do anything he was brushing her lips very, very gently with his own.

A quiver of sweet delight ran through her. She had never expected when they had come out tonight that she would end the evening being held tight in Luke's arms, never mind being kissed by him. But deep down inside herself and in secret, she *had* thought about Luke holding her and kissing her, hadn't she, Katie made herself admit.

The last dance and the evening were over. Silent, her eyes brilliant with emotion, Katie queued for her coat wrapped in a cocoon of happiness.

It was only when they were all leaving the dance hall that Seb made another reference to Katie's work, catching up with her on the stairs whilst Luke and Grace stopped to speak to someone they knew.

Putting his hand under her arm, Seb drew her to one side, saying approvingly, 'You handled things very well earlier.'

Katie blushed. 'Oh, thank you. I mean, I know that Luke was only teasing me.'

'It's only human nature to want to reply honestly and openly when someone close asks questions. Not that Luke is the sort that would ever want you to do the wrong thing, mind, but it's easy to let something slip without meaning to, and you never know just who might be listening. It isn't easy doing our sort of job – that's why I feel I'm so lucky with Grace. She understands that sometimes things are going on at work that I can't discuss with her. It's all about trust in the end, you see, Katie: the Government's trust in us and our trust in those we love and theirs in us. People in our line of business know how important that trust is.

'If you have any problems at work then the proper person to discuss them with is your superior, of course, but if ever anyone outside your work starts to make you feel uncomfortable or ask you questions and you want to talk about that to someone, then I'm always here.'

'You're very kind,' Katie thanked him shyly.

Luke had no idea how things had moved so far so fast. One minute, or so it seemed now, he had been thinking how wrong he had been about Katie, and then the next she had felt so sweet and soft in his arms that he had just not been able to resist kissing her. But then he had been thinking about what it would be like to kiss Katie for what felt like a very long time, hadn't he? Right from the first time he had seen her, in fact.

They were in the middle of a war, Luke reminded himself, and he was in uniform. Falling head over heels in love with a girl and hoping that she would fall head over heels back just wasn't a responsible thing to do.

The chivalrous instincts Luke had inherited from his father were a very strong part of his personality. They warned him now that Katie was a sweet girl, a girl whom he needed to protect from the heartache that came with falling in love and then being separated in wartime – or worse. She had been so darling and sweetly responsive when he had kissed her. So much so that he desperately wanted to do so again.

Just before they left the Grafton, Grace tapped Luke on the shoulder, saying quietly to him, 'I take it that you're over Lillian then, now?'

'Lillian?' Luke pretended to look blank. 'Who's she?'

Grace was delighted that her brother was finally over the heartbreak caused by Lillian Green, the nurse who had started her training with Grace, and who had made it clear that she was only interested in finding herself a rich husband – but only after she had stolen Luke's heart. But even so . . .

'Katie isn't like Lillian, Luke,' she warned her brother. 'I don't think she's so much as been out with a boy, never mind been—'

'Katie's safe with me, Grace, so you don't need to go giving me any warnings,' Luke stopped his sister firmly. 'I'll be looking out for her just as much as I'd be looking out for one of my own sisters.'

'You weren't looking very brotherly towards her when I saw you smooching her during the last dance,' Grace felt bound to point out.

'That's mine and Katie's business; just as you

265

and Seb smooching is yours,' Luke informed his sister.

Grace was tempted to point out that she and Seb were engaged, but remembering what her mother had said to her about her hopes with regard to Katie and Luke, Grace recognised that it would probably be better to say nothing.

Luke could be stubborn and he had his pride – he was a man after all – and he wouldn't want to think that his mother and his sister were standing on the sidelines and keeping their fingers crossed that he and Katie recognised just how perfect they were for one another.

FOURTEEN

'Bettina and her mother are lovely, aren't they? And so very brave. It must be terrible to have to leave your home and your country behind and go and live somewhere else, not knowing where you might end up.'

Bella and Laura had just left the church and were heading back to Bella's house along Lancaster Road.

'Obviously the Polanskis were fortunate because they were billeted with you, but anyone can see that they must have been very comfortably circumstanced in their own country, and it must be dreadfully hard to bear if one ends up billeted somewhere grim,' Laura gushed, patently unable to stop talking about Jan and his family.

Torn between irritation over Laura's praise for the Polanskis, and pride that Laura had recognised the superiority of her own home, Bella was forced to produce a lukewarm smile instead of giving vent to her real feelings about her billetees.

'And wasn't it lucky that Jan was home on leave and kind enough to go down to the school with us and help us sort out that delivery we got yesterday?' Laura continued happily.

Now Bella could feel her irritation growing. It hadn't pleased her one little bit to see the new friend she had been so proud of so plainly impressed by a Polish fighter pilot yesterday when the Polanskis had arrived back at Bella's house whilst she was entertaining Laura. In fact, she had felt obliged to point out several times during the evening that Jan was a refugee and that it was only thanks to the British Government that he was safe and able to fly anything.

Laura had ignored her, though, to say enthusiastically to Jan, 'I've got a cousin in the RAF and he was full of praise for the Polish pilots for their bravery during the Battle of Britain.'

Long before the evening had ended, Bella had been regretting inviting Laura to have supper with her and then stay for the weekend. When she had given that invitation Bella had envisaged an evening discussing Bella's own plans for building up her role as Laura's assistant to the point where it carried a proper title that Bella could use to let her parents know how important her war work was compared with Daphne's. However, when all three of the Polanskis had come in unexpectedly, Bettina and her mother having apparently met Jan from the station, and Laura had immediately somehow or other taken it for granted that the billetees were welcome to sit down and have dinner with them, Bella had had no option but to grit her teeth and let herself be swept along by Laura's enthusiasm.

Before too long Laura and Jan had been laughing together as Jan claimed to be an expert chef, his self-confidence greeted by adoring smiles from his mother and amused ones from his sister, whilst Bella had found herself without any role to play and virtually relegated to the role of ignored onlooker of the fun that everyone else, but especially Laura and Jan, seemed to be having.

Of course, the fact that Jan was visiting – something she had not been consulted about or had her permission requested for – had meant that there was no proper spare bedroom for Laura, and even now Bella didn't know just why she had felt that savage stab of anger when Jan had grinned and said that Laura was welcome to share his bed.

Of course, Laura had done no such thing. Naturally she had slept with Bella in Bella's room. That had meant that Bella had hardly had any sleep at all, her rest disturbed because she just wasn't used to sharing a room with anyone. Nothing to do with the fact that she had been listening to make sure that Laura didn't take advantage of the sleeping household to take Jan up on his offer.

'You must let me know the next time Jan's home on leave,' Laura told Bella enthusiastically, now.

Bella had originally planned to make sure that Laura sang her own praises in front of her mother after church, but she had been so irritated by Laura's constant references to Jan and his family that she hadn't bothered. And now Laura was still going on about him.

'I bet he's a good dancer, Bella. Have you ever danced with him?'

'No,' Bella answered her shortly.

'Maybe we could get up a party for one of the Tennis Club dances? Oh, I wonder what's going on over there.'

Relieved to have a change of subject, Bella looked across the road to where a work party of three men were working frantically and at much greater speed than was usual, to remove some of the rubble of a collapsed building.

Laura crossed the road, leaving Bella no option but to follow her.

'What's happening?' Laura asked the closest of the men.

'We think there's a kiddie still alive under this lot. We heard it crying a while back. Thought it were a cat at first, we did, and then Harry there said, no, he thought it were a kiddie. Then someone came along and said how there'd bin a new baby born to the family wot lived here.'

A baby buried under all those tons of rubble and still alive. How could that be possible? Babies were so fragile and vulnerable. Bella placed her hand against her own body, filled with a mixture of anger and pain.

The man who had been speaking to them broke off his conversation to take a pack of Gold Flake cigarettes from the boy on the bicycle who had just cycled up to him saying, 'Here you are, Uncle Billy. Our nan says that's nine pence you owe her.'

'Come on, Billy,' the other two men working on the rubble with their picks called.

'These houses were bombed four nights ago,' Bella pointed out. 'It's impossible for anyone still to be alive under the rubble, never mind a small baby.'

The nearest of the men replied, without stopping working, 'Aye, we thought that an' all, until we heard it crying.'

'Do you think Jan will still be at your house? I know Maria said that she'd have a Sunday lunch waiting for us when we got back, but she didn't say anything about Jan being there, and I'd like to thank him for all the help he gave us.'

Bella looked at Laura impatiently, on the point of reminding her that she had already done that, and more than once, when one of the men gave a shout and delved into the rubble, pushing it aside with his bare hands.

Within seconds the other two men had joined him and nothing could have wrenched Bella away from the spot where she stood, the whole of her attention focused on what was happening in front of her, totally oblivious to everything else.

Other people had come to see what was going on, but it was Bella who was the closest and she was the first to see when one of them lifted the child – a few months old, no more, Bella guessed – from the rubble.

She – it was a girl from her clothes – was filthy and covered in dust, her mouth and nose rimed with soot and soil.

A first-aider had stepped forward to take the baby and was deftly removing the dirt from her mouth, allowing her to cry lustily.

'Can someone hold her for a moment?' the first-aider asked, and without thinking Bella stepped forward to take her.

She was filthy, her face and clothes covered in dust and earth, but Bella still held her close.

'Yours, is she, love?' an elderly woman, who had stopped to see what was going on, asked Bella sympathetically.

Bella shook her head. The baby was nuzzling her, and grizzling. A sharp pang of pain gripped Bella inside as though her womb had tightened, her breasts suddenly aching.

'Thanks ever so. I'll take her now.' The first-aider was reaching out to take the baby.

Bella frowned, holding the baby tighter as she stepped back until she realised what she was doing. Angrily she thrust the baby into the first-aider's arms and then turned on her heel, hurrying to rejoin Laura, who was standing several yards away and looking impatient. Several yards away – and yet Bella had no memory of having moved closer to the rubble or of having left Laura, and yet she realised she must have done. Why? Just because of the baby? No, of course not. What did she care about babies? Nothing! It was girls like her cousin Grace who went all soft and misty-eyed over babies, not her.

'Goodness, I'm ever so hungry now. Poor Maria will wonder where on earth we are. Oh dear, you've got dirt all down the front of your lovely coat,' Laura told Bella. 'What a shame. We must get overalls for the nursemaids to wear at the crèche. Will you make a note of that for me, please, Bella?'

*　　*　　*

'And like I said before, we wouldn't have been late back for our lunch if Bella hadn't gone and got involved by holding the baby.'

They were all in the morning room-cum-dining room at the back of the house next to the kitchen, and Bella's dining table had been extended to accommodate the five of them.

Bella had been very proud of her reproduction mahogany dining-room furniture when she had first seen it in Gillow's Furniture Emporium, the exclusive furniture shop just off Bold Street in Liverpool. The square table, which extended into a rectangle, could, when both its leaves were in place, seat eight. In addition to the six matching chairs, with their claret and cream Regency-stripe damask seats, there were two 'carver' chairs, and an elegant Georgian-style sideboard.

Even her own mother had been envious of the stylish elegance of her choice, Bella remembered. She had planned to hold dinner parties and show off her furniture and her Royal Doulton dinner service, but that that never happened. Bella looked down at her plate on which most of her lunch still remained. Not because there was anything wrong with her food – grudgingly Bella had to admit that Maria was a wonderful cook – but somehow the delicious smell of roasting lamb that had met them in the hall on their return had filled Bella with nausea instead of tempting her appetite.

Laura had insisted on telling the Polanski family all about the baby that had been rescued from the rubble, the minute they had all sat down for their lunch, and Bella had flinched angrily from the pity she had seen in Jan's gaze as he looked at her whilst Laura was relating the story.

He would remember, of course, what had happened to her own baby and to her; they all would. Well, Bella didn't want his pity. She did not want anyone's pity.

'What a shame to waste such lovely food. You aren't dieting, are you, Bella?' Laura asked. 'Only I know that some girls have said that they're worried about putting weight on with this war diet. I'm lucky, I never put on so much as an ounce.'

Normally Bella would have been so astounded at the suggestion that she, with her twenty-two-inch waist, might need to diet that she would have made a very sharp retort, but today her struggle not to think about the rescued baby and how holding it had made her feel was taking precedence over putting Laura in her place. That and the angry churning in her stomach at the thought of anyone, but most of all Jan Polanski, pitying her.

Bettina and Maria were getting up and removing the plates, swiftly helped by Laura, who went immediately to take Jan's plate, Bella noticed cynically.

There was rhubarb crumble and custard for pudding, but Bella shook her head and refused a helping.

'Bella and I were just saying whilst we were out, Jan,' Laura began eagerly, 'that if you've got leave over Easter it would be lovely if we could make up a party to go to the Tennis Club dance. I'm sure that Bettina would like to go, wouldn't you, Bettina?'

'There aren't any tickets left,' Bella interrupted her curtly. 'My mother asked me to get a pair for my brother and his fiancée-to-be and I couldn't.'

'Oh, I'm sure the committee will be able to find tickets for a party that includes a Battle of Britain hero,' Laura insisted warmly.

'Charlie is a Dunkirk hero,' Bella told her angrily. 'He saved Daphne's brother's life,' she pointed out, ignoring the fact that it was less than a week since she had been telling her mother that she was sick of hearing about her brother's heroism.

'But that was just one heroic act, Bella, and after all, everyone knows that the Polish Air Force accounted for over 600 enemy combat kills during the Battle of Britain. There was a huge amount in the papers about it, and everyone was saying how marvellous they were. Any tennis club would be proud to have a Polish Air Force pilot attending their dance, and any girl would be very proud to be his partner.' Laura's voice had softened as she had added these last few words.

Bella frowned. Laura making such a fuss of Jan, and going on about him being such a hero, made Bella feel as though she was out of step over something important that she ought to have known about. She didn't like being made to feel as though she had missed out on something – or indeed someone – that other girls had taken up, and which had made it – or him – and themselves extremely popular.

Bella had been so caught up in her own resentment about the Polanskis being billeted on her that she hadn't been aware that Jan being in the Polish Air Force made him the social asset that Laura was now implying. All this time, when Jan had been coming to visit his family and she had been shunning him, *she* could have been the one fussing round him and basking in what Bella was now beginning to suspect would be the reflected glory of partnering a Polish Air Force hero, she acknowledged crossly.

'I suppose I *could* get some tickets,' she told them, quickly changing tack. 'After all, me and Alan were the most popular couple at the Tennis Club. I'll have a word with the Treasurer.'

She certainly didn't want the Polanskis thinking that it was because of Jan that tickets were forthcoming. No, she intended to make it clear that they had only been granted as a favour to her. That was the way to keep a man on his toes.

Laura might think that she could attract Jan by flattering him and making a fuss of him but she, Bella, the most beautiful girl in Wallasey, if not in Liverpool, knew that the best way to get a man interested was to pretend that you weren't interested in him. That always brought them running.

'But I thought you just said that you couldn't get any for your brother?' Laura pointed out.

'Well, I couldn't, not officially, but of course I have got them a pair.' That at least was true since her mother had insisted that Bella ought to hand over her own to Charlie and Daphne. No way was she going to do that now. If there were only two tickets going, then they were for her and her partner of choice – Jan – but she needn't say anything about that now.

She'd have to have a new dress, of course. The one she had worn last year wouldn't do at all. She had been a girl then, now she was a woman – married and widowed, and thus entitled to wear something rather more ravishing and seductive than a mere girl might be allowed do wear. She would need to book a hairdresser's appointment as well; perhaps have her hair styled like Vivien Leigh. And she'd need a new lipstick, something a bit darker than her usual pink. Maybe she should have lilac satin for her dress. Lilac was, after all, a sort of mourning colour, wasn't it, and so perfect for someone with her colouring. She would look stunningly pale and fragile, Jan's protective arm around her as they made their entrance; the handsome Polish Air Force hero and the tragic but oh so very loyal and brave widow, whom everyone wanted to see rewarded for the unhappiness she had endured so courageously and silently in her marriage.

Bella could see it all now. It would be wonderful. *She* would be wonderful.

She came out of her daydream just in time to hear Jan saying that he must leave soon otherwise he would miss his train back to his base.

'I expect Laura and Bella will want to do the washing-up for you, Mama, by way of a thank you for cooking lunch. That will mean that you and Bettina can come and see me off.'

Bella looked at him, about to announce that there was no way she intended to do any washing-up, but Laura was already agreeing and simpering stupidly at him, leaving Bella with no option but to agree.

* * *

'Well, that was a turn-up for the book, you and Andy's corporal being at the Grafton on Saturday night. You could have knocked me down with a feather when we saw you,' Carole announced on Monday morning when the two girls met up in the cloakroom at work. 'You and him together put on a really good show on Saturday night. Everyone was saying so. Fair gave me a surprise, you did; after all, you never said a word to me about the two of you.'

'That's because I didn't know I'd be going to the Grafton with Luke and his sister and her fiancé until Friday teatime, when they asked me,' Katie told her truthfully.

'Andy says that the corporal is ever such a good sort; all his men think well of him. Looks like you thought so too from the way you was cosying up to him during the last dance.'

Katie blushed furiously.

'Oh ho, like that, is it?' Carole teased her knowingly.

'Katie, Anne's just been asking if anyone's seen you,' one of the other girls interrupted them. 'When I told her you were in the cloakroom with Carole she said to tell you to hurry and that it's important.'

The enjoyment that had coloured her weekend and lifted Katie's spirits every time she thought about the dance at the Grafton, and more importantly about Luke himself, was swiftly banished by Rachel's words. Katie's anxiety grew stronger when she reached their table to find a grave-faced Anne waiting for her with the news that she was to present herself immediately to their supervisor.

'What's going on?' Carole demanded curiously, then nodding understandingly when Katie shook her head, indicating that she couldn't say.

She was bound to have been wrong about the letter and now she would no doubt be in all sorts of trouble for wasting other people's valuable time. Katie was feeling so apprehensive that by the time Anne had guided her to where a supervisor was waiting for her, her knees were knocking and she had convinced herself that she was about to be dismissed in disgrace.

The supervisor, though, was not 'Frosty', who was on leave, but a tall thin middle-aged woman who introduced herself as Linda Philpott. She greeted Katie with an unexpected and disconcertingly warm smile, thanked Anne, and then took Katie into a cold windowless room off a long corridor, illuminated only with one bare light bulb, which revealed the wooden panelling on the walls and an oil painting hanging over the fireplace.

Instead of seating herself behind the imposing wooden desk, the supervisor sat down instead on an upright chair on one side of the fireplace, indicating that Katie was to take the other chair.

'This room was originally the office of one of the directors of Littlewoods Pools,' she explained conversationally to Katie. 'I dare say it must have looked very imposing in its day but sadly now the war has stripped it of its glory. War has a habit of doing that. It strips the life of those of us who must bear it right back to the bare essentials. In wartime, Katie, those essentials include loyalty, courage, the ability to put others before ourselves, the ability to put our country before ourselves. We see those virtues displayed every hour of every day in our country's brave fighting men, and we see it too in those who have volunteered to do their bit for the war effort here at home.'

The supervisor was obviously leading up to something, Katie realised, but what?

'Sometimes when we think that we are already doing our bit, things happen that require us to do even more, and even to put ourselves at risk.'

Katie's stomach, which earlier had been churning with the apprehension that she might be dismissed, only to quieten when she had recognised the warmth with which she was being received, had now begun to churn again but with a different fear this time.

'You have already shown commendable devotion to your work, Katie. Thanks to your quick-wittedness in spotting that error in the letter you referred to the head of your table, another department within this organisation has been able to break the code being used between the letter writer and its recipient. The sender has already been traced and is now under arrest. It is now, Katie, that I must stress to you how important it is that you understand that what we are discussing here must not go beyond this room; it is no exaggeration to say that the lives of many brave men and women may depend on you adhering to that.'

'No, of course, I shan't say a word,' Katie told her quickly. She was beginning to feel rather sick and desperately anxious to escape from the slightly sinister room and the supervisor's talk of secret codes and people's lives being at risk.

'No, of course you won't. It is obvious to me that you are the kind of young woman who places her loyalty and her duty to her country right at the top of her list of things that are most important to her.'

Was the lecture nearly at an end? Katie hoped so.

'As I have already said, the person who sent the letter has been apprehended. However, it has been decided that the recipient of the letter – and no doubt others – will now be used as a means of conveying false information to the other side via letters that we shall construct here using the code we have now broken. We shall pass on false information in response to the questions that the letter asks. To that end it has been decided that you will become part of the team that will construct these letters.'

'Me? But—'

'Obviously, Katie, I can only give information to you on a need-to-know basis, and that means that whilst I can tell you that it is now clear that a knowledge of popular music and those involved in it plays a vital role in the code within the letters exchanged, I cannot tell you any more than that.

'Your role within this team will be to write a letter incorporating certain pieces of information that will be given to you by using a code, which will also be given to you. You will write this letter very much in the style of the letter you read, that is to say, in the style of a young woman replying to a letter from a young man in a mildly flirtatious manner that refers back to dances the two of you have attended and music you have enjoyed.'

'But my handwriting will be different,' Katie protested, 'and—'

'As I have just said, Katie, I can only give you information on a need-to-know basis. Your task is simply to write a letter using the information you will be given. The fact that your handwriting is your own handwriting is not something that needs to concern you.'

The supervisor's voice was very firm now and Katie could only assume that she meant that someone else, possibly a forger, would copy what Katie had written in handwriting that mimicked that of 'the person who had been apprehended'.

Another girl might have found the whole thing exciting but Katie found it daunting.

As though she could tell what Katie was thinking Linda Philpott reminded her calmly, 'It is for your country that you do this, Katie, and for the lives of all those you will help to save.'

She paused for a few seconds and then said briskly, 'Now, I want you to return to your desk and get on with your work. Not a word about any of this to anyone, mind – not that you will be asked. We all know why we are working here, after all. Your instructions will be passed to you later on today. Just to be on the safe side it has been decided that you should write your letter in your billet. I dare say it will take you several attempts, given the complexity of the code and the nature of the information to be relayed to the recipient of the letter. However, time as always in these matters, is of the essence.'

The supervisor was standing up so Katie did the same.

Having escorted her to the door and opened it so that Katie could step out into the corridor, she shook Katie's hand and said firmly, 'Good show.'

As she made her way back to her desk Katie felt almost light-headed with a mixture of disbelief and shock – a feeling that was strengthened when instead of asking her what had happened Carole behaved as though she hadn't moved from her desk, and instead of questioning her started chatting about the dance at the Grafton, in between complaining about the food they were served in the canteen.

'Andy's asked me to go to the pictures with him on Wednesday. What about you? Has the corporal made a date with you?'

'What? Oh, no. Well, not exactly.'

'Not exactly? What does that mean when it's at home?' Carole teased her.

'Well, Luke did say that he'd enjoyed dancing with me,' Katie told her, deliberately withholding the fact that Luke had also said sort of casually, in a way that made it clear that he wasn't being casual at all really, that he'd got a bit of leave coming up and that, since Katie was new to the area, he'd be happy to show her around if she'd like that.

Katie had been equally studiedly casual in her response when she'd replied that her parents had asked her if she'd seen much of the countryside around Liverpool and that she'd like to tell them that she had.

The result had been that Luke had said that

283

he'd let her know when he could get his leave so that they could sort something out.

It was a prosaic enough arrangement but there had been nothing whatsoever prosaic about the kiss they'd exchanged when Luke had hung back to let Grace and Seb get ahead of them on the walk home, or the other kiss they'd shared when Luke had left his scarf on the table and Katie had seen it and run down the back garden in the dark to give it to him. That kiss had been the sweetest and the most headily intimate of all because when she had shivered in the March air, Luke had opened his greatcoat and drawn her inside its warmth so that they had been standing body to body, her heart hammering and racing at speed against the heavy fierce thud of his.

She'd never French kissed before, nor ever thought she might want to, but somehow it had just seemed so natural and so – so very exciting and wonderful with Luke. She had been trembling when they had finally stopped, and so had Luke. Something special was happening between them, so very special that Katie wanted to hug it to herself for now and only share it with Luke in the way that they had done when they had exchanged special looks and a final brief kiss before they had finally parted on Saturday night.

Fran leaned out as far as she could from the side of the boat taking them along the Nile, through the Valley of the Kings. It had been Marcus who had suggested the three-day trip, and Fran had accepted with a delight that wasn't entirely due to her desire to see the archaeological artefacts left behind by the Ancient Egyptians.

'Oh, I can't think of anything I've ever seen to match this, can you?' she asked Marcus excitedly.

As he moved closer to her, slipping his arm round her waist, his affirmative and softly emphatic 'Never' had her turning her head, laughter in her eyes at odds with the mock disapproving look she gave him as she shook her head and told him, 'I meant this,' and waved her hand in the direction of the shore.

'It is magnificent,' he agreed, 'but I would rather look at you.'

'Be careful,' Fran warned him softly, her own focus on the shore fading as she looked into his eyes. 'If you keep on saying such delicious things to me I could start to take you seriously.'

'I want you to take me seriously, Fran, because I am serious about the way I feel about you.'

He had moved closer to her now, fitting her body alongside his own, his action and its intimacy reminding her of how well they had fitted together last night in her bed.

Even now Fran couldn't quite believe how quickly and easily she had broken all the promises to herself she had vowed to keep, promises like never ever falling in love again, like never ever again risking the betrayal and then the disgrace she had suffered as a young girl.

But this was wartime and she was living in a different world from the one she had grown up in. Everyone said so, all those men and pretty girls who flocked to Shepheard's Hotel each night to

285

escape from the tensions of war and the fear of death. She was a woman now, not a girl, and this time with Marcus there would be no risk of the conception of an unwanted child; both of them were determined to make sure of that.

It had felt so strange at first, discussing the raw brutal facts of sexual intimacy before they had so much as touched one another, but Fran had known from the moment Marcus had suggested this trip and spoken of the elegance of the river cruiser's staterooms that he wasn't planning on them sleeping in separate rooms and separate beds, and by that time she had been as fiercely hungry for him as he had been for her.

Both of them had admitted that the intensity of their mutual desire had caught them off guard. It had whirled up out of nowhere like a desert storm, obliterating everything that stood in its path. In fact it had been as though fate had decreed that they should have this time together since it had been a real live desert storm that had put on hold the troupe's planned trip out to one of the most outlying desert camps, thus giving them an unexpected gift of over a week together. A week in which they had socialised separately and discreetly, but always acutely aware of one another, always managing somehow to be together for a few short precious minutes. And now they had this: three days away from the rest of the troupe.

Last night their 'boy' had served them dinner in their stateroom, and Marcus had fed her soft balls of spiced rice and lamb with his fingers, and they had drunk the worst champagne in the world whilst bubbles of giddy delight had fizzed through Fran's body.

They had made love not once but several times, and Marcus's skill and tenderness had opened Fran's eyes to the reality of what true sexual desire and intimacy could be. She had never been happier, and at the same time never more sharply aware of how rare and fragile true happiness actually was.

Con looked up apprehensively as the door to his 'office' banged open, only relaxing enough to say grimly, 'Shut that ruddy door, will you?' when he saw that his visitor was only his nephew, Kieran.

'Strewth, finding you is like getting hold of the invisible man,' Kieran complained as he dropped down into a chair, putting his feet on Con's desk and reaching into his pockets for his cigarettes. 'What's going on?'

'I'll tell you what's going on,' Con answered dramatically. 'What's going is that I've had the ruddy heavies from the debt collector round, that's what.'

'Well, pay him off then. Your old woman's swimming in money – everyone knows that.'

Con glowered at his nephew. Kieran was wearing what looked like a new suit, grey with a white stripe – not exactly a spiv's suit, but pretty close to it, like the black trilby that he had perched on the back on his head instead of having removed it respectfully.

Getting a sight too big for his boots, his nephew was, Con decided, acting as though he was cock of the walk all of a sudden. Con had seen the girls eyeing up Kieran and that hadn't pleased him one little bit.

It was all right for Kieran. He hadn't got all the worries hanging round his neck that Con had – nor the debts.

'Aye, well, everyone might know it but what I know at the moment is that she's being as tight as the proverbial duck's arse with it,' Con told Kieran angrily. 'It's ever since she took in that stupid kid. Treats him like a little prince, she does, wi' nothing too good for him, whilst me, her husband, she treats like muck on her shoe.'

Kieran grinned and shook his head. 'I allus thought that you'd got her under your thumb?'

'So I had until this so-and-so kid came along. Wimmin. If you'll take my advice you'll do yourself a favour and keep well away from them. They're nothing but trouble.'

'Aye, well, you'd certainly know about trouble and wimmin,' Kieran agreed. 'It's bin all over the theatre about you and that nifty little high-kicker that's just given you the heave-ho.'

Con glowered at his nephew. He had enough to worry about without being reminded of the additional blow to his ego caused by the fact that his latest girl had gone and found herself someone else.

'Never mind about that. I've managed to get the old man to call off his heavies by promising that we'll cut him in to this dance contest thing, so instead of wasting your time hanging around here I want you out and about using them good looks of yours to get the right kind of girls clamouring to enter the competition. We've got them twins lined up, of course. They've bin round here a few times doing that dance of theirs. It's good too – not that I'm telling them that – and I reckon what's more that it would be a good thing if they was to win.'

'They won't like it in Blackpool if you go ahead with a competition. Like I told you, they gave me a right old mouthful and as good as said that there'd be trouble if we tried butting into their market. Seemingly they don't bother charging any dancers to enter; they just use the competitions to get them into the dance halls.'

'Well, in that case they haven't got a leg to stand on, have they, and the pitch is all ours. Hey, get that?' Con joked, his good humour returning. 'Haven't got a leg to stand on and we're talking about dancing? Proper lame duck partners they'd have been.' He laughed even more heartily.

'Get yourself over to Lewis's, Kieran, and get sweet-talking them girls. Tell 'em that we'll be running the first heats the first Saturday in May – no point in doing it over Easter since we'll be busy here then. We won't hold them here neither. We'll ask around and find a bit of an empty warehouse we can borrow for next to nowt, we'll charge them two and sixpence on the door to get in, and another bob to dance. Anyone wot brings in a party of ten or more gets themselves in free. We'll use a gramophone, not a band – cheaper. I'll sort out getting some bills done; you can get your kid to take them round all the schools. We'll make them look glamorous; put a photograph of that Vivien Leigh or someone on it. I reckon we can easily count on having two thousand there.'

'Two thousand?' Kieran queried.

'Why not? The Grafton holds that many. It's full every night and they don't offer any prizes. Oh, and pass the word to as many of your mates as you like that there's going to be any number of girls there and that they can come and watch them for two and sixpence – tell 'em that they'll have to bring their own drink, mind. Here, give us a fag, will you, Kieran?'

Once his nephew had obliged Con slumped down into his own chair and reached for a grubby bit of paper and the stub of a pencil, laboriously working out the profit he could expect to make if he filled an empty warehouse with two thousand eager dance competitors, and a couple of thousand young men, just as eager to watch them.

The figures spoke for themselves.

'Get yourself off to Lewis's, and remember, Kieran, they'll be a big attraction, them being spitting images of one another. The more the pair of them fall out over which of them is going to win, the more folk we're going to get coming to watch them.'

'That's all very well but what if they don't make it through the first heat?'

'I thought you reckoned to be a bit of a knowing 'un?' Con stopped his nephew scornfully. 'Of course they'll ruddy well make it through the first heat, and every ruddy heat after that an' all, until they get to the last one. I'll see to that. What you've got to see to is that by the time the pair of them get there they're ready to scratch one another's eyes out.'

Sasha saw Kieran first, her whole face lighting up with excitement and delight. From the moment they had first seen him the twins had talked together about him, giggling self-consciously as they took an increasing interest in the kissing scenes on screen at the cinema, egging one another on as they whispered about what it would have been like if Kieran had been playing the leading male role. What was not said was that both of them were imagining themselves in the leading lady's role and thus in Kieran's arms.

Add to the mix of emerging sexual awareness the excitement and allure of the promised dance contest and the chance to appear on stage in a real production, and it was no wonder that for the twins Kieran and the dance contest had become the perfect antidote for the boredom they were beginning to feel both with the war and the restrictions it placed on them.

At fifteen they might be legally old enough to have left school and gone out to work, but in the eyes of their protective parents they were still too young to indulge in such grown-up pastimes as going out to public dances and socialising with young men.

In vain they both protested that girls they had been at school with were now going out to dances and wearing lipstick and court shoes whilst the twins were only allowed to do boring childish things and then only in a gang, and when their parents knew exactly where they were and who they were with. Jean, normally soft-hearted with her children, was if anything even firmer than Sam when it came to reminding the twins that they were only fifteen.

When Grace had tried to plead the twins' case, suggesting that perhaps they could be allowed the odd grown-up dance, chaperoned by herself or their brother, Jean had sighed and shaken her head, pointing out to her eldest daughter that the twins attracted trouble like jam attracted wasps and that as yet they had not learned the wisdom of trying not to attract it.

Kieran was not his uncle's nephew for nothing, and within minutes of his arrival the twins were ignoring the department manager's grimly warning looks to bask in his attention, their giggles accompanied by delighted squirms of pleasure as he complimented them and promised them that he would soon have some good news for them with regard to the dancing competition.

'When's it going to be?' Lou asked him, mindful of the necessity of making sure that they could compete without arousing any suspicion at home. After much discussion on the subject she and Sasha had reluctantly agreed that there was too much risk of being refused attached to asking permission, and that therefore they would have to keep their intentions a secret.

'First Saturday in May,' Kieran answered her promptly. 'And I've got a bit of a job for you as well. My uncle wants posters putting up to make sure that we get plenty of folk going in for it.'

Kieran looked over his shoulder. Normally it would have been beneath his nearly eighteen-year-old dignity to be seen hanging about with what in effect was a pair of schoolgirls, but in this instance he had no option if he didn't want to get himself in his uncle's bad books.

'I'd better scarper,' he told the twins, 'otherwise I'll be getting the pair of you into trouble and we don't want that, do we?' He gave them a wink and a look that made them burst out into fresh giggles. Everyone knew that it was very saucy for a boy to talk to a girl about getting her into trouble.

'And mind you wear something stylish for the competition,' he told them. 'Something that shows off them pins a bit. I'll help you choose your outfits, if you like.'

Another wink and he was gone, leaving the twins to look at one another and then down at their long slim legs.

FIFTEEN

Easter Saturday, April 1941

'I don't know how we're supposed to put a decent meal on the table, what with meat rationing and everything, I really don't.'

Jean shook her head sympathetically as she listened to the complaints of the woman in front of her in the queue at the butcher's where Jean was registered for her own family's rations.

'Of course, it's all right if you can afford to buy stuff on the black market,' the other woman continued.

'My husband doesn't approve of buying black market,' Jean told her firmly. 'He says there'd be more to go round for all of us if there wasn't one.'

The weather had started to warm up and, like everyone else, Jean had exchanged her heavy winter coat and her jumpers and woollen skirts for something a bit lighter. She looked down at her own button-through red dress with its white spots, with a small smile. It was one of Sam's favourites, even though it was all of five years old. She was lucky,

Jean admitted, in that she had kept her figure. She might not need a jacket today, but Jean was still properly dressed with a smart little red hat and white gloves. Just because there was a war on and rationing, that was no excuse for the women of the country to let their standards slip, was the message that the Government were giving.

And they had a point, Jean admitted, even if she had had to spend an hour last night darning the thumbs of the twins' second-best going-to-church white gloves. It fair lifted the spirits to see people dressed in bright summery clothes again.

'Well, I dare say he's right, but that won't stop some folk – them wot's got the money and wot don't care about the rest of us.'

Jean would much rather have had someone cheerful to chat with whilst they waited in the long queue, but then, she acknowledged fair-mindedly, she herself was luckier than some. Sam worked hard on his allotment to provide them with salad stuff, veggies and fruit, then there were the hens the allotment holders had clubbed together to buy, and the occasional rabbit that appeared now and again, no questions asked. They'd been lucky where they were, with only a few bombs falling, and none in their street, or on their allotment.

There was nothing like a good roast on a Sunday, though, to get the week off to a sound start, and the meat they were getting now was nothing whatsoever like a good roast.

Normally they'd have been having a nice chicken tomorrow, seeing as it was Easter Sunday, but with both Luke and Grace now living away from home, and neither they nor Katie going to be eating their dinner at home tomorrow, Jean had decided that she wasn't going to waste a chicken just on herself and Sam and the twins.

Thinking about Katie and Luke being together and starting courting made Jean feel especially happy, and not just because it proved that her son was finally over the heartache he had suffered with Lillian.

Grace might tease her about having a soft spot for Katie, and Sam might caution her against matchmaking, but that didn't stop Jean getting a real warm glow inside at the thought that Katie could become her daughter-in-law. Jean couldn't think of a girl she'd be happier to see her Luke married to. But she was also ready to admit that when a man married it was his own happiness he should put first, not that of his mother. Not that it did any harm when a family liked the new person that was joining it. Jean could still remember how much her own mother had liked Sam. Vi, of course, always liked to say that their mother had been as proud as punch when Vi had announced that she was marrying Edwin and thus marrying 'up', but Jean knew that their mother had never really taken to Vi's husband. Not that she would ever say so to her twin, although there had been times when she had been tempted, when Vi had been getting uppity. It was hard now to remember sometimes that they were actually twins, especially when Jean looked at her own pair and saw how close Lou and Sasha were.

They'd been a bit quieter than usual just lately.

Jean hoped that it was a sign that they were finally beginning to grow up and get a bit of sense. She and Sam had certainly made it plain enough to them that they wouldn't entertain any daft ideas about them going on the stage. Dancing at home for their own entertainment was one thing; doing it on some stage was another. Jean didn't have to remind herself of what had happened to her younger sister to recognise the dangers that lay in wait for naïve young girls with dreams of fame in their hearts.

Not that the twins could ever be described as 'dreamers'. No, they were far too active and noisy for that. The lads who married that pair were going to have to have the patience of saints and not mind their closeness either. Children; you didn't realise until they came along how much they would turn your life upside down and how powerful their tug on your heart would be. There still wasn't a day went by when she didn't think of that little lost lad of hers and Sam's, nor little Jack either, even though he hadn't been her own.

That had been a terrible thing to happen: for him to have been evacuated against Fran's wishes by their Vi, and then to have been killed. No wonder Fran had turned her back on her home.

'Oh, Luke, it's so pretty.'

There in front of them was the lake in the pretty Cheshire village of Ellesmere that Luke had told her about, and on the grass in front of it couples and families were already enjoying the Easter holiday.

'Mere means a bit of a lake, like, you see,' Luke explained earnestly. 'That's what they call them in Cheshire.'

Katie had been upset and disappointed at first when her father had told her not to even think of travelling back to London whilst there was still so much danger of it being bombed, even though she knew that her parents wanted to protect her, but then Luke had suggested that since he had leave, they should spend the weekend together, and he had managed to borrow from somewhere a pair of bicycles for them and book them rooms – one each – at a couple of pubs that had been recommended to him so that they could have a 'bit of a cycling holiday', as he had put it, and he could show her something of Cheshire.

Although she hadn't known Luke long, Katie knew that she could trust him. As the eldest son of the family he took his responsibilities to his siblings very seriously, and he would look after her and protect her just as determinedly as he did them, Katie knew – including if necessary protecting her from his own male desires.

Almost comically it had been Jean and not her own parents who had raised an objection to them sleeping under the same roof unchaperoned by a watchful parental eye, and she had made it plain that her concern was for Katie's reputation, not her own son's.

Whilst Luke had looked embarrassed, Katie had told Jean gently but firmly, 'I know that I can trust Luke to be a gentleman, and I do trust him.'

'When we used to come here as kids we'd come

on the train and the first thing we'd do when we got off was ask for an ice cream,' Luke was saying now.

'Mm, don't torment me,' Katie laughed. The war meant that there was no ice cream today, but there were blue skies and sunshine, and the grass was warm beneath their backs as they lay down, wrapped in the old-as-time special privacy that all lovers feel, sharing that silent communication that needs no words and speaks heart to heart. The whole of the grassy bank that led down to the water might be busy with other people, the spring afternoon filled with the sound of other voices, but they were oblivious to them.

Luke reached for Katie's hand, winding his fingers through hers.

'I was a fool for getting it all wrong about you when I first saw you,' he told her.

'Well, you did hear me saying that I wasn't interested in men in uniform,' Katie reassured him. 'You weren't to know that I was just saying it because I didn't want Carole egging me on to flirt, and then getting annoyed with me when I wouldn't.'

'You were in the right of it, really. It's plain daft for a girl to go falling in love with a chap who's in uniform when there's a war on.'

Fear clutched at Katie's heart.

'I reckon that sooner or later our lot will be seeing some action.'

'But you are seeing action. You're on home duties, and look at all the bombs we've had,' Katie protested.

Her fingers had tightened on Luke's now, and he returned the pressure, trying to soothe her.

'Defending the country isn't like going into action. Stands to reason that them that are fighting will have to be stood down and brought home at some point, and that we'll be sent out in their place.'

Katie sat up and looked down at him anxiously. Had he already heard something but wasn't allowed to tell her? War brought so many secrets that had to be kept, as she knew all too well. Her own role in fighting the enemy was causing her plenty of sleepless nights. Following her first letter, a response had been received, and now she had been asked to write back to that. She knew that what she was doing was for the benefit of the country but somehow it didn't feel right, keeping the fact that she was writing to another man – for they knew now that it was a man – from Luke, even though there was a good reason for what she was doing. The whole business of having to fit the messages she was being given into the code that had been broken, and then turn them into letters that read as though they were from a woman engaged in the beginning of a love affair, made Katie feel very uncomfortable, and would have done even without Luke in her life, she suspected. There was no one, though, with whom she could discuss her feelings – not Luke, as she was forbidden to talk about the letters to anyone not directly involved, and not her supervisor either, at least not without seeming unpatriotic.

Only the previous week Grace had commented

on the secret nature of Seb's work, saying that she knew it was difficult for him not being able to talk to her about what he was doing.

'He feels guilty about it, I know, but like I've said to him, it's his duty and he's saving people's lives with what he's doing just as much as we are at the hospital with what we are doing.'

Seb, though, was intercepting messages, not writing letters to another girl. Or maybe it was just that it was easier for a woman to accept a man's duty to his country than it was for a man to accept a woman's, Katie reflected, because something told her that Luke would not be as understanding. He had already shown signs of jealousy, and didn't like it at all when they were at the Grafton and another chap looked at her or, even worse, asked her to dance, not realising that she was with someone. Of course, it was flattering that he cared enough to feel possessive about her, but Katie had grown up aware of the damage her parents' jealousy of one another, and the quarrels and discord that had led to, had done to their marriage, and she didn't want that in her own marriage.

Marriage. Who had said anything about that? Certainly not Luke.

Katie pulled up a blade of grass and leaned over, tickling Luke's face with it until he reached for her, pulling her down towards him.

Katie's laughter died as she looked into his eyes and saw the passion there. Her heart began an unsteady excited flutter of small thuds. This was the time when she should pull away and suggest that they get back on their bikes. If she stayed here now then she would be inviting all those things, and all that temptation that Jean had been so anxious for them to avoid.

So why, instead of pulling back, was she leaning closer until her curls brushed Luke's cheek and his hand reached up to hold the nape of her neck so that he could bring her down within reach of his kiss?

It was the sensation of a child's ball bumping against her legs that brought Katie back to reality. The big grin the child's parents – only a young couple themselves – gave them both as the father retrieved the ball made Katie blush and Luke look very male and protective.

'Come on,' Luke told her. 'Let's walk for a while.'

The village was very pretty in that traditional English way that catches at the heart, with narrow streets filled with a jumble of Georgian, Queen Anne and Tudor buildings in soft red brick. There was even some bunting up across the street for an annual rowing regatta, for all the world as though there was no war at all, and indeed, here today it was almost possible to imagine that there wasn't, Katie conceded as she and Luke walked hand in hand.

'Do you still love her, Luke, the girl who was so mean to you?'

Katie's face burned a fiery red. She had no idea where the words had come from because she had certainly not intended to spoil the day by asking them, even though they had been niggling at her heart for quite some time now.

For a minute Katie thought that Luke was angry with her, and so she said contritely, 'I'm sorry, I had no right to ask you that. It's none of my business.'

Immediately Luke squeezed her hand and told her firmly, 'Well, I should hope that it is, seeing as I happen to think that any lad you might have had a soft spot for before you met me is very much my business.'

'But I haven't been out with any other boys.'

'But was there any you wanted to go out with, a special one perhaps?'

Again Katie could hear that sharp note of jealousy in his voice. It was easy to reassure him, though, by telling him that she hadn't, since it was the truth.

'Well, I'm glad about that because, you see, Katie, feeling the way I do about you I don't want to think that you've got a soft spot for anyone else. And as for Lillian, I did fancy myself in love with her, it's true, but I reckon I was more in love with the idea of being in love than with Lillian herself. Once I found out what she was really like I was glad she'd got herself someone else. I was just a boy then; I'm a man now, and it's as a man that I'm telling you that I reckon I've fallen in love with you, Katie.'

Katie's chin tilted. 'Well, if you only reckon . . .' she told him pertly.

'All right then, I know,' Luke corrected himself softly, making the words a deliberate challenge that Katie herself had to meet.

'I – I feel the same way about you,' she admitted,

objecting breathlessly when Luke seized her in his arms, 'Luke, you can't kiss me here . . .'

But it was too late because that was exactly what he was doing.

Charlie was well pleased with himself. His parents were certainly well pleased with him, even if his sister, Bella, hadn't stopped pulling a sour face from the moment he and Daphne had arrived on Good Friday to spend Easter with Charlie's parents.

Everyone knew that it wasn't just because it was Easter that he and Daphne were here. The ring he'd borrowed the money off his father to buy, a single diamond – a single very expensive diamond, in fact – was now shining brightly on Daphne's finger. He and Daphne had chosen it together, or rather Daphne had chosen it and he'd whistled silently under his breath and hoped that his father was feeling generous. He certainly ought to be, with a hero for a son and a double-barrelled with a father a 'name' at Lloyd's as his daughter-in-law-to-be.

Lord, but it had made Charlie grin to himself to see Bella's expression when she had realised that he was now the perfect son and she was the one who got the parental frowns. After all, he'd had enough years of it being the other way round. Poor old Bella, she wasn't even going to get a look in at the wedding either. Daphne had as good as said that she wasn't going to ask Bella to be one of her attendants.

'It doesn't seem right somehow, with her being widowed, and as Mummy has already said, with me having two cousins of my own and there being a war on . . . Oh, Charles, I'm so happy,' Daphne had told him. 'And so are Mummy and Daddy. Knowing how close you were to dearest Eustace makes you and me so very special.'

Charlie had agreed, of course he had, but in reality he was getting a bit fed up of the constant references to Eustace, and Daphne's eyes filling with tears every time she mentioned him, which seemed to be hundreds of times a day. Eustace was dead now, after all. Charlie had tried jollying Daphne along, and hinting to her that he preferred girls who were fun, although of course he hadn't told her that he preferred them so much that he'd already been tempted by one very jolly girl indeed who lived in the village close to the base. Luckily she was married, so no danger there of any problems, should Charlie find himself in the kind of situation a chap would be a fool to deny himself.

For now, though, he was on his best behaviour, the perfect newly engaged young man, a hero, whose father-in-law-to-be had shaken his hand with tears in his eyes when he had given him permission to propose to his daughter.

'Bella's been able to get tickets for you and Daphne for the Tennis Club dance, Charles, haven't you, Bella?'

Bella gave her brother a thin smile. 'Yes.'

Just as Laura had predicted, the committee had been almost ready to fall over themselves to provide tickets for a hero of the Battle of Britain – a full table of six of them. Bella had spent a lot of time thinking about Jan since Laura had commented on how good-looking he was. She was looking forward to showing up at the Tennis Club dance on the arm of a Battle of Britain hero, all the more so because she knew how much Laura wanted him to partner her.

Not that Bella had any personal interest in Jan. How could she have? He was, after all, a refugee with no country and no money. It was unfortunate that Laura had included Bettina in her invitation to Jan to go with them to the dance. Bella was well aware that Jan's sister despised her. Well, Bella didn't care.

She didn't care much either for the manner in which Laura had now taken to ordering her about, like she had done earlier this week when the crèche had been officially opened, but Bella had been forced to remain in the background whilst Laura greeted the dignitaries and smiled for the local press photographer.

They had now been inundated with enquiries about places at the crèche, and it had been Bella who had had the dull and time-consuming job of taking all the names and addresses of the mothers applying on behalf of their infants and then preparing a typed list in alphabetical order to include the names and dates of birth of all the children.

Bella had been seething when Laura had complained that Bella hadn't put the children, when there was more than one to a family, in date-of-birth order.

'You never said that you wanted me to do that,' she had defended herself.

Laura had simply said firmly, 'I thought you

would have known to do it without me having to say, Bella. You are my assistant, after all, and it is what I would have done.'

As Bella was quickly discovering, there were two sides to Laura.

There was the Laura who treated Bella as an equal and who linked her arm with Bella's and wanted to be her friend, especially when it came to talking about Jan, and then there was the Laura who was very quick to let not just Bella herself, but also the world at large, know that she was the one in authority and Bella the one who had to obey that authority.

Well, tonight Laura was going to learn that when it came to attracting men it wasn't having the most authority that counted, but having the prettiest face. And she, Bella thought smugly, was beyond any doubt the prettier of the two of them.

Bella was jerked out of this pleasant mental confirmation of her own unassailable status by her mother, who was still going on about June being the perfect month for a wedding, and the importance of not wasting any time in getting things organised.

'You'll want to get married in your own parish church, of course,' Vi smiled, her mind busy with plans. In one sense it was a pity that Daphne's home was so far away because that meant that Vi herself could not be as involved in the wedding preparations as she would have liked. After all, she already had the experience of having organised Bella's wedding, which everyone had said had been the wedding of its year, and Bella quite definitely

307

Wallasey's bride of the year. Daphne was a lovely girl and sweetly pretty, but her looks in no way rivalled Bella's, and with the war on it would be next to impossible for her to find a wedding gown that could rival Bella's.

'It's such a shame that you are so much taller than Bella,' Vi gushed, 'otherwise you could have worn her wedding dress.'

'Oh, that's very kind of you but I think that Mummy is planning to have her own gown altered for me. Mummy's going to ask her cousin if we can borrow Great-grandmother's lace veil and tiara.'

Any sense of dissatisfaction Vi might have felt at not being able to have a say in Daphne's wedding dress was swiftly forgotten when Daphne uttered the word 'tiara'. Vi felt positively light-headed with the joy and pride that filled her. Just wait until she told her WVS group that her son's bride would be wearing the 'family' tiara. She would only mention it casually, of course, just dropping the information in so as not to sound boastful or awaken any resentment.

'Well, of course, naturally your mother will want you to wear it,' she managed to agree.

It was just as well really that the South of England was too far away for her twin sister, Jean, and her family to be able to travel to the wedding, Vi decided. Such refinements as a double-barrelled surname, Lloyd's and a tiara would all be wasted on Jean and her down-to-earth husband, Sam. Sometimes Vi actually felt that Sam, instead of being in awe of her Edwin, was actually slightly contemptuous of him, but that, of course, was impossible.

'I must write to your mother, Daphne, and offer my help. After all, I have organised a wedding myself and I may be able to give her some little tips, and June isn't that far away.'

'Mummy and Daddy think that we should wait for a while,' Daphne told Vi. 'They were engaged for a year before they got married and, as Daddy says, with Charles feeling so strongly that he wants to continue in uniform even though he's been told that medically he's not really fit enough to do so, we should perhaps wait.'

Vi looked at Edwin, who immediately looked grimly and meaningfully at Charlie. It had cost Edwin an arm and a leg to find a doctor who was prepared to state that Charlie's 'bad back' meant that he should be dismissed from the army on the grounds that he was medically unfit, and now here was ruddy Charlie over-egging the bread as usual, by the sound of it, and damn-near getting himself stuck in uniform.

'Well, of course, I hate the thought of not staying in uniform,' Charlie informed them all, correctly interpreting his father's grim look, 'especially when I'd been looking forward to fighting for Eustace as well as for myself.'

Bella rolled her eyes when she saw the way in which Charlie's claim had Daphne reaching for his hand, a look of blind adoration in her eyes. Daphne really must be stupid to be taken in so easily by Charlie, Bella thought unkindly.

'But since the doc has as good as told me that

my back could give out altogether if I'm not careful, I don't think I've got any choice but to accept that from now on my contribution to the war effort will have to be whatever I can do whilst working for you, Dad.'

'Well said, son,' Edwin approved over-heartily.

'Daddy's worried about us being able to find somewhere to live,' Daphne continued, still clinging on to Charlie's hand.

'Well, that's no problem,' said Vi immediately. 'Bella has that lovely house right here in Wallasey that her father bought when she got married. It's far too big for her now, and to be honest I've been thinking for a while that it would make much more sense for Bella to come back home. If you and Daphne were to move into it, Charles, we'd probably even be able to get rid of those wretched refugees. After all, Daphne's parents are bound to want to come up and visit her.'

Outraged, Bella protested, 'But that's my house!'

'No, it isn't, dear,' Vi pointed out in a far more steely tone of voice than she normally adopted with her daughter. 'It was Daddy who bought it, remember?'

'But—'

'To be honest, Bella, Daddy and I have both been concerned about you living on your own, now that you're widowed. You've still got your lovely bedroom here at home, after all.'

'You mean the one that Daphne's sleeping in?' Bella pointed out sourly.

Vi tittered. 'Well, of course she's sleeping in it for now, darling, but once she and Charles are married she won't be, will she? No, Daphne dear, you can assure your parents that they needn't worry about you and Charles not having a house. Mr Firth and I were saying only the other night how perfectly things are working out.'

Her mother might consider that things were working out perfectly but she certainly didn't, Bella fumed, as she made her way home from her parents'. And as for her giving up her lovely house to Charlie and Daphne – well, her parents could think again if they thought she was going to do that!

Laura had been hinting for several days that she wasn't keen on her billet and saying how much nicer Bella's house was. She had even been buttering up Bettina and her mother, asking them to show her some Polish recipes, and making comments about how much easier it was to make decent meals when there was an extra ration book to add to the rations. Not that Bella was taken in for one minute by her behaviour. The only reason Laura was making such a fuss of Bettina and her mother was because she thought it would make her more appealing to Jan.

'They are ever such a close family, aren't they?' she had commented to Bella after she had first met them. 'I reckon that Jan would do anything to make his mother happy.'

Her own mother might think they could get rid of the refugees, but it would be a different matter trying to get rid of the supervisor of the local crèche, Bella decided grimly, and since she certainly wasn't prepared to give up her home and her independence to return to live with her parents, she would just have to bite on the bullet and invite Laura to move in with her. But there was one thing that Bella did intend to make clear, and that was that when they were at home it was what she said that went, since it was her house.

When she passed the site where the baby girl had been found alive in the rubble of her bombed home, Bella slowed down slightly. There'd been a big mass burial of some of those who had been killed in the March bombings. Bella had attended the service with her mother, and she had also – very reluctantly – done a stint down at the community kitchen on St Paul's Road, where those who had been blitzed out could go and get a hot meal.

Right now, though, she had far more important things on her mind than her grievances against her parents. The dance tonight would be her big opportunity to dazzle Jan and ensure that he was totally smitten with her and no one else. Bella had everything planned, right down to the new red nail polish with which she intended to paint her finger- and toenails. And since her mother had not been able to persuade her father to increase her allowance, Bella had not been able to buy herself a new dress, which was why she had been obliged to do something she had never imagined she would ever lower herself to do, and that was to buy a second-hand dress.

A smirk of female triumph curved Bella's mouth. She had come across the dress by accident when she had been given the job of sorting through boxes of clothes donated to the WVS for the homeless. Full-skirted, with a strapless fitted bodice, it was made of an iridescent silk that looked black but that shone peacock blue and dark green when the light was on it. There was a matching bolero jacket and a crumpled pink rose attached to the waist.

Bella had recognised what treasure-trove it was the instant she had seen it, quickly bundling it up and wrapping it inside her own coat before anyone else could spot it. There was no reason why she shouldn't have it – it wasn't suitable for someone who was homeless, after all – and she *had* put two shillings into the WVS charity box for it.

Later on in the week, when she had heard about the poor little dressmaker who had come to the hall in tears to ask if anyone had seen the couture silk gown that had been brought to her to alter, Bella said nothing. It was just a black dress, that was all. It fitted her perfectly too.

Laura had been going on all week about the yellow and white piqué cotton frock trimmed with white and yellow rickrack braid that she was planning to wear, as though it was something really special. Well, not when she put on her black silk, it wouldn't be, Bella thought happily.

The house was empty when Bella got back. There was a note in the kitchen from Bettina explaining that Jan had arrived with a male friend, and that the four of them had gone out to visit some other friends who were billeted locally.

The sight of two RAF kitbags leaning against the wall in her spare bedroom had Bella's heart doing an unexpected back flip of excitement. Two

313

kitbags, that meant that Jan could partner her, and his friend could partner either Bettina or Laura; Bella didn't care which of them bagged him, just so long as she had Jan.

The Polanskis and Jan's friend arrived whilst Bella was still upstairs in her bedroom getting ready.

Normally Bella would have hogged the bathroom and run off all the hot water, getting ready for the dance, but grudgingly on this occasion she decided that she perhaps ought to be generous, given the fact that Laura was fussing all over Bettina and her mother, so she had left a note on the kitchen table saying that she had left them plenty of hot water, and that since there would be a buffet at the Tennis Club she knew they wouldn't be expecting any tea.

Bella timed her entrance perfectly. Having waited to make sure that Laura had arrived, she checked that she herself did indeed look as wonderful as she had thought the last time she had inspected her appearance in her bedroom mirror, all of two minutes earlier, her lips a perfect soft red with just a hint of gleam, thanks to an expert dab of Vaseline on top of her lipstick, her eyelashes long and dark, her hair falling elegantly to her shoulders in waves worthy of any film star, and of course her dress. She must wear black more often, Bella had decided as soon as she had recognised how glamorously the fabric contrasted with the pale pearly sheen of her skin.

Carrying her evening bag and her bolero she headed for the stairs, deliberately dropping her bag just before she reached the last stair, exclaiming loudly as she did so.

Naturally Jan, ever the gentleman, came out of the sitting room to see what was happening, the others crowding in the doorway behind him.

'Silly me, I dropped my evening bag,' Bella pouted, 'and I daren't bend down to pick it up because I can't fasten the hook and eye at the top of my zip. Would you be a darling and fasten it for me, please, Jan?'

Bella couldn't quite analyse the look in Jan's eyes as he came towards her. It could just be awed appreciation, of course. How could it be anything else? And how clever of her too to have positioned herself on exactly the right stair for his gaze to be on a level with the creamy exposure of the soft flesh that swelled discreetly before disappearing beneath the bodice of her dress.

Jan's brief, 'You'll have to turn round,' had Bella batting her eyelashes and giving a small practised giggle before she started to turn, just catching as she did so the movement of yellow and white floral cotton as Laura appeared in the doorway.

'Is everything all right?' Laura's question was followed by a cool and very disconcerted, 'Oh', as somehow Bella lost her balance and had to cling to Jan's shoulders for support, her soft breathy, 'Oh, goodness, I am being silly tonight,' answered by Jan's calm, 'Not at all,' as he waited for her to regain her balance and then turn round so that he could fasten the hook and eye for her.

'You should have called me up to do that for you,' Laura told Bella in a voice that Bella was delighted to recognise was decidedly hostile.

315

'I was so busy worrying about Charlie's fiancée enjoying the evening and not feeling left out that I never gave it a thought until I was on my way downstairs,' Bella lied happily, tucking her arm through Jan's as she reached the bottom of the stairs, and telling him, 'I think I'd better hang on to you until we get to the Tennis Club, Jan. These silly heels are a bit higher than I'm used to.'

'Then perhaps you should change them,' Laura suggested tartly.

'I can't. They're my only pair of black dancing shoes.' Bella's response was sweet and triumphant.

Bettina and Maria had come out of the sitting room now, accompanied by a tall, thin, dark-haired man of a similar age to Jan, but nowhere near as good-looking.

'Bella, please allow me to introduce Jonas to you.' To Bella's irritation Jan had to disengage himself from her hold to introduce his friend, who promptly shook her hand.

'I hope you enjoyed your visit to your friends this afternoon.' Bella's smile swept Jan's family and his friend. 'You'll be meeting my brother later at the Tennis Club and I must tell you that he and his girlfriend are newly engaged so tonight will be a very special evening for them.'

Somehow or other, whilst Bella had been talking, Jan had offered his arm to his mother, and Jonas had offered his to Bettina, leaving Bella and Laura to walk together as they left the house and made their way to the Tennis Club.

'I am praying that we don't have an air raid tonight,' Bella announced.

'Well, you'd certainly have trouble running for the shelter in those shoes,' Laura remarked unkindly.

'Jan would help me, wouldn't you, Jan?' Bella cooed. 'It's so thrilling to be going to the dance with two heroes of the Battle of Britain. I shall feel quite jealous if you dance with anyone else, Jan.'

There! That should make her own claim more than clear to Laura, Bella decided as she tucked her hand through the other girl's arm with false friendliness.

'Steady, Bella. That's your fourth tonight. I didn't even know you drank gin,' Charlie complained to his sister, as she emptied her glass.

'That's because I don't,' Bella told him truculently. It was the truth, after all. She didn't drink – normally. But tonight things had gone so horribly wrong that having another drink seemed like a good idea.

It had all started just after they had arrived and she had discovered that the committee had decided to put Jan and Jonas, along with Bettina and Maria, on the top table, which had meant that she and Laura, along with Charlie and Daphne, had been relegated to a horrid little table that barely accommodated four in a dark corner where no one could see them.

Someone had seen her, though – one of Alan's mother's cronies, who had taken one look at her and then made a comment about shameless young women who flaunted themselves in a very vulgar way, which not just Bella herself, but everyone who was within hearing range knew had been directed at Bella.

Matters hadn't been helped when Laura had said disapprovingly, 'Well, I must say that I did think myself that your dress is a bit much, Bella, especially given our position and the crèche and everything.' Laura had then promptly taken herself off to the top table where she had somehow or other managed to get a seat, which had left Bella on her own with the newly engaged couple.

'You can't possibly really be in love with her, Charlie,' Bella had challenged her brother when Daphne had excused herself to visit the cloakroom. 'She's so dull.'

'Of course I'm in love with her,' Charlie had grinned, adding mockingly, 'How could I not be? You've seen the way the fact that I'm marrying her has got Dad opening his wallet, haven't you?'

When Daphne returned to their table Bella gave the ring on her future sister-in-law's left hand an extremely sour look. It was twice the size of all three of the stones in her own engagement ring put together.

Bella had to wait until suppertime to push her way to Jan's side and remind him in a little girl voice that he hadn't danced with her yet.

'You haven't looked as though you've been lacking dance partners,' he pointed out.

Bella pouted. 'Oh, well, they're just ordinary boys, not like you, Jan. You're a hero, and very special.'

Bella had always known how to flirt but she hadn't until now recognised just how dangerously close to the edge she could take that flirting now that she had a wedding ring on her finger.

One of her partners had already called her a dashing widow, so why shouldn't she be exactly that? Fired up by four gins and her determination to best Laura, Bella was enjoying the heady elixir of power that came from knowing that she no longer had to obey the 'rules' that came with being an unmarried girl.

'Mm, I'd love another gin,' she told him.

'I think you ought to eat something first,' Jan told her firmly.

'If you want me to eat, then you'll have to be very nice to me.'

As she leaned closer to him, Bella swayed and almost lost her balance – and not deliberately this time – causing Jan to frown as he caught the scented sweetness of her breath and wondered just how much she had had to drink. He put down the plate he had been holding and took hold of Bella's arm.

'Come on,' he told her. 'I think you need some fresh air.'

'No, what I need is you,' Bella told him giddily as he guided her across the floor and then outside.

No light shone from the windows of the Tennis Club, thanks to the blackout, but there were stars in the sky and enough light from the moon for Jan to glance up and say grimly, 'Looks like it's a bomber's moon tonight. Let's hope the Luftwaffe don't take advantage of it.'

'The war! Is that all everyone can talk about?' Bella complained.

'It is pretty much to the forefront of most people's minds, Bella,' Jan pointed out drily.

'Well, it isn't to the forefront of mine, and it shouldn't get to the forefront of yours when you're here in the moonlight with me,' Bella rebuked him softly.

Jan had gone very still but Bella hadn't noticed. This was it, her moment, her chance to ensure that when they went back inside Laura knew that Jan was Bella's. She moved closer to him, putting her head on his shoulder and her hand on his arm.

'It's all right to kiss me, Jan,' she whispered. 'I know you want to, you know.'

'Bella . . .'

'And I want you to as well.' Bella was astonished. Where on earth had those words come from? Certainly not from her scheming brain. It would never ever have allowed her to say anything so betraying. So where, then? Bella's thoughts had become very cloudy and confused, but not so much that she didn't know what she wanted.

'Jan,' she whispered, and now there was a pleading softness in her voice as well as an invitation.

Jan didn't move.

Bella's gin-soaked senses were oblivious to the message contained in Jan's still silence. Instead they were urging her to do what she wanted to do. Bella raised herself up on her tiptoes and placed her lips on Jan's, kissing him softly and then with increasing passion.

His arms lifted, his mouth moving against her own . . .

'No!'

Bella blinked drunkenly in disbelief. Jan had

just rejected her and pushed her away. But that wasn't possible.

'I'm sorry. This is all my fault. I should have said something earlier.' His voice was clipped and angry. 'I'm engaged to be married.'

'You can't be.'

Ignoring her denial Jan continued quietly, 'Anna is the daughter of some old friends of my parents. We knew one another as children. We didn't know until just before Christmas that they'd managed to escape as well. We're getting married next month. My mother is delighted. It's something she'd hoped for before – before the war.'

Bella had gone from being drunk to being stone-cold sober in the space of less than five minutes. It felt like being all wrapped up in a delicious blanket and then having not just that blanket but also a layer of skin ripped off you whilst you stood in a cold so bad that it physically hurt. She had no idea where such a feeling had come from or why, she only knew that she was in pain.

She turned away from Jan into the darkness.

'Bella.'

How was it possible for the sound made by someone saying her name to cause her so much physical pain?

'We must get back; people will wonder where we are.'

How odd that she should be able to speak so normally through such pain, a bit like when someone had a limb amputated but thought it was still there because they could feel it, perhaps.

*   *   *

A few minutes later, when she stepped into the warmth and light of the Tennis Club foyer, Bella recognised that she had no recollection of having made the physical movements that had enabled her to walk back to the Club. But she must have done so, of course, since she was here.

For the rest of the evening Bella danced and laughed as though her life depended on it, but not with Jan, and nor did she have anything more to drink.

Katie and Luke's rooms at the pub where they were staying were next door to one another, and somehow, when the time came to say good night, neither of them wanted to leave the other, and besides, as Katie reassured herself, they weren't doing anything they shouldn't, at least not strictly speaking, even if what they were doing was rather a lot more than she suspected they should. She didn't feel guilty at all, though. Not lying here in Luke's arms, where she felt so safe and loved, and where for tonight at least there was no war and nothing to come between them as they touched and kissed and loved.

Heavy petting, she had heard other girls calling it, and it was certainly hard to make themselves stop when all those lovely kisses and touches were urging them on, but both of them knew that they must. There *was* a war on, after all, and neither of them was the type to feel comfortable with the idea of a rushed marriage and all the speculation that would accompany it.

'If you do get sent into action . . .' Katie whispered from the shelter of Luke's arms.

'You'll be the first to know, and I won't be going anywhere without putting my engagement ring on your finger, Katie, if you'll wear it.'

'Oh, Luke, of course I will. I'll be so proud to.'

'Nowhere near as proud as I'll be that you're my girl,' Luke responded.

SIXTEEN

Easter Sunday

'There's someone asking to see you, Charles. He says he was at Dunkirk with you. Apparently he's read about your engagement in the *Liverpool Post*, and he's here to offer his congratulations. I've put him in the front room, although I must say that I'm surprised that he's calling at lunchtime on Easter Day, when he must know that we'll soon be sitting down to our lunch,' said Vi. 'Mind you, he struck me as a bit of an odd sort altogether, and rather down at heel and shabby-looking. I wouldn't recommend that you go with Charles, Daphne dear. This fellow looks rather a rough sort. Probably one of the lesser desirable sort of enlisted men.'

The whole family, including Bella, had attended the Easter service at the parish church, and of course they had been delayed leaving, with so many people wanting to congratulate Charles and offer the young couple their good wishes. Vi was disappointed that Bella had not made more of an effort to behave in a sisterly way towards Daphne, but then Vi was forced to admit that Bella had disappointed her on several occasions recently, and it was her opinion that her daughter was not the sweet-natured girl she had been. Everyone knew that she had been widowed, but there was really no reason for her to go around being so quarrelsome and difficult. Vi was sure that Daphne's mother would expect a girl in Bella's position to put a braver face on things, especially when there was a war on and one had to do one's bit.

It was not, after all, as though Bella had any reason to behave as she was doing. Another young woman in her position would, Vi thought, have been making sure that her parents and everyone else knew just how much she owed them and how much she had to be grateful to them for.

Vi was beginning to think that Edwin was right when he said that Vi had spoiled Bella too much. Any other girl, Vi told herself, would have been only too glad to step aside to allow her brother and his wife to move into a house that they needed and she did not. Vi had been dreadfully embarrassed by the way Bella had behaved in front of Daphne. What on earth would Daphne's parents think? Vi dreaded to think what Daphne's mother might say to her bridge partner about Bella's ungracious behaviour. She really must do something about learning to play bridge herself, Vi decided. Really, she owed it to Edwin to do so, given his position.

As she went to check on the vegetables, simmering on top of the Rayburn, which, like everything else in the house, Edwin had bought her new when they had moved into the house just before the war, Vi drifted off into a pleasant daydream in which she was graciously accepting Daphne's mother's praise for her skill at the bridge table.

Charlie was quite glad of an excuse to escape from his dutiful attendance on his fiancée, and was already mentally trying out a few possible plausible reasons as to why he might need to meet up with his unexpected visitor later on in the day, and thus escape the boredom of being cooped up on his best behaviour with Daphne and his parents, as he pushed open the door to his mother's precious 'lounge' and walked in.

The man who had come to see him was sitting down in what the family knew to be the chair that Edwin had claimed as his own and on which no one else was allowed to sit. Broad-shouldered, with his thinning dark hair slicked back with so much brilliantine that it looked like patent leather, his high flat cheekbones, thick, bull-like neck and a nose that at some stage must have been broken, he had a hard-edged aggressive look that said he wasn't the kind of man to get on the wrong side of.

He was wearing a good-quality navy-blue suit and a shirt and tie, although the collar of his shirt looked too tight and was digging into his neck. He had a look about him that said he had probably hung around the city's boxing clubs as a youth. Despite the quality of the suit, his nails were ragged and dirty. He was smoking, and when he inhaled he lifted the cigarette to his lips between his thumb and his forefinger in a cupping movement, rather than between his index and fore-finger.

He was reading a copy of *Picture Post*, a maga-zine that Charlie's mother refused to have in the house, and he grinned widely at Charlie over the top of it, telling him cheerfully, 'Well, well, here he is, the big hero and newly engaged man. Congrats, mate.'

Dougie Richards! Charlie eyed him warily. They had been in the same unit, and right from the start there had been the kind of guarded hostility between them that came from recognising that they shared a similar disposition and a set of values that meant that they put themselves first and others second.

There had been no actual falling-out between them, though, just an unspoken understanding of what they were and the need not to tread on one another's toes. The very fact that Dougie was now here in his parents' front room was enough to make Charlie feel very wary indeed, but those feel-ings didn't show when he held out his hand to shake the other man's and exclaimed cheerfully, 'Dougie, it's good to see you. How have you been?'

'Not so good, Charlie. Not like you,' Dougie Richards answered, shaking Charlie's hand and then relaxing back into Edwin's chair, explaining as he did so, 'Hope you don't mind if I don't stand up, only I got me leg buggered on the way back from Dunkirk, so in reward for being damn-near killed by the Germans and then nearly having me leg cut off, the Government's gone and had me chucked me out of the army as unfit.'

'Well, never mind, I dare say they'll have given

you a bit of a pension, and then you've got those family contacts of yours down on the docks, haven't you?' Charlie pointed out unsympathetically.

Dougie had been fond of boasting to the other men about his family and the influence they had. One of his uncles was in charge of one of the dock 'pens', as the areas were called where the dockers queued to get work, and two others ran a nice little business organising supplies off the ships for the black marketeers.

'Yep, bin good to me, my family have. That's wot families are for, ain't it, Charlie? I reckon that your dad's good to you, an' all, isn't he, and doesn't mind putting his hand in his pocket to help you out? Especially now that you're marrying into money and going to have a posh wife.'

Charlie had had enough, and besides, if he didn't get rid of Dougie soon he'd probably have his mother coming in, going on about her Sunday roast. Dougie certainly wasn't someone he wanted to arrange to meet up with to talk about old times.

'Well, it's very good of you to come round to offer us your best wishes. But I expect you'll want to get on your way now, Dougie.' Charlie's voice was over-hearty as he turned towards the door.

'Give me a real surprise, it did, when I read in the *Liverpool Post* about you getting wed,' Dougie told him, ignoring Charlie's hint. 'Especially when I come to that bit about you being a hero and saving some poor bloke from drowning off Dunkirk.'

'Well, you know what newspapers are like,'

Charlie told him. He could feel the uncomfortable beginnings of alarm gripping his stomach.

'And this girl you're marrying – she's the sister of this chap you was supposed to have saved, is she?'

'Look, Dougie, we're just about to sit down for our Sunday lunch and—'

'Come off it, Charlie boy, you'd never save no one's life if you lived to be a hundred. You ain't the type. Finish 'em off by walking over them to save yourself, is more like it.' He laughed at his own joke, but then stopped laughing to tell Charlie pointedly, 'And I ain't the only one that thinks that neither.'

Charlie turned back towards his visitor, all thoughts of his lunch forgotten. His unease had now turned to a definite sense of queasy alarm.

'Now see here, Dougie. I don't know what this is all about, or what you're trying to imply,' he began to bluster.

But Dougie quickly stopped him, saying cheerfully, 'Course you do. You ain't a fool when it comes to picking up on what's what, Charlie, we both know that. Got plenty of money, has he, your fiancée's old man? Sounds like it from the *Post*. You done pretty well there, mate. And all on account of you lying about saving her brother. I was on that boat with you, don't forget.'

'You were down the other end; you couldn't possibly have seen anything.'

'You reckon? From what I've bin told, you was trying to stop him from hanging on to you in case he drowned and took you with him, rather than saving him.'

'You can't prove that,' Charlie defended himself furiously, his face burning a dark red when he saw the triumphant grin Dougie was giving him.

'Pretty nifty, him going over the side like he did, eh, Charlie? That way he couldn't say whether or not you was trying to save him or push him off of you, could he? It says in the *Post* that he went whilst you had your back to him.' Dougie shook his head. 'You see, the thing is, Charlie, you and me, well, we remember things differently, 'cos I definitely remember seeing you giving him an almighty shove. And you know what I reckon? I reckon you give him that shove because you was feared he'd spill the beans about how you'd tried to push him off you, so you thought you'd make sure that he couldn't.'

Charlie went pale. What Dougie was suggesting was a complete untruth, or at least the bit about him pushing Daphne's brother off the boat was. It wasn't his fault, after all, that Eustace had gone and banged his head on the side of the boat when Charlie had been trying to kick himself free of him. That had been a genuine accident, just like when he had gone overboard and drowned once they were on board.

'I wonder how that posh fiancée of yours and her mum and dad will feel when they know that you killed her brother? Do you reckon she'll still want to marry you then, Charlie? No one going to think you much of a hero then, are they? More like you'll be banged up inside for murder.'

330

Charlie was sweating heavily now. 'It wasn't like that.'

'Come off it, Charlie. I saw you kick him in the head meself, even if you did turn it around smartly and reckon that you was trying to save him when the two of you was pulled onto the boat.'

'I didn't kick him,' Charlie protested frantically, but Dougie wasn't listening.

Instead he shook his head admiringly and said, 'That was proper smart of you, Charlie, and quick thinking as well. I admire that in a man, Charlie, a bit of smartness. Now let's hope you'll be smart enough to know where your best interests lie, because if I was to speak up about what I saw—'

'No one will believe you; they'd want to know why you hadn't spoken up before, if you really had seen something. They'll know that you're lying.'

'Nah they won't. 'S easy to explain, innit? I had me loyalty to a mate, didn't I? And then with it being Dunkirk I couldn't bring meself to talk about it, with seeing what had happened to so many good men. It was only when I read in the papers about you passing yourself off as a hero and deceiving that poor girl that it come to me that I had to say something.'

Charlie was sweating now, an ice-cold sweat that had begun with a sensation of crawling sickness in his belly, and which was now bathing his skin in icy fear.

Folding up his magazine, Dougie put it in his inside pocket and then stood up and put his arm around

Charlie's shoulders, telling him with a smile, 'Aaw, sick as a parrot, you look, Charlie mate, and no mistake, but don't worry. You see, the thing is that mates like you and me, we want to do the right thing by one another, don't we? We aren't the sort that wants to see a mate done down when we can help them, and I reckon you and me can help one another, Charlie. It's like this, see? You want your fiancée to go on thinking that you're a hero, and I want a bit of a helping hand with a hundred nicker. Problem's easy solved, innit, Charlie? You give me a hundred quid and I forget what I seen on that boat.'

'That's blackmail,' Charlie told him, shrugging Dougie off.

'Blackmail? Nah,' Dougie laughed. 'It's what you might call a bit of an insurance policy. You ask that posh chap what's going to be your dad-in-law. I reckon he'll know all about insurance policies, him being with Lloyd's. Meet me down at the Ship's Anchor off the East Dock Road tomorrow teatime, Charlie. Just go round the back door, knock and ask for me. It's a cousin of mine runs it. It's close to the landing stage, so you'll be back on your side of the water quick as you like, before anyone knows you've gone. And think on, if you don't show up your fiancée and her dad will be getting a letter telling them what really happened at Dunkirk.'

'I didn't kill him,' Charlie began furiously, only to stop as the front-room door opened.

Charlie stiffened but it was only Bella.

'Mummy says to tell you that lunch is ready, Charlie,' Bella informed him.

'It's my fault on account of me keeping him talking about old times,' Dougie chipped in, leering at Bella, who glowered at them both and then gave Dougie a haughty look of distaste.

'I'll see you then, Charlie,' Dougie warned meaningfully, giving Bella a wink and telling her cheerfully, as he limped out, 'Pity you ain't my type, otherwise I reckon you and me could have a fair bit of fun together.'

Dougie might have gone but his going hadn't brought Charlie any relief, quite the opposite. Charlie might know that he had not killed Eustace but there was still enough truth in the rest of the story to thoroughly discredit him. He could imagine all too easily how Daphne and her family were likely to react to the discovery that, far from rescuing her precious brother, Charlie had actually tried to break free of his clinging hold in his desperation to save his own life and secure a place on the boat.

He really had no option other than to give in and pay Dougie off. But where the hell was he going to get a hundred pounds from at such short notice? Even with notice he'd have the devil's own job getting it. His father had already loaned him money to buy Daphne's engagement ring, and wasn't likely to be willing to lend him any more. Charlie enjoyed playing cards and the men he played with liked putting on good-sized side bets, illegal for serving troops, not that anyone paid any attention to that law. The fact was that Charlie lost more often than he won and was not therefore in the kind of financial position that meant that his bank manager was likely to look favourably on any request for a loan – even if he had time to make such a request.

'Charles, really, you might have asked your friend to leave a bit sooner.'

Charlie looked blankly at his mother. The over-refined voice she'd taken to using whenever Daphne was around was beginning to grate on his nerves, just like the gentle wistful droop of Daphne's mouth followed by a sad smile that meant that Daphne wanted him to know that he had hurt her feelings in some way. Charlie looked down at his dinner plate and was seized by a surge of fear-induced nausea.

'Well, I'm not having that, I'm not. He could see that you were with me but he still smiled at you as bold as brass, and as for you saying he was just being friendly . . .'

'Luke, he was.'

'Well, you would say that, wouldn't you, seeing the way he was making eyes at you.'

'I don't want to talk about it any more.' Katie's voice was quiet but tense.

How had it come to this, Katie wondered miserably, knowing that her attempts to placate Luke were only making things worse – and especially after last night, when they had been so happy and when she had felt so loved and so safe. If anyone had tried to tell her then that not much more than twelve hours later Luke would have quarrelled with her so badly and been so unreasonable that she actually wished she was not with him, Katie would have laughed at them. But like yesterday's blue skies, last night's happiness was now marred by heavy threatening clouds.

It had all started so innocently. She and Luke had had their breakfast and got on their bikes ready to head back to Liverpool. They had stopped at a pretty country pub for some dinner, then had set off again and been cycling for over an hour when they had stopped for a rest just outside a small village. Luke had just disappeared to 'obey a call of nature', having already stood guard in a very gentlemanly way so that Katie could do the same, when an RAF dispatch rider had come roaring round the corner on his motorbike, slowing down as he spotted Katie. Luke had re-emerged from the bushes well before the rider had finally stopped to ask if they needed any help.

Katie hadn't been able to believe it when instead of thanking him for his offer Luke had been curt and offhand with him, positioning himself in front of Katie and staying there until the motorcyclist had ridden off. But there had been worse to come when Luke had started to suggest that the driver had had an ulterior motive in stopping and that Katie had not been averse to his admiration.

If there was one thing that upset Katie more than anything else it was arguments. She had grown up dreading the sound of her parents' raised voices, and the nasty churning sensation she got in her tummy whenever she heard them. As a little girl she had clapped her hands over her ears to blot out the sound that upset her so much.

When she had grown older, each time her parents

rowed, hurling insults, one threatening to leave the other, Katie had been sickeningly sure that they meant it and had never been able to understand how the furious storms could magically disappear and their threats be forgotten when they lingered in her heart, shadowing it with anxiety and pain.

Katie's feelings were very strong and ran very deep; she was acutely sensitive to the moods of others and dreaded the private misery that rows always brought her. Where her parents, especially her mother, could shrug off the darkest of moods and angriest of shouting matches, it took Katie days to recover fully from the pain of witnessing her parents' fall-outs. She had grown up with the fear that one day her parents would make good their threats to one another and that one of them would walk out on the other. They always seemed to manage to pull back from the edge of the chasm that led into this darkness, but what if one day they could not? What if one day Katie herself became involved in an argument that would separate her for ever from someone she loved? Surely it was better not to argue at all?

So reasoned the young girl that Katie had been, and so too reasoned the young woman she had become. Difficult subjects were best avoided in case they led to arguments. That was what Katie felt, but she was unable to explain any of this to Luke; she barely understood the reason she felt the way she did herself.

What she did know, though, was that she hated hearing Luke raise his voice and that it made her feel afraid in the same way that she had felt afraid as a little girl. Now, just as she had done with her parents, she felt the safest thing for her to do was to pretend that it wasn't happening, and distance herself from Luke until he had calmed down and things had blown over.

Luke frowned. It had really upset him when Katie hadn't agreed with him that the dispatch rider had stopped because he had thought she was on her own. It had been so obvious that that was what had happened, and Katie must have known it too, but by not supporting him Luke felt as though she was acting as though she felt that he was the one in the wrong, and not the dispatch rider. If Grace's fiancé had accused someone of flirting with her she would very quickly have reassured Seb that she wasn't interested in anyone else, so why wasn't Katie reassuring him? If she was really as committed to him as he was to her she would have done so, surely? He would never ever want her to feel unsure about his love for her. In fact, he'd want to do everything he could to reassure her. Was it perhaps because a part of her wasn't fully committed to him that she wasn't doing so? Had she secretly got reservations about 'them'?

Luke desperately wanted to ask her, but he had his pride. If Katie wouldn't give him the reassurance he longed for then he certainly wasn't going to ask her for it. He couldn't. He was a man, and men did not do things like that. So reasoned Luke.

'We'd better get a move on otherwise we won't make the pub by teatime, and we don't want to get there and find they've given our rooms to someone else.'

Katie was so relieved that Luke wasn't continuing the argument that they had cycled several miles before she realised that he hadn't spoken to her at all. That could, of course, just be because they were cycling, and because she had fallen a bit behind him, and not because he wasn't speaking to her because he was still angry.

Katie endured the silence for another few minutes, but then her own emotions got the better of her and she deliberately cycled harder until she had drawn alongside him.

'How much longer do you think it will take us to reach the pub?' she asked him.

She had been rehearsing the question for the last couple of minutes, not wanting to risk saying anything contentious just in case he had stopped speaking to her because he was still annoyed, but to her relief he answered her straight away, saying calmly, 'I'm not sure, but if you're feeling tired and you'd like a bit of a rest, we can always stop.'

'No, we may as well press on,' Katie assured him.

On the surface nothing was wrong but Katie still had the feeling that in reality things between them were not 'right' and that both upset and scared her.

'Well, I'm not the one who's keeping you here,' Emily pointed out truthfully to Con.

She had been surprised at first and then irritated when she and Tommy had got back from church to find Con still in the house. Normally on those nights when he did sleep at home, he'd lie in bed

338

until dinnertime and then get up and take himself off to the theatre or somewhere with his latest girl.

Emily had grown so used to him not being around that now when he was she was finding that she didn't really want him there and that he got on her nerves, with his sulks and his complaints, she admitted, especially now that she had Tommy to keep her company. She'd planned to take him over the water to New Brighton this afternoon, seeing as it was Easter, but now with Con sitting at the kitchen table still in his pyjamas and his dressing gown, his face unshaven and his eyes bloodshot, it looked as though she was going to cancel those plans. She certainly didn't want to go out and leave Con in the house on his own. As Emily had already learned the hard way, if she did he'd be going through everything to see if she'd got any cash tucked away anywhere, and of course she had. Only a little bit, of course, for emergencies, since you never knew what was going to happen these days.

A much more pleasant sight for her to look at than her husband was her adopted 'nephew', who'd grown a whole inch and a half since he'd been with her and had got a bit of decent flesh on his bones now as well. A handsome little lad, he was, an' all, and Emily's heart swelled with pleasure when she heard others saying so, and saying how nice his manners were.

Of course it worried her that he still hadn't spoken, and she knew that sooner or later she was going to have to take him to the doctor to see what was wrong. There was no rush, though. After all, it was obvious that he was healthy and happy. He might not say anything, but the smile he gave her when they were out and he tucked his hand in hers, said more than any amount of words. She'd much rather have Tommy's silence and the love she could see in his eyes than all of Con's slick lying speeches that in the end meant nothing other than that he wanted something from her.

Besides, Emily had another reason for not being over-eager to hear Tommy talk. Who knew what he might say about his past, which could mean that she could end up losing him? Just the thought of that stripped away every bit of Emily's happiness. He was everything to her, was her lovely little lad – absolutely everything – and it would kill her to lose him now.

By rights of course he should be going to school, but from what Emily had heard half the schools were closed and those that weren't didn't have enough teachers, so that mothers were having to teach their children at home as best they could. Not that Tommy could have gone to school anyway, him not speaking.

Con's head ached from the drink he had had the previous night. He had got involved in a card game in a 'private club' and had ended up losing close on five hundred pounds, as a result of which he was now in a filthy temper. Con didn't like problems or trouble. All he asked from life was a full house, a wallet stuffed with money and a pretty girl on his arm. Instead he'd got debts, and a ruddy wife who thought more of some dumb kid than she did of him. Right now Con was feeling very sorry for himself indeed. Sorry for himself and more than a little bit afraid. Con wasn't the stuff of heroes, and the moneylender's heavies leaning on him had scared him. Now thanks to last night's card game he owed even more money.

If the kid hadn't been there Con was pretty sure he'd have been able to talk Emily into opening her purse. Con was the kind of man who always looked for someone else to blame for his problems and right now he blamed the boy, and so it was Tommy that he took his temper out on.

Glaring at him, Con told Emily bluntly, 'I'm sick of having that kid around. He gets on my nerves. I reckon he's not right in his head, with him not speaking, the way he does.'

'If there's anyone around here not right in his head, it's you, not Tommy,' Emily retaliated sharply.

'You want to get him to a doctor and see what he has to say. It ain't normal him not speaking. There's special places for kids like him and he should be in one, and if it was up to me he would be, instead of living here getting on my nerves.'

'Well, it isn't up to you, is it?' Emily told Con, but Con's comments had made her feel very uneasy. She was still Con's wife and a husband had certain rights. The last thing she wanted was Con starting getting difficult about Tommy, making a lot of fuss and trying to get the authorities involved.

So far she'd got away with claiming that Tommy was related to her but if anyone in authority was to start checking up on her story, they'd soon discover that she'd lied, and then Tommy would be taken from her. Emily could feel herself going cold all over and starting to feel sick and shaky inside.

SEVENTEEN

'Well, I can't say that I'm sorry to be leaving. Too ruddy hot for me, Egypt was. Pity about you and the major, though, Fran. The way the pair of you were carrying on I thought at the least that you'd be leaving Cairo with an engagement ring.'

Fran had to grit her teeth to stop herself from betraying her feelings. She hadn't wanted to come up on deck for their send-off, as the ship taking them on the first leg of their journey back to England cast off from the dock at Alexandria, but the two chorus girls with whom she was sharing a cabin had insisted and so now here she was, stuck right up against the deck rail with the cast's pianist and the biggest busybody that ever drew breath at her side, all eager to get as much information as she could about the break-up between Fran and the major.

The white silk dress she was wearing, with its polka dot pattern and semicircular skirt, was clinging uncomfortably to her. She had had to make a new hole in the belt that cinched the shirt-style top in at her waist, because of the weight she had lost. Her hair curled damply over the collar of the dress. She longed to remove the small, head-hugging, polished straw hat sitting neatly on the back of her head, to let whatever breeze there was cool her, but it was part of the ENSA women's role to look as glamorous as they could for the benefit of the men. The truth was that Fran had absolutely no idea why Marcus had changed towards her, and so dramatically, between the most intimate, passionate and loving hours they had spent together and their next meeting only a few hours later, when he had been so icily cold towards her. Because that second meeting had taken place in public at a party that had been given to thank the cast for their visit to Cairo and to wish them 'Godspeed and safety' for their journey home, there had not been any opportunity for Fran to talk privately with him. She had tried, discreetly at first, and then with increasing despair, to persuade him to meet her privately but he had as good as flatly refused.

Even worse, her humiliating attempts to beg him to tell her what was wrong had been witnessed by Lily, who had come up to her later and mocked, 'You'd never catch me running round after a chap who's made it clear he isn't interested, but then some folk are so desperate they can't take a hint.'

Within hours of the party Fran had learned – second-hand – that Marcus wouldn't be accompanying them on their journey home but had instead requested a transfer to 'other duties'.

It was over a week since the party now, since when Lily had been going round with a smug look on her face, like a cat that has had the cream, whilst Fran had been applying increasing amounts of her precious Max Factor pancake makeup to her face in an effort to conceal the effects of her misery. Just as well that Cairo had turned out to be a treasure-trove of all those female things that were so important and so very unavailable at home. Fran had bought makeup, lipstick and mascara, as well as silk stockings, not just for herself but for her family back home in Liverpool. She had even bought a wedding dress – not for herself, but for her niece Grace – just in case the war wasn't over by the time Grace finished her nurse's training and could marry Seb.

Fran had been such a fool, and really taken in by Marcus, believing everything he had told her, believing that they shared something special. She had even begun to think in terms of them having a future together once the war was over.

The pianist, bored now with Fran's lack of response to her questions, had wriggled her way back from the railing, leaving a space that was quickly filled by one of the dancers anxious to wave her goodbyes to the young admirer down on the dock waving up to her.

On the dock side the final preparations were being made for them to cast off. Marcus was down there with the officer to whom he was handing over the responsibility of accompanying this ENSA troupe back home. Was it really only eight nights since she had lain in his arms and then later had lain watching him sleep, Fran thought emotionally, her heart so full of love that it spilled through her, colouring her every thought.

'There's the major,' the dancer told Fran unnecessarily. 'I thought it was ever so mean of you and Lily, what you did, making a fool of him like that, and having a bet on as to who could get him to fall for them first,' she added disapprovingly.

Fran stared at her. 'What . . . what are you talking about?' she demanded.

The girl gave her a look that was a mixture of uncertainty and a determination to stand her ground, even if Fran was the second lead singer and she was only in the chorus.

'I dare say it was supposed to be a secret between the two of you but everyone's bin talking about it, and most of them have bin saying how they thought you was out of order doing what you did. I've heard Lily saying that she wanted to call off the bet but that you wouldn't.'

Fran felt sick. She ought to have realised that Lily would try to get back at both Marcus for rejecting her and Fran herself for being the one he had chosen. Fran had had enough experience of the kind of malicious, manipulative behaviour that could go on in a tight-knit group of entertainers to work out immediately what had happened. Lily had never liked her and was certainly spiteful enough to have deliberately planned to spoil things between her and Marcus just for the fun of it, never mind for the added pleasure of getting her own back.

But surely Marcus must have known she wouldn't do anything like that? She loved him and had as good as said so, even if she had held back the words, afraid of saying them too quickly, waiting for him to say them first to her.

And that last night he had almost done so when he had spoken of the future in a way that had made it clear he wanted them to spend that future together.

But he was a man, Fran reminded herself, and men had their pride. Marcus had said more than once that he was surprised that she had chosen him out of all her admirers.

Fran looked down at the dock. It wasn't too late. If she could only talk to him . . . explain. He was too far away to hear her if she called out, and would probably ignore her anyway. She turned round and started to force her way through the crowd on deck.

'All ashore that's going ashore,' someone was calling.

The companionways were filled with serving men and sailors coming on board, and those who had come to wish them *bon voyage* getting off. Fran got held up between a large woman – Egyptian and high born by the looks of her – and her retinue, who were obviously all travelling with the ship.

She wasted several valuable minutes struggling to get past them all, reaching the companionway to the dock just as the officer standing by it was nodding to the men below to remove it.

'I have to go ashore,' Fran told him frantically.

'Sorry, miss, but we're just about to cast off.' The officer was firm but unmoving.

'No!' Fran looked down onto the dock and felt the ship begin to move.

She could see Marcus standing less than ten yards away. Desperately she called out his name, not once but twice, her voice thickening with tears when he didn't respond.

All around her on the decks people were singing and ticker tape was being thrown. The ship's horn was sounded loudly.

'Marcus . . .' Fran wept as she cried his name, and watched as he walked away and out of her life.

Her final view of him was obscured by both her tears and the excitement of her fellow passengers, so that she did not see as he stopped walking and turned round to look at the ship. And, of course, even if she had done so she would not have been able to see the anguish in the gaze with which he searched for a final glimpse of her. So much loved by him and so very treacherous in her behaviour towards him.

'Charlie, don't be ridiculous, of course I can't lend you a hundred pounds,' Bella told her brother, looking at him in disbelief that he should think she would be able to do so.

'Well, I don't see why not, seeing as Dad bought this house for you, and gives you an allowance.'

'A very small allowance, Charlie. I can barely manage on it as it is, and now that Daddy's giving you a job he's flatly refusing to increase it for me.'

'But Alan must have left you something.' Charlie was growing desperate, but Bella was too intent on airing her own grievances to hear the despair in his voice.

'Oh, yes, Alan left me something, all right – his father's debts and the shame of being married to a man who was about to divorce me so that he could marry someone else. No, the only thing I got from Alan that's of any value is my engagement ring. Not that I bother wearing it much any more.' Bella looked down at her left hand. 'After all, it isn't anything like as nice as the one you've given Daphne. I dare say that all my jewellery put together, including Alan's mother's and grandmothers' engagement rings is only worth about two hundred. Mummy said you paid nearly a hundred for Daphne's engagement ring.' Her resentment of her future sister-in-law's superior position within the family showed in Bella's voice.

'I don't know why you're asking me for a loan, Charlie,' she told her brother petulantly. 'After all, the way Mummy and Daddy are carrying on about you marrying Daphne I would have thought Daddy would be only too pleased to help you out. Or are you worried that he's going to ask what you want the money for?' Bella guessed. 'I suppose you've lost at cards again, have you? Hardly the right kind of behaviour for a man who is marrying the daughter of a member of Lloyd's, is it?' Bella taunted unkindly.

'Leave it out, will you, Bella?' Charlie demanded sourly. 'Look, you must be able to lend me something? Fifty?'

'Fifty shillings, yes; fifty pounds, no,' Bella told him truthfully.

Charlie glowered at his sister. He had been banking on her help, but Bella could be awkward when she wanted to be and it was plain to him that she wasn't going to budge from her refusal.

It was selfish of her as well when she had just been boasting about how much her wretched jewellery was worth. Charlie toyed with the idea of telling her how desperate his situation actually was and why, and then acknowledged that it wouldn't be a good idea to do so. You never knew with Bella, and he had learned when they had been growing up not to trust her. As a child she had always been ready to go running to their parents to spill the beans on him if she thought it would be to her own advantage.

He had to find that money. Charlie was under no illusions about Dougie's ability to make good his threat. Daphne's parents idolised the memory of their dead son, just as Daphne herself idolised her brother.

What had started as a bit of a joke when a comment about Charlie's 'heroism' from one of the other men on the boat had led to Charlie being publicly hailed as a hero, had now turned into a total nightmare. Charlie hadn't minded basking in all the reflected glory of his supposed heroism, even though, as Dougie had said, he'd been trying to push Eustace out of the way to get into the boat ahead of him, not save his life, and when Charlie had seen Eustace bang his head against the boat, in his own desperation to get on board he'd have quite happily let him drown if it hadn't been for the fact that he had felt the weight of the now unconscious man might drag him down with him.

It wasn't true, though, that Charlie had deliberately pushed Eustace overboard. But if Dougie started to make public accusations against him, who knew what might come out? Charlie hadn't exactly acquitted himself with gallantry on the beach at Dunkirk, and if the wrong people started asking the right questions, it wouldn't just be his fiancée Charlie stood to lose; there was also his reputation and his 'heroic' status, and the fact that his father wouldn't be so keen to get him out of the army and into a cushy job working for him if he found out that the son he was so proud of wasn't the hero he believed him to be.

Trust Dougie to have spotted that notice his mother had insisted on putting in the papers. But for that he wouldn't be in this ruddy mess. The trouble was that you didn't mess around with families like Dougie's. A hundred quid, though, and by tomorrow night. Charlie could feel himself starting to sweat.

'You know, Charlie,' Bella warned her brother too sweetly, 'you really shouldn't play cards for money, especially now that you're going to be a married man. Poor Daphne. I do feel a bit guilty about keeping something so important from her.'

'Cut it out, Bella. You're as jealous as hell of Daphne.'

'No I am not. Why should I be jealous of Daphne?'

'Because Ma's making such a fuss of her, for one thing, and because Dad's giving us this house, for another.'

Charlie was losing patience with his sister. He was pretty sure she could have helped him if she'd wanted to, and he was equally sure that she was in one of her sulks for the reasons he had just given. Well, he wasn't going to give up. He'd still got time to talk her round. He *had* to talk her round, Charlie admitted, because there was no one else he could ask. His father was already complaining about the amount of money he'd had to lend him to cover the cost of his engagement to Daphne.

'So we'll be round in half an hour, Bella. Daphne is so excited about seeing the house. I've told her how nice you've made it. It's a pity you have to go out, but I've got my own key.'

Bella was seething. She had never really thought that her mother would allow her father to take the house from her and give it to Daphne and Charlie, but now here was her mother, insisting on bringing Daphne and Charlie round to 'have a look' before Charlie drove Daphne home and then returned to his barracks.

Well, she most certainly wasn't going to be there. She'd decided to go down to the school instead, on the pretext of checking through some of her supplies lists.

Things were still a bit cool between her and Laura at the moment, but that was Laura's fault, not hers, Bella assured herself. At least she wasn't having to endure the presence of Jan and his family. They'd gone to Liverpool to listen to a concert at the Philharmonic Hall. Bella thought she had never hated anyone as much as she hated Jan Polanski. The very thought of his name was enough to make her face burn with fury.

Wallasey Village was relatively quiet, most people who could making the most of the Easter weekend to enjoy what respite from the war they could.

Bella had a key for the school and, in spite of the bad temper in which she had left the house, to her own surprise, once she had started work on the lists she was compiling she actually found the busyness helped to soothe her crossness.

Charlie was on edge and irritable. He hadn't wanted to accompany his mother and Daphne round to Bella's. Discussions about curtains and bed linen was of no interest to him.

'And this is the main bedroom.'

'Oh, how pretty. And a double bed.' Daphne blushed, looked down at the carpet, and then up again at Charlie, to give him a shyly adoring smile, which in turn was rewarded with a glowingly approving smile from Vi.

Really, Daphne was going to be the perfect daughter-in-law. Already she had proved more than willing to put herself under her future mother-in-law's direction, unlike Bella, who sadly had become very difficult since she had been widowed. Vi had spent several happy hours with the family photograph albums basking in Daphne's admiration of Charlie as a baby. So much so, in fact, that Vi had quite forgotten now that she had ever seen Charlie as anything less than the perfect son.

Vi and Daphne had even shed tears together over little Jack. Such a sweet little boy, Vi had told Daphne, and his loss still very hard to bear, which was why she preferred not to talk about him.

Naturally, darling Daphne had totally understood.

Daphne was really the sweetest little thing,
Charlie assured himself as he basked in the adula-
tion of her smile and the sexual *frisson* brought
on by her bashful comment about the double bed.
Charlie reckoned that he would put it and his
married status to far better and more frequent use
than his late and unlamented brother-in-law had
done. It did a chap's ego any amount of good to
be admired in the way that Daphne so obviously
admired him. The only trouble was that Charlie
was used to rather more earthy girls than Daphne;
girls who did rather more than look at a man adoringly. But they, of course, were not the sort of girls
a chap married. Most especially not if one had a
mother like his.

Bella's dressing table was cluttered with bottles of
nail polish and scent, and a packet of cigarettes,
Charlie noticed absently, whilst his mother and
wife-to-be talked enthusiastically about new
bedding. His glance eventually alighted on Bella's
jewellery box. Was all her jewellery in it? Her
engagement ring and those of Alan's mother and
grandmothers? The whole two hundred pounds'
worth?

Charlie could feel his heart starting to thud with
a mixture of desperation and hope. He'd find a
way of paying Bella back and making it up to her.
She'd never made any secret of the fact that she
felt that Alan should have bought her a better ring.
Once he'd got himself sorted out and Dougie off

354

his back, he could buy her something she'd like – give it to her as a surprise and to make up for her having her own jewellery 'stolen'. No one would ever know that a real thief hadn't taken it, not the way things were now, with looters stealing from bombed-out houses, very often during the blackout when there was no one there to see them, and nipping into people's kitchens whilst the door was open to nick food. No, Bella wouldn't lose out in the long run. He'd see to that.

When his mother was heading towards the bedroom door, Daphne trailing behind her, Charlie rushed forward to open the door for them. He accompanied them to the top of the stairs, where he stopped and patted his jacket pocket, exhibiting faked disbelief as he exclaimed, 'Dammit, I'm out of cigarettes.'

Whilst Vi was still saying disapprovingly, 'Language, Charles, please,' Charlie was already turning back.

'There was a packet on Bella's dressing table,' he said over his shoulder. 'I'll just nip back and get them. She won't mind and I'll replace them for her later. You two go downstairs and I'll catch up with you in a tick.'

The rings *were* there, and Bella's pearls. Charlie scooped them all up and stashed the jewellery boxes in his inside pocket, only just remembering in time to take the cigarettes as well.

'Ta, sis,' he grinned jauntily to his own reflection in the mirror, his normal self-confidence returning.

Poor Bella. What a shock she was going to get

when she got home to find she'd had looters in and they'd stolen her jewellery. Of course, he would immediately own up to having forgotten to lock the back door after he'd stepped outside to take a look at the back garden.

And even if Bella did manage to put two and two together and link his earlier request for a loan with her missing jewellery, and from that accuse him of taking it, she could make as much fuss as she liked but their parents would never believe her. Not now that he was engaged to Daphne. It would be her word against his, and Bella wasn't their parents' favourite any more. Mind, if she did look like accusing him he'd make sure he headed her off by pointing out the benefits of her claiming the insurance money from a genuine theft. Bella was shrewd enough to see the advantage of that.

Having made sure that the back door was indeed unlocked, Charlie waited until they were all outside to tell his mother casually, 'Me and Daphne will need an early start tomorrow, so I thought I'd just nip out later and go down to the drill hall, where I did my training when I was in the TA to see if there's anyone there from the old days, to catch up with. A few of the lads like poor old Dougie, who came round earlier, haven't had things as good as me and I thought I'd stand them a drink and slip them a bit of something, to make things a bit easier for them.'

'Oh, Charles, that's so typical of you.' Daphne's eyes shone with emotion, and even his mother was looking pleased and proud.

*   *   *

'Hello there.'

Bella almost dropped her list. She hadn't heard anyone entering the room, but someone definitely had and a very self-assured someone, at that, she acknowledged as she saw the way the man was looking at her.

He wasn't exactly young – somewhere in his thirties, she guessed – or good-looking or particularly tall, but what he didn't have in physical attributes he more than made up for with his smooth self-confidence and the aura he carried with him. Wearing a navy blazer, a white shirt with a paisley cravat, and light-coloured trousers, his shoes – brown brogues Bella noted with approval – were well polished and his nails clean.

His dark brown hair was cut short; his bearing upright and square-shouldered – as though he was someone important. Bella was glad that she was dressed in one of her favourite frocks, pretty blue cotton, which matched her eyes, patterned with pink roses, its sweetheart neckline drawing discreet attention to her smooth creamy skin, whilst its fitted skirt emphasised the curves of her waist and hips. She'd removed her matching blue hat with its cluster of pink roses when she'd started work, which was a pity she decided, because the pink of the roses exactly matched the pink Max Factor lipstick she was wearing. Still, she could see that the man – whoever he was – was studying her very appreciatively.

'I saw that the door was open and I thought I'd take a chance and see if I could jump the queue.' Both his words and his smile might not be openly suggestive but there *was* something there, Bella recognised, some sense of a message being given by someone who was supremely good at the giving of a certain kind of subtle man-to-woman communication, that was like arnica applied directly to her pride, bruised by Jan. Not that Bella intended to let him know that he had any kind of effect on her, not for one minute.

'If you're talking about the nursery,' she began, 'then your wife—'

'My sister,' he corrected her swiftly. 'She's desperate to get her two little ones enrolled here.'

'I'm only the assistant supervisor,' Bella told him depreciatingly. 'I'm afraid your sister will have to apply to the supervisor.'

'Can't you give me any hope that you might intercede for me, and get me into my sister's good books?'

'It isn't up to me, although I could write down their names and pass them on to the supervisor.'

'You are an angel and should really be rewarded with nectar and ambrosia, but alas in these dull times all I can offer is a cup of tea at the nearest tea shop.'

Bella was already beginning to shake her head, when he added softly, 'Or perhaps dinner somewhere a little more exciting.'

A distinctly heady feeling was taking hold of her, Bella admitted. This man, whoever he was, was making it plain that he found her attractive. His flattery proved that, and, when all was said and done, it was after all her due. She knew that. This was what her beauty deserved – a man who appreciated it and her, and who was prepared to show that appreciation. Unlike some men, or rather one man in particular, whose rejection of her had affected her so badly that she wanted to blank the whole episode from her mind.

'I'm afraid I don't accept invitations to dinner from strange men.'

What a delicious game this was.

'Perhaps you will allow me to introduce myself then?'

Bella inclined her head.

'Well, if I am to make a note of your sister and her children's details, I rather think that you should, Mr . . . ?'

'Ralph,' he corrected her silkily. 'Ralph Fleming.'

'You aren't in uniform, Mr Fleming?' Bella asked coolly. 'Only we give preference to the children of our fighting men.'

The look he gave her was both mocking and challenging.

'Commander Fleming,' he corrected her. 'And no, on this occasion I am not in uniform.'

Bella had had the most wonderful afternoon. The commander, Ralph, had insisted on driving her out into the country to a pub he knew, where they had had a drink and he insisted on Bella talking to him about herself whilst he had listened.

At one point when he had stopped her, Bella had waited suspiciously, remembering how both her father and Alan claimed that her chatter irritated them, but she had been totally disarmed when Ralph had said softly to her, 'You know,

I have to tell you that you really are the most beautiful girl I have ever seen.'

After that she had needed a second drink to cool her down, but she had refused a third. She wasn't going to repeat the mistake she had made with Jan. Not ever.

Not that Ralph had attempted to do anything he shouldn't. No, not for one minute. He had been most gentlemanly but yet at the same time managing to imply that he found her so attractive that he would like to be anything but gentlemanly. And he had done so without having to resort to any of the crude vulgarity that Alan would have shown. Poor Alan, he would have put up such a poor show against a man like Ralph, who was obviously very sophisticated and used to only the best of things.

When she had asked him about himself he had said simply that he couldn't really talk about the purpose of his presence in the area, as much as he'd like to be more forthcoming.

'National security, you understand,' he had told Bella with a small rueful smile.

Well, of course she did.

Mindful of her neighbours and her mother, Bella refused to let him drive her all the way home. She had been thrilled, though, when he had leaned out of his car window to ask her, 'May I telephone you?'

So thrilled, in fact, that she had almost walked off without giving him her number.

Bella had reached the gate to her front garden before she remembered that he hadn't given her the name of his sister or her children. Not that it mattered. It wasn't them she was interested in.

After the heady excitement of her afternoon, it wasn't at all in accord with her mood to walk into her kitchen and find Jan there. It reminded her of what she wanted to forget.

Coincidentally he was dressed in almost exactly the same way as Ralph had been, only the dark grey in the paisley pattern of Jan's cravat almost exactly matched the colour of his eyes. Bella had always recognised that Jan was an extremely handsome man, probably the best-looking man she had ever seen. Tall, dark-haired, his hair thick with a slight wave that kept it close to his well-shaped head, the high cheekbones, olive skin and strong facial bone structure he shared with his mother and his sister, on him translated into film-star good looks. And yet oddly Jan did not behave like a good-looking man. There was never any small knowing smile, no oblique look, no sense in any way of him knowing that he was extremely handsome in the way that Bella knew she was stunningly pretty and that she was aware of the value of that asset. That confused Bella. They should have been two of a kind, two people who knew that their good looks set them apart from and above less attractive members of the human race; that they belonged to an exclusive group, and that their looks gave them the power to influence the decisions of others in their own favour. It both piqued and irked her that Jan seemed perfectly happy to behave and be treated as though he was merely an ordinary Joe. His behaviour made her feel as though he was mocking and scorning her in some way that she couldn't understand; as though he thought her beauty was something amusing and unimportant. He had already proved to her that he was immune to it. She needed desperately to get her own back and make sure that he understood the status her beauty gave her instead of laughing at it, and her.

Now, seeing him unexpectedly just when she was congratulating herself that Ralph found her attractive, brought back everything she had felt when he had rejected her, causing her to want to hit out at him.

'What are you doing here?' she demanded nastily. 'I should have thought you'd have been with your fiancée.'

Ignoring her rudeness, Jan said calmly, 'My mother and sister have been invited to stay with our friends tonight. My mother was concerned that you might worry and wonder why they hadn't returned so I said that I'd call round and let you know before I set off back for camp.'

Oh, how typical of him to try to wrong-foot her, with his pretend courtesy and good manners. As though he or his mother and sister really cared anything about her.

For some reason that made her even more furious.

'Me worry about them? It will be a pleasure to have my house to myself,' Bella told him sharply and pointedly. 'Oh, and whilst we're on the subject, I'll thank you to give me my door key. That sister of yours had no business giving you one in the first place, and so I've told her,' she added before skirting round him to go into the hall and then upstairs into her bedroom.

It was typical of her luck that Jan should be there to spoil her happiness just when she had had the loveliest afternoon. Mind, it was perhaps a pity that she hadn't invited Ralph in – that would have shown Jan something, and no mistake, seeing another man and not just any other man but a man as worldly and charming as Ralph, so taken with her and so flatteringly attentive to her. Not like him. Pushing her off like that. Bella started to clench her hands into angry fists and then discovered that she couldn't because of the way they were shaking – with anger, of course, that was all.

Automatically she reached for her cigarettes, frowning as she realised that the pack she had left on her dressing table had gone. And then she saw that the jewellery box was open, and that the jewellery had also gone.

Gone? How could it have? Unless . . . Bella looked towards her bedroom door.

Someone had stolen her jewellery. No, not someone, she corrected herself, her heart pounding with a mixture of shock and conviction. There was only one person who could have stolen it, wasn't there? A savage hot feeling that was a mixture of anger and triumph burned through her veins. She had been right all along not to trust those Poles, especially *him*, Jan. She ran downstairs and wrenched open the kitchen door.

Jan was putting on his coat, his kitbag on the floor beside him.

'Stay where you are,' Bella told him fiercely. 'I'm going to call the police.'

'What?'

'You heard me. I'm going to call the police. Someone has stolen my jewellery and we both know who it is, don't we?'

He had picked up his kitbag, the sun through the window making his dark hair gleam like silk. Bella wondered what it would be like to touch it and if it would feel warm from the sun or—

Shocked by the sudden slide down the secret shadowy path her thoughts had taken, like a tunnel that had suddenly appeared out of nowhere, she swallowed hard as she clamped down on them.

'What exactly is it you are trying to say?' Jan demanded quietly, so quietly, in fact, that it was odd that she should shiver and feel alarmed. He was the one who should be afraid, not her.

'You understand English, don't you?' she threw at him wildly. 'It's plain enough what I'm saying. What happened? Couldn't you afford to buy your fiancée a ring of her own? Oh, I'm sorry, I was forgetting you're a refugee, aren't you, and of course refugees have to steal things from other people?'

He had put his kitbag back down and he was standing looking at her, not saying anything or doing anything, just looking at her in such a way that a feeling of nausea, the kind she remembered from a childhood ride she had insisted on having at a fairground, despite her mother's warning that it would make her ill, was gripping her stomach. Now, though, the nausea was outweighed by the

364

fierce thrust of exhilarating pleasure her defiance of her danger had brought her.

She wanted, she realised, to insult him and humiliate him as he had done her; she wanted to accuse him and watch him beg her not to report what he had done to the police. She wanted to hear him begging her to forgive him.

But he wasn't doing either of those things, Bella realised. He was simply standing there looking at her with pity and contempt darkening his eyes.

He felt pity and contempt for her? How dare he? Didn't he realise that she was the one who should be viewing him with contempt? He was, after all, a thief. And he was at her mercy. She didn't really care about the loss of her jewellery, Bella recognised; what mattered far more to her was the power over Jan that his theft of it gave her.

'It's because we know that we can't trust you that decent people don't want refugees in their homes,' she taunted him. 'That's why someone like you has to marry another refugee. It's because it's like to like. I dare say she's a thief as well, is she?'

Now at last she had got a reaction from him.

'You will take back that insult,' he told her coldly.

'What?' Bella was beside herself with fury now. 'You steal my jewellery and then you have the gall to say something like that? I always knew that, for all others might fuss round you saying that you're a hero, you haven't got much sense,' Bella told him with contempt. 'Because if you had, right now you'd be down on your knees to me pleading with me to forgive you and begging me not to report you to the police.'

To Bella's utter chagrin Jan threw back his head and laughed.

'Ah, so that's what you're after, is it? You want me to plead with you for your forgiveness, and not just your forgiveness I think perhaps.' Subtly his accent had become just that little bit stronger and the look in his eyes very definitely and unsubtly extremely knowing. Now she could see in the grey eyes the awareness she had looked for and had so bafflingly never seen before with regard to his own good looks. 'You want me perhaps to buy your silence for this supposed theft with a kiss or two, no?'

Bella couldn't speak past the tight ball of fury blocking her throat. Her heart was pounding fiercely. She felt hot, and then cold, angry and then excited, her body and her thoughts pulsing with fierce energy.

When had he moved? Bella didn't know. All she did know was that he was now standing right in front of her and that he had reached for her hand and was holding it in his own.

She looked up at him. He was looking back at her. She gave a small gasp, her body trembling. Jan's thumb rubbed gently across the back of her fingers, and she trembled more violently.

He was bending his head towards her. She couldn't take her gaze off his lips. She could feel her own softening and parting. He was smiling at her as though he knew all about that treacherous exciting ache inside her that had suddenly become so very intense.

'Poor Bella.' He placed his index finger against her lips and shook his head.

Her body was awash with so much giddying sensation that her mind couldn't spare the time to grapple with the meaning of his words.

'What, nothing to say? Perhaps you want more than just merely a kiss or two? Perhaps you want me to take you to bed and give you what your husband never did, is that it?'

Why was he still talking? Why wasn't he kissing her instead of talking about doing so, Bella wondered wildly.

He was still smiling at her, giving her a smile that curled the corners of his mouth in such a wicked way that her heart was jumping around inside her chest cavity like a fish out of water.

'Perhaps you even hid the jewellery yourself, did you? Ah, poor Bella, to be so desperate for a man.'

His voice was still soft but it was a softness that raised the tiny hairs at the back of her neck in swift alarm. His words had the same effect on her as a jug of cold water being thrown over her, leaving her reeling and gasping under the shock.

'I am not desperate for a man,' she denied angrily. 'And if I was, that man would not be you.'

'At last – something we are agreed on,' he told her, his voice suddenly cold and hard, as he released her hand and stepped back from her. 'Because I cannot be bribed or bought or threatened, Bella. I have not touched your jewellery.'

'You must have done. It's missing, and you're here. You're a thief, Jan, for all that you're trying to pretend that you're not, and I'm going to make sure that everyone knows it,' she threatened him furiously.

He was doing it again, putting her in the wrong, making her look bad, but this time she wasn't going to let him get away with it.

When he stepped towards her she goaded him triumphantly, 'Go on then, hit me. I know you want to.'

There was a small silence as he looked at her without a smile this time. Instead there was a gravity mixed with revulsion in his gaze that made her heart jerk painfully.

'You know, Bella, despite everything I feel sorry for you. Sorry and rather sad. You're so blind to reality, and blind to the fact that the rest of the world, unlike you, can see past your lovely face to the ugliness inside you. And you are ugly inside, Bella, very ugly. But it isn't all your fault. Your parents are a great deal to blame. I'm sure if they had loved you more and the outward trappings of success less, then you would have learned from them that true beauty is something that comes from the heart, and that it's that beauty that really counts.'

Ugly, her? That was a lie and anyone could see it. She was stunning; beautiful.

'And no, I am not going to hit you,' Jan continued quietly. 'Using violence to make my point would make me contemptible in my own eyes. How sad it is that someone with so much potential to be a truly worthwhile and lovable human being should throw all that away and instead become a person that others dislike and avoid.

You know, I'm surprised that someone as intelligent as you obviously are hasn't worked out yet that treating others badly, hurting them and being unkind, simply means that they will behave towards you in exactly the same way. I feel very sorry for you. It must be very lonely being you, Bella, a woman without friends or kindness or love in her life, who shows only meanness to others.'

'That's not true,' Bella denied. 'I have got friends, and . . . and people do love me.'

She was humiliatingly close to tears – of anger, of course.

'I haven't taken your jewellery,' Jan continued. 'So if it is really missing and this is not just some silly game you're playing because—'

'Because what? Because you think I want you to kiss me? Well, I don't. Your fiancée is welcome to your kisses. I certainly don't want them.'

'And I don't want your jewellery. So, are you sure that it *is* missing?'

'Yes.'

How had it happened? How had it come to this – that Jan was now the one accusing her, and she was having to defend herself from those accusations?

'Then someone must have broken into the house,' Jan told her. 'Presumably no one else has a key?'

'Only my mother,' Bella began impatiently, and then stopped.

'Well, I think we can safely assume that your mother won't have stolen your jewellery,' Jan told her wryly.

369

'No. Of course she wouldn't,' Bella agreed sharply. No, her mother wouldn't have taken her jewellery, but Charlie might have done, Bella realised with a sickening jolt of awareness. How humiliating it would be if she had to tell Jan that, after what she had said to him. She longed for him to be the thief, and right now nothing would have pleased her more than to send for the police and accuse him in front of them before seeing him being handcuffed and marched off.

However, an inner voice was warning her that he was not lying when he claimed he had nothing to do with the disappearance of her jewellery and that same inner voice was telling her that her brother could have done. Bella knew Charlie well enough to know that he was perfectly capable of taking her jewellery, and of being able to justify to himself his need to have done so.

She needed time to think – and alone. And time too to find out if she was right about Charlie without alerting Jan to her suspicions. He'd love that, being able to taunt her about her brother being a thief just like he had taunted her about wanting his kisses. Which, of course, she most certainly did not.

'I don't want to discuss it any more,' she told Jan in a flat voice. 'I just want you out of my house, and the sooner the better.'

EIGHTEEN

'I can't wait for it to be May and the dance competition,' Lou told her sister excitedly.

'Me neither,' Sasha agreed.

'Do you think we should add something a bit more fancy into our routine, like a bit of Latin American?'

They were up in their bedroom, having spent the earlier part of the afternoon supposedly going for a walk in Wavertree Park, but in reality very daringly going into Liverpool to meet up with Kieran, who had told them that his uncle had offered to provide them both with new costumes for the competition.

'Something a bit racy,' he had told them with a wink, adding, 'You're to go to the theatre and ask for Ma Jenkins. She's in charge of all the costumes and she'll run you something up.'

Now Sasha shook her head in response to Lou's question. 'No. Kieran says that we need to keep something back for later in the competition. The next heats, you know.'

Lou nodded vigorously. They were united in

their unshakeable conviction that every word that fell from their idol's lips was spoken with irrefutable wisdom and truth.

'I think Kieran's a bit disappointed in you, though, Lou,' Sasha felt obliged to tell her twin.

Instantly Lou was bristling with angry defensiveness. 'What do you mean?'

'Well, when you went to the ladies, he told me that he was worried that you might let me down because he doesn't think that you keep time quite as well as me.'

They had always been so close and so much in agreement that there had never been any reason for them not to speak their minds openly to one another. But that had been before.

'You're making that up,' Lou accused Sasha furiously.

'No, I am not.'

'Yes, you are, because last week he told me that my voice is much stronger and better than yours, only I didn't say anything at the time 'cos I know how much you like him and I didn't want you to be upset. Besides, I thought it might put you off when we do our number and spoil our chance of winning.'

'I don't believe you,' Sasha announced flatly. 'You're just saying that because you're jealous, because it's me that Kieran likes best.'

'No he does not.'

'Yes he does.'

Since he hadn't been able to find a pawnbroker who looked respectable, was open for business over Easter, but was a safe distance away from Wallasey whilst *en route* to the run-down part of Liverpool where he was supposed to meet Dougie, Charlie had decided that he would have to offer Dougie the jewellery in lieu of cash. Not that that should be a problem. With his connections Charlie was pretty sure that Dougie would get a far better price for it than he ever could.

He'd already found the pub, on the corner of a shabby-looking street of terraced houses, in what was obviously a very poor and rough area of the city, with a gap here and there courtesy of Hitler's Luftwaffe. But he was a bit earlier than he had planned, having allowed extra time for negotiating with a pawnbroker. The street was empty, or at least it had been until the door to one of the houses had opened and a girl had stepped out, and a very pretty girl too, Charlie recognised appreciatively. Her hair was black and curled luxuriantly down onto her shoulders, her face pale and heart-shaped, with gorgeous full red-lipsticked lips and large dark brown eyes. The girl had got to have Italian blood in her somewhere, Charlie decided, but he reckoned she couldn't be full Italian because everyone knew that they didn't let their sisters and daughters out on their own and especially not dressed like this girl was dressed, in a short-sleeved blouse with such a low neck that it was falling off one of her shoulders, and a skirt pulled in tightly round her tiny waist.

The brown eyes were surveying him as boldly as he was her, and quite plainly she liked what she saw as much as he did, Charlie thought appreciatively, as she continued to study him, one hand on her out-thrust hip, her head thrown back as she tossed her hair and eyed him challengingly, before asking mockingly, 'Lost your way, have you, soldier boy? Only if it's Seacombe barracks you're looking for you're well in the wrong place. This is Toxteth. You need to be going north of the city, not south. What you want is the ferry terminal just past the Cunard Building. You can get the ferry there that will get you over the Mersey to Seacombe. Round here isn't the place for the likes of you.'

Since he was supposed to have been going down to the drill hall, Charlie had felt obliged to put on his uniform instead of wearing civvies.

'The wrong place for the barracks but the right place for the prettiest girl in the city,' Charlie riposted with a knowing wink.

She was younger than he had thought at first, no more than seventeen or eighteen, he guessed. She was still standing on the steps to the house, but now she was leaning against the doorframe in a pose that showed off the delicious curves of her breasts. Charlie could feel his blood heating and roaring through his veins.

Being in the army had given him a taste of what life was all about when it came to girls. The confidence that went with that made it easy for him to swagger over to her and place his own foot challengingly on the step below hers as he looked at her.

She wasn't very tall, he was standing below her

and she had to tilt her head back to look up at him. She was very, very pretty.

Lena looked up at the soldier. He was good-looking, she had to give him that, tall and broad-shouldered too, and with that confidence about him that said he knew a thing or two. She'd been half shocked and half thrilled when he had come over like that in response to her comment. The kind of comment she'd heard her cousin Doris making more than once, before she'd hooked up with her new steady. Lena's heart did a small excited dance inside her ribs. She was going to get in a lot of trouble if her cousin came back and found her parading around in her clothes, and she'd get the strap from her uncle an' all if he caught her doing what she shouldn't, but she was tired of being treated like a kid. She was sixteen, after all, and prettier than her cousin Doris – much prettier. But Lena knew that her late mother's family didn't approve of her because of her dad being Italian and him only marrying her mother when he had had to, and even then spending more time with his own family than he did with his new wife and child.

Her parents were both dead now, killed in the November bombings – not that she missed them much. Why should she? Her dad had never been around and her mother had been ashamed of her on account of her having inherited her dad's Italian looks. Bad blood, that's what her mother had always said she'd got, and her mother's family as well – her aunt and uncle who had taken her in after the bombing. Not that they'd wanted to take her in, not for one minute. They'd only done it because the council were paying them to house her.

They'd certainly got the best of the bargain in Lena's eyes, at least. She had to hand over her wages from her job, and her auntie Flo had taken her ration book off her.

Lena's thoughts turned from the unpleasantness of her family and her situation to the far more pleasant matter of the handsome young soldier standing on the step in front of her. The way he was looking at her made her feel just like those girls she'd read about in love stories she collected from the library for Mrs Watson, one of the women her aunt made her go cleaning for. She'd gone all sort of swoony, just like the girl in *Love at First Sight*, the story she'd been reading only last week. She'd been swept off her feet by a rich man with a title who'd rescued her from her cruel stepfather and married her. Lena wasn't so silly as to think that a rich man with a title was going to come walking down her street, thank you very much, never mind marry her, but the prospect of a handsome young soldier falling for her and taking her away from Bessie Street and her mean aunt and uncle and her cousin was certainly an appealing one.

In all the stories she'd read, the man almost always fell in love with the girl once he'd kissed her. Lena hadn't kissed anyone yet, but she'd seen how it was done at the pictures, and it had looked very nice too. Had the soldier moved a bit closer to her? She was wearing her cousin's borrowed heels and she wobbled on them a bit with them being too big.

As the girl lost her balance and leaned towards him, Charlie seized his chance, grasping her firmly round the waist. And what a waist. His two hands met easily around it, but his attention was focused more on the lushness of the breasts above her narrow waist. Lust, scalding hot and insistent, poured through his body. Charlie pulled her closer, his arms fully around her now, his body pressed purposefully into hers, with its male message of desire, his mouth taking possession of her tempting red lips.

Ooohh, it was just like in the films, only she hadn't realised that kissing involved having a man push his tongue into your mouth, Lena acknowledged. Once you got used to it, mind, it was nice, especially when you touched his tongue with your own.

A messenger boy cycling across the bottom of the road saw them and rang his bell cheekily, bringing Charlie back to reality. A quick glance at his service watch told him that it was time for him to leave.

'Very nice,' he smiled appreciatively. 'Maybe next time you'll invite me in and we can get to know one another a bit better,' he joked, giving the girl a meaningful wink.

'Maybe I will or maybe I won't,' she responded saucily, before slipping back inside the house and closing the door.

*   *   *

377

'What do you mean, you couldn't get the cash?' Dougie wasn't smiling now, and nor were the two men standing behind him, big solid dangerous-looking men of a type spawned by the boxing clubs that proliferated in the poor areas of the city.

'I've brought you these instead,' Charlie continued without answering Dougie's question, as he opened his hand to show him the rings. 'Courtesy of my sister. There's over a hundred quid's worth there.'

Charlie had kept back Bella's own engagement ring and her pearls as a bit of an insurance policy for himself.

Dougie looked at the rings and then at Charlie. 'Give 'em to you, did she, or did you help yourself?'

'They belonged to her late mother-in-law,' Charlie told him, again not answering Dougie's question.

'I reckon there's only seventy quid's worth there, maximum,' Dougie told him, 'and we agreed on a hundred.'

Charlie managed to resist the temptation to say that he hadn't agreed to anything.

'Got any more, have yer?' Dougie asked him, his gaze going to Charlie's pocket in a way that said he'd guessed that Charlie had.

'Only this,' Charlie told him, reluctantly showing him Bella's own engagement ring.

'All right,' Dougie grunted after inspecting it for several seconds, 'it will have to do, I suppose.'

Well, at least he'd got to keep the pearls, Charlie comforted himself ten minutes later, only too glad to be able to put the pub and the men in it behind him. The evening hadn't been completely wasted, though. There'd been the girl, after all, and what a corker she was. Pity he didn't have time to go back for a bit more of what she'd had on offer.

From her bedroom window Lena had seen Charlie go into the pub and then come out again, and was impressed. Everyone in the area knew that the pub doubled as the headquarters for the gang who ran the local black market business. Bad people to get on the wrong side of, Dougie and his men were, but *he* was obviously well in with them, she decided when she saw Charlie come out of the pub all in one piece and walk off down the road. He was the business, he was, and no mistake, anyone could see that. He talked proper posh and he'd smelled nice too. Just imagine having a man like that fall in love with you. Lena was imagining it. He'd buy her nice clothes and take her nice places, and they'd get married. Her cousin might be full of herself because she was walking out with a merchant seaman, but she wouldn't give anyone tuppence for her cousin's beau, for all the airs and graces she was giving herself since she'd taken up with him. He certainly didn't compare with her lovely lad, Lena decided happily. And her soldier boy had been ever so gentlemanly as well, not making them cheeky suggestions like so many other men had started doing since she'd filled out a bit. That sort must be daft if they thought she didn't know what they were after. Well, they wouldn't get it from her, for all that her aunt and uncle kept going on about her having bad blood. She'd better get out of her borrowed finery, Lena realised. Because if her cousin came back and found her parading around in her clothes she'd be screaming the place down and ripping her clothes off Lena's back. She'd felt ever so nice, though, all dressed up, and she'd seen how much the soldier had liked the way she looked.

As he got on the ferry, Charlie acknowledged that he had felt far worse than he had expected when he'd handed Bella's jewellery over to Dougie, but what choice had he had? At least he'd got Dougie off his back now. Better to think about that pleasurable little interlude with the girl than feel guilty about Bella's rings. Charlie's smile broadened at the memory of her.

She'd been a knowing one and no mistake. Pity that messenger had come along just as things had been getting hot. Charlie liked sexually aware girls who understood the score and who knew that a man like him simply wanted a bit of fun with no strings attached. Of course, girls like that would be off limits for him once he and Daphne were married. And getting married would bring him plenty of compensations to set against the fun he'd be missing out on. He'd be out of uniform, for one thing, and his own boss, well more or less, but Charlie reckoned his father would be willing to give him a lot more authority and leeway than he had done before, and if the prospect of sex with Daphne wasn't particularly exciting then so what? Marriage wasn't about exciting sex. Charlie only had to look at his own parents to know that.

He'd got a lot to look forward to, including the

fact that since Daphne was her parents' only child, ultimately a pretty decent inheritance from them when they died. Yes, all in all he had every right to feel pretty pleased with himself, Charlie decided happily.

NINETEEN

Thursday 1 May

'Nearly going home time, thank goodness. I'm whacked,' Carole complained, pushing her hair back from her face and leaning back in her chair to stretch her neck muscles, and then lifting her hair clear of the white collar of her pink and white striped shirtwaister dress.

It had been a warm sunny day and the late afternoon sunlight coming in through the windows showed the drowsy dance of the dust in the air.

'Thank goodness it will soon be the weekend. Me and Andy thought we might go and have a look at that dancing competition that's being held. Mind you, I reckon that two and six a ticket is a bit steep.'

'What dancing competition?' Katie asked.

Carole shook her head. 'You must have eyes only for your Luke if you haven't seen the posters for it. They're all over the place, and there's been an advertisement for it in the paper as well. You and Luke ought to enter; I reckon the pair of you would have a good chance of winning.'

Katie smiled obediently, but it wasn't easy. Things had been very tense between her and Luke since the Easter weekend. Not that anything had been said by either of them, but Katie just knew that Luke somehow blamed her for the motorcyclist having stopped, whilst she still felt desperately hurt that he so obviously didn't trust her after the way they had been together and the promises they had made one another.

Carole yawned. 'I'll be ever so glad for a bit of a lie-in as well. I overslept this morning, and of course Frosty caught me coming in late. I reckon she was hanging round hoping to catch me out.'

The supervisor probably had been, Katie acknowledged. 'You really must be careful,' she warned Carole worriedly.

Carole laughed and shrugged dismissively. 'I know she's got it in for me, but I reckon she won't do anything.'

Katie certainly hoped not. She liked Carole and would miss her bright and breezy company if she were to be dismissed.

She was looking forward to going home time herself today. She had been called into the supervisor's office earlier and given instructions to write another letter to the spy, using the code she had been given and keeping to the dance music theme he used, and she was already feeling anxious and worrying about bearing the responsibility for something so important.

She already had the beginnings of a headache, and felt hot and uncomfortable, despite the fact that she had caught her hair back from her face with a bandeau to match her royal-blue and white patterned skirt. Her short-sleeved white blouse, which had felt so crisp this morning, now felt tired and wilted – like her, Katie admitted, and having to wear her court shoes without stockings because of the rationing had resulted in an uncomfortable blister on her left heel. All the girls were wearing their summer clothes, filling the room with a riot of brightly patterned fabrics, which normally would have lifted Katie's spirits.

Was it wrong of her to wish that she hadn't seen that coded letter and recognised what it was?

Whatever she wrote would be checked, of course, but whilst the code could be checked she was the one who knew the most about the actual musicians and dances that formed such a vital part of it and if she got that wrong then it could alert the spy to the fact that he had been found out and was now being fed useless information.

Katie knew that she wouldn't be seeing Luke this weekend and she was both disappointed and relieved.

'I dare say them twin sisters of your Luke's will be entering the dance competition,' Carole remarked.

'They wouldn't be allowed to,' Katie told her. 'Their dad is very strict about things like that, and they are only fifteen. Mind you, I'm surprised that they haven't said anything about it, or tried to get permission to give it a go.'

'Perhaps they have but you was too busy with their big brother to notice,' Carole teased her.

Katie managed a stilted laugh but her eyes were stinging with tears. It had been a week since she had last seen Luke, and then only briefly when he had dashed home to explain that he'd volunteered for extra duty so that one of the other corporals could have leave to go home to Shrewsbury to see his wife and their new baby.

At Jean's insistence Katie had gone to the door with him but the brief kiss they had exchanged hadn't really done anything to ease her misery. It had even occurred to her that Luke might have deliberately tried to pick a quarrel with her because he had changed his mind about her. In the cold light of day, had her behaviour the previous night put him off her? Had he decided that she was too fast perhaps? The kind of girl he couldn't trust because she had allowed him such intimacies?

She would never know, Katie admitted, because Luke obviously wasn't going to tell her and she certainly wasn't going to ask him.

Charlie looked at the letter. There was no need for him to read it again. He had already read it twice and his heart was still thudding in fast heavy beats with a mixture of fear and anger.

Dougie had written to him to tell him that two of the rings he had given him were worthless, and that if Charlie knew what was good for him he would make up the difference between what Dougie had got for the remaining ring – a mere twenty pounds, he claimed – and the hundred pounds he had demanded originally as the price of his silence, and by the coming weekend. Otherwise, Dougie would be paying a visit to Charlie's sister, to talk to her about her engagement ring, and writing a letter to Charlie's fiancée and her father.

'Hellfire and damnation,' Charlie swore savagely. Now he was going to have to drive up to Liverpool or risk Dougie making good his threat. Not that Charlie was convinced that Dougie was telling him the truth about the rings. More likely he was after more money, but Charlie couldn't afford to call his bluff. He could insist, though, that he and Dougie went together to have the rings valued. But if they did turn out to be duds, what then?

Charlie looked out through the window of the rough-and-ready corrugated iron hut where he was standing, one of many that served the camp. Across from it he could see the officers' mess. He'd already been approached by a still-wet-behind-the-ears newly commissioned captain, who wanted to buy his car from him.

Charlie's scarlet MG roadster was his pride and joy, but not so much so that it meant more to him that his future. He needed the MG to drive up to Liverpool to see Dougie, but Charlie was pretty confident that the young captain would give him a deposit on the car. He could use that to pay off Dougie, get back to camp, hand the car over to the captain and collect the rest of the money, and then he'd just have to convince his father that the car had gone AWOL – 'borrowed' by one of the other men and smashed up.

With him due to go before a medical board for assessment of his back injury, followed, with luck, by his dismissal from the army as medically unfit, his mother would soon see to it that his father got him another car. He'd need it for work and, of course, for seeing Daphne, and the old man could certainly afford to buy him one with the money he was raking in from his military contracts, if all the boasting he'd done to Charlie was to be believed.

Charlie screwed up Dougie's letter and tossed it into the small stove that served to heat the hut. Just as well he'd got some leave to use up, and who knew, he might even have time to pay a call on that willing little brunette.

'You're taking a bit of a risk, aren't you?'

Bella frowned at Laura's words.

The crèche had opened earlier in the week and already they were being begged to find extra places by desperate mothers.

To Bella's own astonishment, instead of being irritated by the children as she had expected to be, she had been surprised to realise just how much she enjoyed having to help out when the nursery nurses were busy. The children made her laugh, with their quaint little sayings, and she adored the fact that they told her that she was pretty. One of the senior nursery nurses had even grudgingly told her that she had a 'way with the little ones'. It was the babies who drew her the most, though, although she resented her own unwanted feelings, and tried to keep away from them. Sometimes she found that she was standing looking down into one of the cots at a sleeping baby without knowing how or why she had got there, and, even worse, battling against a longing to pick the baby up and hold it tightly.

Bella didn't like having feelings she couldn't understand. Far better to pretend that they simply did not exist than to dwell on them.

'What do you mean?' she asked Laura.

'I mean you going out and having dinner with a married man.'

'I haven't been out with any married man,' Bella denied.

'That's not what I've heard,' Laura insisted, adding sharply, 'In fact, Bella, I think I ought to warn you that the person who saw you – one of our mothers – made the point that she wasn't very happy about the thought of her children being in a crèche where there was a husband-stealer around. She said that it lowered the tone and that other women would think twice about leaving their children here if they thought the crèche was employing the kind of women who thought nothing of breaking up marriages.'

'The only person I've been out with is a personal friend, and I can tell you that he most certainly is not married,' Bella defended herself and her relationship with Commander Fleming. She had been thrilled when he had telephoned her three days after their initial meeting to ask her out to dinner the following weekend. A man who rang midweek to secure a weekend date had to be keen.

As he was a commander, Bella had half expected that he would take her to one of Liverpool's exclusive officers' clubs but instead he had taken her into the country again, this time to a small hotel. There had been other diners there, of course, but the gardens had been very private – and dark – when they had gone out into them to 'walk off' their meal.

She had permitted Ralph to kiss her but nothing more, even removing his hand from her breast when he had placed it there. He hadn't objected or said anything, but the smile he had given her when he had lit them each a cigarette had told Bella that he wasn't going to give up and that he fully intended to seduce her into giving in. A man who wanted her . . . Really wanted her, not like Alan, who had just used her and then turned his back on her, or Jan, who hadn't wanted her at all, and who had then been so very unkind and untruthful about her.

Bella had spent the days since their dinner date basking in the pleasure it gave her to know that a sophisticated man like Ralph wanted her. No one was going to take that away from her and certainly not some stupid woman who mistakenly thought that Ralph was married.

'Bella . . .' There was a new note in Laura's voice, and a look of concern in her eyes that offended Bella's pride. 'Look, it's none of my business, I know—'

'No, it isn't,' Bella agreed sharply.

'But are you sure that this chap you're seeing really isn't married?' Laura asked her. 'Only I know that there are some men about who are using the war as an excuse to, well, get what they want with no strings, if you know what I mean, and that they don't mind lying about being single to get it.'

'You don't really think I'm stupid enough to be taken in by that sort, do you?' Bella challenged her scornfully. 'I have been married, you know, and widowed. I dare say this woman, whoever she is, thinks that Ralph is married because she's seen him with his sister.'

'Oh, he's got a sister?'

'Yes.'

'Have you met her yet?'

'No,' Bella told Laura defensively. 'Why should I have done? We've only been out for dinner, that's all. He just happened to mention her to me.'

It just wasn't possible that Ralph could have lied to her. She would have known. And she had asked, hadn't she? He had said straight off when she had referred to him having a wife that he wasn't married. He was taking her out to dinner again on Saturday and this time he'd suggested that since the hotel he wanted to take her to was a fair distance away, they stay overnight, and she had agreed.

Of course he would be booking two separate rooms, and she would tell him too about that stupid woman who was spreading rumours about him being married.

He had upset Katie, Luke knew. But it was only natural for a chap to want to protect his girl from the attentions of other men. Luke certainly didn't think there was anything wrong in him doing that. He was aware, though, that he needed to do something to put things right between them and show Katie how much she meant to him. If he had been angry then it had only been because he wanted to protect her – and their relationship, he mentally defended his own behaviour. That he might have overreacted and be guilty of an unacceptable level of jealousy was something that the stubborn streak in his nature wouldn't allow him to consider.

Instead he had looked around for a way of showing Katie his love, and when he felt he had found one he had been like a dog with two tails.

Now he couldn't wait to tell Katie about the treat he was planning for her. It hadn't been easy wangling another weekend off so soon after Easter, but somehow he'd managed it. Today he'd managed to grab a few hours to catch the ferry from Seacombe to Liverpool; hurry up through the town, walking at top speed, covering the distance in less than half an hour, just so that he could lay his 'gift' before Katie and see her excited delight when she learned that he was taking her to London to see her parents. She never said anything, but he knew that she must be missing them, and besides, it was only right that he should introduce himself to them and ask her dad for his permission to court her properly.

He whistled happily, enjoying the extra hours of daylight and the early evening sunshine, as he walked up to his parents' back door. His dad would be down at his allotment, and Luke decided that he would go down there after he had seen Katie and have a few words with him.

'Luke!' his mother exclaimed happily when he walked into the kitchen. 'We weren't expecting you.'

After he had returned her hug Luke asked, 'Is Katie in?'

She would be, of course – he knew that – and he hadn't come home without saying anything to check up on her or anything like that, he reassured himself.

'Yes, she's upstairs in her room. Luke . . .' Jean protested as he headed for the hallway.

'It's all right, Mum, I'm not planning to do anything I shouldn't,' he teased her. 'It's just that I've got something special to tell her.'

Jean sighed as she heard him running up the stairs. She supposed she should have stopped him – her own mother would certainly never have allowed Sam to go upstairs into her bedroom – but times had changed and these young people now lived a very different kind of life to the one she and Sam had lived. Besides, it was Luke's home and she was down here in the kitchen and Katie was not the sort to misbehave or allow a young man to do so with her.

Katie had been struggling for the last half an hour with her letter. The sun streaming in through the window was distracting her, tempting her to go outside, but of course she couldn't. Katie was tidy by nature, and the court shoes she had worn for work were now placed side by side next to the wardrobe with shoe trees inside them, waiting for her to clean them ready for the morning, the silk coverlet on her bed neat and straight just like the rag rugs either side of it, and the toiletries on the glass-topped dressing table.

Her desk was under the window and she looked

out of it longingly, and then made herself look back down at her letter.

She had started off all right with her 'Dearest Peter', and the first sentence, writing as she had been instructed,

I long to be in your arms as much as you say you long to be in mine, especially dancing to our favourite band, the Orpheans, although I have heard that they will be moving out of London early in May to play at a new venue in Yorkshire. As yet I haven't heard who will take their place but I shall let you know as soon as I do.

Katie had guessed that the Opheans was a code name for someone or several people very high up in the British Government, and that the move out of London she was to refer to was intended to fool the enemy into thinking that this person or persons would be leaving the capital.

She looked up as the door to her bedroom suddenly opened.

Luke! She looked at him in consternation. It had been stressed to her that no one other than her supervisor must know what she was doing or see a letter. Quickly she pushed it underneath her writing paper but it was too late, Luke had seen her, and now he was frowning and pushing the door closed, before coming over to the dressing table to demand, 'Who are you writing to?'

'No one. I mean my father.'

She was lying to him, Luke knew. A sick feeling

of mixed anger and despair was churning his stomach and tearing at his heart.

'Let me see.'

'No. No, Luke, you mustn't,' Katie protested, but Luke had already removed the writing pad and seen the letter.

Katie felt sick with guilt. She had been told not to let anyone know what she was doing as a matter of national security.

Luke picked up the letter and read out loud, '"Dearest Peter . . ." "Dearest *Peter*" . . . ?'

Katie stared at him. Luke thought that she was writing a love letter to someone else! In her anxiety over the security aspect of what she was doing she had completely overlooked the fact that Luke might completely misinterpret the purpose of the letter.

'Who is he?'

'Luke, please, it isn't what you think.'

'Of course it's what I think. It's all there in black and white. "Dearest Peter".'

His face had gone bone white, his blue eyes so dark they were almost black. Katie flinched back from his furious anger almost as though it was a physical blow.

'I might have known. In fact, I did know,' Luke stormed at her, 'but I wouldn't listen to my own good sense. Something told me all along that I couldn't trust you.'

He was being so cruel and so unfair. Katie felt shocked as well as hurt and dismayed. Surely he knew she would never ever give her love to anyone else?

'Luke, it isn't what you think,' she repeated. 'I

can't explain but please believe me when I say that I love you and only you.' Surely he must believe her. She would have believed him. 'Please trust me, Luke,' she begged him. 'I would trust you if our positions were reversed.'

'Trust you? You're the last person I'd trust now,' Luke told her bitterly. 'Here,' he threw a piece of paper towards her, 'you might as well use these to take your *Dearest Peter* to London to see your parents. Or do they know him already? Better than me, is he? Someone posh and not in uniform? Well, he's welcome to you, 'cos I don't want you now.'

He was gone before she could say another word, leaving her feeling sick with distress and hurt.

Jean, who had heard the raised voices, looked at Luke worriedly as he came storming into the kitchen.

'Luke, what's happened?'

'Not now, Ma . . .' he told her, brusquely pulling open the back door, gone before she could stop him.

Jean looked at the still open kitchen door. There was silence now from upstairs. The twins were out at the pictures and Sam was down at his allotment. She waited half an hour and then, when there was still no sign of Katie, she put on the kettle.

'I've brought you a cup of tea.'

Katie's red-rimmed eyes and pale set face showed her feelings.

'All young couples have words now and then, Katie love,' Jean tried to comfort her, but Katie shook her head, tears spilling from her eyes.

'This wasn't just words,' she told Jean, and then compressed her mouth against her tears.

'Oh, Katie love,' Jean protested, her maternal feelings overwhelming her as she sat down on the bed beside her and put her arms around her. 'Luke will come round,' she tried to comfort Katie. 'It's just a lovers' tiff, that's all. You'll make it up.'

Katie shook her head. 'I won't come down for supper tonight, if you don't mind, Jean,' she said woodenly. 'In fact I think I'll have an early night.'

She couldn't explain to Jean what had happened and she feared that when Luke did tell his mother about the letter she was bound to think the same thing as Luke had done. Jean was Luke's mother, after all, and he her only son and favourite child, so she couldn't blame her.

Jean nodded. Poor girl, and poor Luke too. Lovers' quarrels were so painful in the early stages of a relationship.

Jean reached the kitchen just as Sam came in.

'Luke and Katie have had a bit of an upset,' she told him ruefully. 'Katie's upstairs in her room, crying her eyes out, and our Luke's gone back to camp.'

Sam gave a small grunt in acknowledgement of what she had said as he washed his hands under the kitchen tap, careful not to use more than one rub of the small sliver of soap Jean had instructed everyone had to last for at least another week.

'They'll make it up, of course.'

'What was it about?' Sam asked her, drying his hands on the towel attached to the wooden roller he had made himself.

'I don't know, and I didn't like to ask.'

Sam grunted again and then informed her, 'Toms are coming on well, and with any luck the early lettuce should be ready in a couple of weeks.'

'I'll be glad to have a bit of salad stuff again,' Jean told him as she set about getting their supper ready. Sam never talked about feelings – his own or those of anyone else.

Upstairs Katie stared at her bedroom wall, engulfed by her unhappiness.

If Luke really loved her he would have listened to her. He would have let her say that it wasn't what he thought but that she couldn't say any more. He would have remembered her work then and guessed surely, as she would have done if their positions had been reversed, that the letter must be something to do with that work. He would then have said to her, as she would have done to him, 'Is it your work?' and she would have said, 'Yes.'

After all, when you loved someone it was their behaviour towards you on which you judged them and their love, and she had shown Luke nothing but love.

After Jean had gone back downstairs Katie had gone into the bathroom to wash her face and compose herself before the twins got back and started asking questions.

Now in her bedroom she sat on the bed. Jean had referred to what had happened as a lovers' tiff that would be made up and forgotten, but Katie couldn't see it like that. The truth was that Luke couldn't see her, the person she really was,

397

because of the feelings Lillian's betrayal of him had caused. If Luke knew her then he wouldn't need to suspect her because he would know that she wasn't the sort of person who would give her love to one man whilst she was involved with another. And if Luke didn't know her, then how could he really love her?

Katie heard the twins come in and then the sound of voices from the kitchen. Katie could visualise Jean giving the twins and Sam their suppers, but her own stomach churned sickly at the mere thought of food, never mind having to face Luke's family. Jean was bound to have told them what had happened.

She really ought to get ready for bed, Katie acknowledged, but she knew already that she wouldn't be able to sleep.

She could hear the twins coming upstairs, but for once they didn't pause on the landing to speak to her, continuing instead straight up to their own attic room.

It was over between her and Luke, Katie told herself bleakly. How could it not be?

She couldn't stay here now at the Campions'. It would be too painful for her and too uncomfortable for Luke's family, and for Jean most of all. Was there a procedure in place for when a person wanted to change their billet, Katie wondered drearily. Would she have to explain? Would—

The sudden urgent wail of the air-raid alarm cut through her thoughts. Her reactions, honed now by previous air raids, had her moving automatically to collect what she would need, and then heading for the stairs just ahead of the twins, who were hurrying down from their room, as Jean called up anxiously from the kitchen.

Sam shepherded them all out of the house and onto the street to join everyone else hurrying towards the shelter. The night sky was crisscrossed with the powerful arcs of searchlights from the city's defences, the low thrumming noise of the incoming planes growing louder by the second.

A volley of anti-aircraft fire from the gun batteries, followed by an explosion, thankfully not close at hand, had them all running faster for the shelter.

'Be careful, won't you, Sam?' Jean implored before she followed the twins and Katie into the shelter, knowing that her husband couldn't join them in the shelter as he had to attend to his duties as an ARP warden, which meant, amongst other things, checking that everyone was safely in the shelter, and then checking the houses themselves for anyone who for any reason had not headed for the shelter.

'I was hoping that we'd seen the last of this, now that we've got double summer time,' one woman complained grumpily as she settled herself on the side of one of the bunk beds. The air-raid siren had obviously woken her from her sleep, because she was wearing her dressing gown and her hair was in rag curlers.

The door to the shelter had been closed now but they could still hear the sound of the anti-aircraft guns and the bombs exploding.

'Sounds like they're after the docks again,' one

of the men commented, and automatically they all tensed and listened in silence whilst outside incendiary bombs rained down from the sky and the anti-aircraft battery waged war against those who were dropping them.

The air-raid shelter was barely big enough to house everyone, which meant that families had to sit cheek by cheek with one another, so to speak, the younger children put to bed in the upper tier of bunks whilst the adults crouched on the bunk beds below. Seated next to Jean and her family were the Whites from number eighteen, an elderly childless couple.

Just as she sat down Nancy White complained to her husband, 'Bert, I've gorn and left me false teeth behind.'

'Never mind, love,' he comforted her. 'It's bombs they're dropping, not ham sandwiches.'

Jean laughed dutifully at the now well-worn joke, but she noticed that neither Katie nor the twins joined her.

'There'd better not be any bombs on Saturday night,' Lou whispered fiercely to Sasha.

'Well, even if there are, it won't matter because we'll have to be back home before it gets dark. You know what Mum's like. Kieran says he's going to put us on halfway through to make sure that there's plenty of people there to clap for us, and so that we can leave before it gets too late.'

'When did he tell you that?' Lou demanded jealously.

'On Monday when he came into Lewis's. You were serving someone, remember?'

'I remember that you were so keen to talk to him that you went off and left me to serve your customer,' Lou agreed bitterly.

'No, I didn't. I didn't think she wanted anything, that's all. We've got to win this competition, Lou. Just imagine us being on stage in a real production. Kieran says that his uncle is going to be one of the judges, and the leading lady of the Royal Court's current production another, and they've got a pair of real professional dancers coming over especially from the Tower Ballroom at Blackpool to make up the judges.'

'Well, Kieran might have told you when we were going on, but it was me he told about our costumes,' Lou told Sasha triumphantly. She was the younger of the two of them, and she didn't like the way that Sasha, who was becoming very bossy, always claimed that she was the one whom Kieran preferred.

The pounding the anti-aircraft guns were giving the German bombers reflected the fury in his own heart, Luke acknowledged. How could he have let himself be made a fool of a second time? But then hadn't a part of him suspected all along that something like this would happen, he thought bitterly.

Orange glows from the fires started by the falling bombs had lit up the night sky, when Luke had been on patrol on the perimeters of the camp, the scream of fire engine sirens mingling with the explosions and the anti-aircraft guns. It was the job of him and his men to be ready for action if they were needed in the defence of the city, and the whole camp was on the alert following several rumours that the Germans weren't just dropping bombs but that they were dropping parachutists as well, with instructions to work from behind the English enemy lines.

The air in their hut was thick with cigarette smoke and gun oil as some men sat smoking and playing cards, whilst others read, and some cleaned their guns.

Although the men looked relaxed, you could almost feel the tension of their coiled ready-for-action muscles and minds.

'It isn't what you think,' Katie had told him. Luke's mouth twisted with bitterness.

He hadn't needed to think anything, he had seen the evidence of her betrayal with his own eyes. 'Dearest Peter.' He could feel his emotions slipping out of control. There was a war on, he reminded himself, and he had his men to think of. They were more important than his feelings.

TWENTY

Friday 2 May

'Oh, Seb, I'm so pleased you're here.' Grace was out of breath from having walked – not run because nurses were not allowed to run in hospitals in case it panicked the patients – so very fast down to the foyer of Mill Road Hospital, where she was doing her nurse's training. 'Hannah saw you as she came on duty and told me that you were here.'

Hannah Philips had been in Grace's set when they had first started their training and they had remained friends. Hannah worked in the operating theatre as a surgery nurse.

'I just wanted to check that you were OK after last night's bombs,' Seb told her, helping her on with her cloak as they hurried outside for a few minutes in the warmth of the late morning sun.

The courtyard outside the hospital exit was busy with ambulances, and hospital staff and patients coming and going, the number of 'walking wounded'

403

patients more evidence if any was needed of the Luftwaffe's assault on the city.

Grace and Seb had been engaged for long enough now to know all the small private corners close to the hospital and the nurses' home where they could sneak a few minutes' privacy without breaking any of the rules. They fell into step together in that way that established couples do, each moving close to the other, Seb bending his head to smile at Grace with so much love in his eyes that she stopped walking, her breath catching as she reached up and placed her hand on his uniform-covered chest.

Seb had been working flat out for the last week as part of a team trying to break the code on certain Luftwaffe communications. The building where he worked – Derby House – was the Headquarters for the Air and Sea Western Approaches Defence control hierarchy. Churchill himself was sometimes there, and the building was impregnable, but of course that did not stop him worrying about Grace and her family when the city was being bombed.

He was very lucky to have a fiancée like Grace, someone who loved him as much as he did her and as passionately, but who at the same time understood that the nature of his job was such that at times he could not discuss his work with her.

In his heart of hearts, Seb feared that Luke, much as he liked him, would not be as understanding with Katie. Luke had been badly treated in love, and Seb suspected that that would make it very difficult for him to trust a girl, especially when he loved her.

They rounded the corner of the building and slipped into the shadows, turning to one another to exchange a hungry passionate kiss, and then another.

'I was worried about you,' Seb told Grace gruffly, holding her close. 'That's the damnable thing about war. My place should be with you, protecting you, but wearing this uniform means that I can't be.'

'Well, I'm very proud of you wearing your uniform,' Grace assured him, adding practically, 'And I've to do my own bit as well, up here at the hospital. I'm all right and but I'll tell you who isn't.' She gave a small shake of her head. 'Our Luke and Katie. Mum came to see me first thing, and told me about it. She said that Katie and Luke had a row last night and that Luke stormed off and Katie was too upset to tell her what had happened. It's such a shame when they're so perfect for one another.'

Seb knew Grace, so he told her firmly, 'We can't interfere, Grace.'

'Well, no, of course not,' Grace agreed mock innocently, putting her hand on his arm as she pleaded, 'But I was thinking that perhaps you could have a word with Luke, Seb – you know, man to man – and find out what's gone wrong. Mum thinks it might have something to do with Lillian and how she was with him and, like she says, that isn't fair to poor Katie, who's been breaking her heart, according to Mum. I feel ever so guilty, you know, seeing as it was me that was responsible for Luke meeting Lillian in the first place.'

Seb gave his fiancée a rueful look. He knew

when he was beaten and, besides, there wasn't much he wouldn't do to keep his Grace happy. Having come so close to losing her had made her all the more precious to him.

'I'll try,' he promised. 'But don't be surprised if Luke tells me to mind my own business, will you?'

Grace's grateful hug had him hugging her back, and then they were kissing again and so thoroughly that it was several minutes before Grace could bring her mind back to her brother's falling-out with Katie.

'I do hope they make it up. We all like Katie so much that it's as though she's part of the family already.'

'You can't expect Luke to marry a girl just because his family like her,' Seb pointed out, but he knew he was wasting his breath. Luke's mother and sister had plainly made their minds up that Katie was the girl for Luke, and if he was honest with himself Seb didn't blame them. It was as plain as the nose on his own face that she was a really decent sort, honest and steadfast, and loyal too.

'I'd better go,' Grace told him regretfully. 'Sister wants us moving beds round to make room in case the Luftwaffe come back again tonight. Mum said that Dad told her there are still fires burning from last night that haven't been put out.' She looked up at the sky and shivered. 'When will it all end, Seb?'

'I don't know, love,' he told her truthfully,

There was just time for them to share another kiss, each of them reluctant to let the other go, before they had to step out of the shadows and walk back to the hospital, Seb drawing Grace to one side so that he could tuck a stray curl neatly under her cap. The May sunshine burnished the gold of her strawberry-blonde hair and brushed the perfection of her peaches-and-cream complexion. She was everything he could ever want, his Grace, Seb acknowledged, and beautiful inside and out.

They had vowed together that for the duration of Grace's three-year training they would do their duty and put any thoughts of marriage out of their minds, but sometimes knowing how long it would be before he could finally make her his was hard for Seb to bear.

'Them bombers last night was just what I needed, I don't think,' said Carole pithily as she and Katie stood in the canteen queue waiting to get their lunch.

'At least we got the all clear at one o'clock so I managed to get a few hours' sleep in me own bed. Are you all right?' she asked Katie. 'Only you've hardly said a word all morning. I know you had to go and see the supervisor first thing.'

'Yes,' Katie agreed. In fact the supervisor had been very kind and understanding, especially when Katie's emotions had got the better of her and she had started to cry. After the supervisor had coaxed the whole story of the previous night's quarrel with Luke out of her, she had even praised Katie for not giving in to any temptation to tell Luke what she had really been doing.

'You're not in some kind of trouble, are you?'

Carole demanded protectively. ''Cos if you are and I can help . . .'

To her own consternation Katie knew that her eyes had filled with tears. After one look at her, Carole told her firmly, 'Look, there's an empty table over there, you go and sit down and I'll get us dinners.'

By the time Carole was putting her tray down on the table, Katie had managed to get her emotions back under control.

'I've got you shepherd's pie,' Carole told her, 'but you'd better not start crying into it 'cos it's watery enough as it is.'

Her comment forced a reluctant laugh from Katie.

'Come on then,' Carole demanded once she was sitting down, 'tell Auntie Carole what's to do. Then you'll feel better.'

There was no point in refusing, Katie recognised, and besides, with Carole going out with Andy she was bound to find out anyway.

'It's me and Luke,' she told her. 'It's over between us.'

'. . . and the thing is,' Katie finished miserably after she had told Carole as much about what had happened as she felt she could, 'now I'm going to have to find somewhere else to live because I can't stay on with Luke's parents now.'

'Well if it will help I dare say you can share with me at my auntie's whilst you're looking for somewhere,' Carole offered generously. 'It will mean the two of us sharing a double bed, mind.'

'I don't mind that,' Katie told her gratefully, 'but what about your aunt? You'll have to ask her if it's all right.'

'I'm sure it will be, but if you can hang on until after the weekend that will give me time to sort things out with her.'

'Thanks, Carole,' Katie said gratefully.

Outside the sun was shining and the air was warm with the promise of the summer to come, but Katie's heart felt as chilled as though it were the middle of winter.

'Grace asked me to come and see you. She's heard about you and Katie breaking things off.'

Seb removed his cigarettes from his pocket and offered Luke one, but Luke shook his head.

Seb had used some of his precious hours of leave to get the ferry over to Seacombe and the barracks in order to keep his promise to Grace to talk to Luke. They were in the camp Naafi, sitting either side of a small table, the two cups of tea Seb had bought untouched.

Fortunately the place was relatively empty, apart from a steady stream of men coming in to buy cigarettes, and a group of men from one of the Bomb Disposal Units lounging round a table on the other side of the concrete block building.

The Naafi building was a brisk walk from the parade ground, and close to the command post, its walls covered with the usual posters advertising cigarettes and spirits, jostling for space with Government notices and stark warnings about the dangers of having unprotected sex.

It had a smell that was, Seb expected, familiar to British servicemen everywhere: a combination of damp khaki – no matter what the time of year or the kind of weather – crossed with tannin from the tea, cigarette smoke, stale air, male sweat and testosterone. It forced itself aggressively and pungently on the nostrils, and added to the gloom of a building with one small north-facing window. Inside here you'd never know that there was sunshine outside.

'She's worried about you,' Seb told Luke, adding when Luke still didn't say anything, 'She thinks it's because of Lillian and she feels guilty because she introduced you to her.'

'Grace didn't introduce me to Katie, and it's her that's gone and made a fool of me, letting me think it was me and her when all the time she's bin writing to someone else, and not the kind of letters you write to your brother neither,' Luke told Seb harshly.

Seb frowned. Katie hadn't struck him as that type at all. She'd seemed a thoroughly straightforward, decent sort of girl.

'Who told you she's been writing to someone else?' he asked.

'No one,' Luke answered him. 'I saw the letter for myself. Oh, she tried to hide it from me and acted all upset, like it was me that was in the wrong, saying that I didn't understand.'

Seb frowned. 'Well, it's not for me to say, Luke, but Katie didn't strike me as the kind of girl who'd tell a chap she cared about him unless she meant it. And it seems to me that if she was involved with someone else then she would have said so right from the start, before you and her started being an item.' Seb hesitated. He didn't know the circumstances and he didn't want to say the wrong thing, but he had spoken the truth when he had told Luke that Katie hadn't struck him as the deceitful type.

Now it was Luke's turn to frown. He respected Seb, and Seb's words carried a weight and an authority Luke couldn't ignore.

'It makes no sense that she would get involved with you if she was already involved with someone else,' Seb pressed home. 'Anyone can see that she's not the type who'd want to play one chap off against another.'

'You can say that, but you didn't see the letter calling him her "Dearest Peter" and saying that she wanted to go dancing with him to some band or other. She certainly kept quiet about him. Never said so much as a word.'

'But she must have had letters from him and if she did your mother must have seen them,' Seb pointed out. 'Then your mother would have known that she was involved with someone else, wouldn't she?'

Luke looked at him. He hadn't thought of that, but of course Seb was right, and Luke remembered now his mother making some mention of the fact that the only letters Katie ever received were from her parents.

'When me and Grace started courting we had a bit of a talk and I told her then that because of my work there'd be things I couldn't share with

411

her,' Seb continued. 'Katie's working in a similar line to me, and it strikes me, Luke, that there could be a different explanation to this letter from the one you're thinking, and that it might have something to do with Katie's work.'

'Well, if that's the case then why didn't Katie say so? Why didn't she explain?'

'She can't, Luke, just like I can't discuss my work with Grace.'

Seb could see that Luke didn't like what he was hearing.

'It seems a bit of a rum do to me, getting a girl to write love letters to another chap behind her own chap's back,' he complained.

'She can't discuss her work with you, Luke, but there's nothing to stop you from asking her if the letter you saw had something to do with it and that you understand that she can't say any more than "yes" or "no". It wouldn't be fair of a chap to start badgering a girl when he knows she's doing her bit for the country.'

The last thing Seb wanted was to provoke Luke into upsetting Katie with lots of questions she wouldn't be able to answer.

'When a couple become an item,' he continued carefully, 'I reckon they have to sit down together and lay their cards on the table, tell one another what's what and make a promise that they'll always be honest with one another and trust one another. I reckon Katie's the sort a chap can trust, if she's given him that promise. And you know what, Luke, I reckon that a chap who gets jealous and starts accusing a girl who loves him of things she hasn't done, because of some other girl who let him down, is a fool to himself,' Seb finished warningly. 'If you do love her, Luke, then don't risk losing her. Life's too short, and Katie's no Lillian.'

It was over an hour since Seb had left, but Luke couldn't get his warning out of his head.

'You don't understand,' Katie had told him. What if that was the truth? But what was there to understand? He had seen the letter, after all, and he wasn't going to be taken for a fool by a woman a second time.

Luke lit a cigarette and drew the smoke deep into his lungs. He didn't know what to think now. But he did know how he felt, didn't he? There hadn't been a moment since their quarrel when Katie hadn't been in his thoughts or when he hadn't ached with misery over her.

He couldn't for the life of him think of any logical explanation for what he had seen, but maybe he should hear from her own lips what it was exactly that he 'didn't understand'. He crushed out his cigarette. It was going to be a long night with no chance for him to see Katie until tomorrow.

TWENTY-ONE

With the money he'd taken off the captain as a deposit on his car in his pocket, a clever plan hatched to explain away its disappearance and get a new car out of his father, along with his elevation to his father's good books for coming home to discuss with him exactly what he should say and do when he went before the Medical Board prior to being – he hoped – discharged, Charlie was feeling confident that dealing with Dougie would be, as he had put it to himself, 'a piece of cake'.

He'd been a bit late setting out for the pub where Dougie had told him to bring the money he still 'owed' him, because his mother had insisted on regaling him with a dramatic account of the bomb damage Wallasey had suffered in the previous night's raid.

'That's nothing to what they've had in London,' Charlie had been unwise enough to point out at one stage, but eventually he'd been able to get away – supposedly to see the family of a fellow soldier who had been injured in an exercise and assure them that their son was all right.

'There you are, Edwin,' his mother had beamed when Charlie had relayed this piece of fiction to his parents. 'Just look how the other men are turning to Charlie for help and advice. I've always said that he's a born leader. Just like you.'

His father had grunted in response but Charlie reckoned that his mother's praise must be worth at least a fiver extra a week in his wages once he started working again for his father.

'Your father's had a bad week at the office, haven't you, Edwin?' she had told Charlie. 'It's this new accounts clerk he's had to take on. A woman – and you know how your father feels about women in business. He doesn't approve of it at all, do you, Edwin?'

His father's only response had been a warning rustle of the newspaper he was reading and a third grunt.

The clear brilliance of the evening sky, with the moon already on the rise suggested that it wasn't going to be the kind of night when you needed a torch, Charlie decided, as he stepped off the ferry along with the other passengers, and then headed down towards the tangle of narrow streets that led deeper and deeper into the slums.

On one street corner a fire was still burning sullenly from the previous night's bombing, despite the fire service's attempts to put it out. Thin, grubby-looking gangs of boys in patched hand-me-down clothes were going purposefully through the wreckage whilst one of their number stood on guard.

''Ere, soldier,' one of them called out to Charlie in a nasal whine. 'Give us a fag, will yer?'

Charlie was tempted to ignore him. He hadn't wanted to come down here wearing his uniform, but seeing as he was supposed to be on a semi-official visit to the home of a fellow soldier, he had felt he hadn't had any choice. If he ignored the kids there was no saying that they might not take revenge by throwing a few bricks at him, but if he did he could end up like the Pied Piper, with them seeing him as an easy touch and pestering him for more.

In the end he decided to play safe, taking a packet of cigarettes from his pocket, opening it to remove the cigarettes and then throwing them towards the boys, telling them with a grin, 'Here, help yourselves.'

It had been a pack of twenty, and by the time they had picked them all up, with any luck he'd be in the pub.

What he hadn't reckoned on was how full the pub would be, with it being a Friday night. The place was packed with dock workers relaxing after a hard week's work unloading freight from the convoys, and getting the ships ready to turn round as quickly as possible.

The sight of an unfamiliar face produced a sudden silence in the tap room, and as Charlie made his way to the bar he was conscious of an atmosphere that, if not entirely hostile, was certainly wary.

Telling the barman that he'd come to see Dougie,

he ordered himself a pint of shandy and gave a friendly nod to the other men standing at the bar.

None of them responded but the barman was already jerking his head in the direction of the door to one side of the bar, telling Charlie curtly, 'In there.'

Dougie wasn't on his own in the small snug, and neither was he smiling. He took out a packet of cigarettes as Charlie walked in, putting one to his mouth, his gaze never leaving Charlie's face as he snapped his fingers and one of the silent men standing with him leaped forward to light the cigarette for him.

He drew on it and then exhaled and then drew on it again, this time blowing a ring of smoke, which he watched ascend to the grimy ceiling before saying softly to Charlie, 'I'm not very pleased with you, Charlie boy. Thought it was clever, did you, passing off them dud rings on me?'

He jerked his head and two of the men standing with him moved towards Charlie to stand either side of him and grab hold of his arms.

'Answer the boss when he speaks to you, *Charlie*,' one of the men told Charlie, jerking his arm up his back.

Pain ripped through Charlie's muscles, fear beading his forehead with sweat.

'It was a mistake,' Charlie protested, gasping in agony as the pressure on his arm was increased.

'It certainly was,' Dougie agreed. 'A big mistake – for you.'

'Look, Dougie . . . Aaaagghhh . . .'

Charlie would have collapsed in agony if they

hadn't been holding him when one of the men doubled up his fist and thumped him in the stomach, warning him, 'It's Mr Richards to you, garbage.'

Charlie retched painfully, trying to drag air into his lungs.

'I've brought the rest of the money,' he managed to gasp out, desperate now to bring an end to what was happening and escape.

Another nod of Dougie's head had one of Charlie's captors going through the pockets of Charlie's khaki battledress jacket to remove his wallet, which he handed to Dougie, who went through it and, to Charlie's dismay, removed all the money from it, swiftly counting it.

'OK. Give him his wallet back,' Dougie instructed his heavies.

'There's damn-near a hundred and fifty quid there. I only owe you— Aaggghhhh.'

Before Charlie could finish his protest a fist smashed into him making him double up in agony again.

'Sorry, Charlie boy. Didn't I explain? There's the small matter of interest, and compensation now for all the trouble you've caused me, as well as the original debt.'

'But you can't—'

Too late to wish he hadn't said anything, Charlie recognised as he received another blow, this time to the side of his face, followed by another that had blood spurting from his nose and dropped him to the floor, fighting for breath and retching in agony.

The sound of the air-raid siren going off might have belonged to another world, for all that it meant to Charlie, but it certainly meant something to the other occupants of the room.

They looked towards Dougie in tense silence.

Lena winced and tried not to feel scared when she heard the air-raid siren sounding. She should have been in the shelter like everyone else in the street, but she was in disgrace, and so she had stayed behind when her aunt and uncle and her cousin had left earlier, her aunt ignoring her uncle's protests that there might not be any bombing, insisting that she wouldn't feel safe unless she was there and that she wanted to go early because she wasn't going to be beaten to the best places again by 'her from three down'.

All she'd done was try on her cousin's new skirt and top, bought for her by her merchant seaman boyfriend, Lena reflected miserably. To hear Doris shrieking you'd have thought she'd have stolen her boyfriend. 'Parading around in them like a trollop' had been Doris's exact words, when she had accused her, and then when Lena had pointed out spiritedly to her, 'Well, they're your clothes,' she had got a slapped face from her cousin, followed by the threat of her uncle's belt if she caused any more trouble.

She was supposed to have put up the blackout fabric on her bedroom window but she hadn't done and now she was so scared with being in the house on her own that she didn't want to.

*   *   *

419

Charlie had virtually been beaten unconscious when the air-raid siren went off.

Dougie, who had been watching the punishment being handed out, put out his cigarette and told his men, 'Time to get down to the cellar, lads.'

The cellars beneath the pub had turned out handy during air-raid alarms, since they saved the pub occupants from having to go into the shelter.

'What about him?' one of the men who had been hitting Charlie asked.

'Chuck him out in the street,' Dougie told him. 'With any luck Hitler will finish the job off for us.'

Lena didn't pay much attention at first when two men came out of the pub, dragging a third man between them. Everyone local knew all about Dougie and his gang, but then the whoosh of another explosion and the fire from it lit up the darkness and she saw the hurt man's face. It was *him*. Her hero. Not that he looked much like a hero now, Lena recognised.

The men had disappeared back into the pub, leaving him lying face down in the street. As Lena watched he tried to get up and then collapsed.

Lena ran downstairs and opened the front door. He was still there, trying to crawl now, and getting nowhere fast. She hurried over to him, coughing as she breathed in the acrid smoke billowing from a burning building in the next street, dodging the sudden hail of rubble as another bomb exploded close at hand.

At first when Charlie felt her hand on his arm he thought it was one of Dougie's men, come back to finish him off, and he tried to push her away, but Lena refused to let go.

'Come on, you've got to get up, otherwise we'll both be blown to bits,' she said fiercely.

A woman. Charlie turned his head to look at her – a moment of clarity amongst all the confusion and pain told him that her face was familiar, and very pretty.

'Hello again, beautiful.'

Lena beamed. It was just like in the love stories she read. 'Come on,' she urged him again.

Somehow or other Charlie managed to stagger to his feet. All he wanted to do was go to sleep, but the pretty girl was pestering him to walk, and it was easier to give in than to argue. He leaned against her, almost knocking her over with his weight, but Lena had seen her aunt help her uncle when he was drunk, and she knew what to do. Draping Charlie's arm around her shoulders she half coaxed and half dragged him down the street back to the house.

Another air raid, and she still hadn't had the courage to say anything to Jean yet about her leaving, Katie thought miserably as she listened to the drone of the incoming aircraft, surely far more than there had been the previous night.

The moonlight had been so bright when they had hurried down the street to the shelter that no one had needed a torch. A bomber's moon, people called such bright moonlight, meaning that the bombers would be able to find their targets far more easily – targets like the docks, and other places where they could do the most damage to the country's resources and its pride. Places such as the army camp at Seacombe? Katie shivered even though it was a mild night.

Was Carole right? Should she have tried harder to make Luke listen to her?

'You're too soft,' Carole had scoffed, 'waiting for him to "understand". Men aren't like that, and if you was to ask me I'd say that him being a bit jealous shows how much he cares about you. You should have sat him down and made him listen, instead of letting him go off. You love him, after all – anyone can see that. And if you want my opinion, sometimes a girl has to work that bit harder to make things right between them than a chap does. See, a chap's got his pride, hasn't he, and it's natural that he kicks up a bit when he thinks that a girl's making a fool of him, 'cos he's got to think of what his friends will think, whilst a girl knows that her friends will sympathise with her if a chap lets her down.'

Did Carole have a point? Carole was certainly far more pragmatic than she was herself, Katie admitted, and talking with her had certainly made Katie begin to question whether or not she was being silly to feel so hurt because Luke had been so quick to misjudge her and too angry to let her try to explain.

A volley of explosions so loud that they drowned out the sound of the incoming planes and the valiant retaliatory thud of the ack-ack gunfire shook the earth floor of the shelter, causing several indrawn breaths.

'No need to worry,' someone called out. 'They say you never hear the one that gets you.'

'Hitler's got it in for us with a vengeance tonight,' another voice chipped in.

'Come on, let's have a bit of a singsong, Dan,' Jean suggested, hiding her own fear beneath a cheery manner. 'You've got your accordion, haven't you?'

Very soon they were all singing 'Ten Green Bottles', and pretending that they couldn't hear the terror being rained down on the city.

Once she'd got him inside, Lena could see that he'd had a real old pasting, but she'd seen worse, living where she did. Her uncle liked a drink and had come back from a drinking session many a time bruised and battered after a falling-out with a mate.

As her auntie always said, with regard to Lena's uncle, a bit of blood went a long way and a bruise was better out than in, for all that it made him look like someone had knocked seven bells out of him.

Charlie, half concussed from the blows he'd received, not really aware of where he was or who he was with, bellowed loudly when Lena applied the cloth she'd soaked in cold water to his bloody face and nose, trying to push her away.

'The ruddy Luftwaffe won't have no problem finding this place if you keep carrying on like that,' Lena told him crossly. 'They'll be able to hear you in ruddy Hamburg.'

A woman's voice. Charlie tried to clear his head,

and then ducked automatically as he heard the whine and then the ear-splitting explosion as a bomb went off close at hand, quickly followed by another.

It crossed his mind that they should be in an air-raid shelter, but somehow he couldn't organise his thoughts properly. His head ached like the devil. He slumped forward in the chair that Lena had managed to push him into.

'You've got to keep your head back,' she told him sharply, 'so as I can clean you up a bit, and it will stop your nose bleeding as well. Made a right mess of your uniform, it has.'

Charlie put his hand up to his jacket and then stared as it came away red.

'Let's get it off you and I'll see if I can sponge it up a bit for you.'

It was easier to give in than object. The pain in his head was so intense that all he wanted to do was lie down and go to sleep.

Somehow Lena managed to drag the battledress jacket off Charlie's limp body. He hadn't moved or spoken since he'd yelled out when she'd started to clean him up. He was going to look a real mess when the bruising came out properly, she reckoned. His eye was already turning purple and there was a gash along his hairline, which luckily wasn't bleeding like his nose had.

Bombs were going off all around them but Lena didn't have time to worry about that. She was too busy trying to get her handsome soldier cleaned up and back on his feet. He wasn't being very helpful, but eventually she'd managed to get all the blood off him, and his nose stopped bleeding.

'Now I suppose you're going to want something to eat,' Lena told him, copying her auntie's favourite comment to her uncle.

But Charlie simply shook his head slowly and told her in a slurred voice, 'Bed. Tired. Want to lie down.'

He was getting up as he spoke, staggering around the kitchen even worse than her uncle did when he was drunk, and lurching into the wall, almost sending the table crashing over.

'Come on,' Lena told him briskly. 'Let's get you upstairs then.'

It took her five attempts, two of which ended up with them both lying in a tangle at the bottom of the stairs when Charlie had collapsed onto her, but eventually, scolding him and urging him whilst supporting him, Lena managed to get him onto the landing, and from there into her aunt and uncle's bedroom, where he clutched the iron bedstead, swaying.

'Bathroom. I need a pee.'

'Then you'll have to use this,' Lena told him exasperatedly, searching under the bed for the chamber pot, ''cos I ain't spending another hour taking you back down them stairs. The lavvy's outside,' she explained when he stared at her.

She'd never heard so many bombers coming over before, Lena admitted nervously, flinching at yet another explosion as she sat crosslegged on the bed where Charlie lay sprawled on his back, snoring loudly.

It was a pity about his face being knocked about,

425

but he was still handsome, especially with that lovely hair, Lena thought tenderly, leaning over to smooth her fingers through Charlie's thick fair hair. It was a good two hours now since she had brought him up here, his body doubling up with pain with every step.

Ooooh, it gave her ever such a funny feeling to touch him, sort of an excitement that she could feel right down inside her, but more than an excitement really, because it made her want to go on touching him. Of course, that was what happened when you fell in love with someone.

Lena's eyes widened as suddenly Charlie muttered something and then reached out and pulled her down towards him. He wasn't asleep any more; his eyes were open. He grunted and said something that again was a mutter she couldn't understand.

Charlie felt really odd. His head was aching fit to burst. The pain that had made it so hard for him to climb the stairs had thankfully eased. He wanted desperately to go back to sleep, but some instinct for survival was urging him not to, that and the sudden fierce surge of lust the sight of the girl on the bed with him had provoked, driving everything else out of his head.

He had a vague memory of being set upon and then struggling up the stairs, but right now he had more important things to think about.

'There's bombs,' Lena whispered, conscious of the fact that by rights they should be in an air-raid shelter, but he obviously wasn't that interested in the bombs because he was kissing her instead.

Kissing her and touching her, and what with the excitement inside her and the knowledge that she had fallen in love, the bombs just didn't seem to matter any more.

She did try to pull back when he started to take off her clothes – she wasn't that daft that she didn't know what that meant – but when she told him worriedly, 'We can't,' he laughed and told her fiercely, 'Yes, we can. You want to, don't you, and so do I.'

'Do you love me?' she demanded.

'Of course I do.' Charlie would have told her anything to get what he wanted. He was on fire for her, burning up for her, his head filled with the sound of his own blood pumping through his veins.

'And if anything happens you'll make sure it's all right?'

'Something is definitely going to happen,' Charlie assured her, misunderstanding. 'And I'm certainly going to make sure it's all right.'

He had no idea where he was or how he had got here – some whorehouse, he supposed, although it was odd that she should speak English when they were in France. Odd but not important enough to come between him and the now urgent drive of his need.

Lena managed to hold him off for long enough to ask him the most important question.

'And you'll marry me?'

Charlie laughed at the thought.

'Of course I'll marry you,' he agreed. 'Now come here.'

*   *   *

427

Emily noticed that the front door was open but she was so tired, what with it being the second night they'd had to get out of their beds and trudge off to the shelter, and tonight with the all clear not going off until gone three in the morning she'd had a job keeping her eyes open at all.

'Come on,' she told Tommy, leading the way to the kitchen. 'Let's get you a nice hot cup of cocoa and then back to your own bed.'

She was in the kitchen before she realised what was going on, the shock of seeing the two men going through her cupboards and piling up her food on her kitchen table rendering her speechless for a second, but only for a second.

'Here, what do you think you're doing?' she demanded, the sound of her voice bringing them spinning round to confront her.

They were both wearing dark clothes and bala-clavas, and the first one to turn said furiously to the other, 'See, I told you we should have left when we heard the all clear.'

'Give over,' the second one told him, for all the world as though Emily herself wasn't there, she recognised indignantly. 'Her and the kid aren't going to cause us any trouble, are they? Get that lot outside and into the car. I'll deal with this.'

'Oh no you don't.' Emily went to block the door. She wasn't letting them empty her cupboards, not after what she'd paid for what had been in them. Not that she'd realised just how the black marketeers had got their supplies when she'd bought them, she acknowledged uncomfortably.

She'd assumed they'd taken stuff from the docks, not from decent folks' houses during air raids.

'Get out the way, love, otherwise you're going to get hurt.'

'You're not taking my—' Emily began, only to cry out in pain when the heavier man punched her hard in the stomach, before pulling her away from the door and pushing her against the wall. His attack had driven the breath from her lungs and cramped her body with sickness and a pain so agonising that Emily could feel herself losing consciousness.

And then she heard it, a shrill, frightened but defiant young boy's voice demanding, 'Leave her alone!'

Tommy. It was Tommy, and he had spoken. Hard on the heels of her joy came her fear for him in case the thieves hurt him.

Then to her relief, from the hallway, she heard the voice of the local ARP warden calling out, 'You've left your front door open, you know,' as he came into the kitchen, just as the thieves took flight and ran out into the back garden.

There was no sleep after that, of course. The police had to be called, and the whole thing told again to them, even though she had told it all already to the warden, and Tommy praised for his part.

The police officer said to him, 'Tried to protect your mum, did you, lad?'

'Yes,' Tommy agreed, slipping his hand into Emily's.

'That was brave of you.'

Yes, she had told them everything, except that bit about Tommy finding his voice, of course. That special miracle wasn't something to be shared with anyone else, nor was the way she had felt when he had slipped his hand into hers when the policeman had referred to her as his mum. She'd have parted with the contents of her kitchen cupboards a thousand times over for that, Emily acknowledged happily.

Charlie woke up abruptly. His head was pounding and he desperately wanted to be sick. The girl lying next to him was deeply asleep. He blinked, not recognising her, but still knowing what she was. The bed smelled of sex and sweat.

He got up off it. He needed to get back to camp. Where was his jacket?

He could hear the sound of planes overhead. They weren't in Paris, then. Dunkirk? No, that's where they'd been told to get to.

He fastened his trousers and put on his shoes. No time to waste looking for his jacket. The girl on the bed stirred but didn't wake. She'd be disappointed when she woke up and found he'd left without paying.

He staggered downstairs and outside, frowning in confusion, and then lurching down the street. When he came to the place where a huge crater had been blown in the ground, leaving a gap between the buildings, he looked at it for several minutes. Where was the pub? What pub? He was in France, wasn't he, where they didn't have pubs? God, but his head ached.

He closed his eyes. He wanted to lie down and go to sleep. He could sleep standing up, he was so tired.

'Oi, you there.'

The sound of the familiar Liverpool accent made Charlie swivel round to watch the man coming towards him. He was wearing a band on his arm. As he approached Charlie suddenly felt violently sick and doubled over.

'Ernie, over here,' the ARP warden called out. 'There's someone in a bad way. Come on, son,' he told Charlie more gently. 'Looks like you've had a bit of a time of it. You'll be all right now, though.

'Reckon he's going to need to be taken to hospital, Ernie. Go and tell one of them ambulance lads on Whiteley Street, see if they've got room for him as well as them others they're taking back to Mill Road Hospital,' the warden instructed the first-aider, who had come running up.

It would soon be morning. Lena had had to hide the jacket away and clean the kitchen and the bedroom before her family came back. Luckily the all clear had woken her.

She'd been disappointed and upset at first when she'd realised that he'd gone, but then she'd recognised that it was better that way. After all, she wouldn't have wanted her aunt and uncle coming back to find him in their bed with her.

Lena giggled nervously at the thought. There would have been hell to pay then, even though he'd told her that he was going to marry her. Doris wouldn't like that. Not with her being older.

Lena wriggled in mute pleasure. She was a bit sore, it was true, from them doing 'it', but then it was only to be expected, what with it being her first time and him being so much in love with her that he hadn't been able to wait. She smiled happily to herself. All she had to do was wait for him to come back for her. She knew he would.

TWENTY-TWO

'What's going on?' Con demanded, looking up the stairs to where Emily was struggling down with a heavy suitcase, whilst the hallway overflowed with boxes that spilled into the front parlour.

'What does it look like?' Emily responded tersely, then answering her own question. 'What's going on is that me and Tommy are off to the country where it's safer. Mr Bindle from around the corner has a sister who's got a cottage in Cheshire she's willing to let out to me. Get out of me way, will you, Con,' she demanded, puffing under the weight of the case, 'unless you're going to make yourself useful for the first time since we've bin married, in which case you can go upstairs and bring down the rest of the cases. I've got the milk float coming round in half an hour to help me get this lot to the station.

'Yes, you bring that one down for me, Tommy,' she called up the stairs to the boy, who was manfully dragging one of the smaller cases along the landing.

'Oh, and you needn't worry about this place,'

433

Emily informed her husband. 'I've been round to the council offices and sorted out for the house to be taken over by the billeting lot. Proper pleased to have it, they were as well. Mind you, I've told them I want it handing back to me just as they found it otherwise I'll have something to say.'

'You can't do that. What about me?'

'What about you?' Emily asked him mercilessly.

'This is my house as well as yours,' Con blustered.

'No it isn't. But I've told the billeting officer that you're to have a room here if you want one, although I reckon you may as well sort yourself out a bed at that theatre, seeing as you've always been so fond of staying there.'

Once Con would have jumped for joy at the thought of Emily going away, leaving him free to do whatever he chose, but now somehow he wasn't keen on the idea at all, and in fact it filled him with a sick feeling of panic.

'Milk float's here,' Emily announced. 'If you want to make yourself useful you can help get some of this stuff onto it.' She turned away from Con towards Tommy, her voice softening as she told him, 'It won't be long now, son. Soon we'll be in the country and it will be just you and me and no bombs or any other kind of trouble.'

Bella wouldn't have noticed them at all if her mother hadn't pestered her into delivering a message to one of her fellow WVS committee members. The fact that this committee member

434

lived several streets out of Bella's direct route home from her parents' house had added to Bella's sense of ill-usage, since it would add a good half-hour onto her walk home. For Sale and For Rent signs were very much in evidence along one avenue of Edwardian semis, which had obviously taken the brunt of the bombing raid on Wallasey, with several houses in ruins and gaps between the buildings where others had been.

It had been a smart area, leafy and green, before the newer areas like Bella's parents' and her own had eclipsed it. It had remained a good address, though, although not as good as theirs. The houses had good-sized front gardens enclosed by neatly clipped hedges, and the road itself was flanked by wide grass verges planted with plane trees. Now, though, since the bombing it was looking slightly forlorn and neglected. There'd been rumours that the War Office were planning to requisition some of the houses but as yet no one knew whether or not it was true.

As she was about to draw level with one of the houses, one half of three pairs that remained intact, Bella saw two little girls, dressed in matching pink and blue floral frocks, their blonde curls tied up in pink ribbons, standing patiently on the front step of one of the houses, plainly waiting for someone to come out. A woman – fair-haired, like the children, and wearing a stylishly cut white dress splashed with scarlet poppies under a red cardigan, emerged from the house, followed by a man, dressed in cavalry-twill trousers, and an open-necked white cotton shirt with a cravat. Bella stiffened, automatically stepping back into the shadow of one of the plane trees that lined the grass verge. The man lifted first one of the little girls and then the other to kiss each of them in turn, before putting them down again and then turning to the woman to kiss her as well.

Bella waited until the woman and the children had walked to the end of the road and disappeared out of sight, and then she marched over to the house and knocked on the door.

If Ralph was discomfited to see her he managed to hide it well, she acknowledged.

'Who was that I just saw you kissing?' she asked him bluntly, 'only it didn't look much like she was your sister – it looked more like she was your wife.'

He laughed and shrugged. 'All right, I'll come clean,' he told her ruefully. 'I am married, but that doesn't matter to us, does it, Bella? You and I, we know the score; we're two of a kind and we take what we want. This is wartime; we might not be alive tomorrow. Why shouldn't we have today what we may not be able to have tomorrow, especially when it's what we both want, and we do want one another, you and I, don't we?'

Ralph's words were an unwelcome reminder of what Jan had said to her. A feeling of anger and panic, almost as though she was trapped in something she didn't want, invaded her. Alan, Jan and now Ralph, none of them had treated her as she had seen other women being treated, women who were respected and liked and . . . and loved.

She had gone weak at the knees, Bella discovered. Inside her head was an image she couldn't ignore and inside her body was an even more insistent yearning. The image, though, wasn't of Ralph; it was of the two little girls, his children.

Yes, she may have gone weak at the knees, Bella told herself grimly, but that was no reason for her to go weak in her head as well.

'What I want is a man who doesn't tell me lies about not being married,' she told him crisply.

A feeling – new to her and somehow uplifting – filled her. Holding her head high Bella walked away without looking back.

What was there to look back for, after all?

She had been betrayed by her husband, humiliated by Jan, and now made to look a fool by Ralph. If she let her, Laura would have a field day when Bella was forced to admit that she had been right about Ralph, and Bella had been wrong.

If she let her. She needed to get away from Wallasey, Bella decided. What, after all, was there for her to stay here for now? Her father wanted her out of the house so that he could give it to Charlie, which meant she'd end up having to live with her parents, and a mother who was beginning to treat her like her personal servant.

It was time for her to live a different kind of life, but just what kind of life Bella did not know as yet.

'Where did you go at dinnertime today?'
'Nowhere.'

'Yes you did.'

Lou and Sasha confronted one another angrily in the street. It was ten minutes past six. They had finished work at six and had just started the half-hour walk from Lewis's in the centre of town, up Edge Lane to their home.

'All right then,' Sasha told Lou, tossing her head angrily. 'If you must know I went to Joe Lyons with Kieran.'

Lou stared at her sister in furious disbelief. 'Are you mad?' she demanded.

'What's that supposed to mean?'

They had stopped walking now, oblivious that other people in the busy city centre were having to walk round them.

'It means that anyone could have seen you and told our mum, and then the fat would be in the fire,' Lou announced, starting off walking again – this time striding out in the sensible low-heeled shoes their mother insisted they wore for work, as though she wanted to leave her twin behind.

'That's not it at all. You're just jealous because it was me that Kieran took for dinner and not you,' Sasha told her, having caught up with her.

They were both wearing their working 'uniform' of plain dark skirts and neat white shirts, the wool serge of their skirts heavy and uncomfortable in the airless warmth of the late afternoon. The air still smelled of smoke, and dust filled the air, getting into everything so that you could feel it in your eyes and taste it like grit in your mouth.

'That's not true.' Lou was now red-faced and even more furious.

438

'Yes it is,' Sasha insisted, her face as white with temper as her twin's was red with angry humiliation.

'You're jealous because it's me Kieran likes best.'

'No he doesn't.'

'Yes he does.'

'Well, let's go and ask him, shall we?' Lou challenged Sasha. 'Because last week, when you'd gone to the first-aid room because of your monthlies, Kieran came in and he told me that it's me he likes best.'

'You're lying,' Sasha protested.

'Come on,' Lou demanded, grabbing her twin's arm, and turning round.

'What are you doing?'

'We're going to find Kieran. Then he can tell you to your face that it's me he likes the most,' Lou told her.

'But what about tonight? We've got to get home and have our tea and then get out again, and Mum was going on this morning about thinking it might be too dangerous for us to go to the pictures tonight like we told her we were doing, in case there's another air raid. Louise . . .' she protested as her twin marched off in the direction they had just come, without her, ignoring what she was saying.

She had to run to catch up with her, automatically grabbing hold of her arm when she did, only to have Lou shrug her off.

'You don't even know where Kieran will be.'

Lou stopped in mid-stride and turned towards Sasha. 'Not so ready to boast that Kieran likes you best now, are you? He'll be at the Royal Court, won't he, stupid? And as for Mum worrying, well, she won't because with going on in the middle of the contest we'll be able to get home before it goes dark and everyone knows that the Luftwaffe don't drop bombs in daylight.'

Lou was off again, striding out at a furious pace, her head down.

Luckily the streets were emptying now of the Saturday shoppers and as yet not filling up with cinema- and theatre-goers.

'We'll never get home in time to have our tea, get changed and then get out again now,' Sasha protested.

'And whose fault is that?' Lou demanded, still walking determinedly.

When she reached the Royal Court's backstage door, Lou knocked on it three times – the signal always given by those 'in the know', wriggling inside the moment the ancient doorman opened it and leaving Sasha no option other than to follow her.

'We want to see Kieran,' she told the doorman. 'You can tell him that it's Lou,' she looked disdainfully at her sister, 'and Sasha.'

'Wait here then.'

The musty darkness of the narrow backstage entrance was sour with the smell of stale scent, food and cigarette smoke.

The twins, normally so full of things to say to one another that they never let one another finish a sentence, stood almost back to back in angry silence.

* * *

It took the doorman ten minutes to climb the stairs to Con's 'office', where Kieran had been following in his uncle's footsteps and entertaining the most junior member of the chorus, whom he pushed ruthlessly off his knee, ignoring her screech of protest, when the door opened.

'Them twins are downstairs asking for you,' the doorman announced.

Kieran cursed under his breath. He'd already had Con going on about how much money the competition was costing him and how it had better be a success otherwise Kieran might as well go and join up, flat feet or no flat feet.

His uncle, who had gone off to the pub for a drink with his cronies, had been in a bad mood all afternoon following the discovery that his wife was upping sticks and moving herself out to the country. In his uncle's shoes he'd have soon found some way to enjoy himself in her absence, Kieran boasted to himself, but of course his uncle Con's wife held the purse strings, and no doubt she was taking her money with her.

Anyway, it wasn't right that his uncle was taking his temper out on him. After all, he'd done his best to follow his uncle's instructions and foster distrust between the two girls, ready to pit them against one another when they danced, to increase audience excitement, but they were beginning to get on his nerves. They were just kids, after all, and he liked girls like the now sulking chorus girl.

Not that she'd keep on sulking for long. He'd learned a thing or two from his uncle, and a pair of silk stockings from that new order that he'd heard from the twins Lewis's had just got in would soon bring a smile back to her face.

He'd better see what the twins wanted. He had to go down to the warehouse anyway.

Conscious of the unpredictability of women in general and the jealous nature of the chorus girl in particular, Kieran ushered the twins outside onto the pavement.

'I was just about to go down to the Queen's Dock to check that the warehouse is ready for tonight,' he told them, grinning at them as he offered, 'Fancy coming with me? Then you can have a bit of an extra practice.'

Since he was already walking towards the main road the twins had no option other than to follow him.

'We want to ask you something,' Lou told him.

'Hang on a minute,' he commanded her, checking the traffic before reaching out and taking hold of Lou's arm with one hand and Sasha's with the other.

Kieran might fancy himself as a dashing young man about town but old habits die hard, and Kieran's mother had insisted on her first-born taking responsibility for his younger siblings from a very young age, threatening Kieran with all manner of punishments if anything should happen to them whilst under his care. As a result Kieran had developed several robust methods of ensuring that his brothers and sisters remained in one piece, one of which was to grab hold of them whenever a road needed to be crossed.

Several roads, busy with buses and other traffic coming from the docks, needed to be crossed before they reached the desolation of the bombed-out streets and buildings that lay close to the docks, all of which the twins were dragged ruthlessly across, depriving them of any opportunity to ask the question they had sought Kieran out to ask.

They were both thinking about it, though, and Sasha, always the more cautious of the two of them, was growing increasingly conscious of the fact that at home their mother would be wondering where they were, and that if they weren't careful and didn't get back soon, they'd be in trouble and probably forbidden to go out tonight.

They were walking south along the dock road now, past the overhead railway. She could hardly communicate this concern to Lou, though, not seeing as they weren't speaking, and not with Kieran there.

By the time they walked down Chaloner Street to where it met Parliament Street, and the Queen's Dock was in view, a surreptitious look at her wrist-watch told Sasha that it was seven o'clock. Her heart gave an anxious thud. Their mother was going to be furious. Tea was at six thirty sharp.

Pain squeezed Sasha's heart. Kieran liked her best, she knew he did, and it was mean of Lou to say he didn't, but right now she wanted to be at home and keeping out of trouble much more than she wanted to be here.

She pulled free of Kieran's grip. 'I'm going home.'

Lou stared at her sister. It was never Sasha who

made the decisions. That was her role. There was only one reason why Sasha wanted to go home and that was because she knew that she, Lou, was right and that Kieran liked her best, but she didn't want to let Lou have the triumph of being able to say 'I told you so'.

'You go then,' she told her twin. 'I'm going with Kieran to look at the warehouse.'

They never ever did anything separately, and it was a funny feeling going off with Kieran whilst Sasha went home. Lou hung back and turned round just as Sasha reached the corner of the street and did the same.

'You haven't forgotten that I'm relying on you two tonight, have you?' Kieran asked her. 'A pair of real stars you two are going to be. Especially in them costumes we got made up for you.' He winked at her and grinned. Lou smiled back but her heart wasn't in it somehow. Funny that all she'd wanted for ages now had been to be on her own with him without her twin, but now that she was, all she could think of was Sasha, going home without her. If anything should happen to Sash . . .

They had almost reached the warehouse. Lou stopped walking.

'What's up?' Kieran asked her.

'I'd better go and catch up with Sasha,' Lou told him, hurrying after her twin without any further explanation.

Kieran watched her go, standing with his hands on his hips.

Females – there was no understanding them.

*   *   *

In the end Lou had to run to catch up with Sasha on one of the maze of narrow streets leading off Parliament Street, which was the quickest way back to Edge Lane, because the minute Sasha heard her twin calling her name she stopped to look round at her and then continued to walk – very fast without waiting for Lou to catch up with her.

'Sasha, wait,' Lou called out. She had to stop because she'd got a stitch in her side. It was horrible round here, she decided, with so many bombed-out buildings. They'd walked along the dock road from the city centre, and she probably wouldn't have noticed anyway, Lou admitted, because her thoughts had been on other things and Sasha had been with her, but now the windowless and doorless houses, some with their roofs gone and even their walls too, others reduced to heaps of rubble, made her feel uncomfortable and jittery. The street was deserted, its residents obviously having been moved out for their own safety.

Sasha didn't want Lou to catch up with her. She didn't want to speak to her twin or to have anything to do with her. She felt funny inside, all sort of scratchy and sore, as though she wanted to shout and scream at Lou and yet at the same time as though she wanted to cry. Why was it that Lou always had to be right? Why couldn't *she* be right sometimes? It wasn't fair.

'Sasha, wait up.'

Lou was gaining on her. Well, she wasn't going to 'wait up'. Her head down, Sasha headed towards what she knew would be a short cut over the debris from a bombed-out building.

Lou watched in horror as her twin ignored the danger sign placed close to the bombed building with its UXB warning painted on it, calling out frantically, 'Sasha, no!'

'Sasha, no?' She was tired of Lou always telling her what she could and could not do, Sasha fumed, ignoring the instability of the ground beneath her feet, as she broke into a half-run, scrambling over what had once been a house and was now a pile of rubble, and coughing in the dust her clambering was disturbing. This time she was going to do what she wanted and Lou wasn't going to stop her.

She was so caught up in her own anger that she'd stepped onto the deceptively solid-looking soft earth before she'd even realised, and by that time it was too late because the ground was giving way beneath her feet, taking her with it.

She tried to save herself but the speed and angle of her descent was so swift that she lost her balance, frantically reaching for the piece of metal sticking up out of the ground to stem her slide.

Lou watched Sasha slide and then fall, her own stomach lunging in fear and despair for her twin as she raced towards her.

By the time she reached her, Sasha was lying on her back on the ground clinging on to the projecting fin of the bomb beneath which the lower half of her body was now lying.

White-faced, the twins looked at one another.

'It's all right, Sash, it's all right,' Lou told her. 'Give me your hand and I'll pull you back up.'

'I daren't,' Sasha told her fearfully. 'Lou, I've looked and there's a great big hole under the bomb. If I let go I'll fall into it.'

'No you won't,' Lou told her firmly.

But even as she spoke Sasha slipped a bit further, and when Lou made her way to the other side of the rubble to look, what she saw made her feel sick. Sasha was right, there was a huge crater beneath the bomb, so deep that Lou couldn't see the bottom of it, but when some small pebbles rolled down into it they made a splashing noise, which suggested that there was water in it.

'I'll pull you out,' Lou announced.

'No, you can't. My foot's stuck now.'

She was right, Lou recognised. Her fall had dislodged the loose earth and rubble thrown up by the formation of the crater and it had trapped Sasha's foot somewhere under the unexploded bomb.

'I'll try and get it free,' Lou told her.

'No, Lou, don't. I'm scared. Don't leave me, will you?' Sasha begged her.

'Of course I won't,' Lou told her. She doubted that she could free her twin. And already, though it had been only a very few minutes since Sasha had first fallen, Lou was certain that Sasha had slipped a bit further towards the crater. Digging herself securely into the rubble behind her twin, Lou took hold of her twin's belt. She couldn't leave her to go and get help; she had promised not to leave, and besides, she was afraid that if she did Sasha might slip right into the crater and drown.

'It's all right,' she told Sasha firmly. 'Someone will see us soon.'

She knew that Sasha was crying and she felt like crying herself. She searched for something to say to cheer her sister up.

'It wasn't true what I told you about Kieran,' she told Sasha abruptly. 'About him preferring me.' Lou knew that Sasha was listening to her even though she didn't say anything. 'He only said it because he thought I was you, because I played a trick on him like we used to do when we were little and changed places. He even called me Sasha,' Lou continued.

It wasn't true. Kieran had told her that of the two of them it was her he liked best, but that did not matter now. Nothing mattered now more than keeping Sasha alive until help came.

Sasha could feel her eyes burning with fresh tears. She knew that she must be going to die because Lou had lied to her to make her feel happier. She knew Lou had lied because Kieran had never called her Sasha. His pet name for her had always been Sassy. 'My little Sassy', he had called her. Not that that mattered any more. Sasha closed her eyes. She'd give anything to go back to before they had ever met Kieran, and she and Lou had been happy dancing together in their bedroom.

Grace smiled to herself as she walked onto the ward past a trainee in mid yawn and struggling to keep awake, who looked at her with envy whilst blushing with guilt.

Grace too had once dreaded nights and wondered

how on earth she would stay awake. She must remember to send the probationer for a cup of coffee once she'd taken over from the day shift.

Her own neck ached slightly from sleeping lying on her stomach with her face pressed into the mattress and her pillow wedged behind her head, just in case a bomb fell. Everyone, it seemed, had horror stories to tell of the injuries those asleep sustained in bombings, especially to their unprotected faces.

It seemed a lifetime ago now since she had been a probationer, although in reality it was only a matter of months. In wartime, though, as Grace was beginning to learn, a day could be a lifetime and bring about the end of many lifetimes, she acknowledged. It was a sobering thought, all the more so with the wards so full of casualties from the last two nights' bombings that you had to dodge between beds filling the corridors.

'Ah, there you are, Campion,' Sister announced with relief. 'Follow me, and I'll go through the new admissions with you.'

The ward was men's surgical, and the beds were filled with men who had either had or who were waiting for operations.

'We've got twenty-four new admissions, all of them suffering injuries of one sort or another from last night's bombing raid, some of them serious, one or two, sadly, that I suspect will prove fatal, despite the best efforts of our surgeons.'

It took well over half an hour for them to reach the end of the ward.

'This is the last one,' Sister told Grace, moving

towards the last bed. 'This poor chap who looks as though he's been ten rounds with a prizefighter is suffering from concussion. A soldier, we think, since he was brought in in uniform but since he didn't have his jacket on there weren't any papers on him so we've no idea who he is. An ARP warden found him wandering around, and so far he hasn't been able to tell us anything about himself.'

'Well, I can tell you who he is,' Grace told her, after looking at the man in the bed. 'He's my cousin Charlie.'

Once she had explained exactly who Charlie was to Sister's satisfaction, whilst admitting that she had no idea what he might have been doing in Liverpool, Sister told her that she'd better go and see the almoner to tell her that they now knew the identity of this patient so that his parents could be informed of his whereabouts.

'Will he be all right?' Grace asked the sister worriedly. Sister's pursed lips reminded her that she was being unprofessional. 'The patient is suffering from concussion, Nurse,' Sister told her firmly. 'Therefore we must hope that he makes a full recovery and regains his memory.'

Charlie stirred and muttered as though somehow he sensed he was being discussed, but he didn't open his eyes.

That was all she needed, Grace thought grimly, her auntie Vi arriving on the ward and demanding to see her son.

The almoner's office was a fifteen-minute walk away from the ward, and Grace had to wait ten minutes to see her before she could tell her about Charlie. Then there were forms to be filled in, and the details to be checked by the almoner to make doubly sure they were correct, before Grace was allowed to go back to the ward.

They were frantically busy, and whilst she'd been gone the new junior had gone into a blue funk, burst into tears and had had to be sent to the nurses' home to calm down, which left them a junior short, and three patients due back on the ward from the operating theatres.

Funny how once she had thought she'd never ever remember the right settings for 'trays', Grace thought with some amusement as she automatically set up the trays she knew would be needed for the evening's treatments, her movements speedy and efficient.

No one was saying anything but she knew they were all thinking the same thing – wondering if the Luftwaffe would bomb Liverpool again.

She glanced at her watch. Half-past eight. With daylight saving they'd got a while yet before it got dark enough for the bombers. Ten o'clock had been the start of them coming in last night and the night before. There was no point thinking about that, though. It was almost time for a 'bottles' round. They were so busy she didn't think she'd get time for her coffee break, but if she could she'd go and take a look at Charlie, Grace decided. Seb was on duty tonight so at least he'd be safe underground at Derby House.

*　　*　　*

'Sam, I'm worried about the twins. They should have been home over two hours ago.'

They were in the kitchen, Sam washing his hands at the sink, having only just come in. He'd called home earlier in the afternoon to warn Jean that he'd volunteered to help out with the heavy lifting work needing to be done to clear away the damage and the destruction caused by the previous night's bombs, and that he'd be late in for his tea. As he reached for the towel he saw Jean's white face.

'They were supposed to be going out tonight as well,' Jean continued.

'Maybe they went straight from work,' Sam suggested.

'No, they wouldn't do that. They'd want to come home and get changed first.'

Katie listened sympathetically. She'd planned to tell Jean at teatime that she was going to move out, but Jean's anxiety over the non-appearance of the twins had made that impossible.

'Katie's already walked down to Lewis's to see if she could see them,' Jean added, causing Sam to give Katie a grateful look. 'And I went down to the allotment in case they'd gone down there on their way home, thinking you might be there. I'm ever so worried about them, Sam. They would have finished work at six, they know we have our tea at half-past on a Saturday, and it's gone half-past eight now.'

'All right, love. I'll go out and have a look meself,' Sam told her. 'Maybe they went to see Grace up at the hospital?'

'They wouldn't do that, not with Grace working.'

'Well, they can't have gone very far. Happen they've bumped into one of their pals and started chattering.'

Jean's smile was wan and strained. 'Not for over two hours, Sam.'

Luke had been thinking all day about what he'd say to Katie when he saw her, how he'd apologise first off and say that he loved her and that he hoped she'd give him a second chance; then he'd tell her that he knew she wasn't the sort that would cheat – because he did know that – then he'd say something about him being a fool and ask for her forgiveness, and then, and only then, would he ask her about that letter. Only he hadn't had the chance to go and see her like he'd planned because of the bombing and all the clearing-up, and now that he had finally managed to get the sergeant's permission to call round at home, seeing as they were in the city, anyway, it was gone half-past eight and like as not she'd have gone out for the evening with that Carole, and he'd have to wait until tomorrow to see her – if he was lucky, he acknowledged as he opened the door into his mother's kitchen.

Jean saw him first, exclaiming emotionally, 'Oh, Luke, it's you. I was hoping it would be the twins.'

'Oh, thanks,' he grinned, his smile fading when he saw the expressions of anxiety on the faces of his parents and Katie. Katie! She *was* here, but he mustn't think of her and how much he wanted to be on his own with her to make things right now, with his parents looking like they were.

It was Katie who stepped into the silence, saying what his parents couldn't.

'The twins are missing. They didn't come home from work.'

Luke and Katie looked at one another, and it was Luke who took comfort from the steadiness he could see in Katie's eyes. He could see how upset his mother was and he was grateful to Katie for acting so calm and sensible instead of making things worse.

'Well, we'd better go and look for them, hadn't we? After all, they can't have gone far,' he said, firmly squashing his own anxiety.

'That's just what I was saying to your mother,' Sam told him, giving him a grateful look, before going over to Jean and ushering her out of the room, obviously wanting to give her a few minutes to get her emotions under control.

They were alone in the kitchen.

Katie tilted her chin and told Luke firmly, 'I'm going to help look for the twins, and before you say anything, I'm not doing it because of you or because I want you to think well of me, or anything like that. I'm doing it because of them, the twins; because I care about them, and your mum as well. They may not be my family, not ever now, but they're as close to me as if they were.'

Luke looked at her, and then before Katie could stop him he had seized her in his arms and was kissing her passionately.

'That's what I think about you,' he told her fiercely when he had stopped. 'I love you, Katie, and I shouldn't have said what I did.'

There wasn't time to say anything more. Sam and Jean had come back into the kitchen, dressed ready to go out and start searching for the twins.

'Had the twins any plans for tonight?' Luke asked his mother.

'They were going to the pictures, but I don't know why since they've already seen the film. I suppose it had some dancing in it that they wanted to copy. You know what they're like.'

Dancing! Katie put her hand to her mouth.

'I've just remembered something. It might not mean anything but Carole at work mentioned that there's going to be a dance competition tonight. She asked me if the twins had entered it.'

Jean and Sam looked at one another.

'They'd have known that we wouldn't let them,' Sam said.

'Where is the competition?' Luke asked Katie. 'Do you know?'

'Not really. Carole said there were posters up and that it's in some warehouse down by the docks.

Sam gave a grunt of frustration. 'We'll have a couple of hundred or more to choose from,' he told them.

'I think Carole said it was in the local paper about the competition,' Katie remembered.

'The *Post*?'

'Here it is,' Luke announced. He'd snatched up the paper the minute he'd heard Katie and now he was showing them the advertisement.

'It's one of them warehouses off Dunton Road, Dad, where all the bombings have been. We were working down there early today, clearing up. We've had to post UXB notices on several of the buildings, and that's just the ones we know about.'

'UXB notices?' Katie queried.

'Unexploded bombs,' Luke told her.

'Well, I reckon Katie's right and that we'll find them safe and sound at this dance,' Jean announced, but they could all hear the tremor in her voice.

'Aye, and when we do and we've got them home, I'll tan the hides off the pair of them,' Sam growled, but all of them knew that he would do no such thing.

Sam and Luke assured Jean and Katie that they were perfectly capable of tracking down the girls on their own but after one look at each other, Jean and Katie shook their heads and announced that they were going too.

It was just gone ten o'clock when they finally reached the two-storey brick-built warehouse being used for the dance. It was one of several close to the Queen's Dock and easily identifiable by the music they could hear coming from it.

At first, Sam's demand to see whoever was in charge had the effect of the men on the door refusing to allow them inside, but once he'd shamelessly mentioned his Salvage Corps status and thrown in some comments about the legality of using buildings for purposes they were not fitted for, he and Luke were grudgingly allowed inside and told to wait with one of the men, whilst the other went off. Jean and Katie remained outside.

The warehouse was typical of its type all along the docks. Separated from the dock road, it had a small foyer area with a set of wooden stairs leading up to the first storey, and a glass-fronted office from which anyone seated in it could observe any comings and goings. The walls were bare brick, and dust was rising from the wooden floors, disturbed by the dancers filling the ground-floor space, and illuminated by the bare bulbs dangling from flexes.

Sam suspected that the excise authorities would be very interested in the legality of the bar that seemed to have been set up on the first floor, although he guessed that the organisers would claim that it was a private party and thus exempt from any licensing laws.

Kieran wasn't best pleased to be told that there was an official from some council department insisting on seeing him.

Con was steaming because the twins hadn't turned up, and nor had half the numbers they had expected, thanks to two nights of bombing.

However, what Kieran wasn't expecting was to be confronted with two tall well-muscled men with very grim faces wanting to talk to him about the twins.

At first he tried to pretend that he had no idea who they were talking about, and he reckoned he might have got away with it if his uncle hadn't come down from the bar, swearing, 'Them bloody twins. If they turn up at the Royal Court again, I'll have their guts for garters.'

'According to the chap we've just seen, the girls were planning to enter the competition and they'd been on their way here with him when Sasha decided she'd changed her mind and was going home,' Sam told Jean when he and Luke had rejoined Jean and Katie, waiting anxiously outside the warehouse. 'He says that Lou then carried on for a bit and then went back after Sasha.'

'Do you think he's telling the truth?' Jean asked Sam anxiously.

'He wouldn't have dared not to,' Luke assured her.

'Something must have happened to them.' Jean's voice trembled with fear.

'We'll have to search every street and every building between here and home,' Sam told Luke. 'It's the only way to find them.'

Luke nodded in agreement.

'You'd better take your mum and Katie home first, Luke,' Sam went on.

Once again Katie and Jean looked at one another. Katie spoke for them.

'We're coming too. We can work in pairs.'

'Katie's right,' Jean agreed. 'I'll come with you, Sam, and Katie can go with Luke.'

Now father and son exchanged looks.

'We'll go back street by street, you can take one side of the road and I'll take the other. We can tell the ARP lot what we're doing when we come across them as well, so that they can look out for the twins too.'

'What if no one finds us?'
  'They will.'
  'You don't have to stay here.'
  'I do, because I want to.'
  'Do you really think someone will find us?'
  'Of course.'
  'Lou?'
  'Mm?'
  'I'm not bothered about Kieran really, are you?'
  'No.'
  'It's almost dark now.'
  'We've got our torches in our bags, we can put them on when it gets really dark, but it won't be that dark because there'll be a good moon.'
  'A bomber's moon. My leg's gone to sleep.' Sasha tried to wriggle into a more comfortable position and then gasped as she started to slip deeper into the hole.
  'Keep still,' Lou warned her twin. She was terribly afraid now that no one would find them, but she couldn't leave Sasha. If she let go of her, her twin would disappear into the cavity beneath the rubble and be trapped there, and even if Lou found some help quickly there was no saying that Sasha would still be alive when they got back. She'd rather die with her twin than live without her, Lou recognised.

It wasn't easy moving northeastwards back towards the city and Edge Lane, combing the streets and bombed-out sites one by one, calling the twins' names, now that it had gone dark, and they'd only covered a very few streets when the air-raid siren went off.

'You and Mum need to find a shelter,' Luke urged Katie.

But she told him scornfully, 'Oh, yes, we'd be likely to do that, wouldn't we? Go and find shelter whilst you and your dad are out here and the twins not found. No, I'm staying right here with you.'

'Where I go you go?' Luke suggested ruefully. There was an emotional catch in his voice that betrayed his real feelings. Katie reached for his hand, unable to think of how she would be feeling right now if it had been their own two children that were missing.

Jean was in despair. 'They'll never hear us now.' She had to raise her voice just for Sam to hear it above the noise of plane engines, the whine and scream of falling bombs, and the fury of the anti-aircraft guns, and he was standing right next to her.

A bomb, dropping several hundred yards away, shook the rubble, dislodging bricks and sending up a shower of dust that made the twins cough. One of the bricks caught Lou's arm, causing it to jerk upwards, her torch falling from her hand.

'What was that?' Katie asked Luke.

'What?'

'Over there,' she told him, nodding in the direction of a barricaded-off collapsed building with a

UXB notice outside it. 'I thought I saw a torch light.'

'Probably some clever little sod doing a bit of pilfering,' Luke told her. 'You stay here, whilst I go and have a look.'

He was striding away from her before she could object, so Katie ignored his instruction and hurried after him.

Luke could see the raised fin of the bomb shining silver grey in the moonlight, its nose buried deep in the heap of rubble surrounding it, but as for any torch light . . . He was just about to turn away when by some miracle there was a split second's silence in the cacophony of destruction and defence that had been raging all around them, and in it he heard quite clearly the sound of Lou's voice saying shakily, 'That's gone and done it now, Sasha. I've lost the torch and it was Luke's. He'll kill me.'

'You're too right I will, you ruddy pair,' Luke announced sharply but his face was wet with tears and he was shaking from head to foot as he yelled, 'Dad, over here. They're here.'

'. . . so you see we couldn't do anything because Sasha sort of slipped under the bomb and . . .' Jean's gulped sob silenced Lou's matter-of-fact explanation of their plight.

Sam said huskily, 'Aye, well, it wouldn't have happened if the two of you hadn't been so daft. I'll stay with them, Luke,' he told his son, 'whilst you go and find help. You'll need to get the UXB lot, I reckon . . .'

'No, I'm staying with them,' Jean said quietly but very determinedly. 'That will mean that both of you can go and get help much faster.'

'I'll stay too,' Katie began, but Jean shook her head, reaching out for Katie's hand and holding it firmly in her own.

'No. Whatever else happens, I want to know that you and Luke will be together and safe, Katie. You two and all those like you – you're the future of this country.'

Katie knew what Jean was saying, but even so, she hated having to leave Jean with her children, knowing what would happen if the bomb did explode.

'You stay here,' Luke told her, leaving her at the first ARP post they came to, where he and Sam explained what had happened and a boy messenger was summoned to alert the nearest UXB team, Luke insisting on borrowing a bike to go with him, whilst Sam organised a team of men to help excavate the rubble just in case Sasha could be moved without risking setting off the bomb.

Grace had just come back from her tea break, ignoring the now familiar roar of the bombers overhead, and not even counting them any more to shiver in fear at their number, even though her brain had registered that it was more than last night, and last night had been very bad. Nor had she done more than glance at the dozens of fires burning throughout the city as she hurried back onto the ward, just as a large bomb exploded in the courtyard at the back of the hospital.

462

Everything in the ward, including the walls, shook, but not one single nurse ran or made a fuss, not even when they realised that they could see down into the courtyard through a gaping hole in the corridor wall. Instead, aided by those patients who were well enough to help, they pushed those who were bedridden out to safety, ignoring the plaster dust coating the beds and somehow managing to sidestep the rubble lying on the linoleum floors.

It did not do any good, of course, to look down into the courtyard at what had once been buildings and ambulances and human beings, and which were now all beyond human help.

Dr Leonard Findlay, the medical superintendent, and the matron, Miss Gertrude Riding, were both calmly giving orders and instructions, despite being injured.

'Hannah,' Grace exclaimed in relief, greeting her closest nursing friend. 'You're all right!'

'Yes, but the bomb got everyone apart from the surgeon and the patient in the operating theatre next to ours, and there's heaven knows how many ambulance drivers bin killed, and some patients. I've got to go. I'm to accompany some of our patients to one of the other hospitals.'

'Grace, what are you doing here?'

Grace turned round to see her cousin Charlie standing behind her in his hospital pyjamas, a bewildered expression on his face.

That was when Grace did something she'd never imagined herself doing in a hundred lifetimes. She went up to Charlie and put her arms round him and hugged him tightly.

'Nurse Campion.'

Sister looked less disapproving than she sounded.

'Sorry, Sister,' Grace apologised.

Up above them in the night sky the bombers were still coming, dropping their cargo of horror and pain. All around her now Grace could hear what she had not heard before, the cries of the injured and the groans of the dying. Angry tears blurred her vision and her throat was raw from inhaling the acrid smoke and dust but she still lifted her fist and shook it furiously and helplessly at the bomber-filled night sky.

If Liverpool could survive this then it could survive anything. And it would survive. It must.

Grace turned back to her patient, lying still in his bed, an amputee who had lost both his legs in a bomb blast on Friday night and who was thankfully sedated with morphine to dull his pain.

She said a little prayer for her family and for Seb, told Charlie briskly that he couldn't walk around in hospital pyjamas, and told the white-faced probationer to go and see if she could get a cup of tea.

All around her everyone was doing what they had been trained to do, fire fighters, police, ambulance crews, salvage workers, nurses and doctors. This was war but it was also life.

It was Luke who got back first with a bomb disposal team, followed within seconds by Sam with a Salvage Corps heavy demolition unit.

464

Jean and Lou were both told they must be moved to allow the men to do their work properly. Both of them protested, Lou fiercely defending her right to be with her twin.

It was one of the bomb disposal team who eventually persuaded her to move over to allow him to take her place. A boy who didn't look that much older than the twins themselves, for all his air of maturity and calm professionalism, Jean recognised.

'What will they do?' Katie asked Luke when he came to join her at a safe distance away from the bomb where she had been sent after refusing to be escorted to the nearest air-raid shelter.

'They can't risk moving Sasha in case it detonates the bomb, so they've got to remove the detonator and then free her.'

'Oh, Luke . . .'

'I know,' he agreed, holding her tight.

'About the letter,' Katie told him. 'I can't say too much. But it was to do with my censorship work. I would say more if I could but—'

Luke kissed the top of her head. 'You don't have to say anything. You should never have had to say anything. I should have known. I do know,' he corrected himself. 'I know that you love me. I know that you aren't the kind of girl who would say that if you didn't mean it, or if you were committed to someone else. I'm sorry, Katie, can you—'

They both looked up as three bombers, flying in formation, swept in overhead, frighteningly low and close as they headed for the docks. The force of the explosion of the bombs they dropped shook the ground on which they were standing, the sound followed by another explosion nearer at hand.

They looked at one another and then they started to run. Where the bomb and Sasha had been there was now only thick black smoke and the beginning of a small fire.

Katie felt acutely sick.

'Sorry if we gave you a bit of a scare, but we decided it would be safer to detonate the bomb after all, because we couldn't get to the second fuse.'

The corporal who had been in charge of the UXB team grinned at them through the thick smoke.

'Sasha?' Katie asked anxiously.

'She's fine. Crying all over young Bobby, though, and calling him a hero. Hero, my eye, all he did was take her place under the bomb so that we could get her out.'

'She's safe?' That was Luke, disbelief and hope straining his voice in equal measures.

The smoke was clearing and through it Katie could see Sam and Jean standing side by side. Sam was holding Sasha in his arms, whilst Jean had her arms wrapped tightly around Lou, who was standing in front of her.

'Those ruddy twins . . .' Luke commented half an hour later after a quick medical examination had pronounced Sasha uninjured and they had all set out for home, ignoring the planes roaring in over their heads. Their threat didn't seem to matter now after what they had all been through, and surely the sky was lightening; a sign that soon it would be dawn and the planes would be gone.

'What on earth did they think they were doing?' Luke asked Katie emotionally, as he stopped walking.

Dawn was now clearly paling the sky but they had fallen behind the others, and were virtually alone in the shadowy narrow street.

Katie looked at him, knowing what he must be feeling. They were his sisters, after all, and he loved them very much. That they had been found and were safe and unharmed was a miracle.

Katie reached out and touched his arm, the tender understanding look of a woman for the man she loves.

'Luke! *Luke!*' she protested, when he took her in his arms and held her tightly, kissing her fiercely. But she still clung to him for all that she had protested, and she returned his kiss equally passionately.

War did that to you. It made you snatch at your happiness whilst you could. She had learned that. It found your weaknesses and your strengths, it made heroes and cowards out of ordinary men and women, it broke hearts and lives and tore families apart.

'I don't know if this has been the worst night of my life or the best,' Luke told her, still holding her.

'Maybe I should ask you which when we've been married forty years?' Katie teased him softly, before frowning and looking up at the sky. 'Listen.'

'To what? I can't hear anything.'

'Exactly. The bombers have gone,' she told him, laughing as the all clear started, swelling in sound until they couldn't hear themselves speak above its noise. No sound had ever been more joyous, Katie thought, as she and Luke held each other tight.

It was five o'clock in the morning and the city of Liverpool had just endured its worst night of bombing of the war. Its worst, but not its last.